BLOOD WAR:
RAGE

Doug Burbey

&

Mel Todd

Blood War: Rage

Bad Ash Publishing
Atlanta, GA
www.badashpublishing.com

Book Layout © 2017 BookDesignTemplates.com
Cover by http://www.ampersandbookcovers.com/

Blood War Rage /Doug Burbey & Melisa Todd. -- 1st ed.
ISBN 978-0-9905182-6-6

Doug Burbey & Mel Todd

To all of those who came home, but never forgot their brothers and sisters who didn't.

Blood War: Rage

Doug Burbey & Mel Todd

Contents

Prologue 1

Chapter 1 – SASC Hearing Testimony 13

Chapter 2 - Hanging it Up 21

Chapter 3 - Scattered.. 29

Chapter 4 - Rage Bubbles...................................... 34

Chapter 5 - When Dealing with Mages 44

Chapter 6 - Dreams... 51

Chapter 7 - Dumb and Dumber 56

Chapter 8 - Demons Attack.................................... 65

Chapter 9 - Allies?... 76

Chapter 10 – Coming Down 86

Chapter 11 - Kayter and Miriam 88

Chapter 12 - Shane is an Ass................................. 94

Chapter 13 – Spying on ICERs 103

Chapter 14 - ICER Offer....................................... 110

Chapter 15 - Offer you can't refuse 116

Chapter 16 - New Toy 122

Chapter 17 - Straps Shrunk.................................. 127

Chapter 18 - Meeting with a Demon 137

Blood War: Rage

Chapter 19 - Puppeteer 143

Chapter 20 - First Assignment................................ 151

Chapter 21 - Tank Rage 157

Chapter 22 - Boss and Picnics 163

Chapter 23 - VFW Scene 168

Chapter 24 - Stooges Call...................................... 175

Chapter 25 - Calling in Reinforcements................. 178

Chapter 26 – Have Chopper Will Travel 181

Chapter 27 - Late to the Party.............................. 193

Chapter 28 - Post Mortem 196

Chapter 29 - Fleeing the Scene 205

Chapter 30 - Escape 209

Chapter 31 - Boss Finds Out.................................. 216

Chapter 32 - We Meet Again 223

Chapter 33 - Dressing Down Kids.......................... 227

Chapter 34 - Toys and Picnics 230

Chapter 35 - Doors are made for Busting 235

Chapter 36 - A Fae Walks into a Bar..................... 246

Chapter 37 - Drunk Fae? 252

Chapter 38 - Phonebooth 260

Chapter 39 - Puzzle Pieces 270

Chapter 40 – Grilling Up the Past.......................... 278

Chapter 41 – Lighten up Georgetown.................... 285

Doug Burbey & Mel Todd

Chapter 42 - Playing Batman 299

Chapter 43 - Truth May Get You Killed 308

Chapter 44 – Reset Raid 315

Chapter 45 – All can die 325

Chapter 46 – Everyone Lies 335

Epilogue - Demons Have Plans 344

Prologue

To fulfill Presidential executive decree for the Demon War surviving United States military personnel regarding LTC Declan Kenner.

[Historical excerpt from Library of Congress of the Demon War complied for general usage]

April 13, 2014 is officially the day Earth became aware of other planes of existence and non-humans, referenced as "Demons", stepped forth and started their attack.

Looking back, we realized they had been popping in and out for centuries, but their presence was only referenced in mythology and fairy tales.

Initially, a glowing oval appeared just above the surface of the ocean about eight miles off Point Baltim, near the Kafr El-Sheikh Governorate on the north coast of Egypt. This immediately garnered worldwide attention. In the space of minutes, it started as a bright speck and expanded to a circle over fifty meters wide. The world tuned in as it glowed, with colors and swirls like something out of a special effects workshop. When the first demonic machine came through, the world lit up with social media, talking about invasions, alien visitors, the end of the world, and the final reckoning. They were all essentially correct.

Large barge like vehicles emerged and began moving towards shore, even as more and more smaller vehicles filled with beings headed directly towards the city. The lore was only half right. Demons were hard to kill, perverted models of the human form,

Blood War: Rage

made to rip humans to shreds and some of them were dangerously smart. At the incoming horde, most people panicked, others watched, filming and streaming on social media. At least until they died, along with most of Cairo.

A bridge of barges was created faster than the Egyptian military could mobilize and the hellish troops descended into the city. Once the bridge was created, the Harvesters were brought in. These tug boat sized, apocalyptic, demonic, tank-tracked mechanizations were part twisted organics and part machine. They acted like a mobile vacuum, extracting the blood and liquid from all dead mammal bodies within a range of eight kilometers of each harvester and it flowed into large tanks towed behind the machine. The rivers of blood talked about in the Bible became real, along with horizontal blood rain, as the blood was sucked towards each harvester through the air. The Demons ran through the streets, efficient killing machines, not doing anything but slaughtering every living thing as fast as they could move.

The Egyptian military fought back but they had been caught off guard and couldn't mobilize fast enough to arrange any coherent response. While they killed Demons, they didn't kill enough to make a difference. In the space of two hours, they mowed through Cairo killing over 75% of all people in the region, then the horde moved towards Jerusalem.

Tacticians, in retrospect, determined that the emptiness between the two cities delayed Jerusalem's fate. Missiles started to fly, and the horde retreated. While we know demons were killed, an exact count of their losses was never tallied. The demon horde pulled back to the portal and it snapped closed, leaving the world in shock. As panic flashed through the world, militaries mobilized, and people demanded answers. The world remained at DefCon 1 for three months and nothing - no portals, no demons. If not for the deaths and ruin of Cairo it might have been a bad dream.

On August 25th, 2014 they came back. A portal snapped into existence outside Minsk, Russia and devastation rolled out. The portal appeared almost dead center of the city and by the time they realized it, the death toll had sky rocketed. Minsk became a wasteland in an hour and the horde - bigger, faster, and moving with a speed even rail couldn't match - swarmed towards Moscow.

The Russian army tried to maneuver into position but they couldn't get organized fast enough. The city was razed by demons, larger than anything filmed in Cairo and even tanks had a hard time killing the biggest ones. Not as much was streamed into the internet as Moscow didn't hold the same tourist population but the pictures taken afterward of the remains were burned into the fabric of civilization. Tanks, missiles, even knives were used against the horde and it barely slowed down. This time, however, with Moscow in ruins, another portal snapped into existence, the harvesters, tanks full of blood, and the ground troop demons streamed back through it and were gone.

What few demons had been killed were snapped up by government agencies around the world for study, everyone trying to figure out if there was a solution to stop them. Many prayed for an H.G. Wells solution but the results all came back negative. Resolutions were passed unanimously allowing the use of any, and all, force by the U.N. member nations to defend humanity. And the world waited.

The world offered aid for Cairo, Minsk, and Moscow but the devastation in those cities could only be compared to Hiroshima. Some of the Demons had been big and strong enough to knock down smaller buildings. People lived who hid in the larger buildings but then our own weapons killed them collaterally when trying to stop the invaders.

It was at this point that strange stories came out, of soldiers creating fireballs, sinking into a berserker state and killing in close combat like the Vikings of old. Where a year ago the stories would have been dismissed as the ravings of people with post-traumatic stress disorder, the scientists listened, everyone wondering about the blood. Why was the blood of people so important? That was when blood became everything, the key to magic, to fighting these invaders, and why we were being attacked. The demons had come to harvest our blood and fuel their demonic magics in some religious zeal for power.

Again, the world waited, but more demons kept coming. Smaller raids, ten to twenty demon soldiers, with portable blood harvesters on their backs, killing and draining, leaving bodies drained of blood, but not desiccated like the larger harvesters, behind them. People fought back, but each raid resulted in dozens to hundreds of dead. One memorable event had a small portal manifest Los Angeles, CA. Street gangs went to war with demons and the death toll was humans five, demons fifteen. But these were only minor engagements compared to the huge portals. The wait for the next major attack wasn't as long and the United States found out the hard way why nuclear weapons would not be the answer to this problem.

On December 1, 2014, a portal appeared outside of Minneapolis. Evacuation procedures kicked in, people knowing that to stay was to die, and the military moved in. Response times had been cut down to minutes and the US military didn't even need to institute the draft as people flocked to join, terrified by what they had seen. Jets took to the air, attacking as the first harvesters came out and it was then that the military found out portals and flying objects, or electronics of any kind, didn't mix.

The US launched hundreds of planes from nearby bases, Canada joined the fight by sending their troops and planes into the fray. As the planes got within three miles of the portal avionics went dead, all electronics failed, and the planes fell from the sky. Missiles fired at them experienced the same fate. Even ICBMs (Intercontinental Ballistic Missile) once within that range simply became a kinetic weapon and they weren't traveling fast enough to do the level of damage needed. One insane helicopter pilot figured out that if the chopper stayed within twenty feet from the ground all equipment worked, letting them use machine guns and rockets on the demons. But only a few pilots could pull that off and not end up killing more of their own people than demons.

Doug Burbey & Mel Todd

The horde rolled through Minneapolis and people couldn't evacuate as fast as the horde moved, so they fought even as the military swarmed in to try and protect them. The US's tactics proved a bit more effective and the military had started equipping and training their own force of novice mages. After embracing the new found human ability to leverage magic, they moved heaven and earth to gather every bit of lore ever written on the subject then put it to use. The decision had been made at the top to use a nuke but the problem became how to deliver it.

In a name that would go down in history, half reviled, half honored, Major General (Retired) Emory Jenkins, volunteered to take a W54 style nuke to the portal. Set up in a high-speed armored dune buggy with a nuke strapped to the back, the general wove through the demons and detonated it a half mile from the portal when his buggy became immobilized, and he was swarmed by the horde. The bomb exploded into the expected mushroom, sending death and destruction with a ten-megaton yield. The world watched horrified and hopeful at the same time. Exultation rippled around the world as the scene cleared and dead demons coated the ground, nothing moving. Hope spurted that if you hit it hard and fast enough, the casualties could be limited. But, the portal had stayed open and demons started coming out, pausing as they stepped into the human realm.

Satellites directed at the spot captured what happened next. The demons swelled, their skin glowing, and they changed. When they started moving they moved faster, stronger, the radiation altered the exposed demons into something even worse. The same demon types that had been destroyed by tanks before were now ripping the American main battle tanks to pieces.

The US managed to force them back to the portal this time, but the costs were staggering. Over 2 million civilians were declared dead or missing. The military strength of the US was now depleted by a third as battalions of men were dropped into the zone, knowing if the demons didn't kill them the lingering radiation would. They killed every demon and none of them made it back through the portal but of the 150,000 service personnel that went into that battle, 131 walked out alive. Within the next 45 days, 29 of the survivors died of radiation poisoning, 74 unexpectedly committed suicide and the final twenty-seven simply disappeared back into the nation's population.

There was another period of silence, with only small portal raids into remote areas of the world by the demons. The biggest, with three hundred demons, happened outside Jerusalem and ended in a battle that all but destroyed the area with most of the buildings within 15 miles. After the consequences at Minneapolis, everyone agreed that nuclear weapons were not the answer but more research was needed. At this point most of the world was focused on building up armies and being ready for the next attack. And the world waited.

January 7th, 2015 humankind was exposed to a new revelation. The U.N. General Assembly was called into session to hear from a man named Lwellyn Ich Salidian. He claimed to have critical information about the war that he would only share with a global body and not a lone nation-state. He revealed that humans were not alone on the Earth and, in fact, he was not human. He was the local leader of a race spread throughout the human world in small numbers, called the Fae, who had been placed in our realm to act as scouts. They monitored our realm's development, assessed possible threats from us, and alerted their home realm of any demon appearances in ours. They had been on earth long enough that their earliest encounters with humans spawned the human mythology of elves before they learned the skills to hide, completely camouflaged in human societies. The Fae have fought the demons through their history, with devastating losses, before they successfully shut off the passage from the demon realm to the Fae realm. They feared that the demons would use the human realm as a possible pathway to once again cross the realm wall using the human realm as a gateway point.

A small number of Fae Embassies were established to allow formal interspecies communications. Fae scouts began to provide the human governments with a trove of information on demonic tactics, weaknesses, and weaponry. But while they had no army in the human realm, and none would ever come from the Fae realm, they would share with humans what they knew of magic to help us in our fight against the hordes. Every nation on earth took up the Fae scouts' offer of aid and began training more proficient human mages quickly.

May 3, 2015, a major portal opened about thirty miles outside Pyongyang, North Korea. Refusing all outside assistance, the leader of Korea didn't listen and drove in nuke after nuke, putting ballistic missiles on flatbeds ordering them to be driven as close as possible before detonating. When South Korea was confronted with the invading horde from the north, the US directed more of its quickly diminishing resources to aid its long-time ally. The deciding factor ended up being rail guns from US Naval Ships, along with troops from China and Russia, smashing into the horde from a second front. The kinetic impact of the rail guns did more damage than almost anything else. Efforts began immediately to create lighter, higher rate of fire, rail guns that could be moved into position with the most advanced power cell storage systems ever developed. By the time the horde was stopped, North Korea was a wasteland of radiation and the dead; the portal collapsed but nothing remained of that country except a handful of survivors.

New rules of engagement were put in place - ground forces only, anything else just wouldn't work. The militaries worldwide ramped up again. By strokes of luck, or planning, these invaders had not taken out any major industrial or agricultural areas. While the world waited and planned, life outside of the hard hit areas proceeded almost as normal, except for the sensation of waiting for the other shoe to drop.

Minor demon raids continued and gun orders went through the roof. Most of the industrialized nations becoming open carry zones but the death toll outside the major portals rarely climbed higher than bad natural disasters. Australia was hit but with typical Aussie fashion they kept the death toll down and beer consumption up. In

Blood War: Rage

July of 2015, another large series of raids hit Guadalajara, Mexico. Over twenty portals opened in that city during the month. By the time the mini raids were done over fifteen thousand people were declared dead.

A massive portal opened inside of the city of Detroit, Michigan on October 25th, 2015 but this time the US was ready. Rapid deployment of tanks, personnel, and kinetic weapons were moved in, the rail lines cleared even as the city evacuated. The joint military ground forces, now including the battle-hardened SSAU "Demon Hunters" and mages, moved in with orders to win at all costs. Those who couldn't evacuate, fought. Gang leaders and law enforcement officers, factory and office workers, hunters and ex-military personnel moved into legendary status as they fought side by side against the demons.

This time with hardened armor, enhanced small arms and artillery munitions, the Soldiers, Sailors, Airmen and Marines understood that no quarter would be given. The military drove them back, not letting a single harvester back through the portal before it collapsed. The Battle for Detroit cost the United States Army the lives of nearly 75% of the 1st and 7th Infantry Divisions. But now, with a survival rate for troops pushing upwards to 25%, it was considered a huge success from previous battles. Even though the demon horde was not completely destroyed and had begun to move westwards down the I94 highway corridor, its size had been reduced by nearly 50%. The biggest win was figuring out where the portals opened and that had been aided by the mini raids. While Ley lines had never been accepted by science, the reality of Becker-Hagens Grid lining up with the portal openings could not be disputed. Small crossings allowed the mini-portals to open enough to let in a few demons but to open the huge portals, all of them required a multiple crossing of lines.

This knowledge let them predict the next portal opening locations, and with Detroit, they were proven correct. While most of the truly major points were out in the oceans or in areas with almost no population to speak of, some of the minor ones weren't.

Then they looked at population density; they had extrapolated from previous encounters that a large supply of blood was needed. That put the next incursion near Ypsilanti, Michigan, a name no American will never forget. It was anticipated that another portal would emerge rapidly along the Ypsilanti Ley line. Another demon horde would emerge, consolidate with the remainder of the Detroit horde and move westwards towards Chicago. The SSAU calculated that the horde convergence would happen within hours and then it would move directly to the population center of Chicago.

Unfortunately, there was no feasible way to conduct a full civilian evacuation. By the time the remaining heavily depleted military combat forces, now under full SSAU tactical command, arrived, the area was too spread out and they had to defend on two fronts with mostly wounded and exhausted personnel. Once again, the Pick-Up Warriors emerged. Originally named by the conventional forces because they came in the backs of pick-ups bristling with guns, then it became a tongue in cheek jibe at the people who would show up for a pick-up game. The name gained honor, as the deadliest ground forces battle ever to ever take place America lasted for two days. Demons kept pouring in at a slow steady rate from the new Ley line portal into the burning remains of Detroit but humanity refused to give up. The SSAU ground commanders enacted what they referred to as "final protocol" tactics. Most of the civilized world called the protocols horrific, or even some, crimes against humanity.

Suicide vests and bombs were ordered to be worn when the ammo ran low, if you could no longer fight, you strapped on a vest and walked up to the enemy and died to take them out. Even the vest's dead man triggers were ordered activated on all wounded. Avoidance of civilian casualties was no longer a consideration. After the controversial actions of the SSAU in Bowling Green, Ohio, the civilian death toll was no longer a constraint. Tales filtered back, videos from people who weren't supposed to be there, teenagers with fierce looks in their eyes as they ran under the legs

Blood War: Rage

of a demon and exploded, taking three with them. Old women in walkers loaded with explosives hobbling out, a grin splitting their faces as they lured demons to them, sure of easy prey. The service personnel still fighting hand-to-claw with mortal wounds.

Nearly defeated, the Department of Defense employed a still classified weapon system with unknown properties. Witness accounts described an intense dome of glowing energy that spread like a nuclear explosion that was centered just south of the city of Ypsilanti. The destruction of the city, the civilian population, the demon hordes and the human combatants was nearly absolute. A miles-long crater was all that remained of the battlefield and the city. The losses that day were estimated at 97%, but the survivors, and watching world, knew they'd finally beaten the demons decisively. The question remained, how much longer could humanity do this? The world's combat effective conventional ground forces were now nearly non-existent.

The worldwide death toll had already topped 250 million. If you lived in an area hit, you were assumed dead because there weren't any bodies to identify. A strange side effect of the huge harvesters, when they pulled the blood from corpses, was that the bodies all but turned to dust; every bit of liquid was pulled out, leaving only clothes behind to let you know a person had ever stood there. That the major incursions left no bodies to rot or be disposed of probably prevented another hundred million in deaths from disease.

Predictions pointed to the next portal opening, this time around February 2016 in the Bío Bío Region of Chile, and the world mobilized. Every nation on Earth with remaining combat power started moving that way. From the previous major attack cycles, it was calculated we had two months to get there and the world made use of that time. Moving people out and moving troops in. When the portal opened humanity was ready, determined to stop them in their tracks. Every nation on earth agreed and the U.N., for the first time since its founding, had not a single dissenting nation. Every nation's remaining fighters would stand together for all of humanity, as one, with everything they had left for a final time.

On February 27, 2016, the portal opened. A single demon, a massive 13-foot-tall bipedal horde leader with hardened overlapping scales and spikes engraved in demonic runes, walked out holding a broken horde leader sword which it dropped onto the ground. With that, the war was over. Negotiations brokered by the Fae took another six months. It became understood that the demons no longer believed the net blood gained by the war was of benefit to them. It is assumed that the demons had unexpectedly depleted themselves in their fight against the humans; they were now vulnerable and needed to regroup in their realm. What they feared as a threat to their own realm was a matter of great debate and of still some concern to the human world leaders.

On August 10th the armistice was signed in blood magic and sealed by the Fae, as Arbiter, making the breaking of it by either party difficult, at the very least. Only designated "communication" portals could now be opened through the realm walls. Doing so required a willing participant from both sides under prearranged constraints. These communication portals were under a select few strict nation states' control with extreme protection protocols in place at all set locations.

Clean up, trying to deal with the emotional and physical fall out took another two years, before most things in America returned to roughly normal levels. The U.S. military consolidated but was grossly depleted; the money needed to rebuild was being directed primarily to ongoing infrastructure repairs. Currently, the world was at a point of unusual peace. The world has turned to rebuilding, grieving, and trying to make sure this never happened again - nation aiding nation as they were put back together.

A portal warning system was created. The demons had exposed that there were several other realms, other than just humans and demons, and no one wanted to face this again. Research and development efforts went through the roof and a special Demon War reconstruction tax was applied to the sales tax, in all states, and it passed with full support. 1% of the cost of all goods was applied to research and making sure we could never be caught off guard again. But as a year went by with no incursions, people relaxed, and the focus changed to trying to rebuild and restore the areas that had been destroyed.

Proof of earlier demon invasions surfaced with the discovery of abandoned harvesters in the Amazon jungle. This gave scientist equipment to study, intact devices that our battles had rarely left. R&D on blood magic became one of the most highly funded areas of research and magic slowly began to slip into the world. As more of the rules of magic was taught to humans by the Fae, such as enchanting and how to use blood, people realized that demon and Fae blood had been in our world all along; people also realized the blood genomes indicated something else. What really perplexed scientists was how the interbreeding occurred because it showed it had happened thousands of years ago. And why was there still another unknown species discovered in our DNA and blood markers.

Chapter 1 – SASC Hearing Testimony

Declan Kenner stopped in front of the hallway mirror on the ground floor of the U.S. Senate Dirksen Building. Through force of habit he came to attention and conducted his own visual uniform inspection. He started his visual sweep at the top of his head to the top of his shiny dress shoes, then side to side and found nothing noticeably wrong with his Army Service Uniform. At forty-five, and a Lieutenant Colonel, he'd better know how to dress properly. The only discrepancy that could be noted resided over the left breast pocket. Where there should have been a soldier's entire career worth of ribbons in neat rows of three, a lone ribbon broke the blue of his jacket. A solid black ribbon with a thin red horizontal line across it.

The single ribbon told everything.

His Demon War, or "Blood War" to veterans and survivors, campaign ribbon. As one of the less than a thousand soldiers who survived to wear the award, custom demanded he wore it alone without any other badges or awards adorning his uniform. Unless you had also earned the Medal of Honor, it ruled the field alone. No particular rule stated this uniform requirement. But it became part of the unwritten military traditions adopted without any need for regulations, orders, or enforcement established that this particular ribbon stood alone on the chest of any Soldier, Sailor, Airman, or Marine in honor of the hundreds of thousands of their

13

brothers and sisters who fell.

It was in the Blood War where he had been given the nickname of DK, for Demon Killer. Declan, the civilian, was a stranger that he didn't know how to be, yet. But he would start to learn that new life after today.

Satisfied with his inspection Declan ran his hand over his clean-shaven head. He felt nothing more than the slight ridges of subdermal mesh implants, a few jagged scars, and the metal grounding tab at the base of his neck. Unable to avoid his next task anymore, with an audible groan he turned and approached the Capital Hill police officer stationed in front of the Senate Hearing room door.

"May I help you, Sir?" the police officer asked politely, and after a quick glance at the uniform name tag added "Lieutenant Colonel Kenner."

"I guess I'm here to testify," Declan responded while handing over a single sheet of a printed email with his reporting instructions.

"First Senate testimony, Colonel? I mean most guys show up here with a bus load of lawyers and well, at least a note pad or something."

"Oh, the last thing I need is a lawyer writing down anything I say, officer."

The officer smiled and handed him back the reporting instructions. Declan pushed open the doors to the hearing room, taking a deep breath and walked into the Senate Armed Services Committee (SASC) hearing room projecting more confidence than he felt.

You're still an officer in the United States Army, you will carry yourself with pride.

His mental voice helped a bit, and he walked eyes front, his stride firm.

A table waited for him, so Declan sat at the only chair provided directly behind the microphone. In front of him the twenty-seven members of the SASC sat at the elevated horseshoe platform

14

surrounding his diminutive table on three sides.

"Please state your name and duty title for the record, Colonel," one of the men on the panel said. He had no idea who most of them were and didn't care.

"Lieutenant Colonel Declan Kenner, United States Army, Special Skills Attack Unit. Currently, no duty title as I'm pending retirement effective immediately after this hearing, Senator."

True at the moment, but a week ago he would have been the Special Tactics Unit's North East Region Commander for the SSAU. He still didn't know if he liked being free of that burden.

"Yes, Colonel, it has been brought to our attention that you have elected to take the separation from service, with immunity from prosecution through the presidential decree for the Demon War surviving veterans." A Senator seated in the middle of the committee table said with a sneer in her voice. Her tone implied scorn as if he had run away during battle, something he would have died rather than doing, unlike others.

"It wasn't really an option, Ma'am. But, yes, I am accepting the rights and privileges as offered under the decree. The last mandated stipulation to that acceptance was to present myself here today for this Senate Armed Services Committee hearing. As soon as this is over I'm done with all of this." He managed to keep his voice flat, these people had no idea.

"Yes, Colonel, we're all aware of how generous the president has been to veterans and covering up for your actions. Healthy retirement with special disability packages and immunity for your possible war crimes tops that list. I'll have you know that we are not all in agreement with these actions, and you will, in fact, be a civilian and held accountable someday. All the veterans we have managed to find so far, have been less than forthcoming. Personally, I believe their accounts are just plain fabrications or lies. I expect you to be more forthcoming Colonel."

Ignoring the direct attack on the SSAU's conduct during the Blood War, Declan replied, his voice calm and matter of fact, even though his pulse pounded. "Ma'am, neither I, nor the other veterans have any reason to lie about our actions."

"Good. Then you're not going to deny that you destroyed the city of Bowling Green, Ohio?"

"No, ma'am, I don't deny that at all." He never took his eyes off her, refusing to look away, to be ashamed of the price he, they, had paid.

"So, you're going to sit in front of this committee now to freely admit that you murdered 47,253 people that lived in the city?" She leaned forward lowering her glasses to peer over them at him, as if he was a school boy to be scolded.

"Ma'am, we were in a direct engagement against a forming demon horde and yes, we did cause the destruction of Bowling Green as a result of our actions. Civilian casualties were high."

"So, you acknowledge that you ordered the Ohio National Guard 134th Field Artillery Regiment to fire on and repeatedly continue to fire on the city and civilians of Bowling Green Ohio? Causing the deaths of over 47,000 American citizens?" She sat back, her eyes wide staring at him.

Does she think I wanted to kill all those people? Or does she not understand most of them were already dead or would have been killed shortly?

"Yes, ma'am, I did." He kept his voice flat and tried not to remember making that decision. It didn't work.

"You acknowledge that you personally ordered the battery commanders to fire Dual-Purpose Improved Conventional Munition rounds into the city? Can you explain to me what the purpose of this round is, Colonel?"

"Yes, I did. The DPICM projectile contains two types of sub munitions. Both types are capable of penetrating more than two and a half inches of conventional armor which is the equivalent to the penetration requirement for killing the demons we were encountering at that time. They are also capable of fragmentation for shredding soft tissue targets."

"And following that barrage, Colonel, you further ordered a second artillery strike against the City of Bowling Green using something called FASCAM rounds? What is the purpose of a FASCAM round?" Glancing at the papers in front of her, then back to him, he knew she had a description of the rounds, but to serve the theater he found himself trapped in, he answered.

"The FASCAM is an artillery deliverable assortment of scatterable mines. Essentially ma'am, those rounds were to kill any survivors left in the kill area still moving around after we used the DPICM rounds on the city. If they were stepped on or moved, they would explode."

"So not only did you murder Americans you sent in, Jesus Christ, booby traps for anybody who might have happened to survive?"

"Yes, ma'am. All organics had to be eliminated from the kill box, humans and demons alike."

"Why in the name of God did you decide to destroy Bowling Green and murder your fellow Americans?" Her voice held a plaintive note, and he didn't know if he felt pity or jealousy that she would never understand the choices made that day.

"Simple logic, senator. The demons were opening a cross realm portal in Bowling Green and it was our intel assessment that they would move directly north to the population center of Toledo, Ohio. Our information showed that if they reached Toledo over 273,000 people were available to be harvested by the horde. We had to stop the horde before it was fully formed to save those lives."

"So, you're telling me that your military incompetence, ineptitude, and pathetic thinking could only come up with a solution of murdering Americans, so that you could justify in your minds the saving of other Americans who clearly were not in immediate danger at the time?" The contempt returned full force and he had to restrain a sigh at the stupidity of people in office.

"No, ma'am, we were using a tactic that we had successfully used three or four times prior. We heavily engage a hoard, when it's found forming at its portal. Then with enough firepower and devastation brought against it the demons will close the portal and try to form their hoard at another location. Our intention was to try and get them to jump the portal to another location where our forces could inflict greater damage against the demons and provide them with less fuel for their harvesters. With luck, it would be a place of our choosing. If that worked successfully then, maybe, only about two thirds of our troops would die on that particular day. We found that when they jumped portal locations, we had a list of places with Ley crossing that were most likely for it to reform. It would then take anywhere from a week to ten days for the portal to re-emerge."

"What? You hoped that by killing tens of thousands of American citizens that maybe, just maybe, you would come up with some future advantage and save your own asses? Jesus Christ, how do you sleep at night?"

"I don't, Ma'am." She flinched back at that, apparently seeing the truth in his eyes.

"So now that we've established you intentionally murdered 47,000 people in the city of Bowling Green, Ohio. Would you like to tell me what the hell you did in Ypsilanti, Michigan just three weeks later?!" She didn't meet his eyes, instead focusing on the papers in front of her.

"I have no recollection of any events in Ypsilanti, Michigan, Senator."

"No recollection? It's a crater two-hundred feet deep and about four miles long. Surely you can tell us what the hell you, and the rest of your incompetent military crew did there?"

"No, ma'am. I can recall none of the events in Ypsilanti Michigan. Either before, or after, whatever it was that caused the crater. That's a period of lost time for me."

"We've heard this lame excuse from several of your veteran buddies already. Lost time. Seems like a very convenient way for you to forget more atrocities you committed."

"Ma'am, the effects of repeated magical attacks and saturation exposure of multi-species blood on the battlefield has caused well-documented effects in most of us. I think I have a paper in my file from a doctor, or something, stating that."

"I don't think anybody buys that excuse. It's been..."

Junior Senator William 'Will' Cheney, interrupted her interrogation, his voice soothing. "Janet, you know this is documented as both magical and scientific fact. These guys took so many rounds to their head between spells, chemical exposure, radiation and demon blood their brains are fried. It's a known fact. What the hell is your point? Are we just here to beat up on the Colonel?"

"I'm here to get to the truth. These guys are lying. Every single one of them needs to be held accountable for what happened." She demanded, her pudgy hand pointing at Declan, and trembling as she held it there.

"Unfortunately, the only people still left alive that know what happened are men and women like the one sitting in front of you, Janet. No matter how much you scream at him, he's not going to be able to tell you. I say we just close this case out and move on. It's taking the country long enough to come to grips with what happened, the discovery of real magic, and another species that is clearly hostile. We have more important tasks at hand, like starting to rebuild. We won this war, let's not start another." Cheney leaned back, looking at her.

Senator Mulkiski reddened. Declan figured it was more of a reaction to how this would play to the C-SPAN cameras if she pushed this too much further than any other reason. Prosecuting the survivors of Ypsilanti, the last Demon War battle, didn't go over well with the public. Either way she relented. "You're dismissed, Colonel. But I want you to know that, pardon or no pardon, or whatever the hell the President claims to have given you, we'll be watching every single one of you."

"I hope you find that very, very boring, Senator" Declan responded as he rose from his seat. With military precision he turned his back on the committee and walked out of the hearing room.

As Declan proceeded down the steps outside the building he

saw movement out of the corner of his eye. Turning, he saw Senator Cheney moving at a quick pace to catch up to him. "Sir, could I have a quick word with you for just a second?"

"I guess I'm officially a civilian right now, you can say whatever you want to me. No need to call me Sir either."

"Well, Colonel, just wanted to say that my wife and family were sheltering in Toledo, Ohio. I can't say that I understand the decision you had to make or what it that meant. I know it must be hard. But I have to admit every night my family says a very guilty prayer for what happened in Bowling Green. Saving their lives and all. It may not be right, to be thankful so many died, but we are all here today because of it. I feel guilty sometimes that we are. But we pray for you every night, sir, all of you. Thank you. Thank you for fighting these terrors and for everybody else who died so I can see my children and wife every day."

The Senator reached out to shake Declan's hand. He accepted it, giving the man a courteous but quick handshake without saying a word. Releasing the Senator's grip, Declan turned and walked away, headed towards the Capital Hill metro station.

Chapter 2 - Hanging it Up

After the war was over, during the swell of national gratitude, the surviving combatants in the US military received a special one-time cash stipend, given in memory and thanks for their unparalleled bravery and heroism in the face of certain death. Since only about a thousand active duty military personnel survived the US battles, the gesture was more symbolic than anything. For the dependents of those who did not survive, their military family members received a double death benefit. Sadly, there were very few of those as many of the families lived near the serving members duty stations and were harvested by the hordes as well.

Declan didn't think twice about translating that monetary symbolism into tangible property. In his case, it translated to nearly three hundred acres of woodland nestled between two state parks in western Maryland and outside the small nondescript town of Jennings. This is where he decided to custom build his retirement home. It would be fully equipped and fortified for him ride out whatever insane apocalypse the universe might happen to have in store for humanity next.

He pulled his F-150 pickup truck off of Jennings Road and turned onto the rugged dirt road leading into the woods. He slowed to negotiate the small bridge that let him go through the open rolled steel swing gate. As he drove up the dirt road he glanced occasionally through the woods at the trees noting where he had placed the cameras. The newly installed security cameras appeared to be a randomly placed but their positioning ensured coverage of each turn and bend of the road.

His truck occasionally crossed over metal gratings laid across the road's drainage ditches and covering irrigation pipes. Nominally these were meant to prevent cattle from crossing them but here they also allowed for remote activation of anti-vehicle tire spikes. Declan smiled as he crossed over the concealed spikes, as they were his idea.

Dammit, those are rather clever, if I say so myself.

Approximately a quarter mile up the road the dirt turned into an asphalt driveway, allowing him to proceed the last half mile further into the woods with ease. He pulled into a spacious blacktopped parking area that looked like it could hold a small fleet of military vehicles if needed. Currently, there were only three construction contractor pickup trucks occupying the large lot. All three trucks had the same markings, Calken's Construction. The subcontractors had been on his property for the last 3 weeks finishing the installation of his full security system for his new house.

Looking up at his house, only about 6 months old now, it would appear to a standard passerby to be some strange Norwegian monstrosity of block construction. Dark concrete block walls, roofs at sharp angles, and deep-set utilitarian windows. It would never win any awards for aesthetic value unless you were in the fjords of Norway. He'd had this particularly ugly house built for other than aesthetic value.

If he'd built this before the Demon War, Declan would have been accused of creating a paranoid prepper's homestead. Within those foot-thick reinforced walls he had a self-contained well drilled directly into an aquifer, solar shingles feeding into the latest and most efficient battery wall and Faraday shielding for electronic interference with meshing for magical intrusion deflection. Now people would regard it as smart. Home protection was a booming business in the US these days.

Declan grabbed both of his bags out of the back of his truck, slinging one over his shoulder and carrying the other one. He waved at the two sons of the construction foreman who had just begun walking out of the woods towards their own truck carrying what appeared to be empty fiber optics cable spools.

Good. Looks like they finished the run to the communications exit point already. I guess they're about done then.

Proceeding up the stairs, to the front of his house, the door was open and held in that position by a large cinder block. Declan remembered that the counterweights on the door kept the heavy steel core primed to swing close automatically when engaged.

"Hey, Charles!" Declan yelled into the house. "You scratch up my fucking door you better repaint it."

"I got it, don't worry about it - not going to fuck up your door, Declan," Charles answered from inside of the house.

"Hey, Mr. Kenner?" Matt Calkens, the foreman, called from the inside control room.

"Yeah, I'm here, Matt. Looks like you guys are making good progress. What's up?

"I just wanted to double-check with you before we do all this old-school bullshit to be sure if it's what you really want?"

"What do you mean old-school, Matt? I'm not having you install a damn moat filled with piranha."

"Not yet, at least. It's all this analog crap. Are you really sure you want us to set the system controls commands using all these multi-digit key sequences to control everything from the panels? You know I can put in a hybrid crossover interface system box inside of here that will directly respond with your vocal and gestured commands. You don't even really have to do much of anything. You just have to wave your hand around and minimally vocalize about what you want turned on and off and the system will do it for you."

"Nope, I like it old school." *Particularly because I don't want anyone hacking my shit. That's why I built a million-dollar house. No way I'm deliberately installing vulnerabilities into it.*

"Alright, Mr. Kenner, figured that was going to be your answer so we're about ready to start programming in your codes. It's going to take you about 2 hours if you want to differentiate between each sensor and switch point of presence within your grid. You've got a hell of a lot of sensors and cameras surrounding the perimeter as well. We need you to decide which groupings to tie together for zone monitoring. All of those are going to need an individual code as you insist on doing it old school but you're the one who's paying us here."

"That's right, Mike, I'm paying to build it, then forget about it with a very nice bonus."

"Yes, yes you are. We are just about ready for you to start punching in command codes soon. Ken and Cory just finished hooking up the lines down on the back end of the property for the fiber ex-filtration run to the antenna array in the woods. It's a pretty nice setup. You should get zero interference, no matter what's going on around your house. Not quite sure who you think is going to be trying to electro-magic jam your communications but this is what I get paid to do and my wallet is highly appreciative of your excessive paranoia, sir."

"I'm glad you appreciate my attention to home security, Matt." Declan snorted a bit as Matt grinned back at him. "Alright, I gotta go drop these bags and put some shit away. Then I'll come back up and start the key punching in for the sequences."

"Got it, we'll clean up the last of the prep now and as soon as you punch in then I'll verify the operations will be ready to go. They we will just need about another few hours."

Declan headed towards the downstairs entryway. A cipher lock barred his way until he put in the access code. It had been part of the original construction and the heavy steel door leading down into the basement opened as soon as he pushed enter. Flicking on the light, he proceeded down the concrete stairs to a wide undecorated cinder block hallway. It led to a series of doors on his left and right. Declan headed down the hallway to the middle door where another cipher lock sat on the wall. He entered that code and then provided his handprint on the control panel's scanner pad. A series of heavy bolt clicks, one after the other, until all four chambered rod braces disengaged, freeing the door. He pulled open the door and proceeded into his armory.

Declan set up his armory a little different than you'd see in most spy movies, where a man walked into a room and the fluorescents overhead would expose row after row and rack after rack of neatly wall mounted assault weapons and workbenches. That seemed rather impractical. Declan preferred a more standard system of safeguarding his kit for long periods of time, or at least what he hoped would be a long period of time.

Along each wall, a series of humidity-controlled steel lockers with individual locks stood waiting for attention. Across from them, on the other side of the large bare room, a stack of green and black cases containing larger pieces of equipment and supplies sat. The end of the hall-like room contained a series of shelves and pallets with various crates of ammunition and sub-munitions that were required for the armaments concealed in the steel lockers.

Declan ignored all those as he walked slowly to a locker set in the corner of the room next to the ammunition crates. This particular locker didn't have an individual lock. With a sigh, he dropped both bags at the base of the locker, then unceremoniously dumped the contents of the bags onto the floor. Stepping over the mess, he opened the locker. Inside, on the left, it held the standard narrow clothes hanging compartment and on the right a bunch of smaller shelves. Declan began to untangle the mess that he dumped on the floor from his bags, extracting things one at a time. He pulled out the dress uniform he been wearing at the Congressional hearing and put it on a hanger. He felt a little off-guard as he hung it up. A sense of uncertainty, sadness even, crept into his mind.

He had no reason to put this uniform on again.

He had retired.

He had nowhere to be tomorrow.

He had no obligation to defend his Nation or humanity anymore.

He was now one of "those guys".

I'm officially an old soldier. What the hell am I supposed to do now?

Blood War: Rage

Nobody counted on him anymore. He had no obligations or responsibilities anymore. Without the Army, his team, or any immediate family, he was alone for the first time since he could remember. For over twenty years he had looked forward to the day he could retire, sleep in and not do shit.

Now, I'm not sure I want to sleep in. I really need to find a hobby or something. Drinking beer is a hobby, right?

Declan pulled his large black leather trench coat from the pile. Scarred, pitted, singed, and gouged it looked out of place next to his uniform. In the strange ways of social trends, this coat has culturally become significant as that of a Demon Hunter - the "Demon Slaying Warrior" that is now nearly a legendary figure. This coat has now spawned fashion trends and copycats. They even made them in funny colors now.

But this one, this one here, is mine. We have taken souls and been soaked in death and the magic fires together. You were my skin. You were my armor. You served me well.

The leather had been soaked hundreds of times in the horizontal blood rains, both human and demon. It's underlying silver mesh magical conductor disbursement system absorbed countless number of physical attacks and magical enchantments to save his life. But now it's just a coat to be hung in a basement locker.

Declan, for a moment, considered burning it not even quite sure why he would want to keep it. He didn't have a single good memory attached to this article of clothing. All this thing should represent is a layer of personal protection that kept him alive. But the hundreds of thousands who died around him in the carnage seemed to cling to it as witness to its importance.

Seems kind of silly not to just throw this fucking thing in the trash.

But out of a sense of attachment to the item, like one might associate to a lucky coin or Saint Christopher medal, this old soldier could not throw it away. Grumbling to himself he hung up the coat; then a few tactical shirts, pants, and a pair of well-worn metal plated boots found a home underneath the hanging clothes. With the second bag, mostly comprised of tactical accessory equipment, he unceremoniously started tossing pieces onto the various shelves: a few tactical lights, a large straight edge heavy gladius styled fighting knife, empty magazines, then Velcro patches.

Wait what's that?

He picked up a patch that was not a normal uniform accessory but lay at the bottom of his bag. One of the few remaining fun memories of him and Shane during their initial training to counter the demon invasion flooded through his mind.

They were having lunch at the food court near the post shopping center, perusing the mall ninja store full of absurd Gucci tactical equipment accessories that vendors would try to sell the soldiers. A singular item had caught both of their attention. A small round patch, light green in color, with a cartoon face of a horned demon on it. It was drawn with black and had the letters MHI underneath it. Both Shane and Doug decided they had to buy this thing and they swore they would wear it in combat. Declan smiled at the memory. But looking down at the patch and seeing that not a single drop of blood had ever touched it he realized neither of them had ever fulfilled that lunchtime promise by wearing it into battle.

He took the patch and gently, compared to his arbitrary tossing of the rest of the gear, placed the patch onto the shelf. He then shut the door on two decades of military experience.

Guess it's time to hang it up, so what the fuck do you do now? I guess I'll check out the Jennings VFW. I hear that's what old soldiers are supposed to do.

"Hey, Mr. Kenner!" The foreman shouted down the stairs. "I think we're about all done and ready for you to go hot and punch in all your activation sequences."

Time to lock down this bunker. Then I guess I'll have a beer and watch some football.

"On my way up. Matt, make sure Charles is repainting my door that he fucked up by the way. I am not paying you guys till my shit is fixed. By the way, do you know what football games are playing today?" Declan said with a smile that wasn't entirely fake.

Chapter 3 - Scattered

Kayter Reynolds pulled up to the Waffle House, parking her van sized RV at the back of the lot. She glanced at the katana lying on the passenger seat and shook her head. Instead, she picked up her .45, slipping the holster inside her jeans. Wearing it while driving became uncomfortable quickly, besides having it in the holster in front of her made drawing it easier. Doing a quick mental check of all her weapons, gun, knife, throwing blades, she opened the door and stepped out.

Standing outside her RV she looked around and then gave her home a once-over. The beige and brown RV looked boring and normal, the motorcycle on the back trailer not that unusual, as long as you didn't spend too much time inspecting it. Not sensing any danger, she pricked her finger with one of her ever-present knives and set the wards with a quick drop of blood. Slipping the knife back into the sheath at her hip, she walked towards the entrance, her stomach rumbling. The last two had lacked any booths where she could sit with her back against a wall, so she'd left. Hopefully, this one would, or she'd have to eat an energy bar and she hated those things.

Walking in, she scoped out the space and latched onto a booth in the corner, where no one could approach her from behind. In a few quick steps, the diner tiny like most of them, she slid into the booth after checking out her escape routes and verifying a clear view of the RV and bike. Perfect.

The waitress, an older black woman missing at least three teeth, waddled over, pad in hand. "What'll you have, sweetie?"

Kayter didn't bother to pick up the menu, it never changed regardless of the state. She flipped her long multicolored braid off her shoulder and glanced at the waitress. "Hash browns, scattered, covered, brown, Texas melt, cheese grits, a pecan waffle, and water."

"Sure thing, sweetie." The endearment rolled off Kayter even as she scanned the room, most of the occupants looking at her, lust or interest on their faces, but too old or too shy to do anything about it. She rolled her eyes and pulled out her phone, scrolling through her email to see if there was anything urgent that needed to be dealt with. Just because she had looks, boobs, and hips that seemed to check most guys boxes didn't mean she cared about any of that. But years of dealing with it had lowered her reaction down to an annoyance and if they didn't approach her she didn't care.

Movement at the corner of her eye made her glance up and fight back a sigh as one of the other patrons in the diner made as if to slide across from her. With a swift move, she lifted her long leg and braced it on the back to the bench across from her.

"Not interested," her voice flat as she met his eyes.

The man, a trucker she guessed from the bloodshot eyes and the rig in the lot, flinched a bit as her mismatched eyes met his. One of her eyes shone a brilliant blue, the other a dark brown that pulled in the light. They made most people uncomfortable, the trucker reacted like most, averting his eyes and focusing on her boobs instead.

He started to talk, addressing her tits, and Kayter sighed.

I don't have the time or energy for this.

"My eyes are up here," she snapped. He jerked his eyes up, red flushing up his cheeks. A decade ago might he have been a handsome man but time and long hours made him look haggard and old.

But even if he had model looks, she wouldn't have been interested. A sex partner didn't appear on her to do list.

"Let me say this clearly. I am not interested. I am not lonely. No, you can't buy me a drink. And no, I don't need any company. Now go away." Her voice remained flat and she never took her gaze away from him.

Kayter watched the mental war going on by the expressions on his face and waited to see if ego or self-preservation would win. There were days she wished she looked like a haggle faced crone except that her looks were a weapon too, just like the rest of her.

I really don't feel like putting him through a window but if he pushes it, I'll try not to kill him.

"Bitch," he muttered, shoving his hands into his pockets. She tensed for a moment but when he pulled out a billfold, threw a twenty down on his table and stalked out, she relaxed.

The waitress came over with her plate, an odd look on her face. "Neat method for telling men to get lost." She set the plate down in front of Kayter, her lips half pursed and half smiling.

Kayter snorted and went back to her food and her email. Incidents had been down, making her life boring lately, so she followed her normal route of hitting all the Ley crossings and checking to see that no one had tried opening anything. But the constant quiet gave her the willies, like all the hair on her body stood on end. When everything was this quiet it meant demons were planning something and that never indicated anything good.

A 'breaking news' alert interrupted whatever mindless show played and she looked up, paying attention.

"We are hearing there has been a rumored realm gate opened outside Baltimore. While at this time it seems to have been a small gate and no demons have been spotted, the very fact that there is possibly a gate open is cause for alarm. Is this a precursor to another invasion? The gate has reportedly already closed, but everyone is on high alert. Statements from both the local law enforcement and Federal ICER authorities claim this is yet another hoax."

Kayter tuned out the rest of the information and pulled up the most direct route to Maryland and what RV parks were in that area. She ate with mechanical movements, needing the fuel, and glad the food tasted decent but she would have eaten it regardless.

She glanced back up at the latest ad for male performance

Blood War: Rage

enhancements, non-FDA approved, that included a promise that your partner would not be disappointed. A shudder rippled through her body at the idea of ingesting anything that contained magic. You never knew how your body would react, especially if you were mixed blood. Most people never realized they were mixed blood until too late.

Kayter mapped out her route, finished the food, and rose, tossing a twenty on the table. She nodded to the waitress as she headed to the restroom. Her RV had a bathroom but one you didn't have to clean always rated higher. Once done there, she headed to her RV.

About fifteen feet away she paused, the smell of stale body sweat reaching her nose where that scent hadn't existed when she got out of the RV.

Fuck. He can't take no for an answer.

A quick debate about a gun versus a knife but if she killed him she'd have to deal with cops, and she didn't have time for that crap. Knife but only if he pulled a weapon.

Shaking her body loose, she kept walking and pivoted towards him as he popped out from the shadow near her camper.

"I knew you couldn't resist me. I'm sure a lonely little thing like you needs a man to give her some real loving."

Kayter snorted. At five-ten, little didn't get applied to her often.

"Are you stupid, or just that desperate? I'm sure if you took a shower and paid well, some prostitute would take your money."

He puffed up and moved closer to her, hands clenched into fists. "I don't need to pay for sex. Women beg me for it."

"Then go find them. I'm not interested." She faced him fully, hands at her side, and began the game of guessing his moves.

First, he'd lunge at her and try to grapple her into a hug; then attempt a slap and then go for her hair to see if he could get leverage on her.

When he moved, he followed her mental map step for step.

Why are people so fucking predictable?

In a fluid motion, she stepped far to his right, grabbed his arm when he went for the slap, moving with the motion as his other arm tried to grab her braid. With a twist of her body, she dislocated his shoulder even as he tried to regain his balance.

"AllEIEI," the scream echoed off the cars.

"Please, quit whining. If I wanted, I could have snapped your elbow and I doubt your health insurance will cover it. Now go away. A good medic can pop that back in but if I don't see you fleeing in the next thirty seconds I'll shatter your knee. Good luck making a living driving after that."

He looked at her eyes, wide, watery blue eyes dilated so much the blue formed a thin rim around his pupils. Whimpering, holding his shoulder tight to him, he stumbled away towards the rig on the other side of the lot.

Men, always thinking with their dicks. I never saw dad act like that, or maybe he just didn't around me. So not worth the effort.

With habit learned via painful lessons, she checked out the area around her vehicle, made sure her protective runes hadn't been touched, and that there were no unpleasant surprises. Other than the puddle of urine off to the side, nothing had been touched.

A touch of her hand dispelled the ward and she climbed back into the driver's seat. Without looking she secured her pistol and made sure the sword would pull easily from where it rested. Another minute to type in the address in the GPS, and she pulled out of the Waffle House. Stomach satisfied and fueled for the drive to Jennings, Maryland.

Chapter 4 - Rage Bubbles

Declan tossed the spatula hard into the sink. Turned the heat off on the stove and shoved the pan to the side. He glanced at the mess he had created all over the counter.

Why the hell is this so hard? Just making soft scrambled eggs. The foodies would be very disappointed.

He tossed the pan into the sink and heard his empty coffee cup break when the pan hit it. Immediately regretting his lack of control, and the pointless abuse of his own property, over some improperly cooked scrambled eggs he reached over, forced himself to calm down. He lifted the pan out of the sink, dumped the remainder of the hardened eggs into the trash and walked back over to the sink where he pulled out the broken cup and washed out the pan.

Smooth. Can you get your shit together long enough to finish breakfast? Crap, that was my 3rd Infantry Division coffee mug too. Now I'm going to have to go all the way down to Georgia just get a new one.

Declan finished cleaning up the kitchen then headed into his living room/man cave. It was just a couple of comfortable leather recliners, a couch long enough to nap on, and an overly large flat screen TV with a matching extensive surround sound system. The only decoration on the wall was a five-foot by four-foot framed canvas map of the world with magnetic Ley lines and major cities depicted. Most people would find the map as stylish but Declan saw it as a reference tool to glance at while watching the headline news of world events.

Doug Burbey & Mel Todd

"Let's see what we got," Declan said to the empty room as he flicked on the television. He then moved quickly through the news channels. Finding nothing of interest he switched the channel over to the National Football League Network. Reruns of yesterday's games.

"Seen that, know the score." Declan stopped his random flipping through the channels and tossed the remote onto the coffee table, then turned his back on the TV and headed towards the kitchen.

"Fuck it. May as well make more coffee." As Declan walked away from his living room and headed back to his kitchen, the ubiquitous deep baritone of documentary narration caught his attention.

"It was here at the intersection of Interstate 95 and 96 where 1st Brigade of the 1st Infantry Division took their last stand against the Detroit demon horde." The narrator began.

Declan glanced back at the TV. The documentary showed stock footage taken after the battle, displaying burned wreckage from the mechanized brigade's Abrams main battle tanks and Bradley armored personnel carriers. All were arrayed in an eastward facing semicircle surrounding the highway interchange. The burned-out wreckage of the vehicles and remains of the desiccated corpses were clearly visible.

"The last remaining unit of mighty Big Red One," the narrator continued "known as the Devil's Brigade, fought its final holding action here for the city of Detroit. The brigade's sacrifice was total. As was common in the Demon War there were no known survivors. The soldiers who fought here are credited with buying the crucial time that allowed the remaining American forces of soldiers, hunters and pick-up troops to marshal thirty-five miles to the west. There they did what they could to stop the Detroit Horde from reaching the fortifications of the Chicago Sanctuary. While the United States government still will not acknowledge what unnatural force they use to eradicate the Detroit Horde near the city of Ypsilanti, it is known that the sacrifice of the Devil's Brigade here in the city bought the critical time needed to employ the still top-secret weapon used in the final battle."

Declan willed his body to move and reached down grabbing the remote tightly and turned off the television. He noticed his hand shook slightly and dropped the remote immediately back onto the chair. His thinking turned hazy. He forced himself to achieve calm as he felt unfocused anger starting to push forward into his mind.

There was no secret weapon. Just death. Yes, the Devil's Brigade bought us some time but it was never part of some grand plan. It was a coincidence. Our stopping that horde outside of Ypsilanti should have never been possible. I should have died there. I still think I did. Are Angels actually real?

Declan felt his physical anxiety rise. He knew it was a psychosomatic response that he needed to control. These emotional triggers started bubbling to the surface of his mind and manifesting in physical anxiety. They seemed to becoming more and more frequent lately, kicked off by even more innocuous-seeming things.

Yeah, I'll just grab a beer to chill out and get my shit under control. Damnit, just relax. There's nothing wrong. It's just a damn documentary. You've seen a thousand of them. Chill.

A subtle, but distinctive, chiming sound emitted from a speaker in the corner of the room. Declan turned his head quickly towards his television and grabbed the remote from the table. He pressed the security menu button bringing up the system's graphic user interface. By habit, he looked quickly at the top right quad of the camera feed which showed the perimeter entry gate from the main road. He saw that it was empty and immediately looked to the left of the screen where it showed a grid layout map display of his property, broken into pre-designated sensor areas. The northwestern block was flashing red denoting the triggering of motion and heat activated sensors.

Damn it, again? This is all I fucking need today.

Declan set the remote control back onto the table then turned to head towards the front door.

Doug Burbey & Mel Todd

I told those Calkens brothers the fucking outer ring perimeter sensors needed to be adjusted tighter. Now I have to hike my ass out there to make more damn deer sensor filter settings adjustments.

He thought about calling up the company foreman and telling them to get their ass out there and reset the sensors themselves but glanced up to look at the camera monitors for the grid momentarily. His eyes locked in on the image of a camouflaged soldier with a rifle moving forward onto his property and towards his house. A second soldier appeared in the field of view, shadowing the lead soldier's movements just a few meters behind. Looking back over to the security grid he noted that by the series of sensors now being tripped they were clearly heading straight towards the house.

I knew this was going to happen one day, I don't know who these people are but I didn't survive this long just to be taken down by a couple of assholes, still pissed off about what they think they heard during my congressional testimony. I told those motherfuckers that when this shit was televised they were putting a target on my back for shit that people didn't understand.

Declan yanked his entry closet hallway closet open and pressed a key code opening sequence on the gun safe inside. He pulled out an AR-15 and extra armor plate carrier harness he kept with the rifle. With movements born of old habits, he pulled the harness over his torso and snapped it in place. He took a thirty-round magazine from the front storage pocket and inserted it into the rifle. With a fluid motion, he pulled the charging handle back then released it, seating the first 5.56 round into its chamber as he moved to his front door.

Declan was only vaguely aware of the warming sensation as his body temperature rose slightly preparing to react to the apparent threat approaching him. He moved through the front door slowly, sweeping the tree line in front of him then veered to the west, crouching slightly while assessing the extent of open field between his current position of cover and the tree line.

Blood War: Rage

Two-hundred and fifty meters of open area. Move fast. Move controlled. Look for targets. Stay low. Be prepared or be dead.

He broke out in a steady jog with his rifle facing forward and pointing to the west where sensors had alerted to the soldiers moving towards the house. His eyes were continually searching for movement behind the trees as he made his way to the point he identified as his next position of cover and concealment. He pressed forward quickly to move out of this exposed danger area. Without drawing any gunfire, or sensing the approaching threats in his immediate vicinity, he reached the cover of the tree line. He dropped to a knee to observe and extend his senses as he felt his awareness rising but he was still unsure of the exact location of the threat. The action was automatic and done without conscious thought.

Alright, I know you're out here. Where are you now?

He pulled out his phone's interface to his home system and opened his security application. Glancing at the miniaturized sensor map screen, he noted the additional sensor activations coming from the west but now angling to the north.

What the hell's wrong with you guys? You lost? Why are you angling away from the house now?

Pushing down the urge driving him to rush forward directly to engage and destroy this threat, he forced his mind clear so that he could survey rest of sensors on the application map.

Are you two a decoy team to draw me out? Clever, that's what I would do - draw me out of the fortified position and bring me into the woods instead making of an all-out assault on the house.

Declan scanned for other tripped sensors but found none.

Is something wrong with sensor the grid? I know those bastards are out there. Maybe they are using some form of magical suppression to interfere with the sensors. But then why didn't other threat sensors alert to magical usage? This makes no sense. There's an assault threat right now. I know it. There is no other explanation. I need to take it out right now. At least I know where the first team is.

His mind locked into battle thoughts, moving to intercept the enemy. You didn't dither in battle situations, you reacted or you died. With quick motions, he brought up a submenu in the security application and ordered his security system to drop the houses shuttered steel window and door barriers. The sound was solid and reassuring.

Try cutting through those, bastards. I will take care of your decoy team then come back to finish the rest of you. I smell blood now and soon there will be more. You will all pay for your mistakes.

He put his phone back into his pocket and raised his rifle to his shoulder and began to move forward in a slow crouch. Fully committed now to destroy the threat.

Okay, time to do this.

Declan let his senses reach out, listening for the sounds of shifting underbrush and focusing his eyes forward for a trace of movement or shifting shapes in front of him. Cracks from the snapping of fallen tree limbs rang out like bells in the woods. He knew his targets had to be only a few hundred meters to his front. Declan slid the fire selector of his rifle from safe to semi with his thumb and placed his index finger lightly over the trigger. He felt his focus sharpening, he had a threat and he would kill it. Anger at becoming a target now twisted and contorted into the heightened sense of battlefield awareness he had not felt in years. His persistent anxiety melted into a solid defined purpose. To conquer his enemy - to kill them and stand in their blood drove him forward.

Yes, this threat will now feed my power. Blood will fuel my ability to protect my home.

Declan recognized the Blood War's rage returning to his mind and body. The Demon Killer, DK, side of him was now in charge again. It had been years since he had to deal with the fact that the blood rains and magic had soaked him to his core, changing his body chemistry. Corrupting him. It had been so long since the rage had pushed forward inside of him that he wasn't prepared to temper it. His ability to think narrowed and pushed to the side by

Blood War: Rage

his need to fight and destroy. Declan learned to control it towards the end of the war but it always came with a cost. He had almost nothing left to pay that cost with anymore but it had begun to take over now and any cost to pay was now just an afterthought. Killing the threat was all he needed now.

DK could almost feel the soldiers in front of him now. His unnaturally charged senses guided him forward.

One-hundred meters to the front. Two targets drifting at an angle away from me back towards the west. That's not right. Are they moving away from the house? I'll close on them in just a few seconds for the kill. These amateurs move like drunk elephants. Easy. They will die nice and easy. Why are they so loud? This is wrong. This definitely is not right. I'll stand in their blood and they will feed my power. Soldiers don't make stupid mistakes like this. Why would they send amateurs after me? Surely they know what I lived through.

He noticed movement in the trees in front of him. A baring of teeth cracked his face as he proceeded to walk slowly but deliberately towards the shifting shadows through the trees. He approached the trailing soldier and closed to about fifty meters. The shifting light and density of the trees made it difficult to get a clean shot. He needed to be able to sight both soldiers nearly simultaneously before he fired his first round, guaranteeing they would not be able to return fire on him. Twenty-five meters in front of him now as his target moved clumsily and noisily away from him. DK no longer cared why they were moving like rank amateurs.

If you come here to kill me, you better bring your A game.

At twenty meters behind his targets, he saw a break in the trees and dropped to one knee then centered his rifle on the back of the first soldier. His senses totally keyed. He sighted down the barrel and caught a glimpse of color through his scope.

What the hell? Orange?

A stripe of orange wrapped around the soldier's hat and another was placed vertically down the back of his jacket. Declan's brain screamed a mental warning. But his finger tightened around the trigger about to release the first round. He shifted his eyes upwards to ensure his second target was positioned for his next shot.

More orange, what the hell?

DK noticed both of the soldiers had a blazing orange stripe on both their hats and jackets. The instant recognition of the standard hunter's orange caused a momentary pause on his trigger finger. His mind screaming to destroy the threat immediately.

Kill them now! Clean shot!

A primal instinct to destroy the threat now drove his mind. Declan struggled to resist it. He tried to retain control over his subconscious actions. Declan forced his body to freeze momentarily. Struggling to clear his mind, the first soldier must have heard him. DK could see him turning in his direction. He fought against the powerful desire to pull the trigger on his target.

The target is right in front of me. Now or never.

"Wait! Please, God! Don't shoot!" The first soldier yelled with desperation in his voice. As the second soldier Declan had under his sight turned, there was confusion clearly on the face of the very young boy in front of him. Declan could see now that the second soldier was merely a child. Confusion clouded his judgment as he fought with his rage, uncertain whether or not he was facing a threat.

"Sir! Please, please, don't!" The tall soldier pleaded.

"What?" Declan weakly responded, not dropping the barrel still pointed directly at the child.

Jesus Christ, these two are just deer hunters. A man and a boy. Not soldiers at all. What the hell am I doing?

The man raised both his hands above his head and held them there. "Jeremy, raise your hands now – real, real slow. It'll be okay." The man addressed his son directly, staring straight at Declan.

"Really sir, we're just a little lost. We were tracking a deer we shot across the ridgeline. We don't mean any harm, I swear."

Blood War: Rage

DK tried forcing himself to lower his weapon, barely moving an inch as he struggled against the rage now screaming into his mind to kill the threat. The rage demanded that he kill the threat and survive.

These two are not a threat.

Declan tried to pull his finger off the trigger struggling against himself. Knowing what he had to do before he killed this child, he focused his energy deep into his core, down into a part of his body that old religious shamans had once called a person's chi. It is the spot within his own mind and body that held a personal energy. DK never knew he had such a force in him until the war. He forced this energy out of his core and directed it to flood into the rest of his body and mind. He forced it to calm and clear his thinking. He felt this energy reserve flow through himself. It flowed, bringing clarity back into his mind. Control over his body seeped back. His finger came off the trigger as he looked again with the fog of the rage lifting and he could see without a doubt there was no threat in front of him. Just a father and a son wearing normal commercial hunting camouflage and tracking a wounded deer through the woods.

No, not a threat at all. There was no diversion or incoming assault team. I was about to murder a child and his father.

Declan looked at the father and lowered his weapon. With his voice barely above a whisper, "Head due west and you will be back towards the state park and the road. Leave now."

He sat on the ground with his back against a tree and watched the father and son quickly move to the west away from him and back towards the state hunting areas and most likely their waiting car. His body and senses returned to normal. A tired sense of mental exertion settled in bringing with it the familiarity of old post battlefield thoughts and sometimes regrets. It had been a long time since he had to repress his rage by burning his personal core energy. Always it carried at cost. The cost was that he had to replenish his core energy or the next time the rage would overtake his mind. He would be powerless to shut it down.

I can't keep doing this. The war always offered me opportunities to replenish myself after fighting back the rage. Hell, I was drenched in blood, power I had in ready supply. But I can't do that anymore. How much longer can I go on like this before I do actually kill someone else because I can't control myself?

Chapter 5 - When Dealing with Mages

Shane watched the demon twitch as blood flowed out of its body into his personal harvester.

Mostly full. I can probably get one more before the battery gets too low.

With expert motions, he swapped out an empty container for the full one as the demon quit moving. It took him a bit, but it was a strong Ley crossing which made it possible for him to summon demons. Fifteen minutes later he reopened the portal, and sure enough, a ring two came racing in, obviously waiting for him.

Shane remembered the monotone voice of the Special Skills Attack Unit training officer giving the intelligence briefing rang clear in his mind though it seemed a lifetime ago.

"Soldier demon. Ring two demon realm categorization. Eight-foot humanoid with fleshy tendrils draping from the mouth. Quantity per Horde, in the thousands. These lobster squid looking bastards are the shock troops for the Horde's bulk forces ripping us to shreds. Lower face area is vulnerable to ballistic weapons. That's your best shot on one of these things. Approximately six hundred pounds. Spined and segmented, hardened, insectoid-like front and backplates. Blades can slide between segments, or at joints but projectiles should be focused on jointed segment areas such as shoulders, neck or hips. Three fingers on each hand tipped with four-inch claws. Avoid that three-foot arm reach. It's a deadly strike from those claws. They've been seen ripping open half inch steel armor plates. Feet have four toes each, thick and wide spread, allowing for excellent stability. Don't try to knock one over unless you are driving a truck at it. Semi-intelligent by human standards. Seen operating some of the simpler demonic machinery. Has not been witnessed operating human machinery. Seldom uses melee weapons, preference appears to be claws. In horde formations, they are not currently known to use explosives or magic. The Soldier Leaders have been known to be adorned with forms of paint like colorations and show some tactical situational understanding. Leaders are believed to command Horde subunits at a ratio estimated at one per one thousand subordinate soldier demons. There have been some rumors of Leader Soldiers using low-level magic. This is unconfirmed as of yet. It is suspected that if this rumor is, in fact, true then it's likely from the use of talismans or demon magic hybrid equipment. Not from any natural ability of a demon Soldier or Soldier Leader, itself."

The advice from the long dead major rattled around his brain almost like a soundtrack to his current situation, timeless and underlying his movements.

SSAU didn't know what I know now.

With an almost bored sigh, he shot it with his high powered taser as he switched on the harvester and shut down the portal. Keeping it open would drain him quickly. Blood began welling to the surface of the demon's hide and flowed into the harvester like a reverse sprinkler. Shane smiled as the screams started.

I love how that sounds. So much pain for my pleasure. Best loot ever. Running into that raid team with a single ring two and two drones. The takedown was fast and I got my own little harvester to play with. Too bad DK never listened to me about how important R&R was. He wouldn't have approved of how I use this though.

His sated smile faded as the memory of his one best friend surfaced. Pushing those memories to the past, that friendship was dead and buried like so many other things in this world. Not worth wasting his time thinking about.

Still amazes me none of the geek geniuses at the DoD have figured this out yet. How portals convert energy still amazes me

Blood War: Rage

and I keep thinking the key is there. I just can't figure it out yet.

His thoughts stayed amused as he watched the demon collapse and twitch as he picked up his specially constructed tasers.

But then most of them focus too much on science, never thinking that religion might hold the answer. You'd think given that we were fighting DEMONs they might actually consider it.

He rolled his eyes detaching the full canister and slipping in a new one, just in case. But the demon lay unmoving next to the three other corpses. Rising he pulled out his ax. Impractical in battle, too heavy to swing for long periods of time, it worked perfectly to decapitate dead demons.

Decapitation kills damn near everything and you don't take a chance with demons.

He grinned as he dropped the ax through the necks or at least roughly the neck area of the demons. Personal harvesters didn't leave the corpses dried and desiccated like the large ones did, so it squished a bit as he chopped. A few minutes later he walked out of the area, his bag full of canisters with blood. The small harvester on his back like a backpack, his ax in a sheath under his coat, and his .45 clearly visible on his hip.

The North Korean countryside showed the merest hint of life coming back to the devastated area. While magic amplified radiation and created demons that acted like berserkers on PCP, it also cleansed the area fast. In another decade this might be nice farmland. With the amount of dead that had been crushed into the soil between human and demon machines and feet, the ground wouldn't need fertilizer for decades.

He moved with assurance through the land, never stopping scanning, looking for dangers, even though he knew there were none. Humans still treated this as a wasteland. Too caught up in what they believed to pay attention to what was.

Granted the demons aren't much more intelligent. Too many assumptions that they understand humans when they don't have a clue. Wonder if this Fae will be any better?

He'd found an old temple outside of where Kumchon existed

before the war. A small camp lay exactly as he'd left it, his warning charms glowing undisturbed. He set down his bag and started to dismantle his charms.

"Interesting. Tell me, exactly how does a human pull blood from the demonkind without killing it first?" The liquid voice that spoke of beauty, sex, and knowledge cut through his thoughts.

Shane spun his hand up, a spell on the tip of his tongue, power flowing through his body from the blood he'd used while killing demons. Military training, aimed at split-second decisions on information let him halt the spell before he'd uttered it, though he seriously considered letting it go.

"You must be the Fae I was to meet." He glanced at his watch. "In an hour, two miles from here."

The Fae shrugged at him with a languid gesture that made him feel awkward and ungainly. "Bored. Knew you were in the area so I decided to follow. So how did you override the need for a dead body to extract the blood? Killing that many demons alone would be impossible for a human."

Shane resisted snorting at the arrogance and narrowed his eyes at the Fae, trying to figure out its game and decide if he wanted to share that info. They had no reason to use it against humans and if a few more demons died, lured out of portals, his heart wouldn't break. The beautiful being, and the Fae qualified as beautiful, looked at him, eternally patient. It had short, perfectly styled blond hair that reflected gold and silver, luminous eyes of green that made him long for emeralds, and a body that most women would lust after. The look in the Fae's eyes made him pause. It reminded him of a cat watching a mouse, trying to decide if killing it would be worth the energy. But then he knew Fae.

"Depends. You have what I'm looking for?"

The Fae waved a hand in dismissal. "It really doesn't matter. But yes, with the right enchantments you can direct a portal anywhere, even a place that doesn't exist though normally not even humans are that stupid. If you go through a portal to a place that doesn't exist, you cease to exist. A waste of energy, and your life, at that point."

Ideas sparked deep in his mind but he kept his face blank. "You have the book?"

"Of course. Not that it will do you much good." The Fae drew out a small book, a journal bound in skin, most likely human or demon, not that he cared. He held it up to him as if taunting an animal with a treat. "You have my payment?"

"Why won't it do me much good?" Suspicion sparked deep within him, his body tensing as he became hyper-alert.

"It's written in my language, in Faelerian. You can't read it."

Shane shrugged. "That's my problem isn't it?"

Please, I learned to read Faelerian years ago. Lewl taught me many things.

He turned his back on the Fae and took down his protections. Moving the bag of blood canisters to sit in front of the tent, he reached inside and pulled a pack out of the tent. "I have your payment."

"Explanation first. This interests me."

No matter how he twisted it, he couldn't see any way the knowledge could be used against him or even humans in general. Killing humans required no effort for demons or Fae so his method seemed immaterial.

"Electrical disruption."

The Fae tilted his head. "Elucidate."

"As near as I can tell the electrical field all bodies contain, which many religions refer to as the soul, holds the blood in. If I disrupt it with a high enough electrical charge, the internal field shorts out for a second, maybe two, but that is enough time for the harvester to grab the blood and start extracting. Once started even the re-establishment of the field won't interrupt it. Granted, the electrical force has to be strong enough to drop an elephant, but creating that didn't take too long"

The Fae looked at him, gaze sharpening and he wondered if the cat had decided to pounce.

"Interesting. I had not considered that as a reason death was required. Payment."

Shane took a deep breath and pulled two feathers out of the silk bag in his hand. They were long, golden white, and radiated in the light of the noon sun as if they could pull the sun's light into them.

The Fae sucked in a sharp breath. "Where did you get them?"

"Not your problem. I have the payment, give me the book."

The Fae moved closer, handing over the book. He could taste the knowledge hiding in it. He traded the silk bag, letting go as his hand closed over the journal, the skin screaming human as his fingers touched it.

"Price paid. Now get out of here." The need to open the book and start reading clawed at him. Curiosity would kill him someday but he would achieve his goal first.

"We'll be watching you, Colonel Shane Michael Gris trained by the Fae Lord Caedrich Arc Irilian and vengeance taker for his children."

Shane didn't think, he didn't even pull power, knowing the Fae would expect it and have protections against it. With a motion he'd spent hours practicing, he pulled his .45 and put three cold iron bullets into the Fae's skull.

The ruins of the beautiful face looked at him in surprise as the Fae crumpled to the ground. "Legends are good for something. Your arrogance killed you. You overplayed your hand showing you knew my full name and rank. You just became too dangerous to be allowed to live. Lewl would be disappointed in me." His voice remained conversational as he walked over and picked up the silk bag with reverence, getting this back did not hurt his feelings.

Huh, no reason to waste power.

He grabbed the harvester, flipped a setting and aimed it at the Fae. Seconds later light pink blood flew out of the body and into the container.

Tucking the book into his inner jacket pocket, he started breaking down camp and loading everything onto the jeep that was hidden in the ruins behind the tent. By the time he finished

Blood War: Rage

the corpse looked drained and he'd gotten three containers of blood. His mouth watered as he looked at the pure power.

Book with the answers I need, angel feathers I get to keep, and Fae blood. Been a damn profitable day. At this rate my world will be constructed before Earth gets invaded again.

He grinned as got in the jeep and headed out. With luck, he'd be in Vladivostok by tomorrow and then he could catch a flight or boat to Tokyo. He had a very interesting book to read.

Chapter 6 - Dreams

The trip up towards Jennings, Maryland took longer than Kayter expected. Between road construction, a flat tire, replacing the tire, and three campgrounds being full, she found herself still a day away and exhausted. The small campground ahead had a space reserved for her. She'd called ahead and paid for the extra days; she pulled in, shutting off the engine with relief.

A night to sleep and get some rest, then she would be in Jennings tomorrow to start investigating. Rising out of the driver's seat, she stretched to try and remove the stiffness the last few hours had caused. Even taking a shower right now seemed like too much effort but her workout couldn't be postponed. If anything, she needed it more now than usual.

Her parking spot faced the woods and the nearest camper couldn't see the small clearing she stepped into. With a picnic table and a fire ring, her workout would be constrained but that made for good practice. The air held so much moisture she felt her skin grow damp even before she started to move. The long-familiar patterns and rhythms to her workout soothed and calmed. Even as her heart rate increased and she started to sweat in earnest, the nagging annoyance and frustration siphoned away. By the time she finished an hour later, her center had returned, and she knew sleep would find her quickly.

Fifteen minutes later, after a quick sponge bath, Kayter hopped into her hammock, pulled the blanket up over her, and fell into dreams.

"DK, I swear by every last drop of blood in my body, if you don't get that stick out of your ass about mages, I'm going to shove another one in there."

"Sir, with all due respect," Declan started to say and John Reynolds cut him off.

"Screw the due respect crap. What the fuck is your problem, DK? Magic is a damn tool and we can't afford to not use a tool, just cause it might bite us at some later point. If we don't do something now we'll all be dead, so it won't fucking matter." John's close-cropped silver blond hair glinted as he got in Lieutenant Colonel Declan Kenner's face. "Figure out which stick is more painful to remove, the one you have, or the one I'm going to shove up your ass." The last words came out as a growl.

"You haven't seen what it does, you don't know the cost," Declan stared back, circles under his eyes, the sun reflecting off his scarred shaved skull.

"And I don't care. There is no cost if we don't fucking survive."

The two men glared at each other and Declan threw up one hand in a sharp gesture. "Fine. I'll let my men know it's available. I'm not fucking using it and there is no goddam way you can order me to, sir." The last word almost a snarl as the men stared at each other.

John sagged, rubbing his hand over his face and feeling the two days of rough stubble. "Understood."

A loud chorus of roars caused both men to turn and look into the distance. A blood harvester started edging through the newly formed portal and the demons surrounding it did their equivalent of cheering. Blood drained from both their faces and John closed his eyes for a brief second, then snapped them back up.

"Go, let them know of the offer. Then let's go send those bastards back to the hell they came from."

"Yes, sir! And John?" Declan said as John Reynolds started to turn away.

John glanced back, arching an eyebrow.

"Thanks for the offer."

"They're my men too, Colonel. Now, go make sure they pay for every drop of our blood they harvest."

"With pleasure, sir." Declan strode away. John followed his path with his eyes and saw him making straight for his men and the cluster of pick-up warriors they'd grabbed as they went through.

John shook his head and headed for the small group of mages. They snapped to attention as he approached.

"The last of the word has been spread. Expect people coming in. Move through as fast as you can, then get ready to do what you can to make sure my men live long enough to extract their piece of flesh. "

"Yes, Commander. Are you ready now?"

"Yes." John sat down in the chair they had waiting, his eyes on the tanks sitting in what used to be a park. The crumbled remnants of swing sets and other playground equipment sat to the side in a twisted and warped parody of their original form.

"Think of whom you want the message to go to. Create an image in your mind of that person, then the message."

John sat there, his eyes closed, face serene.

"Tell us when you have it created." The mage kept his voice low and steady while his hands started to glow a color somewhere between blue and the sound of crying.

"Done," he said, his eyes still closed.

The color sound sparked and the mage sagged. "The message is sent."

"Any idea when she'll get it or how?"

"Best we can figure, in the next few hours. It will be like a vision or a dream but everyone is different and we don't know for sure. But the tests have proved hopeful."

John's mouth pulled up on one side. "And at this point, hope is all we have left." He rose, giving the mages a brisk nod and pulled on his cover, the silver eagle turning red with the reflected light of the portal. With sure steps he headed towards his already positioned tanks. The men stood waiting, alert but not at attention as he headed towards them.

"Ready, Commander?"

Blood War: Rage

"Yes, Sargent. Let's go blow some holes in these fucking harvesters. We're going to make sure they pay dearly for every drop of blood they've claimed.

He climbed up onto the tank, a smile chasing away some of the darkness that shadowed his face. The men sprang up, a rumble of turbine tank engines starting, and the seventy-ton tanks headed towards the glowing portal.

Kayter sat up straight in her hammock, almost tumbling out, as she thought about the scene she'd seen. She'd heard of the pick-up warriors. People in the cities the demons had gone through who'd joined the armed forces, fighting with everything they had to try and stop the demon hordes. Most had died, a few hadn't, but all of them had become folk tales - local legends of the prices people paid to stop the hordes.

She recognized the landscape that had been her dad's last fight. Where he died, a huge explosion had taken out the battalion, and him. He had started the war as a brigade commander, but after staggering losses, he commanded less than a single battalion of what remained of his heavy brigade combat team. He led the 1st of the 66th Armor Battalion on his, and the Iron Knights, final day of combat.

The message had been for her. She received it probably hours after he sent it. It seemed like a waking dream, him sitting there, smiling at her. A real smile, not the guarded ones in the dream.

"Fight, train, stay safe. You are my legacy to the world and you are the key to saving all of us."

No words of love, or sorrow, just his voice and confidence in her.

Kayter reached up to rub eyes that hurt but she lay back down, going over the dream in her mind. Why this dream, why now, and how much of it was real and how much images her mind put together?

Sleep came in fits and starts for the rest of the night. By the time she rose she had no answers but the need to get to Jennings ratcheted higher than ever.

Chapter 7 - Dumb and Dumber

Once again, Kayter blessed her dad's foresight in buying the lifetime membership to three different camping organizations as she pulled the RV into the small spot. The engine shut off and she sat there, window rolled down and listening. The only sounds were birds starting back up and the chatter of some people in the distance. No screams, no gunfire, no scent of blood on the air. As things went, it indicated a better than normal day.

Stretching, she rose and headed to the back of the small RV. Barely bigger than a standard van, it held everything she needed to survive. Guns, ammo, reloading bench, a tiny shower and kitchen, and her weapons.

Habit made her do another spot check before she stepped out of RV, one hand on her hip where her .45 always rode. After ten years of practice with it, she felt naked without it, even to the point of sleeping with it on her hip.

The area remained quiet, and even after listening closely there didn't seem to be anyone close. With a groan she flowed into multiple strikes and kicks, working out the kinks and stiffness in her body. This continued, her still in the leather pants and long sleeve shirt she'd been wearing to drive here, for the next hour. A fine sheen of sweat coated her as she moved, no music, no loud shouts, just hard fast strikes as she moved in the small area.

Her long braid whipped back and forth, a small weight at the end of it hitting her occasionally, but she expected it and ignored it. Finally, the stiffness of driving gone from her muscles, she stepped back into the RV grabbing her sword. The well-worn scabbard attached to her back, and then she shrugged into a loose-fitting leather coat. Practiced movements made sure she could pull her .45 or sword in single swift movements; she locked the door and set the wards. Anyone who tried to get into her RV while she was gone would be in for a deadly experience. Kayter headed to the back where her Indian motorcycle, Midnight, sat on its small trailer. The Indian Dark Chief had been a find a few years back. She'd rebuilt the engine and put tires on it to handle rougher terrain. It responded to her every move, especially since she had an enchantment or two put on it, a payment for killing some demons. Never needing gas had been worth giving up the payment on that ring three demon; when you added in the silence spell, it made her bike a weapon.

A quick flip of the key and the bike purred to life, a low rumble she felt more than heard as she straddled the seat, pulling on a helmet.

"Come on, Midnight. Let's go see if I can get the lay of the land."

Pushing off, the bike headed out of the campground as her eyes and ears listened and cataloged everything. She headed for the crossing to make sure the gate remained closed and that no one had gotten the bright idea to try and open it. Then if that looked good, she would head over to Hunter Gear, and see if her introduction was still good.

When the government had figured out that portals were opened on Ley line cross points they'd set up a system to monitor the minor and major ones. Minor qualified as four or fewer lines and major as five or more. While they didn't make the monitoring system open to the public, they also didn't make it very secure. That allowed anyone with a bit of interest to get access to the site. Outside the major sites, there was always armed personnel, just in case. But the minor only had sensors as they didn't seem capable of supporting large portals.

The problem was that a few demons didn't need a large portal as they'd found out during the war. But any demon appearing on

Blood War: Rage

this side meant someone had called it here. The treaty had tied both hands but people were stupid. And the more powerful the mage the less crossing lines they needed.

The address of the portal, that had set off the sensors, appeared up ahead and Kayter slowed, pulling into an empty lot about a half mile before the address. She would walk up so she could check out the area and maybe catch someone unawares. Parking Midnight, she slipped off, checked her gun and her sword, then moved towards the portal location... listening, smelling, to see if she could sense anything.

While her blood sense wasn't the best, there was something about demon blood that stung her nose. Though with almost a week gone by, unless there had been a large amount of blood there wouldn't be anything left to find. But safe was always better than sorry.

Kayter didn't pull her sword, that would get too many people's attention even in this quiet area of town, but she kept her hand on the butt her .45 as she walked. During the height of the war, everyone went armed as the panic about running into a roving demon band had sent everyone running for weapons. Every state but Hawaii instituted open carry laws. During those years, humans weren't what you feared.

The only thing she heard was normal night sounds, but she hoped to find evidence of mages opening the portal.

She only found the Ley point because of the small sensor the government set up at the point. It worked like a seismic sensor, going off with any detection of magic. From there she spiraled outward looking for a circle.

Found you.

The electric thought sparked as she saw the faint remains of a candle, a few drops of human blood dried brown, and scratches in the soft soil where the circle had been drawn. Clear and easy to see.

Fucking idiots.

She moved back to the portal point and crouched, looking at

the ground carefully.

Huh, small points. So, one of the smaller ones. But I can't tell how many.

Rocking back on her heels she thought, then started to spiral again. When she came across the faint remains of another summoning circle. This one was much older and only because she knew what to look for did she see it at all: a break in the soil making a curve, the impression of boots in a confined area, and a mostly burned black candle.

At least these idiots don't know how easy it is to open a portal and still think they need all the protection and trappings. Makes them easier to track.

Licensed mages were the worst of the worst as far as Kayter could see. No oversight like the military had and too much arrogance because of their blood.

Rising back up she headed back out, the signs were clear, but nothing there to lead her to anyone. The sound of two voices made her pause. The odds of anyone being in this area were low. It wasn't good for making out or hunting and there was no reason to cut through. It really was just land that hadn't been turned into a strip mall yet.

Kayter leaned back against the tree and waited, listening. After a minute the voices got close enough that she could make out words and guess the gender.

Males, it is always dumb males.

"I can't believe they actually want us to summon demons - lesser, small ring one demons, but still. Most other places would arrest you for even thinking about it. And here the government is giving us permission. How fucking cool is that?" The voice came across as young and male, her mental imaged added acne and stringy hair. Kayter cringed just thinking about it.

"I know. They keep telling us we can't summon demons, hah. They just don't want us to know how powerful we are. This is going to be great experience and it will prove to them we are people they can rely on." This voice, just as young, but a bit deeper with no cracks on the high notes of excitement.

Please tell me they are acting out a movie, please? Surely no one can be this stupid.

"With this experience we'll be shoe-ins for the Journeyman license, then we can get jobs that make mad money." The first voice again.

"Please, that is all boring enchanting stuff for the corporations. I'm going to go for my Master's and be part of the demon teams. Oh, maybe we should pull in an extra one to practice some offensive spells on?"

The enthusiastic agreement had Kayter wanting to beat her head on the tree she leaned on.

Nope, they are just apprentice idiots. Yay, me.

As they approached her tree she stepped out from behind it, her hands hanging loosely by her side.

"Gentlemen, I think we need to talk about what you think you are about to do."

They both squawked, reminding her of chickens as they stumbled backward. Both had long black robes on with symbols that she knew meant nothing embroidered on the lapels. One was young. If he was legal to carry a gun she'd be surprised. The other was a few years older, with a small bit of muscle under his robe and dark brown hair matching the scraggly caterpillar of hair under his nose.

"Who the hell are you?" The one that fell on his butt with acne and stringy blond hair squeaked.

Ha, got it. Nailed him in one.

"Someone who knows that summoning demons is illegal, and the penalty of being convicted for it is death. So, tell me why I shouldn't just kill you two right now?" She crossed her arms as she waited, and she saw both pairs of eyes dart to her chest.

Testosterone and males, they never change.

"Cause we have authorization, from the government?" The older one, voice two, the one with the caterpillar.

"Is that a question or a statement? Because unless you have

authorization from the DoD, you don't have authorization."

"The who?" Voice one climbed back to his feet trying to appear taller, even if he still didn't come up to her shoulder.

"The Department of Defense. They have to authorize all interactions with the Hell realm."

"Well, this guy said they had authorization, had a real badge and everything with the letters ICE on it, maybe. He said they needed patriots like us to summon smaller demons to keep people on their feet, remind them that demons weren't gone - but small ones that couldn't kill anyone, just scare them."

"Yeah, so this is none of your business." The blond said, puffing up his chest.

Kayter's patience snapped. With a fluid motion and a twist of her wrist, she snapped the scabbard off her back and snapped it out at the blond. The sword, still in the scabbard, snapped across his forearm snapping it. As she pulled her arm back she elbowed brunet in the nose, breaking it. The twin screams of pain had a sweetness to it that she enjoyed. Blond sank to his knees holding his arm and the other held his nose, now soaking the caterpillar with red blood.

"Now that you understand the power dynamic here, tell me everything you know about who contacted you and what exactly they wanted."

Blondie whimpered too much so she turned her attention to the one still standing. "Really, we were contacted by some ICE guys, or CER, or something like that. They said they needed a little chaos, that people were getting complacent. Just get them a few tiny demons, enough to eat some pets but nothing that would kill anyone." His babble came out fast and hard and Kayter seriously thought about unsheathing the sword and lowering his blood count a little.

"There is no such thing as tiny demons. They are all deadly to humans... hell to anything on this planet. What the fuck were you thinking? Give me your licenses." They both looked at her eyes, theirs wide in horror. If she took their licenses and they were caught casting spells without them, the automatic penalties were steep and getting a magic license replaced made the DMV seem simple and streamlined.

"I can kill you and take them. I don't really have an issue doing that. It might make it easier. Two idiots out here killed and no licenses anywhere. Hmm, I like that idea." She made to unsheathe her sword.

"No, no," they both wailed digging under their robes and a minute later two ID's lay at her feet. With a sigh of disgust, thinking the idea of killing them really might be a better one, she stooped and picked them up.

"Thank you, you'll be glad this happened in the long run. Now is there anything else I should know about before I let you leave with your lives? Anything you heard?" She tapped the sword in her hand as she glared at both of them.

"No really. It was just a job, something to keep people aware," the blond wailed. "Don't take our licenses, we won't be able to even learn until we get them back."

Remember, knowledge is the only way to combat ignorance.

"Do you two know why you can summon demons?" She kept her voice mild, curious as to what they would say.

"Sure," the brunet said holding his sleeve to his bleeding nose. "We can open the portal and we control the demon we summon through the portal. You have to be really strong to control the bigger demons but the little ones are slaved to you."

You know, maybe I should just kill them and save the world from them reproducing.

The thought lightened her mood a bit but their words still made her stomach clench.

Kayter dropped into a crouch, ID's in one hand, the sword in the other, looking at them.

"That isn't exactly how it works. Would you like to know, or should I just kill you now?"

They both paled even more, an impressive feat given how pale they already were.

"Tell us... yes, please." They said voices overlapping.

"Portals take two sides to open, one here and one there, and the drone demons aren't smart enough or powerful enough to open the portal on the other side. That means there is another demon there, holding it and they can send through anything they want. Now because you are both very minorly gifted," she ignored their pouts, "you can only create a very small portal. That means the drones are the only ones that can come through; besides they are attracted to portal energies anyhow. But on the other side, the demon holding it open is smarter and more powerful and if that portal is open long enough, they can make it bigger." Both boys had wide eyes at this point.

"They taught you to close it quickly, right?" They nodded looking at her. "Well, that is because if the demon on other side has time to gather resources he can make it wide enough to send anything through. And drones are only controllable because they seek another mind to control theirs. The rest of the demons?" Her smile, sharp with no humor, spread across her face. "Those demons will bind you, break you, and keep you alive until they have moved through all the demons they want, to then kill everything and everyone. And I mean once they are here, why should they go back? Because trust me, no one, not even master level mages can control another sentient demon. The drones, they aren't sentient - the rest, they have their own plans for us and none of those plans involve us living."

"Oh gods," the whispered words were laced with horror and understanding.

"Exactly. I'm not sure what this government agency is planning but I can tell you a lot of people would die. And it would all be your fault."

"We didn't know. Really. They spun a good story, telling us people were getting complacent and we needed to make sure they didn't forget, so we would never be weak again. I mean we don't want to cause people to die."

"Fine, I'll make you a deal." She snapped her sheathed sword back onto her back and pulled out her phone snapping pictures of their licenses. Then she tossed them at their feet. "I'll let you keep these. But if you hear anything, and I do mean anything, going down or wanting portals open, you call me." She pulled out a card, a number nothing else. It was a VoIP number, not easily traceable, but it would route to her fast enough. "Leave a message if I don't answer. And if I ever run into you calling demons up, I'll let you summon it, let it eat you, then I'll kill it."

She meant every word and she could tell from the paleness on their faces they knew she did.

With that she rose and walked off, leaving the two idiots sitting there and hopefully thinking about their life choices.

Chapter 8 - Demons Attack

In the two years since he'd retired, Declan fell into a routine that provided some structure and social interaction. He performed daily perimeter security checks, making sure he checked for tampering around the cameras and sensors, where the animals walked, and how long it would take someone to walk from each point to reach his house. Declan had no immediate threat against him that he knew of but the better safe than sorry adage had merit. After a month or two, he had decided he needed some human interaction after all. He wasn't looking for a girlfriend or wife by any stretch of the imagination, but he missed the social aspect of life he had back in his uniform days. For that he hung out in the Veterans of Foreign Wars hall a couple nights a week.

He pulled his truck into the parking lot of the Jennings's VFW. He saw a few familiar cars and one or two that he didn't recognize. He glanced at his watch.

Sweet, still happy hour.

Declan jumped out of his truck, locking it by habit, and headed towards the large, single story, white wood building with the largest flagpole in the town proudly displayed out front.

He buzzed in at the door. After a short pause, the door clicked open, and he walked in. It took a minute to sign the membership visit log then he beelined for the bar. He'd paid the lifetime membership fee years ago without blinking. To join you had to have fought in a foreign war and the Blood War counted even if they fought on their own soil. Auxiliary membership was given to the dependents of those who fought in that war.

Declan did a quick look to see if anybody was here tonight that he would be able to tolerate. As luck would have it, at the corner

Blood War: Rage

table in his customary spot, sat a local pick-up warrior from the Blood War. A civilian marksman who survived to tell the tale. It made him a local hero. To Declan, Andrew Cabello was just a friend he could be comfortable around. When the war broke out Andrew worked as an optical engineer developing advanced camera imagery for satellites, pretty high-end engineering stuff. In his spare time, he was an Appleseed civilian firearms instructor. He specialized in long-distance shooting and instructing kids on firearms safety. When the war broke out he became a volunteer add-on civilian fighter. He developed an affinity for the Barrett .50 caliber rifle, becoming an extremely effective sniper.

Warfare had changed its tactics when fighting demon hordes but one thing never changed, even demon leaders tended to stand out and killing them was a good thing. With his weapon of choice, Andrew would single out the horde subgroup leaders, or heavy weapons operators, for special long-range attention. He may not have killed demons by the thousands but he made every shot count. Since meeting each other in Jennings they would often talk about sports, politics, the Food Network, shooting, world events or just nothing at all. What neither ever seemed to talk about was the war. By unspoken agreement, they both decided to leave those discussions behind.

Declan crossed the room toward the well-worn polished wooden bar, glancing over at Casey the bartender and nodded. Without a word, Casey grabbed a sixteen-ounce glass and starting pulling a beer from the Yuengling tap as Declan made his way over to the corner table.

"How's it going, shithead?" Declan asked Andrew as he pulled up a chair and sat down.

"Pretty good. Get your new apple tree row planted?"

"Yup. I've now become a farmer. Well, at least enough to keep my agricultural credit on the property."

"Oh yeah, need to keep that Maryland taxman off your ass. They couldn't snap up that sweet bonus that you got after the war but they sure as hell will get that property tax from you, won't they? You being landed gentry and all now."

"You can count on that, Cabello. You still doing those technical reviews for the new optical sights from Bushnell?"

"Oh yeah. They keep sending me the prototype sights and I do my assessment then give an engineering review. I let them publish the review and in return, I get to keep the hardware if I liked it."

"You know, if you're overloaded on that free high-end glass I can always take some off your hand."

"Sorry, Declan. This is quality stuff. You'd break such pretty kit inside of twenty minutes trying to mount it to that stupid, ugly assed carbine you like to shoot."

"Hey now, I always take care of the pretty things and yes, my Vulture carbine may be ugly, but she's my kind of special ugly."

As both of them chuckled at the standard good-natured insulting ritual, Declan paused for a moment as Casey came up to the table.

"You two loafers going to order anything? Or are you just going suck up space here sitting? Your burger is on the way Andrew, but I'll grab you a new beer in as soon Kenner manages to decipher the complexity of a ten-item menu."

"I'll just have some nachos with extra loafing on the side."

"All right, Kenner. So, it's your normal order then." Casey laughed as he turned and left to go enter in the order behind the bar.

"Who's the new guy over there?" Declan nodding his head to the clean-cut thirty-something in a dark polo shirt and jeans sitting at the corner of the bar facing the door.

Why does he look like he is watching everyone just a little too much?

"Beats me. I asked Casey when I came in. The guy said his name was Chad and signed in with a Springfield D.C. chapter membership card. Smells like a Fed to me."

"Well, he's a bit off the beaten track. But shit, I'm not local so who am I to judge?"

"Hell, Declan, you're local now. Shit, you own more of the land around here than most of the old-timers."

"Ahh, just a small spread to keep me busy in my sunset days. You know that."

"Yeah, yeah. Mr. Kenner the gentleman farmer who doesn't know shit one about farming."

"Shhhhh, don't say that too loud. You'll ruin my rep."

"Yeah right. Apple orchard. Um huh. Last I checked, a man did not need a gun range with pop up targets for growing apples."

"Bite me, Cabello. I'm a hobbyist shooter and I like apple pies. Therefore, apples are needed."

"Speaking of which, Declan, I'm thinking of swinging your way Saturday afternoon. The security desk receptionist at my office finally caved."

"Really? Outstanding, Andrew. The cute blond?"

"That's her. She's never done any shooting and I was thinking of taking her out to your range to do some long gun shooting if that's OK. I can set out the primed reactive targets at your place and I figured her first time should be a big bang event."

"Not a problem at all. Just text me and I'll key the gate for you. You know the way." Declan lowered his voice a little, his voice halting and asks. "You bringing out the Bear?"

Andrews' face seemed to freeze for a second. Declan wondering if he crossed a line. "The Bear... Naw. She needs to stay asleep. Hopefully forever."

"Sorry, didn't mean to... Yeah. Sorry."

"Hey, no problem brother. For your clear violation of man code, I declare your sentence." Andrew said as he motioned to Casey for another round and pointed at Declan with a hand motion of writing a check signaling to put it on Declan's tab.

Declan noted that the smile accompanying the gesture was more forced than normal for the always friendly Andrew. He immediately regretted bringing up The Bear. The Bear was the name Andrew had given to his sniper rifle that he still had stowed away somewhere ever since the war. Its devastation against demon horde leaders was still legendary in this part of the state.

Doug Burbey & Mel Todd

But there were stories, never spoken in Andrews' presence, of how he provided long-range mercy to his fellow fighters when the demons overcame them. Declan understood how that weighed on someone's soul. It was a wound that never healed in a person's mind. Both Andrew and Declan carried that same, and very deep, wound.

What the fuck was I thinking? Damn, dick move Kenner.

Declan quickly changed the subject. "You still toting that .38 Sig around as a carry piece?"

"Yeah. Why? You still on your never-ending quest for the perfect carry piece?"

"Yeah, I guess. I have my Springfield Trophy Match 1911 out in my truck now but I'm still not sold on using it as my full-time carry piece. I just can't seem to find something that I'm as comfortable with shooting as I am with the Vulture. But the last time Donahue came over to my place for shooting, he threatened to take an angle grinder to her, due to his offense at its inelegance."

"Donahue? Oh yeah, Greg, that ex-Air Force Pave Hawk helicopter pilot, with a propensity for cutting down treetops that you used to run with during the war. Well damn, you can't exactly conceal that monstrosity in your pants. Besides, those things are just too damn heavy even for a carbine and I have no need to shoot loads that hot. I have not once been attacked by an elephant. Well, not lately. Ok, maybe a pink elephant last Saturday night after drinking that crap Derick claimed was moonshine. Besides, Greg was right, the Vulture has to be the ugliest weapon man has ever created."

Laughing, as Andrew continued to explain his complicated theory on how Derick must be stealing radioactive waste water and mixing it with pine tar to create his evil beverages, Declan noticed that the polo shirt newbie was still paying way more attention to the people in the bar than he should be.

Something just isn't right about this guy.

Declan had just begun to stand up to go have a chat with the guy when Casey arrived with his food and a new beer.

69

Blood War: Rage

"Here you go, Kenner, one order of nachos. Sorry, we're out of your order of extra loafing by the way. Would you care to substitute that with a side of lollygagging instead?"

Chuckling, Declan replied, "Sure Casey, but I would like my lollygagging a solid medium rare, please."

Putting his thoughts about the strange behavior of the newcomer aside, Declan dug into his nachos and beer and continued his debate with Andrew on the merits and flaws of various absurd items to use as concealed carry weapons. Declan was pretty sure they had this conversation three weeks ago. Neither seemed to care either way if they did. Besides, no one sells chainsaw hand axes anyway.

Declan pulled up the collar of his fleece jacket as he exited the bar about ninety minutes later and started walking across the parking lot to his truck. Warm food in his stomach, some good conversation, and a slight buzz filled the need for human interaction.

Hold on. Is that actual buzzing? Not just my ears?

For a moment Declan thought he may be hearing things but then it started. His senses began to sharpen. He could feel the old reemergence of his magically enhanced battle awareness trying to take hold.

No, no, no! Declan screamed to his own mind. *Not again.*

Turning rapidly, he looked for the source of the noise triggering his physical reaction that he fought to repress. A catalog of old memories, shoved deep into the recesses of his mind, quickly attached itself to the noise and presented itself as a known threat.

Drone. Demon drone. It can't be.

With this realization, he no longer had an option of fighting for control against himself to prevent summoning the battle awareness. His body demanded that he survive, His heightened senses fed his mind with an overlay of his surroundings only visible in his mind but prodding his reflexes without conscious thought.

Declan turned towards the source of buzzing noise and confirmed what his mind already told him. Looking up towards the top of the VFW hall, a squat four-legged, insect-winged demon drone was watching him. The size of a small dog with the general appearance of a great big grey maggot with wings, it glared back at him. A row of protruding black eyes, starting at its small jagged mouth, ran all the way to its blunted tail. During the war, these drones were used as advance scouts for demon sub horde leaders. The demon leaders apparently used some form of an empathic link to see with the drone's eyes and provide direction to the otherwise largely unintelligent larva.

Unintelligent. Controlled. It's not alone then. And now I'm staring right at it so whatever is controlling it knows that I've seen it's scout. Fuck.

Keeping his eyes on the drone, he let his battle senses feed him with hyper-awareness that almost seemed to slow time around him as his mind raced. He began to back slowly toward his truck.

Truck about 25 feet behind me. The 1911 is in the center armrest counsel. Magazine is loaded but there's no chambered round. Doors locked. Truck keys in left jacket pocket. Folding five-inch serrated lock blade hooked to belt behind right hip.

Continuing to step backward, Declan watched the drone track his movement with coal black eyes and flutter its insectoid wings. That generated the humming sounds again.

Truck now 22 feet behind me. Doors still locked. No way to get to the gun. Move my left hand towards truck keys in left jacket pocket. Move right hand towards knife hooked to belt behind my hip.

The drone began to squat its four segmented legs in a movement Declan recognized as a precursor to jumping forward to launch itself either at him or into flight.

Truck now 19 feet behind me. Almost have the truck keys. I have the knife hooked to my belt. I must turn my back on the threat to make it to the truck. There's not enough time to get the gun.

The drone surged forward in a rapid downward arc from the roof towards him. The combat details of the drone snapped into his head. Not efficient in horde combat. When engaged in combat

Blood War: Rage

they stab with their front two legs or bite with the sharp protrusions from the softball-sized mouth. Neither attack is efficient against standard body armor.

Except I'm not wearing any damn body armor right now!

Declan pulled from his memories as he tracked the fast moving drone about to hit him square in the chest.

He dropped to one knee and pivoted, driving the five-inch blade directly under the chin of the drone. Letting the forward momentum of the demon drag the blade across its underbelly as it tore open the soft rubbery flesh before the knife caught and was pulled, wet with blood, out of his hand.

Yeah, you don't have any armor either fucker.

Declan grinned as the drone smashed face first into the parking lot and laid there, unmoving.

Cautiously, he reached down and wrapped his hand around the handle of the knife lodged in the small demon's flesh. He strained his senses to see or feel the slightest indication that the drone might still be functioning. The dead eyes didn't twitch as he yanked the knife free causing the drone's rubbery flesh to ripple momentarily and cover its belly in the same thick yellow blood that coated the blade. The thick blood ran down the blade dripping onto his hand, leaving sparks of power that danced along his sense, muted but there.

Dead. But it was unintelligent and controlled. Who the fuck was controlling it. They could be anywhere, miles away even. But it's not miles away, is it?

Declan saw a shape outlined in the shadows crouching behind the small trailer mounted crab boat that the VFW stored at the back of the lot. He heard the nervous shuffling and faintly made out the smell of... fear.

Human fear?

Declan slowly moved towards the partially concealed individual, acutely aware of the sounds of his shoes on the blacktop and how it could betray his position. Reaching the boat, he began to hear the sounds of a chant beginning.

"Oh, hell no!" Declan yelled and started to run at the target. Risk of an imminent magical attack outweighed the need for subtlety.

Nobody is gonna throw a spell at me!

Crossing the front of the boat, he latched onto a crouched human male chanting and gesturing. Declan tasted and felt the small buildup of energy in the air around them. Nothing else registered before his body slammed shoulder first into the Mage, driving both of them onto the ground hard. The Mage took the brunt of the inelegant assault from Declan and choked on his chanting as Declan's body slammed him to the ground.

With speed born of adrenaline, Declan pushed himself up, grabbed the head of the human, pulling him back by the hair as he placed his bloody knife at the throat of the mage. His mind took in details even as he prepared to slit the throat of the threat.

Declan noticed the mage could not be more than nineteen years old. At most. He wore jeans, sneakers, and a retro Xbox shirt.

Keeping the young mage, who was still panting for breath, pinned, Declan pressed the knife against the human's throat. One pound of effort and a move to the right and the threat would be dead.

Could I really kill him? Am I no better than before?

"I think you need to start talking right now kid, and I mean right now, or I will slit your throat for trying to kill me and for summoning a god damn demon. What the fuck are you thinking?!"

"I'm a licensed apprentice mage, sir, I swear." The mage squeaked as Declan began to let the tip of his knife puncture the boy's neck.

"That doesn't answer anything. No mage is allowed to summon or even communicate with a demon or anything in their realm. The penalty is death. No. You couldn't summon a fucking thing on your own I'd bet. Who gave you the drone and why did you try to kill me with it like an idiot!"

Declan started to lose control as he screamed at the boy. He wanted, needed, to shove his blade deep into his neck. Feel his blood flow onto his hand like that of the small demon. He hungered to drain this human's power into his own. To have the ultimate control over all life and death while gaining power. He must gain more power or he would be consumed by those that were more powerful. He'd defeated this fool and now a price must be paid. It must be paid in blood now. It's the only way.

NO! Help me! No more of it. Not now. I can't. Please make it stop.

Declan moaned and fell backward against the boat releasing both the young mage and dropping the knife onto the ground.

"Please stop. I can't. I won't!" Declan shouted, grabbing at his head with both hands as his body began to tremble as it fought against itself for control.

Part of him saw the mage flee but nothing mattered but the rage pounding in him, crying to get out.

How do I stop it, I haven't had blood in years? Is there even enough left in me now to control it?

His battle sense remained as a side effect of the magic exposure and other realm blood elements. On the battlefield, the sense drew on him constantly. But the blood that coated him got into his mouth and absorbed into his skin, covering the cost and more. It thrived off a human's soul, or chi, and the blood balanced it. But the demon rage was like hitting the gas pedal on a drag racer, emptying the fuel tank in seconds. You received all the power you could want but you burnt out fast and had to be replenished. Replenishment meant blood, one way or another.

Must push it down now or someone will die.

Declan raised his hand slowly and closed his eyes as he began to lick the drops of blood off his fingers. Each drop of demon blood entering his body gave him a bit more control. He felt it merging with him - rewarding him for his kill, recharging his body so he can kill more for more reward. More power.

Yes. I have paid the debt. Now reward me.

Declan moaned, almost as if in pleasure. Then his eyes snapped abruptly open as all of his senses returned to normal.

Looking at his hand Declan noticed they are completely licked clean of blood. Every bit of the demon's blood gone. He choked off an involuntary sob of revulsion.

Pulling himself up in a daze, he walked back through the parking lot and noticed nothing out of the ordinary. He grabbed the dead drone carcass and tossed it into the back of his truck. Declan pulled himself slowly into the cab and drove away from the VFW and headed back to his place.

I don't think I can do this again. They can't be back already.

The battle awareness shutdown began, his senses dulling, oxygen fighting against the lactic acid build up in his muscles. His temples begin to ache as his body started reclaiming its chemical balance within his bloodstream. His reserve of latent magical energy was now almost totally depleted.

It's been too long. I'm burning much faster than I can recover from now.

His face grew rigid as he drove to his sanctuary. Demons were coming.

Chapter 9 - Allies?

She drove Midnight through the streets, cruising with an almost silent purr. Kayter smiled as she felt the vibrations and listened to the streets around her. Everyone took for granted the wars were over but she never had. Her dad had made sure of that. Real enemies never quit, which is why she made sure she knew where her allies were in every city she could. Not friends, but allies. Allies would be more important than friends when shit went sideways.

Up ahead the VFW sign came into view and she angled towards it. The VFW would give her food, good booze, and allow her to scope out possible allies. Even if she would have to deal with men treating her like she was just someone's kid to be humored.

As she pulled into the parking lot, she passed a black F150 pulling out with an older bald man behind the steering wheel. She only caught a glimpse of him but something pulled at her, a memory? Someone she knew? But even as she turned her head to look better, he pulled away leaving her with a fleeting memory of something she couldn't pin down.

Huh, never had that happen before. I'll keep an eye out for that truck. Too bad it wasn't neon pink or something easier to pick out.

Filing the thought away in her head, she came to a stop and shut off the engine but she didn't take off the helmet. Another simple spell let her listen clearly through the helmet though with anyone else, the world outside would have been muffled.

A man in dark jeans and a polo shirt that just struck her as too neat stood there talking on his phone, his head turning to track the F-150.

"Yeah, think he's ready for pick up. He's showing signs of the rage. I'll meet you in two days so we can discuss setting up an incident. That should give him plenty of time to simmer." He paused obviously listening, then spoke up. "If he proves too much trouble, we'll eliminate him. Old demon hunters are flakey anyway, he's just convenient. Sure. I'll file a report."

The man hung up the phone, unlocked the car he stood by, pulling something from the glove box then locked it back up and walked back into the bar. He glanced at her as she pulled off her helmet. The cascade of hair caught his attention as she shook her head, purposefully yawning as if popping her ears. He smiled at her, lingering for a minute, but she completely ignored him. With one more backward glance he went back into the bar.

He'll hit on me when I go in. Wonder why they were so interested in that guy? Hell, why am I so interested in him? And who are they? And why do I smell demon blood?

Her body stock still, she let the sting of the scent invade her nostrils but she couldn't place a location. As if there had been blood there but the body got up and left.

Demons here? At a VFW? How fucking stupid could they get?

Narrowing her eyes, she pulled off her leather riding jacket and tucked it into one of the saddle bags, after pulling out a worn jean jacket. The jacket was threadbare in places but as she pulled it on her fingers gently traced the black bar with a red ribbon through it. A small pin sat below it, a gold star on a field of red. The medal given to a serviceman's family. For all other wars the field had been purple but if they were the eligible survivor of his or her immediate family in the Blood War, it was red. Then, in a ritual years in the making, her fingers continued over to the patch she'd sewed on herself with the 1-66 Armored Battalion crest on it. The last stop in her touch pattern, the subdued eagle patch and name tag with her dad's name. His dog tags had never been found and the idea of reprinting them seemed wrong. But the patch and tag were spares he'd had shipped to her, along with other things that in the long run were more important, when he got word of the imminent portal.

Blood War: Rage

But for now these symbols were paramount, especially here. She started to enter, then stopped. Something about the comments from the man, the twig of memory about the demon hunter, all set the hair on the back of her neck rising.

What the fuck, I don't have anything else to do.

She reached back in and grabbed a small tracking device and slapped it up under the wheel well of the car.

I can track him, see where he goes, and follow in two days. I'll see who he meets - maybe nothing, maybe something.

Dismissing it from her mind, she'd follow up on the tracker back at her RV. Now she wanted food, some information, and some beer. Hopefully, they had more than pale swill on tap.

She buzzed in and signed the log. Conversation died as she strode through the room, the sharp cracks of her riding boots hitting the linoleum floor as she moved for a table in the corner. Dropping into the corner, she let her gaze sweep over the room and men looked back at her. As the only woman beside a waitress, the men assessed her, their gazes snagging on the bar and the medal, then flicking to the patch. Half of them nodded at her, the older ones, turning and going back to their conversations.

A stocky thirtysomething man, with a warm natural smile, detached himself from behind the bar and walked over to her.

"Hey. I haven't seen you here before." His eyes snagged on the name on her jacket. "Your dad?"

"Yeah, part of 1-66 at Ypsilanti."

"Ah. I've got a few other survivors here from that. You never joined?"

The question was common and she smiled, taking no offense. "No. For lots of reasons, but the primary one, Dad asked me not to when I turned eighteen. Besides the war ended a few years later."

"Makes sense. So, what can I get you?"

She glanced at the menu, you never could tell what a given VFW would serve but the quantity never disappointed. "Bacon cheeseburger, medium, fries, and a side salad, please. Large lager? Something dark?"

Doug Burbey & Mel Todd

"You got it." He turned and strode back to the bar.

Kayter pulled out her phone and pretended to check it, even as she scoped out the other people in the room. The man who'd preceded her in sat at the bar but she caught his eyes watching her in the mirror. A few others, younger men, probably caught the mop-up of the Blood War. Since the armistice had been signed, there had been no overseas engagements. While the US still maintained a minuscule presence at some their bases overseas, the world had entered an unprecedented few years of peace. That was mainly because most countries were still trying to recover from the damage, that and no one had any patience with a country acting out. The last one to try had been informed that many countries still had nukes that were useless against demons but they had no issue with shooting them at humans.

The emergence of demons had shattered centuries-old religious feuds. Having real demons invade created a ripple effect on how religions treated the afterlife.

One of the men, youngish, probably did a few years in the Sandbox before the BW started, pushed back his chair and headed over to her. The others at his table were casting grins at his back.

Kayter rolled her eyes and prepared to be wooed. Unlike the idiot back at the Waffle House, this qualified as a potential ally and you never burned that bridge without serious consideration.

Decent enough looking, with an engaging smile, he ambled over, hands in his pockets and shoulders a bit bent. She had to restrain the desire to snap at him to straighten up and walk like a man. Her father had zero tolerance for anyone that didn't carry themselves in a no-nonsense manner. If you walked like a victim, you were a victim. If you walked like you were unsure, you were unsure.

"Hey, haven't you seen you in here before." His eyes snagged on her jacket, registering the emblems there, and his attitude changed. "Dad?"

"Yeah, 1-66."

"I'm sorry for your loss."

Blood War: Rage

She shrugged. "I'm not. He went out and took a hell of a lot of those bastards with them. I know for sure he died well. He wouldn't have wanted anything less."

"How did you end up here?" It sounded like an honest question, so she answered it.

"Heard about the portal rumor out here, figured I'd check it out. I've got some experience with demons."

Understatement of the century there.

He glanced out the windows and looked at the Chief sitting there.

"That yours?"

"Yeah, my baby. I rebuilt her with Dad. Needless to say, she's kinda important." She couldn't stop the lilt of pleasure when she talked about the Chief.

The kid, and why did he feel like such a kid to her, when in reality he probably had a few years on her, straightened up and looked at her closely. She knew he saw her knives and her gun. She didn't make any effort to hide them; she just didn't flaunt them. Then he gave her a real smile, not the come hither one she knew he had practiced.

"My name's Kyle and I came over to see if I could buy you a drink. Even though you're the most stunning woman I've seen in years," he said with sincerity, his blues eyes locked on her mismatched ones, "I'm not enough for you. You've probably killed more demons than I have. I never got any major action and... " he trailed off and shrugged. "You aren't looking for any action. Even I can see that. And I'm not about to go where I'm not wanted. I hope I see you around. Let me know if you need anything." He turned and walked away, this time his posture straight.

Kayter sat there blinking for a moment, thrown off guard and chuckled to herself.

Maybe there is more to the kid than I thought.

Before she had a chance to look after him, the watcher from the parking lot stood and walked over holding two beers and sat down across from her.

Her smile held not an ounce of sincerity but she kept her temper as she looked at the interloper.

"I figured since you chased away the child, you might like a man."

She looked him over, and unlike the kid, he blinked a bit when he saw her eyes, brown and blue locking on to him.

"Who said I wanted a man?" Her voice was cool but she reached out and took the beer; free booze was free booze. She glanced up and saw the bartender nod at her and took a pull, knowing it hadn't been tampered with. Or more accurately, if it had been, the entire VFW would be on fire soon. She knew her body and it would recognize most drugs, so she let the beer wash away a touch of her stress.

"Doesn't every woman? A man to protect her, to keep her warm at night?"

Kayter paused halfway to another mouthful of beer, grateful he'd said that before she took a drink, or maybe she wasn't. If he'd said it, he would have gotten covered with beer in a spit take.

"There are lots of things I need. New tires for my bike, a steady paycheck, and unlimited beer. Nowhere in that list is a man. So, thank you for the beer but I'm just here to get some food, then I'll get going."

Taking that second mouthful of beer, she waited to see how he would respond.

He flushed red. "You owe me, I bought you a beer and you drank it."

"Sure, free beer. But that was your choice. You didn't say I owed you, so I got a free beer. Go me." She flashed him a smile, raising the beer glass in a mock toast and waited to see what he would say or do.

He pushed back from his chair looming over her, trying to intimidate. Kayter didn't care, she wanted to see how the rest of the bar reacted and had to fight to hide a smile. Kyle and his table of other two guys stood up and were headed over as were the two old guys in the corner, the bartender had stepped out with a bat in his hand, and one guy, a bit younger than her dad would have been, reached down to pull a gun and set it on the table facing their direction.

Yes, I could kiss you, you unknown asshole, you just did all my work for me.

"Bitch, just cause your daddy died doesn't mean all you have to do is shake your tits and get anything you want."

"My father gave his life to save assholes like you. But I didn't shake anything. Just cause you served, you think you should get into my pants? That's your problem, not mine. Go away."

"Ma'am, is he bugging you?" Kyle spoke with his friends behind him, and the two old men, Vietnam vets from their hats.

"Bugging? No, but he is about to get hurt." She said her eyes never leaving the sleaze. "Go away. I came in for food nothing else."

His face flushed red and for a minute she thought he would swing at her.

Please swing at me, that would be perfect. Please?

He glanced around to see the bartender looking at him. "Close out your tab. You're not welcome here anymore."

"Bitch," he snarled and Kayter just smiled.

The Vietnam Vet, a man with dark brown skin, and white curly hair snorted. "Give it up. You pushed your luck and she called you on it rather than letting you intimidate her. Good for her, wish my daughter had stood up to her asshole of a husband like that. Get out."

"Or what?" He demanded, belligerent now.

"Really?" She asked looking at him, now more curious than ever exactly why he was following vets. The only one in the room who would have actually done anything in the Blood Wars was the man in the corner. "You have a nice gentleman over there pointing a .38 Sig Sauer at you. Three young men standing behind you ready to kick your ass, two Vietnam Vets who will swear no one saw what happened to you, and then there is me." She leaned forward. "You've insulted me, interrupted my dinner, threatened me, and you don't know a damn thing about me. Go away." Her voice never raised but she saw the smirks of respect from the men in the room and the grins of amusement from the waitresses. That told her he'd probably been an ass but not enough to make it worth complaining about.

He looked at the people around him, swallowed hard and threw a twenty on the table and stormed out. Kyle and his friends followed him.

The two Vietnam vets grinned at her and gave her a saucy wink, which she returned, then headed back to their table. The man in the corner, one she didn't know or recognize but got the same feel from him as from Dad near the end, nodded at each other and his .38 disappeared.

"Morons. I swear. Those jerks did a single tour, get picked up with a government agency, and think they are all hot shit. Sorry about all the drama. Your food will be out in a minute." The bartender stalked way, putting the bat under the counter.

Government agency? Curiouser and curiouser. See Dad, the classics are good for snarky comments in my head.

Kyle and his friends came back in. "He left, we made sure we didn't touch your bike, ma'am."

"Gah," she choked. "I'm not that old. Name's Kayter, Kayter Reynolds. Thanks." Her smile was genuine and each of them blushed as she smiled at them but they headed back to their table and their pitcher of beer as the waitresses brought her food. She tucked into the good basic food, silently crowing at the mission accomplished. She'd created some allies, the entire reason she'd come.

Kayter took a long look around the VFW parking lot before she climbed on her bike, pulling her helmet on. Agent boy hadn't been too pleased when she blew him off and just because he left didn't mean he hadn't come back.

That proved unexpectedly fruitful. I have people on my side, and if I need it, someone, maybe, I can call on. I should have at least introduced myself to Mister .38, but still not a bad intro.

Blood War: Rage

The Chief purred it's almost silent agreement as she wove through the streets back towards the RV park. Curiosity about the man's comments before she came in remained at the forefront of her mind as she drove. The area seemed quiet but she wanted to swear she smelled demon blood in the air. That idea sent cold chills through her.

Getting back to the RV she took the time to put the Chief back on the trailer and secured it. It only took one late night evacuation where she had to spend precious time to hook it up, to make that a habit. Once it was locked to the trailer she pulled out her sword, extra weapons, and ammo from the bags.

Kayter glanced at the RV but shook her head. Checking up on the tracker could wait. Besides, the meeting she cared about wouldn't happen for a few days. That meant she needed to prioritize important stuff. And that meant practice. Walking over to the picnic table, she dropped everything on it but her sword. Even just holding it made the crawling on her skin recede a bit.

Dropping her leather jacket to join her gun, she unsheathed her sword. The *jian* was a double edge sword rarely seen but it fit her fighting style. And with the *sanmei*, or three plate construction, it allowed her strength and flexibility. Dad would never tell her where he got it but he took a half pint of her blood when she turned eighteen and hadn't grown in the last year. Two months later the sword appeared.

"It's yours, made of you and for you. It should protect you better than I can. Never let the edge dull." With that, he'd walked away, and she went to her teacher to learn how to use this new weapon.

Now, years later, she moved into the flows, attacking enemies, practicing her form and working hard. She practiced for an hour, using all the katas her teacher had created for her, all of them with death blows for the various demon types. By the time she finished her heart hammered in her chest and sweat drenched her body, but nothing hurt, only felt nicely warm.

With a bow to the imaginary teacher, she cleaned, then

sharpened the sword, before sliding it back into its sheath. Dad had asked if she'd named it, and she'd looked at him funny.

"It's a sword. Why would I name it?"

He'd just chuckled and never asked again.

The memory of his smile flashed through her mind and she smiled, but that memory pulled back at the dream, the not dream.

Is that where I recognized the bald man? What did Dad call him? Colonel, he had a rank.

But nothing else would come to her mind and she let it go. Forcing it wouldn't bring it up. Stepping into the RV, she headed to the shower, enjoying the heat, and washed with one of her few luxuries, ginger-scented body wash and shampoo. It smelled nothing like demons, had no memories associated with it, so she'd claimed it as hers. Something that meant nothing to her, and therefore meant everything.

Stepping out, dressed and hair at least not dripping, she headed to the computer pulling up her tracking system. She didn't have many of these little toys. A pure tech item paid for with cash and her petty cash was running low.

Pulling up the program on her computer, she typed in the ID of the tracker she'd dropped on the man and pulled it up. The icon lit up outside an apartment building in the area, not too far from the VFW. She set an alarm to let her know where it would be in two days, then typed in an order to store the location of any place it was at for longer than 10 minutes.

With that, she headed to bed. She had some gear to buy tomorrow since she hadn't seen any demons stumbling around the local neighborhood.

Blood War: Rage

Chapter 10 – Coming Down

Declan rolled down his window and punched the lock release code into the control box lifting the gate to his property entrance. He noticed his fingers still trembled as he pushed in the code. Was it the fact that he had the demon body in the bed of his truck when they shouldn't even be in his realm or the fact that the battle rage so quickly took over his body when he was unprepared?

In the final weeks of the war, the symptoms of the rage had become common amongst the veteran hunters. Originally it was discounted as an adrenaline rush combined with residual magic exposure but the symptoms quickly abated after the inevitable splashes of blood and absorption of the demon body fluids into their bodies. It did not take the doctors, or even the hunters themselves, long to reach the conclusion that they were both related. But when coming down from the rage now, Declan had to rely on a trick that the human mages had shared with them about being able to consume little bits of yourself to counter the effects. The mages still called it the human Chi, the Fae had some weird name for it that translated loosely to one's own balancing core energy. Either way, a person's own individual reserves of this energy was finite unless replenished and the only way that humans knew how to do that was through infusion, or absorption, of a demon's own blood. Some of the human mages, what Declan thought of as corrupted ones, directly infused demon blood into their own to enhance their powers. Some did it with syringes like a heroin junkie, the more extreme went so far as to have stents implanted into an artery so they could mainline demon blood from an IV bag directly into their own, giving them a reserve of power on a battlefield. Shane had devised that trick and encouraged it among his Soldier Mages.

Shane, who he could have called immediately for help once. But that friendship had burned with the end of the Blood War.

Even if Shane was possibly still alive there's no way in hell I'm calling him for anything.

Declan drove his truck into the woods at the back of his property and threw the drone's body into the burn pit he used to get rid of wood scraps and fallen tree limbs. After soaking the corpse in diesel fuel he ignited the drone and watched it burn, smelling the conflicting sweet but rancid odor of the burning demon flesh. It was the smell of a Blood War battlefield.

I want more. I need more.

Declan didn't know if the wave of nausea he felt was from the after-effects of the receding rage, the smell of the burning demon, or his own thoughts and desires but it was clear now that a Demon Hunter would never be able to live a long and quiet retirement. If he couldn't control the rage, then it would consume him when his reserves were exhausted and when hunters got consumed they usually took out a lot of other people with them. It was not a question of if, but when. Maybe he should have joined up with some of the other veterans that signed onto mercenary groups overseas to live fast and fight hard on suicide missions. Fighting hungover and high till they died in some third world shithole for a petty dictator's civil war.

"I can't go out like those guys. I'm not ready to quit just yet." Declan turned his back on the fire and started back towards his truck. "There has to be another way."

Chapter 11 - Kayter and Miriam

With the two idiot mages on her mind, Kayter wondered if she needed to pay closer attention to what magic they taught at the universities. She pulled up to a nondescript warehouse, and shut off the bike, looking at it closely.

I hope they have what I'll need, or at least can make it. Dad said he knew them way back when, and since then they've become a name in the close-knit hunter community.

At first glance, it just seemed to be a warehouse, but she noted the reinforced base, the heavy front door with a peep section, and a keypad next to it. The windows at the top had bars over all of them. This place should be able to withstand an assault and if they had the right ordinance, they'd be able to eliminate anyone stupid enough to try.

Taking a deep breath, she flipped down the kickstand and slid off, walking up to the door, hand on her pistol as she approached. Standing to the side and making sure the frame of the door protected most of her body, she knocked twice.

The peep panel slid back but she noted no one stood in front of it, any more than she did. Exposing yourself like that was a good way to die. Kayter appreciated that these people weren't idiots.

"What?" A feminine voice said, though it had no softness in it.

"Looking for Hunter Gear. John Reynolds referred me."

"Oh, how is Johnny doing?"

Kayter snorted. "Johnny would kick your ass if you called him that and he's been dead for three years."

"Ah, killed in Detroit?"

"No. Ypsilanti." Kayter's voice remained flat. At this point she'd accepted her dad's death even if she still thirsted for vengeance,

Doug Burbey & Mel Todd

but a lot of people had as much reason as she, if not more. She just counted each demon she killed as one step towards paying for his death.

"How do you know him?"

Kayter let her eyes drift closed for a second, then snapped them back open. In this new world death held no reverence. Everyone had lost someone.

"His daughter."

"Ah." There was a wealth of information in that word but Kayter had no idea how to interpret it. Before she could start to stress, the peep slide closed and she heard the clanking of locks and the door pulled back.

"Welcome, guest to our home and business."

The old formality had power in the words and Kayter suspected the speaker was a magic user of some power. If she entered it put her under obligation to respect her host and the house.

I can live with that.

Letting her hand drop from her pistol, though she shrugged once to feel the reassuring presence of her swords, Kayter crossed the threshold. The door closed behind her with a clang and she had to resist drawing her weapon.

Dad said they were good people, and they gave me hospitality.

She repeated that over in her mind as her eyes adjusted from the brightness to the more subdued lighting inside. A long counter sat to her right and a tiny woman grinned at her. She didn't even come up to Kayter's breasts. She had tiny bones, inquisitive eyes, and dark hair in a short pixie cut.

She heard Miriam's voice again say, "Welcome Guest, to our home and business.". There was a pause, then in a more normal voice "Welcome, Kayter Reynolds. I'm Miriam. How can we serve you today?"

The friendly tone and small stature did a lot to ease her wariness but she still stayed alert.

"I need some new gear and Dad said this was the only place on the East Coast to shop at."

Blood War: Rage

Miriam's face split in a grin. "He was such a charmer. Come on back and let's take a look at what you might need."

She walked from behind the counter and led Kayter through a door at the back. As they walked, Kayter felt the various spells lick across her skin but none of them reacted. While she couldn't wield magic herself, she could sense it and all of these were intent based spells. Since she intended to spend money, it didn't have any issues with her. She filed the information in her head. All these spells meant someone here had extreme enchanting skills - skills she could use.

The door she walked through lead into a huge workshop. At the far end, she saw a forge but it didn't seem to be in use at the moment. Workbenches were scattered everywhere and the walls were lined with enough weapons and gear that she had to actively swallow the saliva that appeared while looking at some of it. Jackets, boots, knives, swords, gloves, guns, and more things than she had names for.

A huge man, at least a foot taller than her, sat at one of the benches. His large hands were turning metal rings into a rippling fabric of metal, each ring smaller than her pinky nail.

The woman gave her time to take in the shop before speaking. "So Kayter, what brings you to us today? And I assume you know you carry all four blood types?" Her eyes drifted over to the swords and then scanned her body, but more in trying to see what size or style she would wear than looking for weapons. Kayter realized the man had quit working on the mail and was watching them, his body relaxed but his gaze intent.

"Yeah, Demon, Angel, Fae, and Human I've been told. All in me. Does it matter?" Her voice remained flat, even as she waited for the answer.

"Ah, an abomination. No wonder your dad was so tense. Interesting." The woman flashed her a grin. "Nope, it doesn't matter. More making sure you know how interested some parties would be in getting a hold of your blood. But not me. This is my place and nothing touches anyone here that I don't allow, but that doesn't mean I wasn't aware of it."

The man had gone back to working with the rings, and a tightness in Kayter relaxed. The urge to stay and never leave almost brought her to her knees. With a soft growl she pushed it away, turning to face the woman instead.

"I need an armored body suit that is flexible enough for me to use my swords. I need a new long-range weapon, preferably something that will take out a ring three with a headshot. While I can kill them up close and personal, for demons that level, I'd rather be half a mile away."

Miriam looked her up and down, her head tilting one way and then the other, it only served to enhance the bird impression.

"I can do the bodysuit and lace it with dampeners, though they'll only last about a year before I'll need to reapply them."

"I can't feed the spells?"

Miriam arched a brow. "What do you mean by feed the spells?"

Kayter hesitated. That information could be worth something. But she couldn't know if other people could feed them or if it was only her. Since she couldn't cast the spells herself, that meant it really did her no good to keep it to herself.

"If I put my blood on the spells, they recharge."

"Huh." The woman said her eyes drifting off a bit. "I could see how that would work for painted or etched on spells," Kayter nodded at that, "but since I weave mine into the fabric I don't think it would work, unless you soaked the fabric in your blood. That might be a bit much blood to shed. Besides, I can recharge them relatively easily on a yearly basis." Miriam shrugged. "But yes, it would work though I'm not sure how long it would last."

Kayter thought about it. "If I bleed while wearing it, will it help or hurt?"

Miriam started to respond then stopped. "Abomination blood. Huh." She fell silent, then turned and spoke to John in a language Kayter didn't recognize. She spoke English, French, German, Spanish and enough Russian to get by. But it didn't sound like any of those.

Blood War: Rage

"If you bleed on my weavings, it should recharge but for a lesser amount of time, unlike my charges. But it will not reduce the efficiency at all. But the idea of a bodysuit is to protect you from getting cut, no?"

"That would be preferable. When I bleed, things get difficult." It was an understated way to say that Demons went into bloodlust to get to her blood, and the Fae just went weird. Thankfully humans didn't react to her blood.

"I imagine. Abominations are usually killed at birth when they survive at all." Miriam didn't have disgust or avarice in her words, simple academic interest. That interest Kayter could live with. "I'll have to plan something new for you; it will be extra. You'll also need some new boots. Yours are losing their integrity."

Kayter glanced down at her worn, twice resoled boots. "But they're comfortable," she protested. Breaking in new boots took forever.

"So are my boots, though you'll need two pairs, to let them breathe properly. Come back in two weeks. I'll have stuff for you."

Kayter blinked, thrown off balance. "Don't you need to measure me?"

"Full body scan equipment as you walked through, as well as capturing your walk pattern and balance on the floor in the entryway. Everything has been stored and under your name."

"Cost?" Kayter didn't know if she really wanted the answer. This sort of equipment, handmade, enchanted equipment, carried a steep price.

The woman shrugged. "I won't know until I make it. Not more expensive than the .30-06 custom we made and sold your dad."

Kayter choked, that rifle had cost over twenty thousand. It had been enchanted with magically telescopic sights that could sight through stone, could not be used by anyone else outside his bloodline, self-cleaning and had included five hundred enchanted bullets that he claimed would go around corners, once locked on, and had a maximum distance of two miles. Dad had only used it twice but said both times took out an overlord demon from over a mile as they exited the gate.

"I would hope not."

Miriam smiled. "I charge what my goods are worth, believe it."

Kayter nodded. She still had that rifle but she wasn't the shot her dad had been. Her skill set and her strengths lay in melee combat. Her genetics made her stronger and tougher than most humans, though pure demons from the higher rings could eat her alive.

"I'll be back in two weeks." With that, she turned and walked out. She had places to be and needed to stop at the bank.

Chapter 12 - Shane is an Ass

The temptation to throw the book across the room made the migraine pounding in his skull worse. And he didn't know if giving in would help, with either the migraine or the frustration.

"Where is Declan when I fucking need him?" Shane shoved his body up and stalked out of his study/ritual room.

He stood at the window, looking at his non-existent view, a nondescript apartment in Arlington. The only things outside the window were other brownstone buildings with their windows staring blankly back at him. It didn't matter. He didn't see the buildings or the world around him for that matter. His mind was locked on the past when Declan Kenner had been his best friend.

"Why the hell couldn't you embrace this new opportunity? We could have everything and you're too fucking hidebound to accept it."

The throbbing at his temples, the book laying on the table laughing at him, and the need for blood all mixed together, pushing his limits.

Center. You can't blow up another apartment.

Shane inhaled deep and slow through his nose and held it until the pounding of the vessels threatened to break through his skull. Then he released it through his mouth, letting the pressure drop. He repeated this until the inhale and exhale mattered more than anything else. Only then did he open his eyes and look at the book.

The portals are the answer. There has to be a way to create what I want. What I need.

Declan popped back into his mind - the raw power, the test scores - everything he refused to use. He'd only accessed the

94

barest of his abilities to keep the rage in check and then locked out everything else.

Shane's glance went back to the book, looking for something he'd read, a word that maybe, that meant something else. Not power but maybe... potential?

He started towards the book with a gleam in his eye when the alarm on his phone went off. Pulling it out he glanced at it and cussed.

Changing his direction, he grabbed a light jacket and headed out the door instead, setting the wards with a flick of his finger against the door jamb. A tiny needle sat there, pulling out the drop of blood needed to be able to set the wards, something so automatic he didn't even think about it.

He took the stairs two at a time. The elevator had never worked and he doubted it would be fixed before he had moved on from this plane.

Why did I agree to this meeting? Oh yeah... stupid idiots that I can get to do stuff for me.

They'd agreed to meet at a park a few miles from his house. He grabbed his bicycle leaning against the entrance to the apartment and gave a brief laugh at the drops of blood surrounding it.

Don't fuck with stuff that isn't yours. You never know who has enchanted it.

The amusement of some gangbanger growing back the skin on his hand kept him distracted during the ride to the park. A bike tended to be all but invisible. A helmet to keep the cops away, jeans and a t-shirt, and no one ever noticed him. It worked almost as well as an invisibility spell, not that he'd really got that working at all yet. The problem with invisibility is people ran into you because you subconsciously expected them to move to give you room to get by. It had proven very frustrating, not to mention that no matter whatever else it created, a weird distortion hovered where the spell existed.

Shane left his bike at the handy bike rack and tested the protections but they were fine. He didn't need to re-power them, even if he almost glowed with power from the Demon and Fae blood. That would keep him for months if he used the blood wisely.

And even with all that power, I still need these idiots. Were we that bad in basic? What I wouldn't give for Drill Instructor Strauss right now.

He shook his head, trying to chase away memories of a different time, a different person. That person had small dreams, thought he could be happy. That person had been limited in what he could see. He wasn't that person anymore.

Why can't I get the past off my mind today?

Shane kept turning that question over and over in his mind as he headed into a forested area of the park. Magic might be commercially acceptable but people got uncomfortable if they found out you practiced. Magic was dark, bloody, and required a certain turn of mind to be good at it.

And dammit, if Declan had gotten off his high horse he could have been here with me to create this new world.

Again with the thoughts from the past! Why was he thinking so much about it? No matter how fast he shied from that thought though, he knew he'd have to explore this more fully later.

And here I thought I'd already removed all those pesky emotions like guilt or morals.

As he walked across the field a bright orange ball came tumbling towards him.

"Hey, Mister. Can you kick it back to us?" a child yelled. He'd not spent enough time around kids to know the age and didn't care.

"Sure." He gave it a kick back towards them, smiling as they grabbed it and went back to their game. He watched for a minute, their joy and unconcern radiating as parents watched them.

Too bad they are all dead. They just don't know it yet. Stupid lemmings. You can't stop what is coming. All you can do is run but you don't have any place to run to. I will. No matter what.

Shane shook his head, trying to shake the mood off. Turning, he moved with greater purpose towards the copse of trees, wanting to get the meeting over. The book called to him and something in the back of his mind kept pressuring him with pieces.

He stopped at the edge of the clearing and seriously considered beating his head on the nearby tree.

Why does everyone think because you use magic you have to look like a freaking reject from Lord of the Rings? Robes are stupid.

In the clearing four young men, and it almost always seemed to be men, were dressed in robes having finished the 'ritual' circle to open a portal. While he didn't need a circle anymore, most of the young ones needed that pattern. They didn't understand how to channel their power or their blood without the physical representation.

Fucking morons

He stepped up the pace and got there before they could start casting.

"So just a question. Are you trying to start the next invasion? Or do you have a reason to commit suicide? I mean, I can just kill you. It would probably be a lot less painful." He kept his voice dry and repressed his desire to just kill them and be done with it.

One of them puffed up at him, crossing his arms over his chest. "What do you mean? We're doing it right. No demon would dare come over with all of us here."

Shane backhanded him hard, in a smooth motion he didn't even think about. "Next idiotic comment?"

The kid he'd backhanded, none of them even looked old enough to drink, looked up at him. Blood running from the nose he'd hopefully broken.

"What was that for?" The voice sounded thick as he held his robe to his nose.

"A... you're a moron. B... demons don't give a fuck about how many mages might be on the other side. C..."

One of the other mages, a redhead this time.

"Demons can't come in when we are here. We'd be able to control them and they'd do what we say." His tone and attitude were of overconfidence and belief in his immortality.

Shane turned cold eyes on him. "Really? Should we test that?"

A huge smirk as the child responded. "Of course. We'll open the portal now."

For a minute, a full sixty seconds that ticked by in his brain, he considered letting them. Almost walked away and let them open the portal. The laughing child who had kicked the ball stopped him. The child might be walking dead but there was no reason to make him real dead any sooner.

"Sure, tell you what. I'll stand over here and watch you control the demon. But you might want to set a size limit to your portal. Right now it's set to be unlimited."

The three standing went pale and scrambled to set a size limit, while Shane stepped back and readied a few actions and wondered if any of the four would survive.

Don't really care. Why did I need them again? Oh, frag... yeah. They have the contacts to the morons on the other side.

"So, who's the primary contact?" He asked in a casual voice.

"Me?" said one that was covered in the robes but the voice was higher, feminine. She wasn't part of the circle and if he had to judge by her body language she didn't care too much about what they were doing.

A female? Interesting. The last female mage he'd worked with had been Janice. Wicked smart and vicious. This one might be worth keeping alive. Well, that and the fact she was the contact.

"Go for it, let's see how your control goes." He stepped back, flicking a drop of his blood onto the runes, setting up his ability to instantly collapse the portal. But only when the point had been made. They were still making it too large.

Did they forget it is in meters not feet? Damn, I should have brought my tasers. And my harvester. Might have been able to glut myself on demon blood.

He heaved a sigh and braced himself. This would be a deadly lesson for three of them. The girl he needed alive for the contact.

They began to chant, another stupid construct he didn't

understand why they taught it, but whatever. Made it easier for him to interrupt them and the energy they were channeling. The girl heaved a sigh and dropped to sit against a tree. He felt her gaze turn to him for the first time and it locked there, but he couldn't focus on that right now.

The portal opened and from the widening of their eyes, and paling of faces, he figured they really had thought it would be three feet across not three meters.

Morons.

He stood the picture of casual indifference but every muscle in his body tensed ready to go. If he didn't need their power, every demon would be dead, he had no love for them.

A decent sized ring two moved through the portal, not so large it had to bend, but large enough it took up the entire portal. This demon didn't have a face exactly, or at least nothing that Shane could recognize facial expressions on. Humanoid with Freddy Kruger like claws, and tentacles that covered where a mouth probably existed.

One of the idiots stepped forward, raising his hand in what Shane figured he thought was an imperious gesture. "Demon, we have summoned you here to do our bidding. We have a small task for you."

What? What the hell did they think a demon was going to do for them? Why in the world are these idiots in possession of any amount of magical power?

The demon pivoted and looked at the kid, its odd head tilting.

"We must remind people that demons are still there. There is a small building outside these trees, go destroy it." The kid had deepened his voice in an attempt to sound older, more powerful. He sounded like he'd smoked too much weed.

The demon stood there, and Shane readied himself. In a move so fast that Shane only saw it because he'd been looking, the demon slapped at the kid. Seven inch long claws sliced through his body like a hot knife through butter.

The screams started even as the kid's body still pumped blood on the ground. Shane saw another demon starting to come through the portal, crouching to get through.

Yeah, I don't think so.

He collapsed the portal with a pull of power, a severed demon arm dropped onto the ground as it closed, making a wet thwap that made him smile.

The demon shifted its body at the thwap, then whipped around. Its eyes, what Shane assumed were eyes, were locked on him.

Great, got one that can think. Just what I needed.

Even to himself, his sarcasm burned. The female sat against the tree, not frozen but watching him, while the other two men had started waving their arms, and cast something at the demon, who only snapped out an arm towards the other side of its body. The claws on that side punctured straight through the idiot standing there like needles through paper.

Okay, time to stop this before he really gets pissed. Though, mental note, never leave without my tasers again.

Shane let loose the spell he had waiting. Demons were big and tough but they had the same weakness as mammals - their brains were in their head if they had a humanoid shape. Blunt force rarely worked because humans, without the aid of decent machines, couldn't match their strength. So you didn't use blunt force.

The strike of lightning from his fingers impacted in the demon's skull, exploding it with a satisfying sizzle, even as it drained Shane of almost every bit of energy he had. This was why mages didn't fight demons one on one. Sure, they could kill them, one of them. Then they were barely more than drained toddlers and from everything he'd seen, the loss of one demon didn't matter to the Horde.

Staggering from the magical exertion he moved over to the demon, pulling the knife from his waist and stabbed it into the opening at the top of its body. It took almost more energy than what he had but he managed to get past the cauterized flesh to the blood still running through the body. He shoved his hand into the opening and pulled it back coated with blood. With a moan, he shoved it into his mouth and sucked the blood off his hand.

The first drops hit his tongue like bitter ambrosia. Demon blood tasted awful, like a mix between castor oil and bitters. but the power flowed into his body like drugs through an IV. Shaking his head to chase away the last of the cobwebs, he turned while still dipping his hand in and out. He needed to be as powered up as he could get before the body needed to be destroyed. Leaving this body for certain alphabet agencies to find would be unwise.

A whimpering caught his attention and he looked to see the girl staring at him face pale, eyes wide, and her throat swallowing convulsively as she stared at him.

"It is you. I thought you'd never show up." Her voice had an odd tone. She glanced at the others and shrugged. "I told them I could have opened the portal but they said girls couldn't control portals. They weren't strong enough. Oh well." She stood and moved towards him. "They can't control demons. They should have known."

"They should have. Drones will obey, the rest want us dead. Whoever is teaching this crap should either be shot or is a plant by the government to get most of you killed before you learn how to use this power."

The girl had pale green eyes, light red hair, and she was so pale that her freckles stood out on her face. She didn't look scared or upset though and that made him really nervous. She should be freaking out.

"Were you related to the other idiot with the red hair?"

She nodded shakily. "My cousin. The demon cut him. I knew he was dead but I didn't know when."

Is she in shock? What the hell does that mean? I don't care and don't have time to deal with this. But she's useful, which means I need her powered.

"Come here." He reached out grabbed her and pulled her close to him. Still oddly passive she didn't even try to move or fight, just letting him manipulate her like a doll. Taking her hand, he shoved

101

it into the opening. Wiggling the limp limb to make sure it got coated he pulled it out, nodding at the blood dripping from it.

"Open your mouth." His voice held command, the sort of command you needed with a drone or dumb recruits.

Same difference in all reality.

Her face blank even as she never took her eyes off him, she dropped open her mouth and he wanted to roll his eyes, instead, he shoved her hand into her mouth. The taste must have hit her first as she gagged and tried to pull her hand out but he held it there easily. He could see when the power hit her system and she started actively swallowing, color flooding her face.

"More," he ordered as he pulled his hand away. She nodded and shoved her hand back into the demon coating it with blood before bringing it back to her mouth.

Looking around even as he topped off, maybe this had been a ring three with as much power the blood had. Either way, he'd make sure power rolled off him before he walked away. The other kid, the one whose nose he broken had disappeared. The two dead ones lay there, more bodies for him to deal with, and a mage.

Huh. Maybe I should keep her. I need someone to help and she is the demon contact. Thrall her?

Shane wrinkled his nose. Thralling left a taint he didn't like, even with all he'd done. Killing seemed cleaner than that level of mental rape and rape had never been anything he condoned. Rape of any type.

She's a follower, maybe she'll follow me. Worst case I kill her. Or maybe her brain snapped, just as possible.

He pitched his voice low, not seductive but soothing, that of a teacher who knew everything.

"Tell me everything. How did you get into this? How were you made the contact? And who set your goals?"

Shane settled back to listen as, in between sucking blood off her hand, the girl talked.

Chapter 13 – Spying on ICERs

Kayter tucked her hair up under the wig and pulled on the garish shirt over her t-shirt. Between the off-color brown of the wig, the orange, yellow, and purple of the shirt, blue sweats, and glasses that distorted her eyes, she looked like a fashion reject. She'd popped in a contact to change both eyes to brown.

She'd picked up his car outside where she assumed he lived and followed him to a local restaurant, Penn Alps. He'd gone in a minute before but she wanted to wait until he and whomever he met with were seated before she went in, so she stayed in the front area looking at the higher quality kitsch that had exploded all over the place.

Heck, some of this stuff is almost decent. Why can't Cracker Barrels be like this?

She fondled a few more items until she saw a woman, older but still attractive, and another man who screamed career-government-suit come in and join him.

"Hi, I'd like to be seated now?" She quit breathing through her nose as she spoke, her voice instantly becoming nasally.

The young woman behind the podium smiled at her. "Sure, we're pretty empty so do you have a preference?" the server asked she walked her into the room. Agent man and his party sat at a window so she angled for a booth where she could watch their body language where but they'd have to move their chairs to see her easily. Besides in this outfit, you'd have to be blind to even want to talk to her.

The hostess smiled at her, handed over a menu, and moved away, probably to save her eyesight. Kayter glanced at the menu and decided on something that couldn't be messed up. She pulled out her phone and pointed it towards their table, slipping in her Bluetooth headphone, and hit the app that activated the small directional microphone she'd attached. Then she listened, wondering what she would learn.

"I do not understand why you insisted we meet here, Chad." Kayter flicked her eyes up to verify but with only one woman in the group, she knew who spoke.

Agent man has a name. Chad

"Cordelia, I told you. I didn't want to risk anyone else overhearing us. Kenner might be ready to bring him in, but I have doubts about him," Chad said, even as he flicked the menu away from him.

Kayter typed on her phone, taking notes, even as she put puzzle pieces together.

"And the other people in the office are risks?" Even through the headphones, the woman sounded annoyed and unimpressed.

"Risks? Not really. Talk too much? Probably. Look you know how important this is. Demon summoning is on the rise and we need hunters. I'm just not certain he's the right person to bring in."

The second man, the one who screamed either Fed or accountant, spoke. "He fits all our criteria, has the training, and from what information we've been able to gather about his house, still is well armed."

"Yeah but he's unpredictable, doesn't take orders well, is probably a functional alcoholic, and you wouldn't know if he would actually do what you asked," Chad pointed out.

Kayter wanted to look up, to watch, but figured that might be a bit too obvious, so she buried her nose in the phone, pretending to be absorbed in what it said.

"And the rest of my 'employees' aren't like that?" The sarcasm in the woman's voice made Kayter like her. Anyone with that much attitude couldn't be all bad. But then again, she'd been wrong before. With quick strikes at her keyboard, she took notes of her observations.

"Cordelia, the sarcasm is unwarranted. We both know the best contractors are those who have a light leash and are allowed to figure out the best way to accomplish their objectives." The suit spoke again and Kayter wanted to roll her eyes but the waitress came up to her. She gave her order quickly, wanting to get rid of the woman.

"Bacon cheeseburger, fries, no mustard," she rattled off, making sure the app recorded everything.

The waitress headed off and Kayter focused back in on the discussion.

"... he should be avoided." Chad's voice said and Kayter narrowed her eyes.

"If you are both quite finished telling me how to do my job, I would like to know when you think you can meet with him and make an introduction."

"I'm telling you he's dangerous. He killed the demon, picked up the carcass and didn't even blink. He's a wild card and we can't afford that. He'll expose us and get scrutiny down us with his recklessness." Chad said again.

Why doesn't he like this man? This Kenner?

"Really? Because he was efficient, calm, and fought back the Rage, so you want to not use an excellent tool like that? And if that had been you there? You would have died." A long pause and Kayter heard Chad make some mumbling sounds but not clear enough for her to interpret. "If this is some male ego on your side, jettison it. Because I do not give a flying fuck."

"Cordelia," Chad protested then fell silent.

"Is there a reason you are so determined to sway my decision? Is there some valid reason I should ignore one of the few hunters to walk out of Ypsilanti? This, a man that has managed to control the rage for the last three years without any assistance? Someone who killed a demon single-handed? At least half of the agents in our organization have never killed one without superior firepower; superior to the point that usually I have to create a cover reason for the excessive destruction? Whereas Kenner, on the other hand, killed it, cleaned up, and walked away with only you knowing it even happened. Chad, if that is reckless, please give me more reckless agents." Her voice had an arctic dryness to it.

"Your point is made, Cordelia, the sarcasm is not conducive to employee morale. Though I cannot dispute your points, I will arrange to have someone deliver an invitation about ICER and ask him to come see you if he is interested." Suit spoke this time, and Kayter wanted to cheer for some odd reason. She liked the woman but suspected she would not like the company the woman worked for.

"Philip, please do not try and moderate my behavior or the way I treat my employees. If Chad has a problem with my tone, he is free to take it up with HR. Do not forget how, and why, I have my job." Her voice slashed out like a whip and even looking out of the corner of her eye, she saw Philip flinch backward.

I need to run a check on this woman, who the hell is she?

"Of course, Ms. Bennett," he stammered out.

Her food arrived and Kayter flashed a half smile at the waitress, still more focused on the conversation at the other table.

"Chad, I expect you to deliver the invitation and make sure he has a reason to accept. If he doesn't, I will be following up to figure out why. Now that our recruitment of Declan Kenner has been decided, and since I still need to finish eating, perhaps we can address the entire fact that a demon just happened to attack someone we are interested in, in front of you, and in front of a backwoods VFW post?" Her voice had a sharply pointed aspect that reminded Kayter of a dagger.

"Oh, um, there was a mage. Young. Stupid. Apparently, a demon contact had convinced him to summon a demon there."

"Alone and without a contact key physically present? And you were lucky enough to witness this? And there just happened to be a demon hunter there to deal with it?" Disbelief dripped off her tongue and Kayter could almost feel Chad squirming in his chair. "Where is the mage now?"

"I grabbed him. A demon had been whispering in his ear and convinced him that they would never come back if all the hunters were killed. It would keep Earth safe if they killed the ones who took so many lives. It sounds like the demons are trying to eliminate demon killers, all the old guys from the war. So apparently this idiot decided to try and ambush them outside the VFW, figuring that is where most of the old hunters would be."

"And you just happened to be there? And the non-keyed mage was alone?" Cordelia's voice was flat, unimpressed, but Kayter wondered what she thought. Was he capable of setting up something like this?

"Luck happens occasionally," Chad replied and his voice sounded sketchy, even to Kayter.

"And where is this 'idiot mage' now?"

"Uh, he resisted my efforts to capture him, and as he ran he fell, snapped his neck. Sorry I tried to bring him in, figuring he'd have information for us."

If this woman believes that lying sack of shit, she'll lose all my respect.

"Really, how unfortunate. Please make sure you attend all training on how to subdue suspects without killing them. What about the rise in minor portals opening? We know all the major nexus points are guarded but I've seen a spike in mini portals opening at those with 2-5 Ley lines crossing. Have you heard anything to identify which human mage oclaves are communicating with the other side? And how they're manufacturing key tokens?"

"Not yet. We have a lead or two as to which group might be working with the demons but nothing solid enough to make a conviction or even pull anyone in for questioning." Philip replied this time. Kayter glanced up, wanting and needing to see his face and body language.

He fiddled with his fries, not looking up, his shoulders hunched.

"So why exactly am I paying both of you? If luck is why you managed to see a demon get killed by one of our perspective demon hunters? A random young mage found enough connections to the other side to get a demon summoned here, if only a drone, yet my employees can't seem to get ahold of anyone that has information about who is talking to demons on the other side?"

The table fell quiet and all she could hear was utensils scraping on the plates. A quick glance up told her an interesting story.

Cordelia leaned back, watching both men, her salad removed of all the protein but the greens only lightly touched. Both men had ordered hamburgers, fries, and cokes. The image of a lean cat watching from a tree branch over a pack of rats sprang to her mind.

The woman is no fool. She knows something else is going on.

"I think we are done here, gentlemen. When you decide to get your asses gear and actually do your mission, please feel free to contact me. Until then, please do your fucking jobs and quit wasting my time." Cordelia pushed back her chair and walked out. Tossing back as she did. "You can pick up the tab Chad, and I will not be authorizing an expense voucher."

Kayter snorted to herself and finished the hamburger. They had not screwed it up. Amazing.

Philip left a minute later, leaving Chad sitting there all alone. She ducked her head down even farther in case he glanced over at her.

"Son of a bitch, the fucking wench," he muttered in a sotto voice that the microphone picked up perfectly. He gave a huge sigh and pulled out a cellphone.

Brow arching, Kayter waited, curious to see who he would call. Their security protocols were shit but she wasn't going to complain.

"Sir, it's Chad Morant." A pause, then he started to talk. "No, sir, I wasn't able to convince her otherwise. She'll bring in Kenner. I think she's becoming suspicious. She twigged pretty hard to the coincidence of the mage and the demon. I told her the mage died while I was trying to apprehend him. Sir, be circumspect in using him." Another long pause as he rose, tossing a fifty on the table. "Don't worry sir, I can handle her. I'll get rid of Kenner before he becomes dangerous and eliminating a few demons won't hurt our plans. If anything, it might help them. Yes, sir."

She wanted to follow but that would be obvious. Besides, at this point she didn't know if she would get any more information by following. So, she sat back and thought about everything she heard.

Should I warn this Kenner? Would he even believe me?

Chapter 14 - ICER Offer

Declan pulled into the parking lot of the VFW and shut off the engine. He wanted to relax. However, experience and the traces of demon still in the back of his truck told him he couldn't afford to assume anything. He especially could not assume that demons and mages weren't out to get him.

Old habits encouraged him to check his knife, the Glock 17 on his hip, and his phone before pulling on his worn leather jacket and getting out of the truck. Walking around in his demon hunting gear might be a bit much, so leather jacket it was.

If I run into another demon in public though, fuck everybody, I'm wearing it. People can bite me, but I won't get gutted.

Buzzing into the VFW, he relaxed as the familiar smells and sounds washed over him. Glancing around he didn't see anyone he really knew or wanted to hang out with, so a quiet evening for him. Heading to a corner table, he waved at Casey, who nodded and started pulling him a beer.

Good man. Why can't the rest of my life be that simple?

By the time Casey headed over with the beer, Declan had decided on his meal - nothing fancy, steak, fries, and salad. A man did need a little bit of roughage in his diet.

He only gave Casey a half smile, not even enough energy to tease him about who might be up to bat this week. He just wanted a little bit of peace. His house screamed safety but the walls were starting to close in on him.

Casting another glance around the room, he analyzed the vets from one of the sandbox wars. None were demon hunters but all of them were good soldiers in their day. If anything bad happened, he'd have some backup.

And if they need to, they could put a bullet in my brain too.

He shook off the morbid thought, instead shifting his attention to his beer and the TV. No game on tonight, most sports were still getting back to regular schedules. It was set to the news when something caught his attention.

"Casey, can you turn that up?" His voice tight and urgent.

Casey glanced at him, shrugged and turned it up so he could hear the News announcer.

"Cops were called to the scene of a veteran of the Demon War acting odd. Police found him barricaded in his house. They were unable to get in. He was shouting obscenities and threatening to kill them all if they touched his stuff." The scene changed to a house in a cleared area, neat yard, driveway, and a clear porch. But Declan looked at it, saw the barred windows, the clear lines of sight, and multiple retreats.

His mouth went dry and his hand tightened around his beer glass, unable to take his eyes away.

"You okay, Kenner?" Casey's voice startled him and he ripped his attention way to nod at the man setting his food down.

"Yeah, just need to see this story. Thanks."

His attention jumped back to the story.

"We only found out the details after the standoff ended. A government agency, one which we still don't know, stepped in and talked the man out. He seemed calm as they took him away."

Picture shot back to four men, all in black tactical gear, walking a man between them. He looked about Declan's age, in worn fatigues, with a cap shielding his eyes. What struck Declan was the jitters he could see in the man's body, the way he kept looking in all directions as if expecting an attack, then the clenching and releasing of his hands. He disappeared from sight as they put him into the back of a black SUV.

Is it the rage? Did he lose it? How did they get him out? What did they do?

"What has neighbors up in arms, is what the police have found in his residence. The camera showed police bringing out more and

111

Blood War: Rage

more weapons. From my point of view, the man had enough to fight a war. What is going on with Demon War vets?"

The camera panned back to men and women carrying out ammo cans, gun boxes, knives, and other weapons that could have just as easily come from Declan's own armory.

"Rumors are that he lost his composure and screamed about rage taking him over and that he couldn't control it anymore. This is the third veteran in the last six months to devolve into incoherent anger and threats against everyone around them. Is this a form of PTSD we need to research? Or is there some environmental contamination from the Demon War and the blood that is only now making itself known? Do we have ticking time bombs living among us?"

"Huh, and the Vietnam vets thought they had it bad." One of the Desert Storm vets on the other side said to his dinner companion.

"Yeah, Agent Orange's got nothing on this rage crap. What do you think, they got too much blood on them?"

"On them, in them, what difference does it make. All I know is those vets might have a shorter lifespan than anyone expected. Hell, the fact there are any vets at all is both impressive and suspicious."

"Hush, don't you know? There's a few that come around here. They've earned it." They glanced around guiltily but Declan hid his face behind his beer, pretending to not have noticed.

What if that is me, just in another place, and with less control? Fuck it, have a few beers. You know your limit. Then go home, lockdown, and figure it out.

He focused on food, eyes darting everywhere and all too aware of the rage at the background of his mind and his soul. Andrew was not here today to distract him. For the most part, Andrew qualified as the only person he really talked to. Declan fingered his phone, almost wondering if he should call someone.

God, one rage incident and you're ready to call the hotline. Push it down. You know how to manage this. You aren't him, you won't lose it. You've pushed it back, you're in control.

The bravado didn't help. He could feel it bubbling at the edges and made a mental note to avoid Friday and Saturday nights here. Occasionally it got rowdy and right now, rowdy would be bad.

At his limit, he signed his bill, tossing in his normal 20% tip, and headed out, though he still stopped before the door closed, checking the parking lot, reaching for any magic or demons.

Once burned, twice shy, and all that crap. Hell, at the rate my life is going, I'm going to need an eighties montage soundtrack playing in the background.

He snorted and headed to his truck, keys in his hands. Declan slowed to a stop as he saw a man reclining against his truck and his eyes narrowed.

"I don't think I know you well enough to like you leaning against my truck. Get off." Declan stopped a few feet away, more than enough time to draw and put two bullets in his head.

The man stood up, a smile on his face that just had enough insincerity that Declan's hackles were raised. Youngish, not more than thirty, and vaguely familiar but not enough for him to pull out a name for him.

"Sorry about that, but I didn't figure you wanted this conversation in public. My names Chad Morant, and my group has been watching you."

"None of that is geared toward making me feel any better about you leaning against my truck." Declan eased his jacket open, making sure to clear it from his draw.

The dweeb held his hands up. "Really, I'm not here to cause an issue. We just heard a few things, that maybe the rage crept back in, and maybe was causing you issues."

Declan felt like he'd just been sucker punched in the kidney and fought to keep his face impassive even as his mind went into a tailspin.

How the fuck did they know? Could they have gotten into my security systems? Did they set up the demon attack? Or wait, that hunter – did he report it? Oh hell, are they the group that took that other hunter. What if they are here to take me? Fuck them, I won't go quietly.

"Your point?"

"My agency might have a solution to your problem. New drug. Helps counteract the side effects." He reached into his breast pocket and Declan's hand tightened on the pistol grip, everything in him ready to pull and fire as he'd practiced so many times. "Just getting out a business card. See?" He drew a dark card and laid it on the edge of the truck bed. "Go see the lady there. She might have something for you to try, something to push the rage all the way down."

"Yeah? And what's that going to cost me? My soul?"

"Please, this isn't a deal with the devil. We both know he doesn't exist. I have no need for souls, nor does my agency. Think of this more along the lines of barter. But I'm sure the supervisor you speak with will give you all the details." The man smiled a cold smile that jabbed at Declan. "But if you don't want a way to control the rage, feel free to ignore our generous offer. Not my problem if you lose it and kill some kid cause he looked at you wrong." The man smirked and shrugged. "I was told to make you the offer, my job is done. Have fun with the rest of your life, demon hunter has been." With a jaunty flick of his hands, he turned and got into a non-descript sedan. He started it up, leaving Declan standing there the need for violence eating at the corners of his brain.

Asshole, he completely blew away what little fog I had. Need to stop and get more booze before I get home, this will be easier to deal with drunk. Deal with the rage, the booze helps. It has to be a coincidence. There are lots of alphabet agencies. It has to be.

Moving forward he glanced at the card, hand hovering over it as he fought with the options. Then he grabbed it, shoving it in his jacket pocket.

I'll look at it later, now the store, then home. I need to get the rage down before I lose my cool and become what they want me to be.

He spent the whole drive home hoping a demon might cross his path and hating himself for that very thought. The image of the demon hunter in California never strayed far from his mental nightmare.

Blood War: Rage

Chapter 15 - Offer you can't refuse

Declan sat in his truck looking at the business card in his hand and the building across the street. The addresses matched so it had to be the right place.

This has to be a hoax. I mean who the fuck even has business cards anymore.

He fingered the heavy cardboard, all black with white letters with an address, a number and nothing else.

I mean am I supposed to be impressed that they have a business card that cost damn near a dollar each?

That thought caught his mind and he looked at the card again, weighing it. It was a damn heavy card. With a suspicion, he tilted it and let the light reflect off of it.

Ha, thought so.

Indented just slightly into the card were runes, traceries of spells, and now that he paid attention, he could feel the slightest prickling across his fingers. But they were so faint he knew they hadn't activated them.

Yet.

Tracking spell, maybe a compulsions spell, and most likely the real purpose of the card. Wonder if their minions know these spells are on them.

He gave the building a second look - a standard office building, concrete gray with no personality, only windows reflecting the outside. Since he didn't have creepy crawlies running over his body, the odds were not too much magic was currently in use.

Fuck this.

Declan started the car up and felt the wave of rage rise like a geyser in him, tinting his world red, his body shook as he fought through it.

"My agency might have a solution to your problem. New drug. Helps counteract the side effects." The words of the interloper rang through his mind and he switched the engine off, sweat beading and trickling down his scalp.

I don't know what I have to lose, but right now I'm about to lose everything.

Reluctance made his feet drag as he stepped out of his truck, locked it, and after glancing both ways, crossed the street. Only the oncoming traffic made him pick up his pace, though as soon as he got to the sidewalk it slowed again. Sensing carefully, he didn't find anything but then again, that wasn't a skill he used much.

If this keeps up, I might regret that choice.

The bitter thought drew his lips back from his teeth. The snarl still on his face he pulled open the door and walked in. The faint smell of antiseptic hit his nose and he frowned. With a shake of his head he headed up the stairs. The card said suite 301 and being in an elevator made you an easy target. This wasn't enough stairs to make putting himself at risk worth the effort. Besides, it gave him more time to scope things out.

Climbing the two flights all he saw was a cigarette butt and sticky stuff he didn't want to think about on the landing. He walked in and looked around and for some reason was vaguely surprised at the bland office décor. A single door sat in the middle of the hall. The rest of the walls were a dull beige that implied nothing so much as boredom.

The temptation to walk back out ate at him but the rage that bubbled too close to the surface sent him walking down the hall, noting the door sat exactly in the middle.

Odd.

On the door, the logo etched in frosted script on the glass, International Cooperative Element Responders.

He read it twice and rolled his eyes. With his face in a blank mask, he pushed open the door and walked in. An empty waiting area, with an unmanned reception window, lay in front of him. As he walked up to the window a woman came striding out from the back.

"Yes, may I help you?"

He took a minute to look over the woman, she looked to be in her late thirties, but his ability to guess age on females had gotten him in trouble more than once. Rich brown hair lay around her face in a cut that highlighted her sharp features. Her brown eyes reminded him of an Amberbock beer, the rich color that promised oblivion. Then there were her curves. Her tailored dark grey suit did not hide any of them and in any other situation he might have been tempted to see if he could buy her a drink. In this current situation, he wondered how many honey traps she had run.

DK lifted the card and flashed it at her.

"I was told I might find a solution to an issue I have?" He didn't clarify anything. If she didn't know, then she didn't need to know.

"Ah, Declan Kenner, also known as DK. Yes, I was informed you might be coming by. Please come on back." Her voice brisk and matter of fact made him feel like a young second lieutenant being instructed by a Master Sergeant - never criticizing but making it very clear he didn't know a damn thing.

She walked to the side, opened the door and stood there waiting for him, her posture that of a patient DI.

Wonder when she is going to explode and start cussing at me?

He walked through the door. With a brisk stride she turned and walked down the rows of cubicles. The walls were too high for him to see anything, though the silence was telling him something. He kept getting distracted by the snap of her skirt and the ass that filled it out.

I wonder if she'd like to check out all my scars? Or maybe see what duty stations we had in common?

Thinking thoughts about the woman seemed safer than dwelling on why he came here. Besides, she exuded a level of competence and poise he had seen in female master sergeants.

Fraternizing had been strongly frowned on but he still found that sheer 'I can fucking handle anything' attitude sexy as hell.

With a military perfect turn, she went into an office and settled behind a desk.

"Please take a seat Mr. Kenner." her voice cool and calm as she waved at a chair.

Am I in the spider's lair? And why aren't I more worried? Damn hormones. I need to get laid more often.

He sat after casting a sharp look around the place. It looked like any other office, some pieces of paper in frames on the walls, a computer, and a phone, a clear desk, and two chairs. Bland, boring, and not at all fitting the outfit she had on. Her suit had been crafted to fit her body, and he'd lay money the undergarments she wore cost more than his boots.

Red. I bet they are red.

The visual flashed through his head and his arm almost slipped off the armrest as he lowered himself into the chair and she smirked. He swallowed with the sudden conviction she knew exactly where his mind had gone.

Get your fucking head in the game, Declan. You don't know what they want.

The mental slap helped and he settled down, his eyes on her.

"My name is Cordelia Bennett. My job is to assess if you will be any use to our agency and if you have any qualities that make the price of keeping you worth it."

DK arched his brow. "And what makes you think you are capable of assessing my qualities."

"Experience." She reached down and opened a drawer, smirking at him as he tensed. She pulled out a manila folder and opened it. He saw his own military personnel file picture staring at him, upside down. "Declan Kenner nominally called DK for Demon Killer. Retired veteran with over twenty years in. Pardoned from all actions during the Demon War. Lives outside Jennings, Maryland. Owes nothing, visits the VFW, and has no known social groups outside of a few other war vets such as Andrew Cabello and Greg

Blood War: Rage

Donahue. Once best friends with Shane Gris, currently AWOL with whereabouts unknown but believed to be operating outside of the country. You were one of the 3% that walked out of the incident at Ypsilanti alive and were accused of war crimes relating to battlefield actions in Bowling Green Ohio. Granted a TS/SCI clearance, which has not been revoked. Also marked as immune to recall to active duty. Interesting." She slapped the file closed and put both elbows on the table, rested her chin on her hands and looked at him. "So why are you here?"

DK felt his blood run colder with each comment.

She knows too fucking much. How the hell does she know this stuff? Those records were supposed to be fucking sealed. And fuck, is Shane really somehow alive?

He fought to swallow, even as he made sure his face didn't move so much as a fraction and he still got the sense she knew how freaked out he was.

"I seem to be having some anger management issues and one of your people mentioned that I might be able to get some assistance here."

"That is quite correct. But there is no such thing as a free lunch. I assume you are willing to pay for Reset."

He almost sagged in relief but the idea of showing weakness to this sexy piranha in human skin did not seem wise.

"Reset? Is that what is it called? Drugs, sure. How much." Even as he spoke he reached for his wallet. Money he could come up with.

"Oh, Declan. Surely you didn't think it cost something as simple as money. Oh no. I want you to do things for me." Her sweet smile and glimpse of cleavage as she leaned forward made him hope for a brief instant that maybe sex was how he could pay for it. "I need you to kill demons for me. In return, I'll give you Reset."

I knew this was too good to be true.

He started to rise but she reached into a drawer and set down on the desk a single air compressed vial. It was the standard med version, you pressed it against your skin, pressed the button and it pushed the drug into your system via compressed air.

"This is Reset. Guaranteed to keep your rage at bay. And all you need to do is the occasional job for me."

He couldn't take his eyes away from the vial. The answer to at least some of his problems lay right there.

"And what do I have to do to earn those vials?"

She shrugged, her cleavage heaving impressively he noticed from the corner of his eye. "Nothing much. Kill some demons, help us keep rogue mages under control. Basically, keep America free. You'll get a bounty for every demon you kill; extra money is always nice. And as long as you don't refuse a job or die, you'll have all the Reset you need."

It sounded so simple, and he didn't believe it. "Can I have some time to think about it?"

"Sure. Here, this one is on me. Try it out and give me a call if you decide you want to work for us." She slid the vial and a card across the desk. "I'm sure I'll be hearing from you."

He couldn't resist, he picked up both, noting the card had her name embossed on it. Cordelia Bennett.

"Sure thing, Cordy. I'll let you know."

She arched a brow and the displeased look made him smile. "It is Cordelia. And you'll call me. They all do."

With that ominous statement ringing in his ears, she ushered him out, and he headed home. He didn't glance at the vial as he drove. Instead, he waited until he locked and sealed the door to his house behind him before he gave in and pulled the vial out of his pocket. Declan twisted it in the air, looking at the light bouncing off the neon pink and gold liquid.

What the fuck, if I'm dead I won't care anymore.

He pressed the vial against his arm and hit the button. Coldness pressed again his arm and the rage disappeared as if snuffed out. He slumped back against the wall, at peace for the first time in longer than he had realized.

Oh, I am so fucked.

Blood War: Rage

Chapter 16 - New Toy

Shane looked at the bodies lying around while the girl talked. He didn't have any way to store any more blood and the bodies needed to be disposed of. Keeping one part of his mind on the story the girl spun, really, she babbled so quietly about things that didn't make sense, he lost the thread of the conversation. Instead, he prepped a spell to help dispose of the corpses. As he prepped he took more blood. He'd fill himself to bursting, which was possible though improbable, as he didn't want to leave here drained.

The fading note in the girl's voice caught his attention and he realized he'd not tracked her words.

Damn, I'm going to have to get her to calm down and repeat everything.

"Shush," his voice a whisper but still she froze mid-babble, looking at him. Her face was so pale her freckles stood out like vivid dots of orange.

"You can't be real. You were supposed to be a dream."

Huh? What the hell. I'll deal with her later.

"Move over there, I need to get rid of this evidence since I assume you have no desire to face a firing squad?"

Her eyes drifted to her dead cousin, but her head nodded almost dreamily, as if she wasn't actually here. The consequences of summoning demons were draconian, to say the least. If you were found guilty you were taken out and shot. No one could afford to have people that could use magic sitting around, stewing. If you could use it, you had a personal reserve that meant eventually you'd have the power you needed. And that meant eventually you'd break out. The courts didn't like that option.

Mages got very quick trials and there were no appeals.

Shane verified that she stood out of the way and dipped his hand in one more time, then pulled on the power that vibrated in him like a horde of angry bees. A wave of energy rippled out from his hand and settled over the bodies, and they began to decay and rot, like a time lapse, but in minutes they were nothing but dust piles that started to blow away in the light breeze.

He staggered a bit but it passed quickly, the overload taking care of the energy needed for that spell. Shaking his head to try to get his brain working again, he turned to see the girl looking like a pillar of salt as she stared at the remains of her friends, her family, and the demon.

"Come on. I'm not done with you. But we shouldn't stay here anymore."

She bowed her head and fell in step behind him. Shane gritted his teeth at the surge of pleasure at her subservience. That had never been anything that attracted him. He had no desire for sheep, he needed a wolf.

"Get rid of the robe. It's stupid and garners attention. Don't you have any belongings?"

"Oh," intelligence lit up her face and she stripped out of the encompassing robe and darted to the right, grabbing a backpack and stuffing the robe in it. Without the dark colors surrounding her, she looked like spring come to life, bright and wholesome. He wondered why she'd want to contaminate that with blood.

"Do you have a name?"

Not that I know if I care or not but hey you gets old after a while.

"Jane Smith."

"Fine Jean, you're coming with me. You going to argue?"

"Um, no," her voice dropped to a whisper. "It's Jane."

"Sure. Come on." He headed out across the park wanting to get away from the evidence as quickly as possible. He might have people who owed him but there was no reason to push his luck.

She trotted next to him, exuding light and sweetness. He really wanted to ask why she wanted to sully that but her choices weren't his problem.

And I don't give a fuck. Remember, she's dead. She just doesn't know it yet.

He glanced at her sideways.

Well, maybe not. If I can use her, no reason I can't take her with me. Depends on her power levels and what she can do.

"Okay, Janine, start at the beginning. You can open portals?"

"Yeah. I can open and hold them."

"And they didn't want you because you were a girl?" That struck him as the height of stupidity. Who cared what was or was not between your legs?

"Yeah. My cousin said I should be seen and not heard."

"Moron. How long?" This mattered. Some mages could only hold it for minutes, others... well others could do impressive things. Janice had been able to hold it for over an hour before she got stressed.

She shrugged, not looking at him. "Two hours is the longest. But it got closed on the other side."

Shane stumbled a bit but covered. "Why so long?"

Fuck me, two hours and she implied she could have done it longer?

"Oh. Frax wanted to see this TV show I had mentioned. So, I set it up so he could watch my favorite show."

"A demon wanted to watch TV?" His voice contained every ounce of disbelief that existed in his body.

"Well, I was talking about my favorite series, cause the vampires are so well done, while we waited for his boss. I set up my tablet so he could see it."

Fuck me, do these children think they can become our friends?

"How often do you talk to Frax? What ring is Frax?"

"Ring one, he's a lesser. But..." she trailed off biting her lip.

Shane realized they were at his bike. Grabbing it, he started walking. He needed to hear what else she had to say.

"What?"

Doug Burbey & Mel Todd

"I think today's Frax was a different Frax. He didn't know about the TV and seemed awfully jittery."

That idea slapped him in the face. He wondered why he'd never seen it before, but she kept talking.

"But normally I get like a mental knock that they are looking for me. I mean, the first time I had to just create the portal and all the drones kept showing up, like moths to a flame. But finally a demon who could think showed up and I gave him a token so he could contact me."

Tokens were enchanted wooden disks, usually a half dollar size, scored with your initials, then soaked in your blood. It created a sort of link between the demon that had it and the mage on the other side but only let them 'knock' but nothing else. Any mage capable of holding a portal could create them but usually couldn't do anything else. The concentration to hold it took up all their attention and power.

"Why did you do that?" The idea horrified him. Give them direct access to your brain? How insane could you get?

"The angels told me to. Said it was important." She shrugged. "So, I did."

Shane gave her a wary glance.

I know they are real but I've only met one, just one, and he had been here for over a thousand years. They don't normally talk to people. So, she is raving mad. Joy. All that power in an idiot savant.

"Why did you come today?"

"I showed up today cause my cousin said he needed me to contact the guy. I tried to tell him I could pin them but he didn't believe me. He said they had someone to impress today and he didn't want my delusions to ruin their chance to impress." She looked at her feet as she walked and he had to grab her to prevent her from walking into a light pole.

"Huh. The boys," he couldn't remember their names for anything, and boys covered all of them, "said they needed help with some demon negotiations and that the demons were willing to trade something more valuable than blood. I was the only one with the portal coordinates."

"They lied. Boys do that"

Truer words have never been spoken.

"But the demon wants to talk to someone, negotiate about the portals and treaty."

Chapter 17 - Straps Shrunk

Declan walked into his house and set the ICER business card down on the counter. Cordelia's card also had subdued trace runes in it and like the last time, he could feel a slight tingling on his fingertips as he handled it. He knew he could force the runes into activation if he concentrated on them. It would be straightforward but it did not seem to carry any trace impressions of being some form of hostile magic. While still concerned as to what the runes were for, he had delegated figuring that out to a lower priority task. The drive back to his house had been one of the most calming and relaxing he'd had in over a year. Whatever was in the concoction of chemicals that the ICER's have provided him in their Reset drug, it clearly worked as advertised. He could feel that his personal core energy had been replenished and had given him back his sense of balance and control.

"Well sir, I do believe you might have a little bit of your shit back together today. And I guess I got myself a part-time job now if I want to keep it that way. Since it sounds like this part-time job may be of the exciting type, I better go make sure all my gear is squared away." Declan told himself as he took a bottle of beer from the fridge, twisted off the cap, and flicked it towards the open trash can across the room. He missed his target with the bottle cap landing beside several others in the corner of the room on the floor. With exaggerated fanfare, he raised the bottle and took a pull.

Damn, somebody really needs to clean that up. Maybe I should hire a maid.

Turning around, Declan headed down the stairs into his basement and then to his armory. Opening the wall locker

Blood War: Rage

containing all his assorted gear, he glanced at the shelves with a confused look on his face.

Oh, now what the hell does a semi-secret government agency subcontractor for general demon nuisance killing wear on the job? Well, I am definitely not required to wear a uniform. So that's out.

Declan sat his beer bottle down on the workbench. He then reached out and took his heavy hunters coat out of the locker, holding it up and inspecting the damage and wear marks.

You, my old friend, are a definite must. Although it does look like you could use a little tender loving care. Spending some time in the shop could probably do you some good too.

Declan replaced his old coat in the locker, then glanced down at his armored boots. The metal hinged shin plates covering the front and back of his boots, while dented, dull and scratched, were still fully functional and ready to be put back into service with a just a layer or two of lubricating oil. He glanced at the shelf full of combat pants, and the fire-retardant combat shirts, disregarding both.

I'm pretty sure some random demon hunting is not going to entail my being trapped in burning vehicles. Besides, I need to be able to walk around in public without everyone assuming the Army has demon hunters roaming around the streets again. The coat and boots worn with civilian clothes will probably just have people thinking I'm a middle-aged wannabe hipster fashionista. That works just fine for me.

"This here will not be fashionable but will definitely be needed." Declan pulled out his tactical vest from the closet. The nylon and Velcro vest contained the ceramic composite front and back plates, offering protection from kinetic attacks. It also served as the primary load bearing system for additional ammunition magazines, his front chest holster for his backup .357 Magnum revolver, a small individual first aid kit, and finally a combat knife.

"This son of a bitch gets heavy when loaded out and it is not very inconspicuous. But like they say, don't leave home without a full basic load of ammo and a couple of Band-Aids." Declan chuckled to himself as he pulled the harness over his head, wrapped the securing side straps around himself.

"What the fuck! Who shrunk my shit?" Declan tugged on the straps in frustration realizing they were too short now to snap closed properly. Setting the tactical vest onto the workbench, he reached over and took a long drag from his beer bottle, trying to recall how to properly adjust the vest.

This had to of shrunk somehow. I know it was set up perfectly the last time I wore it.

Declan looked down at the beer bottle in his hand, then reached over and tapped at his slightly protruding beer belly; then he sat his favorite beverage back onto the bench.

"I guess this isn't much of a mystery, is it? You let yourself become a little bit of a chubby monkey didn't you, Declan? Well, I guess that just solved two mysteries. First off, the vest did not shrink, I just need to get the straps resized. Secondly, that explains why Cordelia did not throw herself at me immediately in a fit of passion like she clearly should have in a kind and just world."

All right now, tubby you have got yourself a problem. You told Miss Government Sexy that you would do some jobs for her. You need to do the jobs for Miss Government Sexy to get what you need. But, oh no hero, you decided that drinking beer from about 10 o'clock in the morning till 10 o'clock at night is now a national Olympic event that you are diligently training for.

"Well, seeing as how I'm not going on a diet and losing 20 pounds in the next few days, I need to take a trip into the shop for some adjustments. Besides John and Miriam don't judge."

Shit, when did I get a beer gut? Damn it, why isn't there a spell for instant weight loss. Now that would be some magic shit I'd actually consider buying and using.

For a minute he considered stopping drinking but a combat tour "dry" and the nightmares that accompanied that tour flooded back into his memory. Paying for alteration to his gear would be better than drying out. That held true any day of the week.

Two hours later, Declan pulled up in front of an industrial

Blood War: Rage

warehouse, parking his truck in the empty lot in front of the single heavy steel door. He took the nylon duffel bag out of his back seat and lifted it over his shoulder as he walked towards the door. He raised his hand to knock and paused as he heard a series of mechanical clicks unlocking it. Glancing upwards, he noticed the series of cameras spread along the side of the building and waved at them, smiling. He pushed open the heavy door and began to walk down the entry hallway, feeling the rippling wave of magic sweep over him. This process felt familiar, almost safe, and he knew it was just Miriam's way of speeding up her service as it measured and evaluated his body shape. Also made it so she could kill anyone who might be a threat. The tech would be as prevalent as the magic.

Well, at least she doesn't have to run a tailor's tape up and down my crotch. Wait, is that good or bad? Good. John K is fucking scary.

Before he reached the end of the hallway he heard Miriam's voice. "Welcome Guest, to our home and business."

"Miriam, what happens if you don't say that every time somebody walks in?"

"Well, Mr. Kenner, let's just say that having children would definitely be out of the question for you." The female voice answered from inside the warehouse.

Oh please, like that has been an option, ever.

Declan proceeded through the rest of the hallway and into the open warehouse space angling towards the long counter area at the front of the room. The diminutive Miriam was standing behind the counter as Declan took in the room.

"Good to see you again, Miriam, I got some work for you and I got a couple questions for John," Declan said as he dropped the nylon bag onto the counter.

"John, Mr. Kenner's here. He wants to talk to you." Miriam shouted over her shoulder to the back of the warehouse, past rows of metal shelves and towards what sounded like a heavy floor press grinding through metal in the back of the warehouse.

"So what type of ingenious weapon of destruction is John working on back there?"

"I think it's a light aluminum set of Paladin plate mail," Miriam replied, as she unzipped the nylon bag and started pulling out Declan's Hunter coat without even waiting to be asked.

"What in the hell can that possibly be useful for? Aluminum? And who the hell fights in plate mail anyway?"

"You do know this is a business, right? We do have other customers." She said casually, as she ran her hands across the damaged areas of his coat, tracing her fingertips over areas of exposed silver mesh lining frowning slightly.

"If it's someone that fights in aluminum plate mail, then that is a pretty dumb customer."

"It's for sale at the Renaissance fair next week you, dimwit. Like I said, this is a business. You wouldn't believe the markup on merchandise we get at the Renaissance fair."

"You know, I think it's illegal for you to sell legitimate charms in an unlicensed venue like a Renaissance fair. Don't you?"

"Like I said, you wouldn't believe the markup I can get at a Renaissance fair with the right customer. But, what you should be more concerned about is how much markup I charge you for fixing your clearly negligently maintained coat here." Miriam said gruffly as she pointed her finger at Declan's chest. "I've told you before, it's a whole lot cheaper if you just take care of your equipment instead of bringing it to me to fix after you've run off and done something stupid with it."

"I didn't really think I'd be needing it anymore," Declan stated without thinking.

"So, this is not just fixing it up cosmetically for old times' sake is it, Mr. Kenner?" Miriam asked raising an eyebrow slightly the teasing tone of her voice disappearing.

"No, it's not. I need it brought back up to combat standard."

"Now would this have anything to do with that pretty government chippie that's been nosing around lately? Not to mention a new hunter with a name from the past."

Blood War: Rage

"What are you talking about Miriam?" His attention had snapped to her as he processed that bit of information.

"Come on now, Mr. Kenner. No reason to play coy here. John and I do leave the shop here occasionally. It's hard to miss the increase in the number of specialized equipment requests that we've been getting. Not to mention the repairs that we've been having to do on some of our newer customer's equipment."

"Newer customers? Are you taking Government contracts now?"

"That would be none of your concern if we were, Mr. Kenner. But, I was referring to that pretty young huntress in town. She has some very, hmmm, unique equipment requirements indeed. And she seems to need them repaired."

"A young hunter? I'm pretty sure, even if the Department of Defense had restarted a Hunters program, none of them would be on the streets as civilians already. I can ask around for some folks I know, see if they know anything."

Cordy is many things but she isn't a hunter. And Miriam wouldn't regard her as young. Huh, the game is afoot, Declan.

"Oh, she's not a mystery for you to solve, Mr. Kenner. As a matter of fact, I'm pretty sure you knew her father."

"Are you harassing customers again. Miriam?" A large man, a good foot taller than Miriam, wearing a machinist smock and wiping his hands off on an oil-stained rag approached from the back of the counter.

"I was just inquiring with Mr. Kenner if he happened to be needing repairs on his gear because of our government friends who have been making inquiries around the area lately. And he's trying to convince me I should be giving him discounts." She snorted in derision at that idea.

Declan fought back a smile.

"Now Miriam, Declan's businesses his own now. We pride ourselves in respecting our customer's privacy." John told his wife as he extended a hand over the counter to Declan who responded immediately with a firm handshake.

Doug Burbey & Mel Todd

"Good to see you, John. I have an idea that I want to run by you after Miriam's done given me the third degree here. I mean, it's not nearly as interesting as making cosmetic medieval armor to sell to college students spending Mom and Dad's money for role-playing games."

"Hey, don't knock it, Declan. The Paladin with the sweetest armor gets all the wenches. Or so I'm told." John had added the last bit after noticing the withering glare Miriam was giving him.

"Okay Mr. Kenner, before you go off on a tangent about wenches, how fast do you need your coat back?"

"That's not all I need." Declan pulled out his tactical vest from the bag, placing it on the counter. "I also need my vest resized. It's been a long time since I used it and apparently the sizing straps have shrunk a little."

"Sizing straps shrunk?" John smirked as he glanced at Declan's midriff.

Declan tugged his shirt down frowning.

"Hush, John. If Mr. Kenner says they shrunk, then they shrunk. I will make the adjustments based on your new readings from when he came in. The best that I can do for the coat is a re-impregnation of the wards with some of the silver mesh fill repairs. John can do some of the leather overlay patching and readjust the straps easy enough. To be perfectly honest, Mr. Kenner, the whole coat could really use some saddle soap too. You do know upkeep on this equipment is not always complex. Didn't they teach you army folks anything about preventive maintenance checks and services? I mean really, this leather is just screaming for some moisture. All said and done, the vest will maybe take 20 minutes. The coat will take me at least a week to get all the ward reinforcements to set. I can do the physical mesh repairs as the wards are taking hold. So yeah, I need a week."

"If I gave you little cash incentives, do you think you can put my stuff to the front of the line and have it all back to me in 3 or 4 days?"

"Sure, I could, Mr. Kenner. If you don't want the wards set so

Blood War: Rage

that your back gets ripped open by one of those government problems that they are denying they have. Or how about having the wire mesh fail because the wards have not integrated into the disbursement system and your entire nervous system gets fried by a novice level mage throwing amateur magic at you?" She replied sternly.

Declan raised both his hands in surrender, "All right, Miriam, a week it is then."

Miriam folded the coat and placed it back into the bag, then went the tactical vest on top of it and she zipped it closed. She carried the bag off to the back of the shop and placed it on an open workbench.

"Declan, what did you want to run by me?" John asked with a look of sincere interest. "You always have the oddest requests. What is it this time? A beer bottle opening grenade maybe?"

Declan paused for a second in thought "Hmmmm, no. While that would be awesome I could see unpleasant repercussions to carrying that around on a Friday night. What I really need is help with my Vulture."

John groaned "Really? That beast of a carbine is one of the few successful Army R&D efforts during the war. Reliable, rugged as hell and with a barrel built to withstand the hottest enhanced magical small arms rounds. But it is ugly as shit. Which is fine but it can also only carry twenty-one rounds, if you're using the extended double stack clip, and it weighs nearly 12 pounds unloaded already. There's not much I can do with it, buddy."

"That's the problem. The rounds."

"Well, you can stop right there, Declan. I can't extend the mag capacity. It's simply that the force needed to extend the magazine spring is proportional to the distance that spring is extended from its rest position. To push those heavy rounds in a higher capacity magazine you either end up with a two-foot-long magazine, or a drum mag making the weight balance canter to a side and make the weight of the thing just totally ridiculous. Either way, the Vulture becomes just flat out unshootable."

"I don't need more rounds in the magazine. Hell, at the price point you guys have on high explosive rounds, I can't afford them anyway. What I need is the ability to select round types, on the fly, without having to swap out mags. Standard, to explosive, to jacketed loads and so forth."

"Oh, now that is something else entirely." John leaned back and closed his eyes and drummed his fingertips rhythmically on the countertop for a few seconds.

"Earth to John. Earth to John." Declan snapped his fingers in the air in front of John.

"Oh yeah. Round selection." John's eyes snapped back open as he continued, "Interesting concept but also a problem. I mean, the Vulture's reliability is based on its heavy but simple, construction. There's really not much to its guts to allow for the addition of a complex trigger assembly, not to mention that the lower receiver feed and sear cam are in no way suited for a dual-round-ready configuration below the breech bolt. I think you'd be better off with a whole new weapon instead of trying to add round selection to your Vulture. I just happen to have some very sexy new replacement candidates I can show you. Have you seen the Heckler & Koch HK517 yet? It's a 7.62×51mm cartridge: Hybrid tech and magic optics with battery-less infrared d light amplification up to 10x, piston-operated, selective fire rifle with a rotating bolt. It is magazine or belt fed and I could possibly work some form of round selector in there if you insisted. But I can't guarantee that won't reduce its mean time between failures though."

"As sexy, and expensive, as that sounds, I'll have to pass. I trust my Vulture and will have to stick with her. But hey, if you get any cool ideas..."

"Yeah, yeah. I'll call you if I figure out a miracle of magical gunsmithing that turns a frog into a princess. You sure you don't want to give me a fat roll of cash for some sexy expensive German hardware? I mean, Miriam is on my case about taking her to Disney World so I need to pimp the goods, you know."

Declan laughed "Sorry, man. Maybe you can hard sell one of

the Government types on the HKs. Toss in a free three-point sling and a forearm grip and they'll fawn all over it. They dig that Gucci tactical crap. "

"Will do, Declan. I'll keep thinking on your issue, but no promises. I kinda think you're screwed on that idea, but you never know."

"I'll be back in a week to cash out and help you put a down payment on your Disney vacation."

"No checks, Mr. Kenner! Cash business here you know." Miriam yelled out from the back of the shop.

"Damn," Declan looked at John "what's she have? Magic hearing or something?"

"You have no idea, man, no idea. See you back here in a week and we'll have all your kit ready to go."

Chapter 18 - Meeting with a Demon

Shane froze, looking at his toy. Suddenly the vague attractiveness of her red hair and pale skin didn't begin to compare to what her sexy gray matter contained.

"You have the portal connections to a demon who wants to negotiate?"

She shrugged. "Yes. It's a complicated portal but I could hold it in my head."

"And what exactly did he want to negotiate?" Shane kept his voice icy cool even as his mind threatened to overload with ideas.

The girl shrugged. "Something about working with our leaders and small raiding parties. Angry about the loss of some good foot soldiers."

"How did you get the portal info?"

Her face lit up, and for a split second, she glowed. "Some government agent guy gave the demon token to me. Said a small batch of the tokens were provided by the Treaty Arbitrators, to both the humans and demons in paired sets, at the signing. They were to allow the humans and demons to foster a more positive report by communicating across the portal wall. He said it was his gift to me." Her head dropped and she shrugged. "He was cute and called me pretty."

Shane opened his mouth about to tell her how badly she'd been played, then snapped it shut, forcing a smile. "You're more than cute. You might be the sexiest woman I've met in a very long time. Would you be willing to open that portal for me?"

"You think I'm sexy?" She stopped mid-stride to look at him,

Blood War: Rage

and for a split second, he regretted how he was about to use this naive child. It disappeared with the reminder that they were all dead already; they just hadn't physically died quite yet.

"I do believe you are the sexiest woman I've seen in years. First, tell me all about this agent that gave you the token." His voice dropped to a low purr as they walked and he scanned the area, verifying no one paid any attention to them. "Tell me about this demon."

The toy blinked at him. "I don't talk to him. I just open the portal and ring Frax's bell. Frax's boss is scary though. Ring five maybe? So, does that mean you like me? They said you would keep me."

Shane had to blink to disconnect, from someone having the portal numbers to a ring five demon, to a woman seeking reassurance.

"I think I've never liked anyone more. How strong of a Ley line crossing do you need to ring up his portal?"

And when did I become British? Gah. But this toy is proving more useful than I could have expected. A ring five?

A shiver ran through him.

What if it's a ring six? Fuck, can she reach that high? That might be exactly where I need to get the information to save myself, and maybe a few others.

The thorny concept of a sustainable gene pool ate at him, especially as he suspected his balls were firing blanks. But if that was the case, who cared. He could let his universe collapse as soon as he died, he wouldn't care - he'd be dead.

The toy shrugged. "At least two, three is easier."

Shane almost tripped. "You can open a portal on a two crossing ley line?"

"Sure. Really I don't need crossings, but if I do it without one, I'm exhausted for days." She shrugged then stopped as he did.

His mouth dropped open, closed, and dropped open again. Shane took a deep breath and a slow smile spread across his face. "Toy, I hope you like me because I'm not letting you go."

He pulled her close as he walked faster to the building, thoughts whirling around his head.

"First things first Toy, we are going to summon a demon."

She looked at him a bit wary. "It's Jane, and I'm a bit tired. It's been an exciting day. And I... " she trailed off frowning. "I feel weird. Is this the blood? Maybe I'm not tired."

"Was Frax there?"

"No. One of the guys had a different portal token; they didn't want to use mine. I don't think they knew." Her voice trailed off and she swayed a bit on her feet. "I think I should eat something."

They had reached his building and Shane leaned his bike against the wall and then ushered her up the stairs. "Not a problem, I'll order a pizza, heck five. You rest. This building crosses Ley lines. Then you and I are going to summon a demon."

It took a bit to get the food in her, but he had to admit Toy looked better, not as pale after she ate. He'd been making notes and organizing thoughts while she ate and stared at the wall. Not at the TV, not at her phone, not at a book, but at the damn wall. Shane almost asked her what she looked at twice but decided he didn't want to know. Ignorance was bliss. Happy before the demons, miserable afterward. Knowledge made no one happy.

He had the circle constructed, his questions organized, and eagerness bubbled through his veins. This would get him the answers. He could feel it, closer than he had been in a very long time.

"You ready, Toy?"

She ducked her head, not looking at him, her voice a low mumble. "It's Jane. But yeah. I'm actually still buzzing from all the blood earlier."

Shane smiled so widely he thought he might break something as he waved at the circle. "Go for it, Toy."

This time she didn't correct him, just drew a token out of her pocket. One lancet later, the lancet makers were raking in a fortune now, she squeezed a drop of blood on it, centered herself and waved a hand. A small portal about the size of a basketball appeared and Shane felt his jaw drop again.

Oh fuck, Toy. You are mine. I'm damn near tempted to collar you in every sense of the word. You just became a slave, cause I am never letting you go. Fuck the cost, fuck morals, not that I have any. You are a walking portal. And you are mine.

Possession coated those thoughts. Every other mage he'd seen, those few that could call and open portals, took chanting, a cut of blood, and so much effort they could barely hold the portal open for more than a few minutes. His Toy waved her hand and it opened.

"Frax? You there? Got someone that wants to speak to the big boss."

Toy tilted her head looking at the portal and shrugged. "I don't know." She turned and looked at Shane. "It wants to know your name."

Shane blinked and realized he hadn't introduced himself, but Toy didn't need to know his real name.

"Marcus Vipsanius, Mage of the Romans, here to parlay with the boss of Frax."

"You get that Frax? Sure, we'll wait." She yawned and sat back down on the couch and Shane felt his eyes go wide.

"You don't need to stand there and keep it open?"

"Nah, that is only if I'm the only one holding it. But Frax takes half the weight and I take the other half. Kinda like holding a bowling ball in the air, heavy but we brace each other."

Shane mentally made note and addendums to everything he knew about summoning portals. He could do it. But only hopped up on blood, with at least four crossing lines, and a ready supply or blood or sleep afterward. He needed to find out about the demons that were making contact and if this was something he could use.

Toy lifted her head and blinked at the portal. "I assume you only want to talk to Bezzid, not see him?"

"Yes," the word blurted out of Shane before conscious thought registered. "Just talk. My apartment can't handle a what, ring four?"

Toy shrugged. "I think he is a five maybe six. But..." she scratched her head and winced. "Okay communication open. Go for it."

Shane drew himself up, demons didn't see the world the way humans did and their lack of understanding idioms amused him. But mostly he wanted to see what he could find out.

"To what underling do I speak?" And Shane held his breath hoping he took the right approach

"Bezzid is not underling. Bezzid controls a horde." The demon's voice sounded flat, stripped of all intonation, but Shane got the sense he missed something about it. "Why does Marcus Vipsanius, Mage of the Romans, contact Bezzid? Human contact is normally done via Kelvin of the White City."

Fuck, he already has a normal human contact? This is not good.

"I come to offer information about the demon hunters that are prepared to invade your realm."

Toy shot him a look of confused horror but Shane ignored it. All of him was focused on the portal.

"Ah, so the reports from Bezzid's scouts were correct. The Demon Hunters are preparing an invasion. Bezzid's casters talk to your human oclaves and know of all your trickery. Bezzid had heard of one called DK. He names himself after us, mocking our power, trying to steal it. Kelvin of the White City thinks Ze can win this battle. Ze's hunters will not be enough to win against Bezzid's horde. What information offer Bezzid in trade? What do you seek? Why you waste time?"

DK? What the fuck? It can't mean Declan? That level of synergy would be insane. Though...

Shane cut off his thoughts and focused back on the important part right now.

"Lighten up, Francis." He replied abstractly as he tried to process how to direct this discussion. "You're getting upset over nothing. I'm looking for knowledge. I seek books of information about the blood and the Angels. I would learn to create worlds, oh great Abattoir of Knowledge."

"Francis? Ah, one of odd Earth sayings. You seek to overthrow Kelvin? Take Zir's power and servants for yourself?"

"Kelvin is a minor mage, I am a Magnus, I shall remake that which is."

"Ah. You speak of the lost knowledge, the truth in creating the existences. It matters not. When Bezzid's hordes win through, there will be no chance to create more existences as all blood will belong to us, Only the Angels will be left. With three races they cannot stand against us and Demons will retake their rightful spot."

I hate it when Deva was right. But I doubt he's involved in this mess. He said he wanted to stay out.

"You cannot win, not without my information. I know the portals and when and where they will attack. But I will not share without the knowledge I seek."

"Bah. Knowledge is in the blood. Books hold it only for a short time. Except for the Demon Bible but that would kill you, drain your blood. Though it might be interesting to watch. However, you are not worth my time. Leave."

The portal winked out creating a slight vacuum that pulled loose papers towards it.

"Ow. Dammit. I hate it when they do that, it hurts." Toy whined, rubbing her head.

Shane just stood there reviewing what he'd learned.

Who the hell is Kevlin? What had DK gotten himself into? And what did he mean the knowledge is in the blood?

Chapter 19 - Puppeteer

Kelvin Ordonio sat casually in a plush lounge chair located at the end of the United States Capitol Building's second floor main hallway. To a passerby he would look like any other government employee using his downtime to check his emails on his phone. That was exactly how he wanted it. Kelvin liked to ensure that his outward appearance was always designed to fit the situation with maximum effectiveness. He opened his secure link and typed in the appropriate Senate office room number then turned on his earbuds' audio. Immediately he was rewarded with clear video, and audio, from a live concealed feed that originated from the Senate Majority Leader's own office. He had stirred the pot and wanted to watch it boil just a little before he just happened to stop by in to offer his assistance to the Senator.

Inside of the lavish office, Senator Mulkiski turned abruptly and pointed her finger at her Chief of Staff's chest as he shut the door to the Senator's inner office.

"How many times have I told you? One, only one, of these constituent meet and greets each day. That was two before the first session today, you sorry sack of shit. If there's another one on my schedule for today. I swear to God, you're going to be fired."

Her Chief of Staff pulled out his tablet appearing to double check the Senator's schedule. Senator Mulkiski moved over and sat down at her opulent desk set to the back of the room with the windows of her Senate office building overlooking the mall behind her.

"Janet, I reminded you yesterday that we were going to have two constituent meetings this morning. Both of those were family members of big donors, and you know that. Without these smiling photo ops of yours, we have unhappy donors who don't want to give you their money for your reelection campaign. You do remember the elections you still have to do, correct?"

"Yes Mark, I do remember that I have to be reelected. I do remember I have constituents. And you need to remember that I said I would do one of these a day, not two. The party didn't spend the last fifty years gerrymandering the hell out of my district for me to keep wasting all my time now with constituents. You know my seat is perfectly safe; that's why we only need to do one of these photo ops a day. You may know your way around this building enough to keep the ship running as my Chief of Staff, but don't you forget for one fucking second that I've been here long enough to know my way around this whole god damn city. When I say only one constituent photo op per day, it means one fucking photo op a day."

Mark tapped at his tablet aggressively. "I got it, Janet. The next time the harbor authority union vice president asks for a favor of you to just take a picture with his damn niece, I'll make sure to tell him that you're too busy to talk to constituency today." The senator's Chief of Staff said sarcastically.

"Well, don't be an asshole about it, Mark. You know as well as I do, I would've made an exception there. Let's just not make a habit out of this."

"Of course, Janet, one constituent meet and greet a day only. But I do need to point out the two votes that you have coming up this afternoon. We need to have your open floor debate comments reviewed then prepped." The Chief of Staff began as he moved around to the side of the Senators desk while pulling up the prepared text on his tablet.

"We've got both these votes in the bag. The party whip is already done with the counts. He assured me those losers across the aisle have lost five of their Centrists members already, so they are not going to be able to institute any form of filibuster. I don't even know why we have to bother with the formality of either vote, I've got all those sad sacks of shit by the balls and there is nothing they can do about it."

"Janet, I've still got concerns about those rumors of the Midwest coalition block starting to push back against us on the additional provision we included in the fuel subsidy bill for the enhanced medical data gathering authorities being granted to the Department of Defense."

"You know as well as I do those redneck libertarians have nowhere near the clout to go against me as majority leader. They know that if they want the cheap fuel subsidy, that to mooch cheap diesel fuel for their dirt farming constituents they will do and vote exactly how I tell them to."

Kelvin had to fight not to laugh. If he ever let this out to her 'dirt farming constituents,' her term would be over. As fun as this was, he couldn't sit here all day. He rose and headed to the Senator's gatekeeper. It took him a few minutes to walk there, making sure to tuck his phone in as he did. Minutes later he pushed open the door to the outer office.

"Shelia, how are you doing? That dress makes your eyes just sparkle. I'm afraid I need to see the senator. Now, please."

He smiled at her, making sure it reached his eyes.

Shelia blushed and hit the intercom button on her desk. "Yes?" Senator Mulkiski's voice came through the intercom, vaguely distorted.

"Senator, Director Ordonio is here to see you."

"Mark, what's this about? I don't remember anything about him coming here to visit me on my schedule today."

"I honestly have no idea whatsoever."

"I really don't think you have any time to meet with him today, Janet. I'm sure he's just here to hound you about his department's budget request for next year. I'll go out and tell him that he needs to address any of his concerns on his next Program and Requirement Forms submission through the Department of Defense Liaison Office, like he is supposed to. I'll get rid of him. Just because his agency has a fancy name, and only really answers to DoD Special Access Programs oversight, does not give him the right to just freely walk into the office of the Senate Majority Leader."

Kelvin had to fight back a laugh at the horrified expression on the secretary's face as the intercom button stuck and all the words came through to the office. He shook his head holding up a finger to his mouth when she would have interrupted and let them know.

She rolled her eyes and shrugged, going back to her work.

And that my dear senator is why you are never rude to the people who work for you.

"You know it does Mark. Don't be an idiot. His budget is already set, and today's vote on the fuel subsidies, with the enhanced personnel data security to the HIPPA regulations shoved discreetly inside of it, his staff basically wrote themselves. I bet you that this prick is just here making sure I have the votes is all. So go ahead and push my schedule little bit, Mark. Shove everything back about fifteen minutes while I deal with this."

"You want me to stay in here?"

"No, I can take care of this myself, Mark. Like I said, he's just being a pain in the ass government bureaucrat trying to check up on his little pet bill rider we are voting up today. I'll put him in his place and send him back out on his way, this shouldn't take more than 15 minutes. Just send him in when you leave."

Kelvin heard the steps and nodded to the secretary. She clicked the button twice and it disconnected. He'd have to remember to send her chocolate, that had proved more entertaining than he expected.

The office door opened and Mark stepped out, a forced smile on his face. "Go on in, Director."

The Director of the International Cooperative Element Responders, Mr. Kelvin Ordonio, entered the Senator's office still fighting back chuckles. At five feet eight inches tall and slightly overweight, with a Pacific Islander heritage, Mr. Ordonio projected a calm and social exterior bordering on jovial. Something he carefully cultivated. Although his light grey suit and shoes were

146

immaculately maintained, they appeared to be of the same moderate cost as every other suit worn by a government employee grinding through the daily chores of keeping the Washington D.C bureaucracy moving.

He smiled warmly at the Senator's Chief of Staff "Mark, how have you been good Sir? I hope the Majority Leader here is taking great care of you. If not, you know we could always use a man of your stature over with the ICERs. I could make some calls for you." Shaking the Chief's hand then clapping his shoulder lightly as if they were old friends. "We have great dental coverage. Oh, and reserved parking spaces. You can't beat that deal with a stick here in D.C. huh?"

"Oh, I'm just fine where I am, Director, but I appreciate your offer none the less," Mark replied back. But the smile on his face betrayed nervousness and he quickly left the room and pulled the Senator's office door closed behind him.

Senator Mulkiski sat still behind her desk staring directly at the visiting Director, impatiently drumming her fingers on the glossy dark hardwood desktop. "Director Ordonio, what a pleasure to have you come across the river today. What brings you over to the Capital Hill side?" Her words came out cordial, but cold.

"Oh, thank you, Senator," Kelvin began his cheery reply as he pulled a laser pointer sized metal object from his inner coat pocket and clicked a button on its base. "It's always an honor to be given a few minutes of the Senator's time to personally address any of the concerns your office may have in regards to the budget request questions your staffers have requested from my budget management chief." Moving the object slowly back and forth at waist height along the wall, Kelvin continued slowing across the room appearing to study the various displays of Maryland art and photos hanging there. Just because he had the office bugged, didn't mean he wanted anyone else listening in.

"Ma'am, may I ask, is this new? I've never seen this before. It's a great photo and I must know if it's a local artist." He said as he pointed at a framed photo with the metal object in his hand and deliberately ran it slowly over each edge of the frame.

"Why, yes it is, Director Ordonio. So nice of you to notice. It's from an artist that works out of a studio on the Eastern Shore. I'll make sure my staff gets you his information." The Senator responded flatly.

"Oh yes, please do, ma'am." He replied as he looked down at the tool in his hand then clicked its base again as he returned it to his pocket. "You get the best free stuff, Janet. You don't pay the price for anything, do you?"

This is part of the problem I need to solve. Greedy career politicians with no real regard for helping their constituents. It's all about power, and the trappings of it, for them. Decades after decades of worthlessness, problems unsolved and pushed off to be forgotten after the next election cycle. We should have put them in the front lines against the hordes instead of our real best and brightest Americans. Kelvin thought bitterly to himself, making sure his mask of easy civility never wavered.

The Director turned and walked over and sat directly in front of the Senators desk, unbuttoned his coat casually, and placed both his hands folded on his lap as he presented a warm smile.

Clearly showing signs of agitation the Senator pressed the ICER Director, "What do you really want Ordonio?"

"Oh, what we all want, Janet. A world that is safe and free, with the United States of America as the final global superpower and without any of these pesky little demon and Fae issues of course."

Director Kelvin Ordonio knew that behind his crafted deceptive smile and calming demeanor was a man whose soul was committed. He would not hesitate to commit a humanity-saving genocide without a single regret, if needed. He was committed, she was just a weakness to exploit.

"Director, your bill rider goes to vote in a couple of hours. It is buried in a subsidy bill as a provision to the existing HIPPA laws for a DNA repository consolidation, ensuring that any, and all, DNA information collected by any government body or commercial activity, is exclusively stored in a single secure repository to ensure private DNA information is not exposed unwittingly. Therefore, the public/private information is secured and citizens will not have to worry about their personal information being misused."

"That's is absolutely splendid, Janet. I'm glad your staff agreed that using the DoD's secure data repository was the most cost-efficient way to proceed as well. Using an existing, and currently underutilized, facility is absolutely in the taxpayer's best interest - a very wise decision. As a core civilian management reorganization, scheduled for next week, will be shifting the repository oversight to my department, I can assure the information will not be misused at all."

"You'll have what you want this afternoon I assure you. I have full faith the repository will be in good hands under your oversight." It would give him a starting list of Americans that are most likely unaware that they even possess a trace of Fae, or demon, DNA in their blood. When the system is fully synced with all Homeland Security Agencies, the DoD, Medical System Records, Department of Justice and Corrections, not to mention all the commercial DNA collecting services and private security providers, the Director of the International Cooperative Element Responders will be able to sort nearly 80% of the humans in the country by potential blood associations with other realm species - no matter how weak a trace or how many generations back.

"Now that it's done, I expect to be compensated immediately after the vote Director."

The Director could not miss the Senator's quickening pace of her fingers drumming her desktop, or the inadvertent flick of her tongue across her upper lips in the excitement of securing the mother of all bribes. "After the President signs the bill enacting the law, you will immediately receive payment into your account in Manila."

"That will be at least two more weeks! How do I know you won't screw me over after the vote?" Her jowls shook, and her complexion reddened at the idea of a double cross.

The Director stood and reached over the Senator's desk and

Blood War: Rage

took the small pad of post-it notes. He wrote five numbers onto the top sheet (2,783 / 1,528 / 432 / 896 / 176) before he placed the pad and numbers down directly in front of the senator. "Because I never fail to keep my promises, Janet."

The ICER Director buttoned his coat and turned to leave as the Senator picked up the notepad glancing at the numbers that Director Ordonio had written on it. "Well, what the hell do these mean?"

He turned to look at the Senator as his smile disappeared and turned into an icy stare directed at the aged politician. "The first number is the identified number of Demon War Veterans originally confirmed as survived the war. The second number is how many who are alive today. The third is how many I have under my department's employment today; the fourth number is how many we still have under observation and assessment for disposition."

"But what is the fifth number you wrote down here for then?"

"That, Janet, shows you that I never fail to keep my promises. I told you I would eliminate your issue with the War Vets. That fifth number is how many of the Vets that I've already had killed."

"But what about these guys that you've actually gone and hired? You promised to completely take care of my request. Keeping 432 in your private army stable is not what I asked."

The warm smile returned to the Director's face. "When I've done what I need to do to ensure our fine nation's superiority and safety, then the third number you see there drops to zero and the fifth number increases by that same amount. Don't worry, it will only take me a day to adjust the personnel disposition numbers. As an added bonus I'll be able to shut down my Reset factories. I don't much care for loose ends."

Chapter 20 - First Assignment

Declan settled into his recliner, hit play on the perfectly positioned big screen TV, turned it on to the football game which was the first season of NFL since the armistice was signed, cracked his beer, and sighed.

This is perfect. An afternoon watching the game, plenty of beer, and maybe I'll grill some brauts later.

He ignored the itchy feeling under his skin, determined to enjoy a perfect afternoon. The kind of itch they talked about while they waited for the next wave of demons to try and kill them. Out of habit he glanced at his phone and the remote viewer on it, flipping through the camera views, verifying nothing moved as the sportscasters babbled about stuff that didn't matter.

"Shut up and let them throw the damn football," he muttered at the TV. But even the annoyance felt good. He'd missed football.

The talking idiots finally shut up and the ref blew the whistle, kickoff! Declan wiggled a bit more to get comfortable, raising his beer for another drink and his phone rang. Startled he tipped too soon and beer spilled onto his sweatshirt.

"Alcohol abuse, penalty, two yards." he sighed. Setting the beer down he wiped at his sweatshirt, Detroit Lions - always in his heart even if Detroit didn't exist anymore and looked at the phone with the other.

"Unknown? Who the fuck is unknown? I don't think so." He hit decline and got up to go get a towel to wipe up the mess, and another beer.

The phone chimed with an incoming text as he walked back towards his chair and he picked it up frowning.

Answer the phone, Mr. Kenner

Blood War: Rage

Who the fuck?

The question echoed in his mind as the phone rang again displaying unknown again. Glaring at the phone he clicked accept and raised it up to his ear.

"Yes?"

"Mr. Kenner. I have a job assignment for you. Something simple that I am sure you will find in your skill set. It might even give you an opportunity to refresh your memory on how to run a mission." The warm contralto voice told him who spoke instantly, and he didn't know how he felt about the fact that she had been serious about demon hunting.

"Cordy, so nice to hear from you. Miss me already?" He turned and put the beer back in the fridge. Even as he made sure his tone stayed light and flirtatious his mind raced.

Is this a setup? Why is she calling? What in the world could she have for me to do?

"Again, It's Cordelia. I have a demon that seems to have been summoned from a small unsustainable portal and is causing havoc in your neck of the woods. About twenty miles away. I'd like you to remove this annoyance."

The sudden itch to have his gun in his hands made him rub his hands on his jeans, his mind slipping into mission mode.

"How many?"

"Best guess, just one, but sources are not always perfectly accurate."

Declan had to bite back a laugh at that understatement. Perfect intelligence didn't exist; he knew that for a fact.

"Level?"

What am I going to need out of my stash? Can I get her to pay for restocking?

"Reports indicate a level one. Minor. Something I am sure will be easy for you to extinguish."

"And how will you know I've done it?" Declan asked leaning back against his counter, watching the TV without really seeing it.

"You will be expected to deliver its teeth, or an identifying

152

body part, to me. Upon verification of their authenticity, I'll pay."

"I'll need reimbursement for my ammo and any damages to my equipment I might sustain, in addition to the Reset."

"Of course, that is standard for all of our ad hoc contractors. Though if the costs are too extravagant I will require receipts. I assume you know how to use GPS coordinates on your phone for directions."

Declan scoffed. "Of course I do."

"Excellent. I will text them to you immediately. Good hunting." Cordy hung up and Declan looked at his phone.

"How the hell do I load in GPS coordinates to figure out where to go?" Twenty minutes of searching the web, downloading two apps, before he got it to work. "Stupid hi-tech toys. Where the hell is a sergeant when I need one?" The location didn't seem too far away and he ran the ring one demon info through his head.

Normal heavy weapons but takes a decent amount of firepower to kill them. Assume Intel is wrong. There are three of them and ring two. What do I need to load for?

With that in mind he headed down to the armory. Typing in the codes and providing the handprint, he walked in and stood, eyes narrowed as he glanced around at his choices. After a minute he nodded. Striding over he grabbed his modified Vulture Heavy .45 Carbine, a tac vest, ten spare clips, another quick clot kit, a backup piece to ride in the ankle holster, and a combat knife, because you could never go wrong with a combat knife.

Ten minutes later he stood in the kitchen, the unopened beers casting baleful looks his way. "I'll be back for you, promise."

Patting himself down one more time he headed for the door, then paused. With a sigh, he came back and grabbed a battery pack for the phone. With his luck, he'd run out of juice in the middle of nowhere chasing this thing and never get back to his beer.

With nothing else to delay him, DK walked out the door, a smile on his face.

The location sent him outside of Jennings. About thirty miles

Blood War: Rage

from his house- DK found a headache growing and realized he had clenched up, frowning and glaring at the road.

Why the fuck is someone opening gates and pulling in demons this fucking close to my house?

The more he thought about it the more his blood boiled and the more he wanted to kill the fucker who did this. Maybe even more than the demon itself. The GPS dropped him back behind some all but abandoned strip mall. The only advantage was there would be a lower probability of witnesses. He pulled his truck to a stop in the shadows at the back of the building and stepped out, grabbing the Vulture as he moved. Closing the door quietly he stood, breathing deep, and the stench of demon filled his nostrils. Electric adrenaline licked across his nerves, lighting up his brain as it hadn't been in a long time. His eyes closed in pleasure and he breathed in deep and long, taking all of it in - the blood, the brimstone, the taint, and the wrongness of it.

I fucking missed this.

The truth of the words burned, but he smiled anyhow moving forward the Vulture tight at his shoulder.

~*~

No one answered as DK rang the bell on the counter. As a drop of demon blood slid off his nose and hit the counter his patience vaporized. Pivoting with military precision, he'd retired not died, he turned and took the two steps to the door. Pulling back his foot he slammed it just outside the knob. The cheap plywood hollow door shattered, flying apart. He walked through not caring that the knob didn't even have a lock on it. The destruction without having to worry about dying felt good. He needed more. The corners of his vision flashed red, and something in him screamed that meant bad things.

DK didn't care. He stalked through the cubical farm, navigating effortlessly through the maze, his steps taking him directly to

Cordy's office. The door stood slightly ajar but he could hear music coming from the other side. Without breaking stride he shoved it open, his hand shooting out automatically to stop it from rebounding into his face. He'd knocked down more than one door in his career.

The office door, no better material than the one in the front, bounced off the wall with a crack of drywall, slamming back into his hand. Cordy, sitting at the desk with headphones on, spun backward and came up eyes wild and a .38 pointed right at him.

"What the fuck, Kenner," she shouted her eyes so dilated they appeared black. He noted with some small part of his mind her aim never wavered and she held it on his center mass with the air of someone who knew how to use a gun.

"Ring one demon, you said. One demon, best guess, you said. Imply maybe there would be two. I believed you. Why? I don't know. Maybe it was your tits. Maybe because you have something I need. Or maybe I was stupid enough to think I could trust a government whore. There were three fucking ring twos, and one three. I used up every bit of ammo I had, ended up killing the last one, the three with my fucking knife. NO ONE USES A FUCKING KNIFE TO KILL A RING THREE DEMON!" He screamed that last bit leaning over her desk. The .38 pointed at his chest and he didn't give a damn if she pulled the trigger. After tonight the pain of the .38 hitting his vest would be a bee sting. Maybe.

Cordy blinked and put the gun away. "That is NOT what I was informed. I will deal with that breach immediately. Do you have proof?" Her voice calm and cool as if he stood there in a suit, not dripping demon blood all over the carpet.

DK closed his eyes, absorbing the power the blood brought with it, using it to push back the rage, to build his internal power and force calm onto his mind. He dug into one pocket in the BDU's and pulled out three tentacles and set of fangs.

"Here. These ring twos didn't have teeth. "

Cordy looked at the gory bits on her desk, mouth wrinkling in a slight moue of distaste.

Blood War: Rage

"Very well." She reached in and pulled out four doses of reset. "Please send me an invoice for the ammo and I'll have the money deposited in your account." She pulled out some latex gloves slipping them on and picking up the tentacles, her nose wrinkling.

DK blinked, looking at her. "And detailing for my truck."

She glanced up at him, her eyes tracking over his body. He knew she saw every gouge every rip, and the amount of blood that covered him, very little of it his.

"Of course. Your expertise is appreciated. Please do call ahead next time." She glanced at the door. "It would lower the maintenance costs significantly.

DK narrowed his eyes at her. "I don't know if I find you incredibly sexy right now or if I just want to put a bullet in your head."

She didn't even look at him, instead kept picking up the 'trophies' he'd dumped on her desk. "Let me know when you figure it out, so I know whether to kill you or just make your dick quit working."

A bark of laughter escaped without his permission and he grabbed the Reset.

"Will do." With that he walked out, suddenly feeling much better than when he walked in.

Chapter 21 - Tank Rage

Standing inside his large metal work shed, Declan wiped his forehead off with a greasy shop rag and then did the same for his hands. He glared down at the M3 Stuart light tank's 220 horsepower diesel engine block sitting on jacks in front of the open and exposed compartment of the light tank. It sounded like a great idea when he decided to buy a fixer-upper tank and have it shipped to his property all the way from Texas. Right now, that idea seemed less appealing to him as he tapped at the oil return line gauge in frustration.

Why the hell aren't you building pressure?

Declan turned and grabbed a new set of hose clamps, along with a set of heavy pliers, and began to replace the line connectors at the end of the engine along with its sister couplings feeding into the engine compartment.

It's been a long time since I've ground hopped a tank engine. That dude should have told me there was no maintenance manual with this son of a bitch.

Declan checked all the oil lines and then proceeded to do the same for each of the fuel lines. He then ran two power cables from his workshops' power inverter and attached them to the starter leads of the tank's engine. After double-checking his work, and was satisfied that everything was correct, he climbed into the small turret, wiggled his body into the driver seat pushing his head out through the open hatch as he reached down, and squeezed the butterfly starter coil.

"Alright, you fussy little bitch, give it to me this time."

When Declan squeezed the starter, he was momentarily satisfied by seeing the engine shake slightly as the starter

Blood War: Rage

attempted to turn the motor shaft and a cough of smoke puffed out of the manifold exhaust before stopping quickly with a loud clunk.

"Shit."

Declan climbed back out of the tank through the turret and walked around to the front slope of the tank where the engine sat inert on stands. As he passed his workbench he grabbed the small sledgehammer then looked down at the eighty-year-old starter, unsure what to try next.

Well, this used to work with an M1 starter let's see if it's the same on an old M3. My guess is the solenoid is stuck. "So how do you unstick a tank starter? Well Sir, you hit it with the big fucking hammer." Declan spoke aloud to the empty workshop. He struck the front nose of the starter with the hammer hearing a satisfying thunk noise as its internal solenoid disengaged and the spring popped itself back into position. But as the solenoid snapped into place, Declan heard metal bending as the lower end of the small engine begin to slide backward towards him as the supporting jack stand shifted.

"Son of a..."

The small engine sliding off the stand clipped Declan's shin sending pain shooting up his leg. Instinctively he reached down to grab the heavy engine before it fell completely on his leg. The pain radiating up his body began to mute as his eyesight started sharpening and his ears began to hum as his blood pressure increased. He could feel the rage instantly surging forward into his body into his arms as he lifted a weight far beyond what he should be capable of lifting. He knew he could be ripping his own muscles as the rage surged through him, flooding his bloodstream. No longer even thinking, he lifted the engine up a few inches and pushed his body against it, setting it cleanly back on the jack. DK backed away staring at the ton of metal in front of him as the rage pounded against his temples. He grabbed the hammer and began to smash it repeatedly against the hull of its tank breaking the head of the hammer off, then throwing the handle clearly across the room

"Son of a rat's ass!"

Declan knew that if anything, or anyone, so much as entered the room he would lash out violently at them. The pain in his leg was nothing more than an inconsequential dull ache but the raw power surging through his body felt delicious. He could use this power right now and take a life without question. He could own the existence of another, taking every ounce of their blood and power as his own.

No. I can't let it control me for this shit.

By sheer force of will, Declan shoved his hand into his cargo pocket, wrapping his trembling fingers around the small metal cylinder inside of it. It was only in his pocket because he'd found it on the seat of his truck the other day and had dropped it there, meaning to put it away. He pulled out the auto-injector of Reset and quickly slammed it into the side of his neck. The release of the chemicals that flooded into his body cleared his mind nearly instantly, bringing with it a return of consciousness and cognitive thought.

Unfortunately, it also allowed the pain it had been suppressing to jump back into his brain, flooding his bloodstream and making him crumple to the floor grabbing his leg.

"Damn it!" He panted through the pain as he tried not to scream, waiting for the first burst to dissipate.

How long am I going to survive burning through Reset every time I get pissed off or hurt?

When the pain had receded to manageable levels, he saw it was a nasty scrape, and probably a bone bruise, but not anything that needed medical attention, Declan began to put his tools back on the workbench. His mind was locked in worry about how quickly he reached for Reset to solve his problems when the audible alarm of one of the perimeter sensor activations kicked off.

Instinctively he glanced over at the flat screen on the side of his workshop wall and glanced at the cameras pointing towards the entry points to his property. He noticed it was the familiar

Blood War: Rage

Suburban coming up.

Huh, Andrew's here. Wonder if this is good or bad?

When Andrew reached the first road gate his phone chimed, alerting him to a text message. Declan picked up his phone, confirmed that it was from Andrew, and replied "Hold on, I'm opening the gate. I'm back in the workshop the north side of the property." He triggered the gate opening and turned to stare at the recalcitrant tank.

About ten minutes later. Declan heard Andrew's Suburban pulling up to the front of the workshop.

Andrew pulled open the sliding door and walked into the workshop, barely even glancing at Declan as he started to take in the light tank being worked on in the bay. "Holy shit, you really do have a tank in here, don't you?"

"What's really generous is that you consider it a real tank, seeing as how it's in about 400 damn pieces and just about crushed my leg thirty minutes ago." Declan said as he limped lightly towards his workbench.

"What are you bitching about? A little blood is required for every type of maintenance. Didn't your daddy ever teach you that?"

"Way to show up after my damn mounts broke and nearly killed me, Cabello." He said dryly, though if Andrew had been here it might have been very bad.

"Yeah, whatever. Declan, I know you got beer fridge in here somewhere, so *por favor*."

"Yes, in back. Help yourself. Then come back here and tell me why the hell this ground hop kit is not working right."

Andrew came back with two bottles of beers, handed one to Declan, then immediately turned around and looked at how the engine lines were running into the engine compartment of the tank while humming softly to himself.

"What do you think?"

"Well, looks pretty solid. What is the problem?"

"I got a splutter. I got a puff of exhaust and then nothing. Then I got pissed off and walloped on the starter with a hammer and heard a thunk."

"Well, that does sound like it was a starter. My guess is the hammer will have already loosened the solenoid. Did you try to jump it again?"

"Just about to. Hang on, let me climb in the turret and give it another crank."

Declan took another long pull of beer, still trying to regain his balance, before he clambered back into the turret. He reached into the driver's hatch, squeezed the igniter and received a satisfying sputter then the tanks old motor turned over.

"Shit, sounds like you got it. My work here is done." Andrew gave Declan a mock salute with the neck of the beer bottle tapping his forehead.

After shutting off the motor, Declan sat on the edge of the turret, pulling from his beer then looked down at Andrew. "That's the problem brother. I don't think our work is really done."

"Ah, we'll get this thing back together. That's not work. That's going to be fun. Heck, give me a key to your work shed here. I'll swing by when I got free time and fix everything you screw up, because you won't admit you don't know shit about fixing tanks."

"That's not what I'm talking about. Our real work. They've come back."

Andrew's face flushed. "Bullshit! That's not funny. Not one damned bit."

"Sorry. I killed four demons the other night. Then last week another three. Hell, this all started with the drone that attacked me outside the VFW. You know where there's a drone, there's a horde forming. And now I've got a regular gig going out and killing them. And I'm getting busier."

"Aww fuck me, man..." Andrew drained his beer in one long pull then slowly set it down on the workbench. "What should we do?"

"Personally, I'd like to shutter the compound, set all the charges, get good and drunk, and then let the Apocalypse come to

Blood War: Rage

me." Declan noticed Andrew's look at his statement. "But, you know that's not gonna happen. My plan is to take the fight to them wherever I can find them."

"We've both been here before. Too much hard-won bad road behind me to give back one fucking inch of it. Not a single fucking inch!" Andrew nearly shouted. "What do you need from me, Declan?"

"Just be ready when I call. I'm thinking I'll need your pick-up game again."

"You got it, brother. But, you're buying all the beer on this hunt and hopefully we'll both make it out the other side." Andrew headed back to the beer fridge cursing a little under his breath.

Chapter 22 - Boss and Picnics

Mr. Ordonio walked leisurely toward the pair of large black four-wheel-drive armored government utility vehicles idling by the curb. The second vehicle's rear passenger door was held open by an armed tactical agent for the ICER Director.

"Why thank you, Steven. It is Steven, right?" He asked the agent holding the door as he approached the vehicle.

"Yes, it is, sir. By the way, thank you very much for the flowers you sent to my wife when she got home with the new baby. She was thrilled, sir."

Kelvin paused at the door and smiled back at the waiting agent. "Oh, really it was nothing. I'm just glad mom and baby are home happy and healthy. Now we have a new member of the Team ICERs family. I do hope you bring them both to our next department picnic."

"Absolutely, sir. We wouldn't miss it."

"Now, Steven, I do think I told you guys that you really don't need to do this opening the door thing. It seems a bit pretentious don't you think?"

"No way, sir. We know how hard you look after us all. You're definitely one of the good guys and it's the least we can do." The agent responded almost shyly.

"Well thank you, Steven. That's very kind. But you tactical guys are the real heroes here, I'm just an overpaid paper pusher." Kelvin clapped the agent on the bicep as he entered the vehicle and the door was closed behind him.

And that, ladies and gentlemen, is how you get men to kill, or die, for you with a smile.

"Really, Kelvin, you sent flowers to an escort agent's wife?"

Blood War: Rage

The man seated across from the ICER Director, one Mr. Barry Boyd, his Director of Operations. Barry was born and raised to be the next generation of a proud African-American Virginia farming family. He had the strong farmers build for it, at over six foot two, and the body of a triathlete. Even at the age of fifty he still held his own against the interns at lunch on the basketball court. But Barry just hadn't seen himself heading back home after graduating the Virginia Military Institute on an ROTC scholarship. Instead, after a few years in the United States Army Barry had crossed over to the 'Dark Side', as his father put it, and had become a career government civilian. For the last twenty of those years, Barry had worked for Kelvin in some fashion or another.

"Of course, they just had a baby!" Kelvin beamed and rubbed his hands together excitedly. "I really hope they do bring the little one to the picnic. I love babies. Particularly when the mother and father are both certified at 100%." He pointed directly at Barry for emphasis with his smile fading slightly, "That, Mr. Boyd, is what this world needs most."

"I got it, Kelvin. What I was getting at was that you bust my ass over buying extra printer paper for the office and then turn around and buy flowers for a bottom of the org chart employee."

Barry didn't look at him while he talked, which was something that annoyed him to no end.

"First off, language. Second, there's no reason for us to use so much paper. It's not good for the environment. Third, that agent's job is to put his life on the line to protect us. So, if he has to choose who to take a bullet for you, or me... Who just sent the man's wife flowers after she had a baby huh?"

"Damn, I concede. Well played, Kelvin. So on to business then."

Barry turned to look at him and Kelvin sighed. The man had no idea of how much the little actions supported the big ideas.

"Of course, but just a second." Kelvin leaned forward towards the driver. "Mr. Boulder, has the car been swept today?"

"Yes, sir, I cleared it myself at the motor pool this morning, and again two hours ago after we dropped you for your last meeting."

"Excellent, thank you very much, Mr. Boulder." Kelvin reclined back in his seat and pressed a small switch raising a privacy screen between the driver's seating and the passenger's area.

Barry continued, "The International Summit of ICER Directors in Salt Lake is now three months away but I'm still not comfortable with all our secondary members. One in particular."

"The Chinese again, right?" Kelvin frowned. It was critical that each ICER Director was either on-board, or a suitable replacement was immediately on-hand to assume command after the Summit. "I can't allow for any confusion or indecision in Salt Lake. While setting up the ICERs as a global response force, from all the modern military forces, may have sounded good to the fools at the U.N., the politics are tedious to say the least."

Barry nodded, his dark eyes sharp. "Yeah, it's the Chinese. The National People's Congress appointee has proven unapproachable and his second, Mrs. Kim is well... I just don't trust her at all. I'd say our best option is to arrange for them to be replaced by the Chinese before the Summit. We'll just have to take our chances that we'll get leverage quickly over the new appointees."

"No Barry, that's too close to the Summit to risk another hardliner coming in."

Damn Chinese have always been cagey - filling their ICER offices with party loyalist instead of people who understood that humankind is more important than their own government.

"We always knew that Mrs. Kim was questionable. I'm not sure she really appreciates the magnitude of our mission. It is possible she is playing us. Waiting for us to remove her political competition before she turns on us and pushes the Chinese military to embrace their hunger for more and more magical exploitation. They'll doom us all to annihilation by by going down that path. No, I don't trust her. But if we can't get the Chinese to willingly come along, then after each country completes their part of the cleanup, we will all turn together to deal with the Chinese the old-fashioned way. Even if they fill their ranks with aberrations and risk fracturing the very realm wall that protects us with their use of magic, we'll remove the threat of the magic from humanity once and for all."

"So how do we keep Mrs. Kim in line then?"

The Director thought for a minute then lowered the privacy shield between him and the driver. "Mr. Boulder."

"Yes, Sir?" The driver responded, not taking his eyes off the road and maintaining perfect spacing with the security vehicle in from of him.

"Where was it that Mrs. Kim's daughter went to school?"

"Sir? The Chinese chick? Oh yeah. Her daughter goes to one of those Brit colleges... Cambridge I think."

"Thank you, Mr. Boulder." Kelvin closed the privacy screen again. "Now, Barry, I think a call to the London ICER Director is in order. He should have some of his fine team invite and escort Mrs. Kim's daughter to Salt Lake for the Summit. I think mothers are beautiful in how they will do almost anything to protect their children. Don't you, Barry?"

Barry smirked a bit. "Yes, I do, sir. I'll set up a secure teleconference for later today."

"Oh, it can wait till tomorrow morning. Time zones, remember. No need to be rude and make our London friend take a call at some ungodly hour of the morning just for us. Besides, I think it's time we called in a favor from our friends in Boston. Things have been too quiet lately and we cannot have humanity complacent ever again. No, never again. I won't allow it. "

"How many you want let out, Kelvin?"

"Just two or three should do it. Give them about three hours on the ground. Then have our people take care of them in front of local media. Make sure the press gets word that the rogue Mage oclave has not been fully accounted for and that they still pose a possible threat to the community. Run the standard PR reminder spots afterward that the government expressly forbids contacting the demon realm or trying to open portals as both are global treaty violations and capital offenses. That should keep the panic levels moving back upwards and give me a little bit of good PR for the department before my next hearing on the Hill with the funding appropriations bill writers."

Barry typed a series of messages out on his tablet as Kelvin sat quietly and watched through the windows as the Washington Mall moved past slowly, while the vehicles headed back towards the Pentagon.

"Barry?"

"What?"

"You are coming to the picnic and bringing those incredible deviled eggs, right?"

"Oh for fuck's sake, Kelvin. Yes."

Kelvin closed his eyes and smiled.

Blood War: Rage

Chapter 23 - VFW Scene

Declan pulled into the parking lot of the VFW and shut off his truck.

Damn, I need this. Hope Andrew can make it. I need something that doesn't involve demons and does involve booze. Huh, wonder if I should start seeing if I can get a ride to this place. Nah, I know how to hold my booze. Worst case, I'll sleep in the truck. Oh, who am I kidding? I ain't getting so drunk I can't drive. Not here. I got that drunk and I'd be an easy target. I don't like being an easy target.

He climbed out but took a moment to scan the place. Ever since that damn drone, he'd become a lot more paranoid and always carried. No one here would ever say anything. Most of them had weapons on too. Hell, he'd be more surprised if there was someone that didn't come here armed.

You're getting old. Quit lollygagging and get to the food and booze.

His mental chiding made him smile as he walked in, still scanning. Getting jumped once made an impression.

The noise and smells of beer, frying oil, old smoke, and a bit of sweat swamped him as he pulled open the door. Declan smiled and felt some of the stress drop off as he signed in and made his way into the place. It was busy for a weekday but he saw Andrew there in the back and headed in that direction.

Andrew Cabello planned a bit more than he did and usually took a taxi or ride-share to the VFW so he didn't need to worry about what condition he left in. Declan reached the table and pulled back a chair, angling it a bit so he could get a decent portion of the room in his view. Too bad they couldn't make restaurants where every seat had your back to the wall.

"Hey, how's it hanging?"

"Still attached last time I checked. Why? You think you want to check and make sure they're still there?" Andrew asked arching a brow and smirking at him.

"Thanks, but don't swing that way. You can do your own checking." Declan grinned feeling something like good humor settling in.

"How goes the demon-killing business? Still doing that?" Andrew already had a pitcher of beer on the table and pushed a spare glass towards Declan.

Hell, you don't have to tell me twice.

Declan poured the beer and concentrated on that first, more important than answering the question. When at least a third of the glass of beer had slid down his throat he set the glass back down on the table.

"It goes. Too damn busy for my liking. Seems like they've got me running all over the area every other day. It's cutting into my drinking and football time." He groused with humor. Andrew, however, didn't laugh.

"Huh. That busy? Didn't think that many demons had been missed in the cleanup." He twisted the beer glass around and Declan sighed.

"We didn't. I should know. Spent a good six months after Ypsilanti and prior to the final armistice doing that cleanup. These are new. Idiots are opening portals and letting them in. Luckily most mages can't open a major portal or hold it open for more than a few minutes. But yeah, demons." A bit of the good humor faded, and he sighed. "Where's Casey? I need food before I die of starvation."

As if summoned by his words, Casey came out of the kitchen with a tray of nachos headed towards them.

"Andrew, here's your order. Kenner," he nodded as he put the food on the table. "What can I get you?"

Declan's eyes were locked on the nachos and he felt more than heard Andrew laugh. "Help yourself. I figured you would. Casey, can you get me a double hamburger with steamed veggies on the side?"

"Sure," Casey said looking at Declan. "You?"

He had a laden nacho half way to his mouth and paused. "You going all healthy on me now?"

"Hell no. But I figured with the nachos some fiber might be helpful. Gotta stay regular you know."

"Point. Can I get the chicken fried steak with a salad and loaded baked potato?"

"Yep. Assume you want another pitcher of beer too?"

"Always," though it came out more like 'awrarys' as his mouth was full of nachos. Casey rolled his eyes and headed back to the bar and kitchen.

Neither Andrew nor he spoke for the next few minutes. Declan hadn't realized how hungry he was until after he started to eat. By the time they both came up for air, the huge plate was half empty and the pitcher was completely empty.

"Guess I needed that."

Andrew shrugged at his words. "We both did and here comes Casey with more food and beer." His voice trailed off oddly as his gaze remained on the door to the VFW. "Hey, you know that guy?" He nodded at the man that had just walked in.

Declan finished off the beer and followed Andrew's gaze. "Huh. Maybe? Is that Randolph Drimori?"

"Randy?" Andrew asked then nodded slowly. "Yeah, I think that's him. Didn't he do a few runs with us?"

"Yeah, he served. Made it to the other side, but missed the final action after getting wounded. Heard he went merc." Declan watched the man and waited until he caught his eye, then waved him over.

As he got closer Declan knew it was the same man. A few years older, few pounds heavier, but the same ruddy face, strong shoulders, and if he remembered correctly, ice in his blood. The man had never even flinched when the demons were coming through, just aiming and firing as fast as he could and taking down targets as they were called. Andrew had been the one calling a lot of the targets in over the radio.

"Hell, DK and Andrew? Hell, it's good to see faces I recognize. Mind if I join you?"

"Nah, take a load off and tell us what you've been up to." Casey reached the table, dropped the pitcher on it, and looked at the newcomer.

"What can I get you?"

"Another pitcher, but make it a bit darker? Lager? Been drinking so much European stuff the American brew is too light now. Hamburger, fries, and a water?"

"Got it."

Declan helped himself to some more nacho's looking at Randy.

"Where the hell you been you've been working on the Euro-beers?"

Randy sighed and glanced at the nachos.

"Help yourself, if someone doesn't we won't have any room for our food," Andrew commented as he refilled his and Declan's beer glasses, leaning back to watch the man.

He does look a bit exhausted, like he's seen too much shit lately. And here I thought the world was pretty quiet. That's what the news tells us every day.

A vague sense of unease whispered at him but the application of the new beer helped push that to the back.

"So, yeah. You know I went private hire, right? Army didn't want me no more but I didn't have anything else I was good at. Got with a unit doing cleanup work over in Europe and into Russia. God, what was left of Moscow. Seeing that on the TV was one thing, walking through what was left is totally different. Let's say we don't realize how quiet it is here." He took a few bites then shook his head. "The European ICER guys are hiring mercs right and left and I swear it seems like every country thinks they are the best things ever. But so far they don't impress me all that much."

"Why? Not helping with demons? Are there lots of demons?"

Blood War: Rage

Andrew asked even as Declan made his grip on his glass relax a bit. These were strong beer glasses but he didn't need to see if he could break one, that might be a bit stupid.

"More than you would think. But no," Randy paused eating another bite. "Just the causality rates are through the roof. Don't get me wrong. People die. But I swear every time I turned around another squad had lost one or two men. And we won't go into how many just disappeared."

Declan tilted his head. "What do you mean by disappeared?"

"That's it, I'm not sure. They would just be gone. Some were killed other ways, drinking and driving, domestic stupidity, you know. But we all drink and most of us know not to get in a car if we can't drive." He grunted then smiled as Casey set a pitcher of a dark brown lager on the table and disappeared. Randy filled his glass and took a long drink, sighing in pleasure as he put the glass down.

"Then there are the battle mages."

That caused Declan's back to stiffen. "What do you mean?" He and mages didn't get along all that well.

"They're disappearing too, and the ones that are still there are scared. These are ones that served, not the young idiots who think summoning demons is cool. These are the ones who watched all their friends die as they tried to keep the hordes back. These are the hardcore, solid, battle mages. Them being scared of something makes me nervous and you add in the rumors - rumors about a global plan that doesn't involve us? Hell, I don't know. But I figured it was time to get out. I've got money saved and the US still has armed civilians. Lots of European countries rolled that back. I want people to be able to fight and I can't afford to live in Switzerland."

All three of them laughed a bit at that. Switzerland had only ramped up their edicts when the demons showed up. Every citizen carried a gun and most businesses had rifles, not small ones but .50 Barretts available if they were needed. Everyone who had a real understanding of what the demons could do wanted to live in Switzerland. Plus, the landscape made it difficult for a horde to traverse with any speed.

"We all want to live there. So, you here for good?" Andrew Cabello asked.

"Probably. Just a lot of friends have disappeared. Hell, they lost a fifteen-man team in Australia two weeks ago."

"Shit, really?" Declan paused on the way to get more nachos. That was a huge team to lose for anything short of a sub-horde coming through.

And I really hope if a horde does come through we hear about it. Otherwise...

The ramifications of that thought turned his stomach and he decided on more beer instead.

"Yeah. So, I'm out. Got a sister down in Florida and think I'll find a place on the Keys. Too shallow for whatever is bugging ships in the oceans and too soft for any of the really big demons to handle."

"Huh. They still losing ships?" Cabello asked even as he made room at the table. Casey dropped all their food, took the empty pitchers, and left mustard and ketchup without asking.

"Remind me to give him a big tip," Declan said as he directed his attention to his salad.

"Will do," Andrew said but looked back at Randy, still waiting for an answer.

"As far as I know, yes. Mostly subs. Think they've pulled them all back. The huge cargo carriers don't seem to get bugged much. But our ships, the mid-sized ones are there, then gone. They never even get any maydays off. I suppose it's possible there's a coupe going on and they are all held up at some island somewhere but it is affecting all the fleets... well, any fleet that crosses the Atlantic. The Pacific and the smaller ones aren't seeing this level of disappearance." Randy snorted. "At this rate, the entire ocean is going to be declared a no man's land."

"Ouch. That will definitely suck for the East Coast for trade."

"Maybe. A lot of ships have started going up near Iceland, then back down. The best guess, not that the governments will admit to anything actually being in the water, is that whatever it is doesn't like the cold."

"Joy. Good thing I like American beer." Declan smirked at the other two. They both laughed and the conversation drifted into sports, fishing, and other things that had nothing to do with death or dying.

Chapter 24 - Stooges Call

Kayter seriously considered throwing her computer against the wall. All the little Ley line crossings kept having blips of power flowing through them. So low the alarms for a portal didn't go off, but it meant something. The problem? She had no idea what it meant. Checking against other areas of the country they didn't have these low-level pings. Only in this general area.

It makes no sense, what is pinging the Ley lines? It's not at the level the demons would use to tie a portal to, even with human help. It's like someone, or something is testing the lines for throughput of low-level magics.

Throwing her hands up, she grabbed her sword and stepped out of the RV before she threw something irreplaceable. Stripping out of her jacket she started working out, sit-ups, push-ups, pull-ups, anything to burn off the frustration. She broke into a nice sweat and thought she might be ready to start going through sword drills when the ringing from her laptop grabbed her attention.

Frowning she headed back into the RV and looked at the computer.

'Incoming call' flashed on the screen.

She ran through who knew the number in her mind but hit accept even as she mulled it over.

"Yes?"

"Um, yeah this is Gary?"

Gary, who the fuck is Gary?

"Yeah?"

"Um, is this the scary lady in the woods who kicked our asses?"

Ah, the light dawns.

Blood War: Rage

"Hello, Gary. Is there a reason you're calling? Anything interesting to tell me?" Her voice dropped to a throaty purr.

Finally, something to do.

She settled down into the chair grabbing a pencil and paper.

"Well, we talked to some of our professors and they backed up what you said. So, me and Sean decided to tell you if we heard anything. Well, they just got a hold of us and told me something I thought you'd like to know." His voice wavered as he talked and the last word he squeaked.

"And what would that be?"

His voice shook a bit. "Just don't tell anyone I told you okay? Cause I think they might hurt me if they find out I told you anything."

"No one told me anything, I haven't talked to anyone."

"Oh good. Well look, they called us late yesterday and said they might need some help with a little spell they have going on up at this park near a college today. They wanted us to come and promised us we'd never forget. But something sounds off about it. I thought I'd tell you."

"College, which college?"

"Oh, MIT. The magic department. They gave us an address." He rattled off the address and she scribbled it down quickly. "It's at one of the minor crossings up there. They said we should be there by three o'clock."

"Three today? And you are just now calling me?"

The other end went silent and she waited.

"Well, we had to think about it. Decide and well, it's a long drive and I thought it didn't sound like a good idea. So, I called you. At least I did that much, so I've done my good deed. Remember this, okay?"

"Next time, call me sooner. But keep your ears and eyes open, Gary. And just think, maybe you've saved some lives. If I can get there in time."

"Sure." He hung up and she pulled up the maps and cringed as the distance popped up.

How real was this information? The part that made her believe it was the odd phrase of "promised we'd never forget" sounded like a way to get rid of witnesses.

Fuck.

She glanced at the clock and cringed.

That was a nine-plus hour drive. If she avoided cops and barely stopped, she might be able to do it seven. Maybe.

Fuck, I can't afford not to go but I swear if they are yanking my chain, I am going to track them down and skin them alive.

Kayter jumped up and started packing for a horde invasion. Guns, ammo, her sword, her flexible armor (which fit her almost like a body suit), leg armor, and her boots were placed around her body. Packing up the saddlebags, she locked the RV and then cut her finger. With deliberate precision she allowed ten drops of blood to fall on the enchantment inscribed on her gas tank. Then another five on the enchantments on the engine to keep it silent.

With luck, she'd be there before they started. Without luck, well, maybe not everyone would be dead.

Chapter 25 - Calling in Reinforcements

Declan hung up the phone and thought about the assignment Cordy told him about.

So, Boston huh? That's a nine-hour drive. I'm not doing that shit the old-fashioned way. Not to mention that at this point I'd have to be tearing out of here to pull that off.

Declan reached into the ubiquitous junk drawer everybody had in their house and started rummaging around. He pulled out a business card that read Gregory Donahue, Shillelagh Law.

I'm going to need a ride and having a little extra muscle never hurt. Greg is a lot of muscle.

He dialed the number at the bottom of the card of the law office and waited for someone to pick up.

After about five rings a gruff voice answered. "Yeah, what do you want?"

"Mr. Donahue, is that any way to answer the phone for a professional business number, let alone a law firm?"

"Course it is when I don't really want any clients and when I'm hungover."

"Plus, you probably don't really want a client that's not going to pay you anything."

"Holy fuck! DK is that you?" Greg's tone lighted considerably with the recognition of Declan's voice.

"Yep, it's me, Bunyan. How you been doing, brother?"

"Man, I haven't been called Bunyan in years. Not since the war. But hey, not bad. I'd be even better if I didn't have such a pounding headache."

"That's because you're not supposed to drink the entire bottle of Jim Beam in one sitting Greg."

"Well, it's not like I'm saving it for anything. Besides, I got plenty where that came from and if I run out, they'll make more. Or maybe that's the potato chip guy, I'm not sure."

"You do know they put a screw top on those things for a reason?"

"Like you're one to talk, DK. I don't think there's a bottle of beer you've met that you haven't fallen in love with."

"While that is absolutely true, I didn't call you out of the blue to discuss our functional alcoholism traits."

"Good, cuz that's a lame conversation."

"I need a favor, Bunyan."

"Well, fine then, DK. Now that I'm feeling the brotherly love and all. What can Shillelagh Law do for you? And by the way, you're going to get billed whether you like it or not, even if you call it a favor asshole." His voice held humor and interest.

Wonder if he's been as bored as I have?

"I need two things really. First, I need a ride and second, need some muscle."

"Well, my dear friend, I can say two things to your two requests. One, I have all the muscle that three to four women at a time can handle. Two, I do have a ride, but that shit comes with invoiced bill cuz fuel is not free I don't really care if you did pull me out of a burning wreck. I have bills to pay, DK."

"Good, I need you here in six hours or less. Oh, and come loaded for bear. Big fucking bears."

"Well, shit." Greg paused on the other end and Declan all but felt him adjusting his mindset from giving a friend shit, to shit going down. "Got it. I will have to reschedule my pedicure and pop some aspirin, but if you need to call me in for a bear hunt then you know I'll be there. Need the bird fully kitted up?"

"No, the chopper is just so we don't spend three days stuck in Boston traffic. Pick me at my place ASAP. We need to get out to MIT right away."

Blood War: Rage

"Alright, DK, I'll help you go deal with some nerds and bears. Let me find some water, and my damn pants, then I'll go pull my shit together. I'll pick you up in about five hours."

"Thanks, Greg, see you then. Just land out back and try not to muss the grass too much."

"Whatever, shithead. See you soon"

Declan hung up the phone and started a mental checklist of what he needed to get ready.

Ride, check. Extra backup, check. Site Intel, on the to-do list. Now to pick my loadout and pack a lunch.

Chapter 26 – Have Chopper Will Travel

Declan heard the approaching helicopter coming in on a low approach. He hefted his Vulture carbine over his shoulder and walked to the side of the open field behind his house. At first, he thought he was getting a visit from the military as a UH-60 Blackhawk approached his makeshift landing zone but the marking lights and lower body gray/upper body dark brown paint job exposed it as a civilian version of the Blackhawk. A Sikorsky S-70 with external fuel pods. Greg Donahue was on final approach.

Seems Greg couldn't take his war bird with him, so he bought the closest thing to it he could. I bought a house; he bought a sweet ride.

Declan tossed a green soup can shaped object into the center of the field after pulling a pin from its top. A steady stream of white smoke poured from the marker grenade in the center of the field that would show Greg the wind's direction and speed in the improvised landing zone. He then turned his back to the approaching helicopter and lowered himself onto one knee with his head down and the collar of his heavy leather Hunter's coat raised to protect his neck and face from the rotor wash of the landing helicopter. Getting hit in the face with debris hurt.

After he felt the rushing wave of the rotor wash move across his back Declan turned, keeping his body hunched over and his eyes on the figure motioning him forward from the side of the helicopter. He moved to the side door that slid rearwards, revealing the passenger cabin of the helicopter. Declan pulled himself into the aircraft by grabbing a nylon strap by the side of the door. He hesitated a moment, taken slightly off guard by the plush interior that he hadn't expected. He assumed it would be like the military benches that he was used to in a Blackhawk helicopter. Strapping himself into the harness of the plush leather seat and facing forward, he saw the familiar six-foot-five bulk of the pilot sitting at the controls from behind. The pilot pointed at his headphones and then backward towards where Declan was seated. He turned around and noticed a headset hanging from a hook above his seat. Declan took it down, settled it over his ears, then placed his Vulture between his legs with the muzzle facing down. It was an old habit instilled in every soldier since the early days of the air cavalry in Vietnam. Apparently, pilots did not like you accidentally discharging your weapon and shooting through the top of their helicopters into the rotor blades.

Declan still hadn't gotten a good look at the other crewman. He watched him on the outside; then he moved around to the front of the aircraft and entered the co-pilot seat.

He activated the intercom on the headset. "Hey, Greg, I don't get to ride up front?"

"Unless you've been rated to fly an S-70 you aren't getting anywhere near these fucking controls. I will introduce you here in just a second. Sit down and shut the hell up so I can get this bird back up in the air."

"Yes, sir, shutting the hell up for a moment now." Declan settled back into his seat, feeling relatively useless with nothing to do during helicopter operations.

Declan watched the pilot and co-pilot team in the cockpit run through their checks for a few minutes with great interest. While he was never afraid of flying, Declan remained slightly concerned by the fact that the million-dollar machine, with a few thousand points of failure, was being operated by someone who was likely very hungover.

Yay though I walk through the Valley of the Shadow of Death, I shall fear no evil because hopefully, Greg is not still drunk and about to kill us all.

Doug Burbey & Mel Todd

Declan felt gravity pulling against him in the unexpectedly plush aircraft. He glanced out the window and watched his backfield and house fall away from the helicopter. He then looked around the interior of the cabin, noting differences from the commercial version and that of a standard military transport. Lost were the nylon bench seats and weapon clamp-down brackets. The dull gray steel flooring and generally utilitarian interior had been replaced with three rear facing, and four forward facing, leather bucket seats.

Shit, they got cup holders!

Noise cancellation headphones with microphones affixed above each seat and even a reading light was built into each seat back. A center console running between sets of seats was what looked like some form of low table with a refrigerator.

That totally looks like a beer fridge. Would he really have a beer fridge in here?

"You have got to be kidding me." Declan reached up activated the intercom on his headset again.

"Holy fuck, Greg. You have a beer fridge in here?"

"Only the best for my clients, DK. The rich folk don't like their booze getting warm." Greg replied over the intercom.

"So, what the hell do you actually use this bird for? Not exactly standard lawyer stuff I'm sure."

"Well, as I'm diligently working towards establishing my law practice, I have to earn a little extra on the side with specialized clientele. They demand a certain amount of comfort as I securely move them to and from where they need to be." His voice had tones of affronted protestation and Declan didn't believe a word of it.

"Sounds to me like you babysit rich kids and fly them to the fucking Hamptons for the weekend." Declan goaded his old friend.

"I've been known to do that. Pays the bills anyway. Mostly I get paid to make sure that the rich kids don't get beat up, or killed, or kidnapped." Greg answered as he signaled his copilot and pointed at a blinking gauge in front of him. "Hey, before we get anywhere, what the hell is that giant metal barn over there for?"

Declan took a moment to glance around the back of the chair towards where he thought Greg was pointing. The large sheet metal building, with doors big enough for a tractor-trailer truck to enter, was partially concealed in the woods at the north end of his property. The metal structure had caught Greg's attention as he vectored the helicopter in the general direction of their destination. "That's just my storage shed."

"What the hell are you storing in there a small herd of cattle?"

"That's where I keep my restoration project and my lawnmower. I needed a little hobby besides drinking and watching football."

"I remember you talking about wanting to restore a World War II half-track if you ever got the chance. You finally doing that?"

"Even better. I ran across a guy willing to part with a mediocre condition M3 and started to restore it."

"Are you fucking kidding me, you got a Stuart light tank in there, DK?"

"Well most of her is still light tank. I got a bunch of boxes of shit that are supposed to be the rest of it. I've been fiddling with it on and off for the last year."

"Damn, that sounds fun. I'll come out and give you a hand with that, in-between babysitting gigs." Greg spoke as he adjusted the complex array of controls in the helicopters dash.

"I can always use a hand. And by hand, I mean you move all the heavy shit around and lift it into the tank while I supervise you, all while drinking beer."

"You know a Stuart isn't worth a shit against a horde right, DK?"

"I'm out of the Horde fighting business brother. Well mostly. Sort of. Now I'm kitting up for the Zombie Apocalypse." Declan smiled as he settled into the ridiculously comfortable passenger seat.

"Ah right. And what are we flying off to fight right now?" Even through the headphones, his sarcasm couldn't be missed. "Though

I guess you owning a small light tank makes total sense now. Flipping zombie menace."

"Damn right it does! I'm gonna be the King of the Zombie Apoc. So long as I can find a few hundred crates of 37mm main gun rounds for it. And we aren't going to fight a Horde, just a few lost blood bags."

Greg laughed out loud. "Well good luck with that shit. I'm fresh out of early WWII munitions."

"Well, I may know a guy," Declan said as he lifted his feet up onto the table between the seats.

"I bet you do, DK. I bet you do. You're making some strange friends lately, it seems. So, as I'm flying you to Boston to likely meet our certain, and horribly gruesome deaths, are you going to tell me who we're working for today?" The humor his voice had started with faded a bit as he talked.

"Sure, the ICERs."

"What the fuck is an ICER? Sounds like a refrigerator repair company." Greg responded, over the headset intercom, with a slight chuckle.

"Stands for International Cooperative Element Responders. So yeah, ICERs."

"Oh, government dudes. OK, got it. Didn't figure you'd be joining back up. Actually, I'm just surprised."

"I haven't joined shit. I'm strictly an independent contractor using my unique skills for some extra cash. A man does need beer money." Declan protested. And he almost believed himself. Almost.

"Uh huh," Greg replied, sounding totally unconvinced.

"Well, I got them to agree to reimburse you for fuel."

Or at least I will as soon as I file an expense report for it.

"Well now, that is so generous of them. I'm thinking of joining the Ice-T team now."

"ICERs." Declan corrected.

"I like Ice-T team better. Oh hey, almost forgot." Greg pointed at his copilot. "This is Joe, Joe Kling."

Blood War: Rage

"Nice to meet you, Sir," Joe responded with a flat voice without looking back at his passenger.

"Joe's a big conversationalist as you can see. But trust me you want to party with this guy!" Greg reached over and lightly cuffed the copilot on the shoulder.

"Yeah, right, Mr. Donahue," Joe responded again with the same disinterested inflection in his voice.

Curious Declan asked, "Joe since you're along for the ride on our little adventure, what's your flavor in the fight?"

Declan, sitting behind Joe and unable to see his face, saw the copilots head tilt slightly to the side. "Sir, I don't understand your question."

Declan glanced out the window and watched the rugged hills of western Maryland pass underneath the helicopter as they flew east. "I mean, what's your preferred method of fighting? You a long gunner, grenade tosser, sniper, AK-47 prey and spray type? I need to know how you like to fight if we get into anything."

Joe responded back over the intercom hesitantly "Well, I don't..."

"He's not in this fight DK." Greg cut in quickly. "Joe is the best crew chief in our business but he's not in the ground fighting side of the business. He keeps my bird at a fully mission capable status and if needed, provides close air support when I have my baby all pimped up with the add-ons."

"Got it, Greg, good to have you on board, Joe," Declan noted the barely perceptible nod of the copilot's helmet.

"OK, Declan, you may as well kick back and take a nap. We got a couple of hours before we get to Boston. Where exactly is it that you want me to land? Please don't tell me it's a 7-Eleven parking lot."

"I want you to land at Pacific Street Park, near the Plasma and Fusion Research Center at MIT. We'll make a quick visit to the graduate student residence hall across the street. Land, we go in, we settle the business, we get back on the bird and get out."

Greg manipulated the navigation panel between his and the

copilot's seat adjusting and tapping on the screen. Apparently, he was engaged in a conversation with Joe on the selected landing point. After two or three minutes, he banked the helicopter slightly on a course correction then reached over and reactivated the internal intercom.

"DK, the park looks big enough and clear enough to land. Only problem we might run into is people in the field, so we may have to shoo them away a little bit when we come in for landing."

"How do you shoo people away from the landing zone from the air?"

"Well, Joe's got the idea that he'll just push you out from the side of the aircraft to fast rope rappel in when we're about 150 feet off the deck and let you walk around and tell people politely to get out of the way."

"Hey, Joe, that's a dumb assed idea. I'm not doing that. I haven't done any real rappelling for over twenty years. Not sure what you think my current skill sets are but rappelling out of helicopters is not on that menu. "

Declan heard both Greg and Joe laughing over the intercom. "Don't worry about it, Declan. We are just going to head straight in and land. You be surprised how quickly people will get out of the way on their own."

Great, smart asses flying me. Why do I hang with these people? Oh yeah, cause I'm a smart ass too.

Declan spent the ride talking to Greg, bullshitting about the old days, and arranging to go out for drinks. Assuming they lived. As they got closer the conversation faded and he watched Greg and Joe manipulate the helicopter across a quick, low approach over Boston towards the Massachusetts Institute of Technology campus. Guided by the GPS navigation, Greg had no problem identifying the cleared park field across from their objective. Declan used the time on the approach to try to get a look at the building they needed to move to as soon as they landed.

"I really can't get a good visual on what's going on in that open courtyard between the buildings right now. Greg, you see anything?"

"No, I can't see what's going on there either. I thought I saw a glimmer, maybe even a faint glow. You know that's never good. But I think you're right, that courtyard area between the buildings might be the objective. You want me to run a racetrack orbit around the top of that building, so we can get a good look in between?"

"No, let's go straight in for a landing and move in from there. If we start to circle around the top of the building we're giving away any element of surprise, we might have."

"You know DK, this bird is not exactly small and whisper quiet. Not sure how much of an element of surprise we're going to get. I'm pretty sure MIT's not used to big assed Sikorskys landing in their parks."

"That's why we got to land and go in fast. I want to go in and quickly bust up whatever shenanigans these idiots are up to. Put the fear of God in them. Then get the hell out of here." DK paused and grinned, " Shillelagh Shenanigans. That's what you should call your firm."

"Ha, ha. Not. Fine, you're the special tactics boss DK. Who am I to second-guess your ridiculous plans like a sane human being."

Declan felt the nose of the helicopter dip forward and the tail rotor slide to the side as Joe and Greg lined up the big helicopter to angle downwards into the park. He looked out the window for obstructions and any civilians. Greg leveled the bird and began a slow vertical descent. Declan felt the connection of the landing gear as it cushioned the body of the helicopter when they met the surface of the park. Declan unhooked his harness and looked forward, seeing Greg pointing towards the road at the end of the field. In front of them, across a two-lane street, sat the buildings they were about to head into. Apparently, Greg was giving Joe some form of instructions that seemed to become an animated conversation. Declan heard Greg chime in over the intercom as he was reaching up to take off the helmet.

"All right DK, Joe's got a serious question. We clearly have just attracted attention. Response times of campus or local police may vary but someone will undoubtedly be here to check us out, within the next 5 to 10 minutes. What is Joe supposed to tell any cops that show up?"

"That's a very good point. I should've thought of that." Declan thought about this for a moment, then reached into his pocket pulling out his wallet and rummaging around for the ICER card. Pulling it out, he reached forward and handed it to Joe.

"Right Joe, this number on the bottom here is a very nice lady called Cordelia. She's the government bigwig in charge. I hope you're good at stalling. No pun intended. You just need to bluster anybody who comes up and hand them this card. Don't try to explain anything, just point to the number and say 'Call her'. This is where you need to pour on the aloof bravado with a touch of bureaucratic boredom. Oh, and try not to get arrested before we get back."

"Yes, sir. Hand card over. Act bored and annoyed. I don't know anything. Take off and leave you guys stranded if it appears I could be arrested. Got it." Joe responded and really did sound like he was bored and annoyed with the whole thing.

"I prefer you didn't ditch us, but you got the idea, Joe. Time to motivate, Greg. Let's unass this bird and gear up."

Declan pulled open the side door and stepped out onto the park field yanking the door closed behind himself. He noted that Joe was already outside of the aircraft doing what appeared to be some form of flight checks as Greg exited as well. Greg grabbed what looked like a 7.62 variant of the standard military M-16 rifle, called the AR-10, from a clamp point next to his seat. He draped the weapon's sling over his shoulder, settling it in front of his chest. Greg never carried what he would consider baby weapons. To amplify this fact, in a leather cross draw holster on his chest, he also carried a Ruger Super Redhawk revolver chambered for .44 caliber rounds. The Redhawk could take out a bear, or a low-ring demon, with a single shot but it was not exactly a dainty weapon with low recoil.

Blood War: Rage

"Still packing light. I see?" Declan said as he pointed to the Redhawk on Greg's chest.

"Always safe to assume if I'm shooting something, then I'm probably going to need to make a big damn hole. I keep telling you to dump those .45s for some man gun." Greg said with a smirk on his face.

"I'll leave the burning desire for man gun all to you, Greg," Declan replied as he reached down and clipped both sides of his heavy hunter's coat open, allowing free access to his additional magazines stored on his protective chest plate carrier and the backup side arm riding in his thigh holster. He then pulled his Vulture around to the front of his chest and chambered the first round.

Greg noticed several people on the fringes of the park apparently taking pictures of the helicopter and talking on their phones. "I think it's time to move, DK. We've become popular already."

With a quick nod of his head, Declan turned towards the small line of trees in front of the street, between him and the building. He moved quickly towards them with Greg easily keeping pace slightly to his left and behind him. From his map recon, Declan knew that behind the trees they would have to cross the street and be able to move directly into the entrance-way of the graduate student residence hall. They both reached the trees then hopped the small fence that separated the park from the sidewalk. The sound of shattering glass came from the entrance of the residence hall. With a quick glance in both directions, DK and Greg rushed across the street towards the front of the building entrance. Without glancing over his shoulder, knowing Greg would be doing the same thing, Declan raised his carbine to his shoulder, looking for targets in front of him as he jogged towards the doors.

"All right Greg, you get left. I got right. Should be a set of double doors as we come in the hallway. The left side of the entryway is yours, the right side is mine. Then there's the second set of doors going to the courtyard. Once we clear hallways on the right side of the entryway, we'll see which way we're going - left, right or into the courtyard." Declan instructed as they approached the front of the building at a trot.

"Shit, contact! One forward!" Greg yelled loudly from Declan's left as he immediately lifted and fired three rounds through the glass door in front of Declan. The first round shattering the storm glass as the heavy rifle's round exploded through the door and into the blur of moving orange off to Declan's left side. Knowing the target was engaged. Declan focused on his field of engagement area to his front right. Greg would take care of his left. Declan shouldered through the intact door on the right as Greg vaulted through the broken door on the left, getting a clearer look at his target. The crumpled mass of the type one demon was on the floor, struck by all three of Greg's rounds.

"Son of a bitch. Eyes up, Greg. There's never just one of these bastards!" Declan saw the broken glass, probably the noise they heard earlier, that once belonged to the door leading out to the courtyard and between the buildings. He could hear and feel, the screeching hum a magical portal emanated from a very close proximity.

"Shit, they got a portal held open. We need to shut it down before these guys pull anything else through for God sake. We'll push straight into the courtyard right now and take it out." Declan shouted as he turned to sprint towards the outer doors to the courtyard but before he took two steps a hold on his collar yanked him nearly off his feet. He glanced back at Greg, confused.

"Too late, too late, we got incoming. Back up!" Greg yelled releasing Declan's collar and raising his AR 10 and immediately started firing through the doorway into the courtyard as Declan was caught unprepared by the blisteringly loud retort of Greg's heavy rifle as he emptied the magazine shooting at new targets. Greg reached for a replacement from his combat harness. As Greg reloaded Declan could feel his battle senses kicking in with an awareness of targets in front of him that cleared and sharpened. In his limited scope of vision, he could see at least three ring one demons and a ring two demon closing in on the door he been about to rush through. Choosing his first target he fired two rounds from his carbine striking the closest ring one demon in the chest, collapsing it about ten meters from the glass door. Then he shifted to the second ring one demon following its ill-fated companion. As he fired the first round, he heard Greg engaging from his left with both weapons hitting the same target simultaneously ripping a gaping wound in the center of the demon knocking it backward onto the ground. The ring two demons sensed the unexpected threat in front of him and quickly moved to the side, away from their field of direct fire.

"Son of a bitch, we have got to get in there. You get a look at where that ring two went?" Declan shouted at Greg, his ears ringing.

"No, I just saw two go the right. I did catch a glimpse of a glow from the courtyard. And I can feel that portal myself. That means we got some dumb fuck mages out there also that I guess we need to assume are hostile."

"Yeah, this sucks - mages and demons. I wasn't planning on this. Figured we were only going to have to break up some college kids trying to expand their horizons."

"Well let's go, DK. No time like the present to break up this budding inter-realm relationship."

DK and Greg began to move forward in a crouch and hesitated momentarily as they spotted the ring two demon again. This time it was falling back into their field of vision apparently deflecting an attack from something.

What the fuck? Somebody is hacking at it with a damn sword!

Declan paused on pulling the trigger as the demon's assailant appeared in view. A woman, wearing what looked like a bulky leotard, attacked a seven-foot-tall, yellow skinned, over muscled and long clawed ring two demon with some sort of sword. She even pushed it backward.

Chapter 27 - Late to the Party

The drive to MIT passed like a surreal nightmare for Kayter. The invisible clock was ticking down in her head and she had to stop to get food, to hit the bathrooms, to stretch. Showing up at a battle tired, hungry, and having to pee would be a recipe for disaster, and that usually got you killed. So, she ate, drank liquids and about thirty minutes out she stopped and did a full stretch as fast as she could. She didn't know what she would walk into and being stiff would not be smart.

She felt the portal pulling at her as she drove up. She parked the bike deep in the trees and let the eddies of magic pull her toward it.

I'll never understand how other people can't feel this but most are acting like nothing is going on.

A quick backward glance showed students still milling about, though a few seemed edgy. She stepped through the trees which did an excellent job of completely hiding the small quad from the rest of the area. The glow of the portal snagged her attention as soon as she cleared the trees.

Fuck. Really? Already fully set up? Argh.

Kayter tried to locate the mages. Someone had to be holding the portal open, even as guilt lashed at her. Should she have driven faster, skipped the breaks, gone hungry? Each thought ratcheted her stress and guilt up. How many people would die because she wasn't good enough?

Her sword in her hand, she started to run as she saw a demon coming through the portal. A ring one as far as she could tell. She needed to kill it now. If she let too many get through she wouldn't be able to take them all. One on one, even two on one, she'd normally win, as long as they were lower ring demons.

Gods help us all if a ring four comes through.

Running toward the emerging demon she caught a flicker of motion, a tail disappearing down an interconnected walkway to another building.

Fuck, more already. Kill this one, then go after the other. Where the hell is the mage?

A bad feeling flickered through her, making her gut clench, but she didn't waste time on it. Instead, she lashed out with her *jian*, moving faster than an Olympic athlete, cutting and slicing. The *jian* had two sharp edges and a point. It was one of the few swords good for both stabbing and slashing. The custom *jian* had a razor edge and she'd practiced with it for so long it moved as if a part of her body. Something about the sword not being made of normal metal, it cut through the demons' flesh easier than anything else she'd ever tried. She knew her life depended on this odd weapon, so she took very good care of it.

This specific demon had the more insect-like build, with multiple legs and arms, so aiming for a head strike would be useless. This would she'd have to dismember and deal with killing it later. Kayter darted in, her speed making the demon's attacks seem slow. Aiming for the shoulder she slashed down and removed the first arm like trimming branches off a sapling.

The demon let loose a screech that cut through her brain and she flinched, almost losing her own arm as it lashed out with the other three arms. Each arm ended in four long serrated claws and all of them came at her face.

Kayter dropped to the ground, rolled, and came up with an underhanded strike and severed one of the two legs at the hip connection. The thing, gushing greyish red blood, toppled over and she moved in, slicing fast and hard. It felt good to use her skills; it had been a while since she had to stretch herself. It took less than forty-five seconds before the demon lay there screaming, its limbs all separated.

Another quick look around and she still couldn't find the damn mage. With an internal growl, she took off after the demon she'd seen going into the walkway. Running full speed, she almost slammed into it as it turned a corner and headed back her direction. Trying not to fall over, her adrenaline pumping and the knowledge that the portal kept emitting its siren song on the other side, made her reckless not to mention that she figured her chances of living through this were low. So all her being was focused on the now, which made her reckless, slap-happy, and deadly as hell.

This demon followed the humanoid lines, though it had a lizard-like tail which gave it incredible balance. But that meant head detachment for a sure kill. With that in mind she went at it, using jabbing strikes to push it back as it tried to figure out how to attack her. She made damn sure she didn't leave any openings.

Movement to the side caught her eye and she glanced that way as the demon ducked one of her slashes. Two men, eyes wide and jaws open stood in a doorway watching her. She dismissed them, concentrating on the demon. Ducking under a swing of long claws, she came up for a strike, only to miss as the demons' head exploded.

Kayter recovered her balance, then looked back at the two men. What she had dismissed as spectators were obviously demon hunters. She glanced back at the courtyard and saw another demon starting to come through.

Fuck, fuck, fuck. Stay cool. You know what you're doing. Deal with them and either find out if they know anything or get them out of here.

With that final thoughte and trying to act like she didn't think she'd die today, she backed up towards them, still checking the portal in the courtyard.

195

Chapter 28 - Post Mortem

"Greg, watch out for the civilian!"

"Got it." Greg took a breath and held it in as he caressed the AR-10 trigger lightly, sending a single shot through the head of the demon which caused the woman to halt mid-swing as it collapsed at her feet. After a split second of confusion, the woman glanced towards the doorway and noticed the two new arrivals. She turned her back to them, facing out towards the courtyard, and backed up quickly through the door and into the entryway joining Declan and Greg.

This is now a total shit show.

Declan watched the young leotard wearing - okay maybe she had leather body armor on with boots, but still, it looked like a leotard it fit her so closely - sword-bearing, pony-tailed young woman back into the relative safety of the entryway. He watched her slow, then control, her breathing as she kept her eyes on the broken doors leading into the courtyard in front of her. Her unusual outfit was splattered with a fair amount of yellow blood, with her sword dripping some of the fluid onto the floor beneath her.

"Excuse me, ma'am, I don't mean to be rude, but you need you to leave as quickly as possible. My friend and I have some serious work to take care of right now. This is no place for a sword-wielding college student." Declan shouted at the back of the new arrival.

The woman spun quickly towards Declan with her sword pointing at his chest and a strange grimace on her face, "I don't think you understand what's going on here old-timers, you two wannabe Rambos are out of your league and should just move along. I got a problem I need to figure out. Plus, I still don't know where the damn mages are." she said, then paled, her eyes wide locked on Declan.

"I've… I've dreamed about you." The words stumbled out of her mouth, and from the look on her face, she hadn't meant to speak them.

Greg continued to watch the courtyard in front of them trying to angle his head to see further into it but his view was blocked. He glanced to the left and right at the hallways and what appeared to be stairwell doors to the sides of the entryway in rapid succession, his entire body coiled tight. "Hey there, lady, don't worry. We're professionals. Kind of. Looks like you got lucky up there, but we have an old saying never bring a sword to a gunfight."

The woman caught her bearings and a half smile crept back onto her face as she laughed. Standing up as tall as she could, "I don't run out of ammo, or let everyone in the world know where I am though." She replied with what Declan recognized as bravado.

Never taking his eyes off the field of fire in front of him, Greg responded "Maybe, but I do believe I have two kills to my credit already and I'm not covered in nasty shit. Hey, DK, look. The millennials all still appear to think that dry cleaning is free or something."

Not letting the verbal challenge go unmet, the strange woman snapped back. "Some of us have enough intelligence to not want to advertise our presence to everyone in the world. Any time you want to see who's the better hunter, let me know. But for now, we need to deal with the fucking portal." She shifted back and forth on her feet like a hyped-up junkie and glanced at DK. "And talk to the guy haunting the dreams about my dad."

"DK, where did you get this Ritalin addict?"

Trying to get his bearings on the changed situation, DK responded. "I swear I've never met her."

"Uh, huh. Then why is Xenia the Warrior Princess here dreaming about you?"

"Seriously? Can you two shut the fuck up for a second so I can

197

think?" Declan snapped back harshly.

"Whatever, you cradle robbing freak." Greg barely controlled his laughter.

Declan turned to look directly at Greg, "Can we just get back to killing demons? Damn it, this is not going as planned at all."

"I don't know, maybe you should ask your little protege if that's okay first, DK."

"I told you... Shit, where did she go?" Declan noticed that the young lady was no longer standing next to them and had moved towards the edge of the building trying to peak around the corner to get a look into the courtyard.

Quickly, glancing back over her shoulder, she commented. "I'm doing my job killing demons unlike you two comedians sitting there talking. Have fun when they come in there to get you. Me? I'm gonna be over here clearing a path through those three demons, as I just figured out where the damn mages are. They pulled them to the other side of the portal to keep them safe, or at least prevent us from killing them. So now, not only do I have four demons but some stupid fucking mages to deal with. Are you going to do anything or just stand there?"

"Fuck. Alright Greg, ready?" Declan said as he quickly released his magazine from his carbine and replaced it with a fresh one, slapping it into place.

"You know it, brother. Time to get to work." Greg said just as the crazy woman took two steps back and swung her sword barely deflecting a long talon strike of the lumbering demon that had rushed at her from her blindside, pushing her off balance. She ducked and weaved in between the demon's continued attacks, cutting at them with the blade. It glided through the demon's flesh and muscle like butter. Declan had never seen anything like it and kept getting distracted, not by her ass but by that blade.

Who the fuck was she? And why the hell would she be dreaming about me?

The young lady strongly parried the demon's arm with her sword spinning and thrusting. It cleanly between its armored chest plate and neck, partially severing it with a fatal attack.

She's got moves, I'll give her that.

She turned with an insane grin on her face towards Greg and Declan, still laughing. "You two old dudes going to get your asses in gear? That portal isn't going to collapse by itself."

With her back turned to the courtyard, she couldn't see the small mass of demons spilling through the portal, growling at the mages. The mix of ring one guard dogs and a spattering of ring twos had started to gather into a cluster that would attack as one wall of tightly packed claws and teeth.

"Get your ass back here right now, move it. You got a really good way to die going on. Get the fuck over here right now!" Declan yelled at her in his old army 'command voice'. It was a voice that demanded attention.

The lady didn't blink, but apparently realized that she had lost focus. She didn't look back but sprinted to the entryway as ordered.

Just like a damn newbie. Reckless as shit, but at least she knows how to listen occasionally.

Declan let the random thought rattle in his skull as a plan took shape in his head.

"Why? You two finally done playing with your dicks?" she snapped back, but her face stayed serious as she looked back at the portal when she reached them.

"Enough bullshit. Time to shed blood." Declan let his mind slip into acceptance of the coming battle. He felt it tap into is core and start consuming his own inner self to feed and enhance his senses. *No, worries. A hit of Reset later and I'll be right as rain.*

"Hey, Greg, watch that left hallway. I got a twitch." Declan motioned past Greg.

The rushing noise of scraping claws on tiles from at least two demons could now be heard approaching from the hallway on the left. "I'll take these," she yelled as she ran into the hallway alone. Without a moment's hesitation, the young lady turned and ran in front of Greg. The action blocked his field of fire and forced him to lift his weapon upwards to avoid hitting her as she barreled into the hallway sword in hand.

"Fuck, get out of the way lady!" Greg screamed at her as he pushed around the edge of the wall to angle his weapon down the hallway after her.

DK watched in astonishment as the young lady just did what made no sense at all.

Son of a bitch! Is she insane or something?

Declan ran to the wall opposite of Greg as they both tried to get a shot off into at least one of the two demons. "Fucking kid keeps dancing into my shot and that group behind us in the courtyard is not gonna forget we are here."

Dammit, she isn't group tactic trained. Fuckity fuck. If I don't reign her in, she'll get hit with friendly fire and that is never friendly.

"Lady, get your fucking ass over here! We don't have time to do this tragic hero crap. This is now a group tactic and I'm in charge." His voice sharp, she glanced back at him, blocked a blow from some claws, removed the head of the demon, and dropped to the ground. Greg took the shot, the next demons head exploded and covered her with even more blood. With a motion that made DK's back and knees hurt, she flipped to her feet and made her way back to him.

"Fine. Got a plan?"

Greg turned to begin moving towards the courtyard. "Bunyan, hold!" Greg stopped immediately at the use of his old call sign from the war, then dropped to one knee and faced forward with his weapon.

DK pointed directly at the sword-wielding maniac looking her straight in the eyes with a sudden coldness.

"You will stay exactly three meters in front of Greg and me. We will move forward as one. You will keep your spacing. We will engage all targets up to five meters in front of us. Not an inch more. You will kill anything inside of five meters as we move forward. You are the close kill box. You will keep any demon that we don't kill from killing us. Don't question me here. This is how we fight. This is how we don't die. So yes, or no, answer only. Do you understand?"

"Got it. I'll stay in the kill box, defend, while you kill everything else." She winked at both of them and moved to her directed position in the team.

Declan waited until she was situated in the directed spot three meters in front of them. "OK, forward slow. As soon as we round the corner we take it slow and steady. If we can kill them all at range, then great. If not, then you're up kid."

As the small group rounded the corner, stepping around the dead ring two demon, Declan clearly saw the humming portal. Approximately eight feet in diameter, this portal was not the work of a few novice mages playing around after school. It hummed and vibrated so deeply that they could feel it 30 meters away. These MIT idiots had some juice and knew how to use it.

No question as to which human is the key holding this side open. He's the one that has his neck surrounded by the claw of that soldier demon standing behind him preventing him from running away.

Two additional mages at the portal were screaming and trying to pull away from the small guard dog demons that were in the process of dragging them back through the portal into the demon realm. Several more demons began to emerge and join into the ranks of the small mass of demons slowly increasing in size.

"Help them or kill them?" The lady asked as she looked back and forth at the scene. The small knot of six demons stood between them and the mages being dragged into a demon hell realm.

"This portal is a capital offense so they're essentially already dead and of no concern to me," Declan said as he began to fire round after round at the cluster of demons now surging forward at his team in a mass of flailing claws moving faster than should be possible for a biped. Declan could hear Greg's AR kick out three rounds bursts tearing into the demons in front of them.

Blood War: Rage

Neither Greg nor Declan spoke anymore as their old survival reflexes, and familiarity with fighting demon clusters, kicked in. Hold, shoot the wall in the weak points. Don't separate, cover as your team reloads, give no ground, fight or die. If you run, your team dies first and then you'll just die second. The demon cluster had thinned considerably before it reached the team but not enough to keep them out of the close kill box. Declan caught glimpses of the sword flashes as the kid did her job. She was holding the team's point and keeping the demons off the shooters. Close enough for him to get hit with the occasional sticky warm spray of blood from her targets, but she was holding.

Good luck kid. Don't die. Was the only thought Declan could spare before his mind devolved into "Aim, fire, reload. Give no ground, fight or die."

Fifty seconds after it had begun, the team stopped as the cluster of demons was now no more than a semi-circle of corpses in front of them. Except for one – the soldier holding the portal's human key Mage by his neck at the edge of the gateway to another realm in the universe. The soldier demon appeared to be struggling between his need to kill this challenge in front of him, proving his power, or to obey whoever told him to ensure the human kept the portal bridge open. As if to answer, the soldier pulled the human by the neck and raised another claw tapping the mage on the head.

"Stop! For the love of God stop! It demands you stop there." The key Mage shouted. "It will kill me if you keep walking or if I drop the portal link!"

Declan kept his eyes locked onto the demon holding the Mage prisoner as he slowly walked forward. "Easy there, Junior. You just tell your buddy here we can deal."

"I can't tell it anything! I just feel what it wants, I can't actually talk to it!" The Mage's voice cracked as he answered. The demon shifted, glancing at each of the threats in front of it. A talon started to drag over the mage's forehead, drawing a line of bright red blood.

"Who's giving the orders for this bullshit? Tell me and we'll deal with your problem." Declan asked the mage in as smooth a voice as he could manage.

"I can't... the agent said they'd kill our families if we..." the Mage sobbed. He glanced towards the center of their team and began to twist his hands and mumble.

"Shit!" Declan barely managed to shout as he turned his back. Stupid chivalric tendencies had him grabbing the chick and spinning them both so his back faced the portal. He felt the hammer blow of a magical ball of energy slam into his spine, knocking him and the woman to the ground, followed by the burning fan of magic spreading quickly through the inner mesh wiring of his coat dissipating it. Greg fired at the mage immediately, with his first round removing the mage's face and the back of his skull. As the mage's brain imploded so did the portal as it's required human and demon linkage was severed. With the magical threat eliminated, Greg emptied the remainder of his heavy weapon's magazine into the neck and upper torso of the remaining demon before it could react.

"All clear! You two can get off the ground and stop with the cuddling now." Greg bellowed as he dropped the empty magazine from his weapon and inserted his last full magazine. Declan stood up with a groan then reached down, offering Kayter his hand, and pulled her up when she accepted it. He reached out with all his senses, searching for a threat. He could not sense anything of danger but the police sirens were definitely getting close.

"I agree, Greg, I don't feel a thing. All clear. But we need to go. I don't plan on hanging out with the boys in blue tonight. You go check out that mage and see if he's got an ID you can grab."

"On it," Greg answered as he started to jog over to the mage's body.

Declan turned towards the young woman, "And you kid, I need you to... Hey, Greg! Where'd she go?!"

"I don't know. I was talking to you, dipshit." Greg answered back as he was rummaging under the dead mages robes. "Got a

Blood War: Rage

wallet! MIT Student I.D. Let's get the hell out of here DK."

Declan scanned the courtyard and didn't see the kid but did catch a glimpse of a woman with a ponytail on an unnaturally quiet motorcycle drive away quickly. Just before two police cars with gumball machine lights flashing and sirens blaring closed off the road in front of them.

Well shit.

Chapter 29 - Fleeing the Scene

The man from her dreams shouted at her and she responded. He had the command voice from her childhood, Dad could shout the same way. It annoyed her. But for now, she'd obey, cause there was no way in the world she could take on that many demons by herself.

From there, everything became a blur. The memories of him in the dreams, whoever he was, let her listen and obey, and she didn't argue. She just let herself ride the adrenaline and the fear that kept her sharp.

The explosion of magic the man had shielded her from, then the gunfire going off above her head when the mage and its demon controller were taken out, made her ears ring. But it also gave her the shaking she needed to get out of survival mode. As the man pulled her up she looked around. Declan, maybe that was his name or DK, she never really listened to the names just the orders, turned to deal with the other man.

Holy fuck, I lived. And made a complete ass of myself. Just cause you did mostly solo stuff, you never block fields of fire. What the fuck was I thinking?

The whine of sirens and the surge of exhaustion that slammed into her made up her mind.

Time to go. I don't need this. He looks like he's got some backup and I can't believe I was that fucking stupid.

While the two men were arguing she turned and disappeared into the trees. Reaching her bike, she cleaned off the sword and used a towel to quickly wipe most of the blood off her body. She'd come out unscathed and exhausted, but somehow uninjured. Better than she'd expected. Within another two minutes she had

Blood War: Rage

slipped on the bike and headed down the street even as she heard the sirens coming ever closer, multiple types from the sound of it.

What the fuck was that? Since when do you rush into a situation like that?

Kayter grimaced to herself. John had trained her to think, to assess, and to weigh the risks. Why had all that training disappeared? Why had she been so driven to prove herself? Stuff from the dreams?

She spent the next twenty miles tearing her behavior apart and coming to some conclusions she didn't like very much. Biological needs, bladder, and thirst gave her the incentive to pull into a rest stop. More than a bit exhausted, she just pulled into the first open slot, not giving the car next to her more than a token glance, noting it was dark, four-door, American.

Parking the bike, she pulled off her helmet, setting it on the bike, and started trudging up to the restrooms. She felt more than a bit sticky and was still upset and frustrated with herself. The entrance to the restrooms was a blind turn but the voices from the other side got through her fog and she stopped.

".. can't believe we have to go to MIT to clean up that mess. You would have thought the demons would have killed the mages before too many got out of the portal." The voice held tones of annoyance and exasperation. It also sounded familiar.

"Well apparently some local hunters got involved. Hell, for all I know your boss sent them up to deal with it."

"Cordelia? That bitch? Nah, no way they could have gotten there in time. Sure, we made plans to verify the report got made, but it's a nine or ten-hour drive. We're only getting sent cause we were within two hours. Hell, anyone she sent would either have to fly or would have been local. You know we made damn sure the local got sent in the other direction yesterday." The arrogance of the voice rubbed at her and she turned her back to them, ducking down to get a drink of water as she heard them move closer.

"Fine but if I have to put down a bunch of demons, I want hazard pay. Just because they gave us some fancy weapons that

206

are supposed to single-shot-kill the little bitch demons doesn't mean I have any desire to put my life on the line. The full-on soldier demons are still gonna needs lots of HE rounds to take out."

"Doubt many of them are still alive. They tend to be their own worst enemy when it comes to the portals, killing the mage for the blood then wondering why the portal collapses. Either way, there will be drama and terror. Perfect for the bosses master pl – " He broke off as his phone rang.

They were behind her now, so Kayter straightened and turned enough to see the two men. One she'd never seen before. Older, military cut dark hair, glasses, a bad suit, and a slight limp as he walked. The other, Chad Morant, the idiot from the VFW and the one she'd followed to the restaurant.

"Chad," he said into the phone, then his step paused and his back stiffened. "They what?" another pause. "Who got there?"

Kayter grinned at the stress in his voice and watched them but she made sure she looked like she was staring at the map of where she was, and what local landmarks were nearby.

"Got it." She heard a beep. "That asshole fucking flew there. I can't believe he got a fucking helicopter and flew there. Somehow that bitch got her own people out there. They're covering up for him now. Boss is going to be livid if this gets out. We need to get up there and see how much we can twist for our own control. Damn idiots. How hard is it to follow instructions? Open the portal, let a demon or two slip out, maybe three, then close it and run. Let the cops find out how bad demons are and remind people why we keep researching this stuff." Chad made a sound between a growl and a grunt. "Let's go. Step on it. If the cops want us, they can pull us over there."

She focused on them as they headed towards their car and backed out fast, neither seeming to pay any attention to anything other than themselves.

That was a setup? Why? What did they have to gain from any of that? Hell, that was more than two or three demons. That was enough to possibly level the town.

Kayter used the restroom, cleaned herself up a bit, and for the rest of the drive home, she went back and forth between chewing on herself and trying to figure out what that ICER agency was doing.

Chapter 30 - Escape

Declan watched the motorcycle race away feeling both confusion and admiration for the young lady's skills in the fight.

"Well, that was a hell of a thing wasn't it, DK?" Greg said as he slung his rifle over his shoulder.

"Turn around and get on your fucking knees now! Hands straight up or we will kill you!"

Well shit. That didn't take long. Impressive response time.

Declan thought as he and Greg both raised their hands above their heads and turned slowly as instructed to face the four figures in what appeared to be police tactical uniforms spread out in front of them. The figures pointed rifles directly at them and the blinding flashes of the dazzler devices mounted to the rifle barrels prevented either of them from getting a good look at the new arrivals.

"Boston PD, down on your knees! Face down, hands in front of your body!" Barked the armed individual standing in the middle of the small group. "You move and you are dead, do you understand?"

"Absolutely, officer, we are not a threat and will comply with all of your instructions," Declan responded as calmly as he could, knowing he was a hair trigger away from a nervous police officer killing him by mistake. "We are both legally armed officer but are not a threat. We will not touch any weapon in any way. We're here on a Department of Defense sanctioned operation." Even as he spoke, he and Greg lay down on the ground.

Would truly suck to save the city just to get mistakenly killed by over keyed cops.

"Jesus Christ, Steve! What the fuck? Are those demons? And a human? Demons aren't supposed to be able to come here anymore." His voice had a trace of hysteria and Declan glanced up to see a police officer on other the side of the formation was now pointing his weapon, not at Declan and Greg, but directly at the cluster of demon corpses in the courtyard.

The officer, not taking his attention off of his two armed suspects, said "Go check it out, Daryl." The leader directed the officer nearest the demons. "Tracy and Jones, you two zip and clear the suspects here. I'll cover."

"Yes, sir." One of the remaining officers responded as two of them moved forwards towards the prone demon hunters. "Both of you, keep your hands down with arms straight out and palms down on the ground. Do not so much as twitch or you will be shot!"

"Understood, officer. We are not resisting and will comply with all your instructions."

"Steve, we have a dead civilian here too. Holy... His face and half his head is blown off!" Officer Daryl shouted over from near where the portal circle had opened a few minutes earlier.

Tilting his head, the lead officer pressed his radio handset. "Tac ops we're at the 10-35. We have the 10-32s down. One known civilian DOA and a pile of, fuck I don't know, demons I think." He paused while listening to the response. "Yeah, that's what I said and no, do not put that on the dispatch net!"

Officers Tracy and Jones both reached down and smoothly wrapped nylon riot cuffs around Declan and Greg's outstretched wrists locking them together.

"They said what?!" the lead officer snapped back into his radio microphone. "You have got to be shitting me! We have a dead civilian, piles of not human looking dead things, and two armed to the teeth fucking psycho suspects right in front of me! No way am I doing that."

Declan felt his Vulcan being pulled away from his body as one of the officers placed a knee firmly down on his back and began to expertly pat him down for more weapons.

210

He fought back a growl, no one touched his weapon. Rage licked at the edge of his mind and he pushed it down. The demon blood the chick had occasionally sprayed him with helped to keep it to a low roar.

"On whose orders? ... Yes, in fact, there is, in fact, a real fucking helicopter across the street in the park. No, the pilot gave that number to the campus cop, not us. Why in the hell would we detain the campus cop? All right, all right. Yeah, I got it already. Out." The agitated lead officer took his hand off his radio. "You, jacket boy, what's your name?"

"Declan Kenner," Declan responded after assuming the endearment of 'jacket boy' was meant for him.

"Tracy and Jones, back off and cut them loose. Daryl, back away from that shit and don't touch a thing!"

"No need to tell me twice, Steve." DK could see Officer Daryl quickly move away from the bodies out of the corner of his eyes and let out a relieved breath.

"You sure about this boss?" The officer holding Declan pulled out a small set of wire cutters but hesitated to cut the cuffs off him. "Their damn guns are still hot and they're covered in blood, or some shit. I'm positive these are our guys."

"Yes, just cut them loose and give them back their gear. Somebody cleared that guy's name. Apparently, they're government or something. And clearly these are dead fucking demons!" The lead officer shouted while pointing at the bodies. "So, listen up guys. This is screwed but Daryl, you need to go out to the helicopter right now and detain the campus police officer and put him in the truck. If it gets out that demons are coming through portals again, we'll have a riot on our hands." His voice didn't sound all that steady as he glanced at the pile of the dead.

"What?" Daryl began to protest.

"Just do it! Be polite, do it quietly, but do it now. Nothing goes out over the general frequencies. Everything stays on our tactical network only. More of these government clowns should be here any minute now to take care of 'cleanup and public affairs'.

Blood War: Rage

Whatever the hell that means."

Pointing at Declan and Greg, who had both gotten to their feet grabbing their weapons as they rose. "You two just get in your helicopter and go. Leave right now and don't come back."

Declan made damn sure to not even accidentally point his weapon near a cop. Greg didn't have the same survival instinct.

"Sweet! Later, Bean Town." Greg said with a smile and a wave to the officers as he started moving to leave.

"Appreciate the help, officer," Declan said gravely as he started to follow Greg back out towards the helicopter.

The lead officer watched the two government gunmen leave then surveyed the carnage in the courtyard around him. "Fuck my life, the demons are back." The bleakness in his tone clear.

I almost feel sorry for the guy. Almost.

Declan and Greg walked through the smashed glass doors, exiting the residence hall out to the street.

"Well, that's a hell of a lot of gumball machines," Greg muttered as he surveyed the chaotic scene that had formed outside of the campus building. Each end of the street was blocked by not one, but two sets of emergency vehicles. The outer cordon was local police cruisers blocking the road with the inner cordon consisting of black government Suburbans with large white 'ICER' letters stenciled to the sides.

"Seems your boys are here, DK. From the sounds of that shouting over there, I don't think they are in total agreement with the local Leos on our little situation going on here. "

Declan looked over in the direction that Greg was pointing and saw a line of police patrolman gesturing at both Greg and Declan, then pointing at the aircraft, then back towards the courtyard. They were being held back by heavily armed, grey and black urban camouflage wearing ICER agents. The individual who appeared to be in charge of the ICER agents had a radio in one hand and was gesturing towards the police in what appeared to be an effort to get them to move their vehicles farther away. Declan and Greg quickly moved away from the heated law enforcement discussion

212

and towards another small group of ICER agents that had set up a perimeter around the helicopter with road flares. They were in the process of keeping both the local police officers and civilians away from the aircraft.

"Well, I'd love to stick around and help these good people with traffic control Greg, but I might have an unpaid parking ticket or two that I'd rather not have to address at the moment. So, my vote is let's get in your bird, call it a day, and grab a beer."

"I concur. This sounds like the first good plan you've had all day. Let's get the hell out of here. It so happens I might just have a 12 pack of beer in the cooler on the helicopter."

They headed towards the chopper at a trot. Joe waited for them, leaning against the door, his body tense.

After a quick glance at Declan and Greg, the ICERs waved them through their improvised perimeter around Greg's helicopter without asking any questions. After a short scolding from Joe about tracking "disgusting and unearthly filth" into his aircraft, they did a quick preflight then got the Sikorsky airborne and headed smoothly westwards.

Declan activated his headset intercom. "So Greg, I believe you mentioned beer?"

"Yup, right under the center table in front of you. The top lifts up."

Declan reached over to the table, lifted the lid and extracted the cold 12-ounce object of his desire from the concealed mini fridge.

"Wait a second, you said you had beer. This is Corona! What's with this pretentious yuppy fake beer? You got a lime in here somewhere too? I'm horribly disappointed in you, brother. How far you have fallen." Declan's feigned indignation was not enough to prevent him from opening the bottle and draining half of it.

"Yeah, I can see how broken up you are about it. Oh here." Greg tossed the dead mage's wallet over his shoulder to Declan.

"Yeah, thanks. Let's see what we got. Five bucks says there's a Starbucks card in here." Declan pulled out the student ID, noticing

Blood War: Rage

the age of the young dead mage. Twenty-two.

Damn it. Only twenty-two. What a waste.

He continued to pull items from the wallet and tossed them into the seat next to his after a quick inspection of each item.

ID.

Nothing special. Idiot was from Florida.

Tossed.

Medical Insurance card.

Was on Mommy and Daddy's coverage plan.

Tossed.

Discover card.

Only a college student would sign up for this 20% interest rate credit card.

Tossed.

Declan pulled out a familiar looking business card made of heavy cardboard, all black with white letters, with an address, a number, a name, and runes that tingled his fingers. Chad Morant.

"Son of a bitch! That fucker."

"What? The beer's warm?" Greg responded to Declan's outburst.

"No. I think this whole thing was a trap, Greg. We were set up by the ICERs to take the fall for today. The dead mage had one of their cards on him, one of Cordelia's guys. That lying bitch!"

Declan pulled a slip of notepaper, with a name and phone number, out of the wallet.

"Shit, DK. That is not good." Greg said from the front, paying attention to flying the bird.

Declan read the name on the slip of paper and he could almost feel his blood run cold.

"No Greg, we just went from not good to total shit show. This dead guy has the phone number for Marcus Vipsanius in his wallet."

"Who the fuck is Marcus Vipsanius?" Greg looked back over his shoulder into the passenger compartment from his cockpit seat.

Declan paused for a few seconds and closed his eyes before

214

responding. "Marcus Vipsanius was the name of a famous Roman general. Also, an internet pseudonym used by an old friend to stay out of trouble for drunken online rants... Shane Gris."

"Oh, fuck me, DK."

"Yeah. Fuck me. Get me home, Greg. I need more than this shitty overpriced Mexican beer. A few demons may be the least of our problems if Shane is mixed into this. We could all be very dead, very soon. All of us."

Chapter 31 - Boss Finds Out

The Office of the Director of International Cooperative Element Responders reflected Kelvin Ordonio's status as a Senior Government Executive Tier Three. The walls were adorned with precisely centered awards and memorabilia he'd collected over his decades of government service. He ran one of America's most powerful semi-independent agencies but it's hybrid structure and authorities were so closely intertwined with the Department of Defense that it forced him to primarily work from this office in the Pentagon. Working in the Pentagon had distinct advantages for him. First and foremost, he did not have to waste any of his internal department funding on paying for the security infrastructure and the personnel required to maintain his own headquarters. No one ever accused Kelvin of wasteful spending. His personal motto of "Mission, Efficiency, and Effectiveness through a balanced Team" reflected how he lived his life.

The director finished typing his reply to the Secretary of Defense with his thoughts on the executive summary distributed by the Emergency Operations Center based on the incident last night at the Massachusetts Institute of Technology.

Well, that didn't go as planned, at all. Clearly, there are some issues with the synchronization of team efforts. That won't do. No, it will not.

The knocking at his office door interrupted the Director's chain of thought. "Please, come in." He responded to the knock in his usual cheery voice.

"Excuse me, Sir, I need a minute of your time." The man was only about 5 feet 5 inches tall but stocky and muscular. His face was scarred with the signs of a rough life and more than a few

216

fights. The man's name was Jonathan "Johnny" Boulder. Unfortunately, Johnny had a tendency to wear a scowl on his face that tended to frighten the office staff. Or it could be the fact there were always quiet rumors surrounding the Director's driver's additional duties. It was hard to hide the fact that as a driver, he spent an exorbitant amount of time with the Director beyond what would be thought is necessary. It amused Kelvin to think that if his staff really understood the additional services Jonathan provided the agency, they'd be truly terrified of the man.

The Director politely turned away from his computer screen and gave his full attention to the new arrival. "Oh yes. Jonathan, come on in son. You know you don't need to hold on to all these formalities with me. As a valued employee you know I have an open-door policy. What can I do for you?"

Johnny shut the door and waited until it had closed fully. "Sir, it's about last night's operation. I really think we have some issues."

"I absolutely agree, Jonathan. But first off young man what have I told you about pride in appearance for professional government employees?"

"Oh shit, sorry, sir." Johnny quickly reached up to his loose and poorly knotted tie, tugging at it and then attempted to pat down his hair. "I'm working on it."

"I know you are Jonathan, but when a person reflects pride in his appearance it reflects the pride that he takes his job. I know you take great pride in the excellent work that you do. It is also important to maintain a professional image if you ever want to move up in the reins of government service." He said with warmth and sincerity.

"Absolutely Sir. I swear I really am trying. Are you sure I can't wear clip-ons? Really not getting the hang of this tying the knot."

"Clip-ons? Now, now, Jonathan. Come over here let me help straighten you out."

Kelvin found Johnny's discomfort at him taking such a hand in his appearance amusing. But when you owned people down to

Blood War: Rage

their soul, they didn't have the ability to say no to you. After all, Johnny owed the director his literal freedom. Without the Director's influence, and his taking him under his wing, Johnny would have been only a few years into a 30-year Federal sentence by now.

He got up and walked around his desk to Johnny, straightening his tie and tapping him gently on the shoulder, even as he fought a smirk at the man's flush. Kelvin returned to his desk and leaned back in his chair with his hands on his lap.

"Jonathan, I know things didn't go as planned last night and I value your opinion. What do you think the principal issue is that needs to be addressed? As well as how we should address it?"

Johnny paused, and Kelvin preened as the man remembered to think and formulate his responses before he answered.

Johnathan has a bright future. He learns from his mistakes. So few really do.

"Well, sir, I think the issue here is that we have a third party involved that has completely fucked up a plan that took weeks to put in motion. I think we need to find the hunters that shut down the operation then stomp them into a bloody pulp."

"Ah, that's what I like about you, Jonathan. You have a direct way of looking at things. Now if I asked my own staff planners for such an answer, they would have taken three weeks to research, and formulate a 20-page course of action analysis, with footnoted responses. Then, they likely would have presented it to me in a PowerPoint presentation a week later."

Johnny adeptly waited quietly for his boss to continue, knowing how he loved to monologue his "teaching" points.

"But there are a few data points you are missing. First, the plan wasn't a few weeks in the making, it's been two years. Those young mages at MIT have been a long-term investment for this agency. Scholarships don't fall out of the sky you know. But when I adjust the numbers, I'll determine a proper business analysis on whether that investment provided any actual returns in the long run. But I do concur in your assessment that the hunter's involvement was quite an unexpected problem. The executive summary I just read from in the emergency operation center said that this response mission was coordinated by one of our very own regional division chiefs."

"But when did you authorize that sir?"

"This is, in fact, the problem as I did not request a response. It also stated that over a dozen demons had traversed into our world through the portal. This is highly unacceptable. The direction was for only two to three demons, of no more than ring two power, be allowed in to cause a minor ruckus. There is a point of inverse effect with regards to the quantity of demons allowed over. Just a few here and there and we are granted more authority and funding to keep a lid on it without much scrutiny. Too many demons and our military friends start clamoring to call the shots and our plans are hindered. They may mean well but they will only get in our way."

"Yes, sir, the response team was well positioned to stop the overflow thru the portal. I can only assume the hunters were brought in as part of that team, based on their ridiculously fast response time. They had to have been in motion well ahead of the portal opening. The team belongs to Ms. Cordelia Bennett." Johnny shuffled his feet avoiding looking at the director while he waited.

"Oh yes, Ms. Bennett. I don't think I've actually met her in person but the performance evaluations I signed off on her, which came up through the channels, were very glowing. She seems to be very effective and efficient at organizing while utilizing her resources prudently. Now Jonathan, unfortunately Ms. Bennett is not part of our special team. Who's our inside agent with her team?"

"It's that pompous dickweed, Chad Morant, sir."

"Now, now, Jonathan. Language, please. Mr. Morant may be somewhat overly opinionated of himself but he's one of our assets. You should not disparage your own. That is not professional."

"Yes, sir. Still a dickweed though." Johnny mumbled quietly but

Blood War: Rage

flushed when Kelvin frowned with as much fatherly disapproval he could muster at the use of bad language.

Foul language is the refuge of the weak. I don't have weak people working for me, well not for long.

"Very well, Jonathan, I don't need you to intercede here. Not personally. I have other things that need attending to with your special skill sets, so you're going to leave this extra task to Chad to take care of. I think it's time we readjusted the numbers and give the senator a little more of what she asked for. It's always nice to feed the machinery a little oil every now and then. So have Chad oil that squeaky wheel for us, will you?"

"Yes, sir, I'll give him the word. I'd rather take care of it to myself to make sure it's done right though."

"Jonathan, always the meticulous professional you are. Except for your appearance unfortunately, that's still a little bit on the tisk, tisk, tisk, side. But I need you to head to the factory instead."

"What do you need there, sir? It's moving along pretty good. The crew hasn't been giving me any trouble. Not after I took care of the last incident. They are squeezing every drop they can to meet your quota."

"Oh, I've seen your reports. While you could benefit by learning how to use the spelling and grammar check functionality, the numbers are clear enough. What I need you to do is to take inventory on how many assets will need to liquidated and how many resources you will require for that mission when it comes time to shut down the Reset factory. We need to have the perfect amount of stock on hand so that we can feed our little junky assets for just long enough to make use of them before they are moved over to the liquefied column on the ledger. The numbers are very delicate now, Jonathan. I need everything to be meticulously precise."

"I think I got the numbers right, sir. But I understand. You need all the hardware and human assets properly accounted for. I have to say, sir, I look forward to liquefying the excess warm bodies stock as soon as you give the word. Some of them do not have the proper attitude even after repeated adjustments."

The director cringed at the implied, but not so subtle, statement of his underling. While Kelvin had never been squeamish in ordering the death of others, he did find it rather ghastly the amount of a personal pleasure that Jonathan took at beating people to death.

That business is all rather unnecessarily messy and inefficient. *Although I'm really going to regret the day I have to liquidate Jonathan as a potential exposure risk. But, the assets on hand versus the resources to achieve mission accomplishment equations are what they are. I just can't take it personally when my saving all of humanity is at stake of course. A few cracked eggs and all.*

"Now what I'm really curious to hear, from our friend Mr. Morant, is about how one of my regional Chiefs requisitioned a helicopter without my signature?" The director said while chuckling. "I mean, I applaud the initiative and find it incredibly damned resourceful. But, this was a very inopportune time for one of my chiefs to show initiative to the scale of somehow acquiring a helicopter off the books. I find it all horribly inconvenient right now."

"You want me to take care of her, sir?" Jonathan asked with a little too much enthusiasm

"Oh no, Jonathan. Every problem is not a nail that needs a hammer's attention. I will simply deal with my over-exuberant subordinate. I like to think that I encourage a climate where my employees feel comfortable taking the initiative to accomplish their missions. No, I can't punish her for such a thing. I think her team may be ready to take on some much greater responsibilities. You just make sure Mr. Morant understands that with greater responsibility, I expect the next missions to carry extreme risk, and unfortunately the results will cause a few reductions in on hand personnel resources."

"Absolutely, sir. I'll order up a cluster fuck op for Ms. Bennett's team." Johnny smiled as he pulled out his phone to begin texting.

"Oh, and Johnathan, don't forget to say happy birthday to Mrs.

Blood War: Rage

Lin outside. She turned 71 today. I think there's still some cake in the breakroom. Grab some on the way out. It was wonderful. Cream cheese frosting."

"Um... sure Sir," Johnathan replied uneasily as he shuffled out the door under Kelvin's watchful gaze.

Chapter 32 - We Meet Again

On the ride back from MIT Kayter hadn't come to any conclusions about the ICER's. But by the time she got back to her RV, she figured she'd proved herself to be the world biggest idiot and hoped she'd never see the old guy again. By morning her mood hadn't improved much but her determination to remember her job crystalized.

Her job was to eliminate scouts, provide close in backup, and not to get herself killed. At no point was she supposed to be bait, the way she'd played it last night. The fact that she'd had fun didn't change the stupidity level of her actions.

In a foul mood, embarrassed, and knowing she needed to improve her gear, she headed to Hunter Gear, hoping Miriam would have her order ready.

A black F150 sat in the parking lot but being a popular truck, she didn't do more than give it a half glance. The owner didn't seem to be lying dead outside of HG, so they were probably a hunter.

That's cool. Miriam mentioned there was someone she thought I should meet in the area. I just never want to run into that guy again. DK? Just yeah, luckily he was up at MIT not here.

Shaking the thoughts off and determined to never see the man again, she pressed the buzzer to get in. A click and the door unlocked letting her into the short hallway. She still hated that walk, knowing all the weapons pointed at her where she couldn't see them.

The second door clicked open as she walked up and she entered the workshop and glanced around. In the back she could see John K and another guy, but Miriam called her name and

Blood War: Rage

pulled her attention over to her.

"Morning, Kayter. How are you this morning?"

Kayter shrugged, small talk had never been a thing with her.

"Thought I'd see if my order was ready. I think things are heating up."

Miriam's eyes darkened and she nodded. "Yes, we were just hearing that. While it might be good for business, that idea does not excite my soul."

"No, but it doesn't surprise me." Kayter commented, following Miriam as she moved across the workshop.

"I can't say it does me either. Stupid loopholes in blood magic treaties. But, the idea of anything we call demons keeping their word is probably just as stupid." She reached down and pulled out a dark green, almost black, bodysuit. "Here, this should fit. John is working on the other part of your order. Come on over. There is someone I wanted you to meet anyhow. He's local and spent time in the military."

Kayter followed, but most of her attention focused on the item Miriam had just handed her. The workmanship was excellent, as she expected, but she really wanted to investigate the enchantments. She could feel them tingling at her fingers.

"What exactly did you manage to enchant into it?"

"Well the material I make it out of is cut and impact resistant. I wove in greater levels of cut resistance, energy renewal, and boosted strength. Given the conversation we had, I altered my pattern a little. If you bleed, the enchantment will absorb it and pull it in for a short-term boost."

"Strength boost? How much?"

"Standard is about ten percent, most bodies can't take more than that. I took a guess that as an abomination you can probably handle up to twenty-five percent. Figured if you got cut under that, you'd need the boost."

Kayter whistled softly, still fingering the material and arched a brow.

"Nice, you even accounted for crotch access."

"I've had catheters setup; they are not fun and active movement can be decidedly painful." Miriam's voice held wry experience and Kayter smiled and looked up. "Besides, I wanted to introduce you to someone. Declan Kenner, this is Kayter Reynolds."

Kayter froze, the smile twisting to a grimace as her eyes landed on the last person on Earth she ever wanted to see again.

I wonder - if I wish hard enough will a portal open up and suck me into hell. That would be preferable to this.

"Oh, we've met." Outside of a battle, his voice had a certain softness to it, a softness that reminded her of Dad. It meant that when the softness went away you were in big fucking trouble.

Miriam glanced back and forth between the two of them. "Why do I feel like there is a story here?"

"Nope, no story." She had to get the hell out of here. "I'll come back later for my boots. Let me get you paid Miriam and I'll get out of your hair." She knew she was babbling, but no way in hell could she handle facing this man right now. As far as she was concerned the only saving grace so far was that he seemed to be alone.

"John, Miriam, do you mind if I borrow your office for a bit? Ms. Reynolds and I need to have a talk." Before she could make her escape, and only the inability to leave without paying for the bodysuit stopped her, his hand gripped tight around her arm above the elbow.

"Is there bad blood between you? You know I won't allow customers hurt on my premises." John had stood up and his gravelly voice filled the air with menace.

"I won't harm a hair on her head. We just need to have a talk about why I am appearing in her dreams and why she crashed a portal opening yesterday." Declan's voice held velvet smoothness.

Kayter wanted to protest, to scream, but she knew to her bones the worst that would happen is she might die from embarrassment and the chewing out her inner father would give her. But, if she was going to work in this area she needed to prove that aside from the other day, she didn't normally act like a reckless fucking idiot.

"Nah, I do need to talk to him. I just hoped I could put it off for a decade, maybe two."

She kept her focus on Declan but she thought she saw Miriam bite back a smile.

"Well, not willing to let you in my office but feel free to use the entryway."

Kayter stiffened and she felt Declan stiffen also but he only replied in that same soft voice. "Thanks, Miriam."

In short order she found herself in the unimposing entryway. Her skin started crawling, and that was before she turned to look at Declan Kenner.

Chapter 33 - Dressing Down Kids

As soon as the door to the main room closed behind him, Declan released the young woman's arm. She moved away from him to lean against a wall, her arms defensively crossed over her breasts and absolutely no expression on her face.

Kayter Reynolds. Fuck, last time I saw her she must have been eight? Ten? Would have been when John and I were still on the same base, way before it got bad. Before the war and Ypsilanti.

As always that one word caused ripples of something to run up and down his spine. But he pushed it away and leaned against the door looking at her.

"John Reynolds was your dad? Commander of 1-66 Armor?"

She jerked her head up and down in a sharp nod.

"Huh. That explains a few things." He never took his eyes off the young woman as she relaxed a tiny bit. "It doesn't explain why any child raised by him would have run into a situation in such a reckless fashion, much less walk into someone's line of fire."

A dull flush crept up her face. The odd colored lights in the room made it look orange.

"While I get that you didn't train in small squad tactics, I cannot believe any child of Reynolds would not understand basic weapon safety and how to not get shot in the head - not to mention running into a situation like that with no damn back up. What the hell were you thinking?"

"Well, I..."

Declan cut her off, visions of her dead body lying at his feet and her dad demanding to know why he hadn't saved his daughter pushed him into saying more than he intended. There had been something about John Reynolds you just had to respect, even when you wanted to punch him in the teeth for being a stubborn monolithic asshole.

"Your dad was a complete hardass and we butted heads constantly on tactics that we had to use, especially there at the last. He didn't like the choices I made and I didn't like how he kept thinking we were going to live through the war. But I respected the hell out of him and he was a brother. Right now, I'm tempted to pretend you are my daughter and set your ass straight."

Her head jerked up and her eyes narrowed.

"Untrained I can deal with, reckless I will not. But, what the hell were you thinking? You couldn't take on all those demons with just a sword. Don't get me wrong, I would have been dead in the first thirty seconds if I had tried that shit. But you must be careful. This isn't a fucking video game where you can hit reset if you die." Declan growled pushing away from the wall glaring at her.

"I don't have time for this shit. You are not allowed to die, or act like an idiot, or cross into people's line of fire. Trust me, I've seen too many good people die because not shooting at the things trying to kill them would have cost them more than the dumb schmuck who got bisected by your field of fire."

He felt his temper rising as all the ways that entire scene could have gone wrong played in his mind and how he would have one more dead child on his conscious. He had too many of those already.

"Look, it might not be my place to school you, but if you are going to stay in this town, on my turf, you need to make some decisions. And how you're going to survive this is one of them. You're going to have to decide if you want to stay a soon-to-be-dead lone wolf samurai or be part of a group. If you choose the group, you need to learn how to work with people, or you're going to be the next Reynolds to fall in battle. Your call but if you stay the lone ranger, just fucking get out of the way when my team shows up."

"I can't use liabilities that put my team and mission at risk and I'm not going to watch another Reynolds die. Get my number from Miriam. Call me immediately if you need me. If you need back up

I'll be there." He fought back rage and frustration at not knowing what to say and with her just looking at him, a stunned look in her eyes.

"And this is why I never had kids, I don't know what to say to them." With a vicious turn, he moved and yanked the back door open and yelled into the work area. "Miriam, give her my contact info. I'm gone and open the goddamn front door please."

A click sounded at the other end of the hall, the signal of freedom, a place away from these emotions.

"I need a drink," he muttered and headed out, brushing past the girl who stood there, pale and guilt-stricken. He just kept walking out to the truck and got in it, headed straight home. He didn't plan on stopping the drinking until the faces of the dead stopped staring at him.

Much later, staring at a college game, he hated college games, it occurred to him that he might have been a bit harsh and maybe owed her an apology.

Giving apologies sucks, almost as much as college football games.

Chapter 34 - Toys and Picnics

Shane had tucked Toy into his bed. He might contemplate seducing her later but right now sex didn't even register in his list of things to do.

And isn't that a sad thought.

The corruption of the blood ate at him, the knowledge of the choices he had made, but none of it mattered. With a new world, a new universe, he could stop the corruption.

Kelvin of the White City? Demons are pretty damn literal. Could he mean the white house? Or someone from DC? That might work, tons of white stone shit there.

Even as he thought he typed into search engines, the name Kelvin would help being relatively unique.

Then what the fuck was the DK thing? Why has Declan been on my mind, how can he be part of this?

His mind shied away from the raw weeping wound that was his actions at Ypsilanti, he'd done the right thing. Maybe someday he'd believe it.

"You can't betray dead men, so get over it," he muttered to himself, but the feelings still lurked. Maybe someday he'd find out how Declan walked out alive. A beer, a talk, if Declan didn't shoot him on sight.

Using search engines, he found the only thing that made sense, Kelvin Ordonio director of a small but oddly well-funded group, International Cooperation Emergency Responders. The subtext of the website screamed Demon Control and he smirked. He'd never get that close to someone that high up but his direct reports might be an option.

Social media provided the answer he needed. People never

locked their accounts so only close friends could see them, which meant it didn't take him to long to find out about a picnic the next day that most of them would be attending.

It's been a while since I've been to a picnic. Guess I better pull out my glamour and thrall abilities.

Those were always harder for him to use but with the supply of Fae blood, he should be able to pull it off for a while.

He spent the evening in preparation for a picnic, then crashed on the bed next to Toy. At least he had a king bed so he didn't have to deal with her snuggling, or so he thought. He woke up the next more entangled in pale limbs and red hair.

Shane lay there looking at the ceiling, trying to remember the last time he'd woken up with a woman and drew a blank. He cataloged the sensations and realized they were nice and his hand started to drift.

Enough. You don't have time for this and taking advantage of a young woman is still beneath you.

He pushed the girl away, speaking as he rolled out of bed. "Up. We have a picnic to go to and you are going to be my arm candy."

Toy looked up at him from under red hair that resembled a chaos theory diagram more than hair. "Okay. I've never been candy before." She crawled out of the bed and Shane watched and enjoying the show.

Just because he didn't believe in forced sex didn't mean he wouldn't enjoy free eye candy.

Besides, she'll distract anyone looking for strangers. She all but radiates innocence and lack of intent.

That thought rattled in his brain but he pushed it down in order to live with his choices, his questions about Declan, and what he would do with his new universe.

"Toy, I think you should move in here."

I can control her better that way and she is a ripe young lamb for any wolf that comes by.

Toy paused on her way to the bathroom turning to blink at him. She tilted her head and shrugged, looking at the ground. "It's Jane.

Blood War: Rage

Just as well, with my cousin gone," her voice caught a bit and she wavered then shook herself, "I don't have a way to afford the whole rent. I'm on scholarship at the university."

Without another word she headed into the bathroom and Shane grinned, ignoring the dying quivers of his morality.

I do love people who let me use them, makes my life so much easier.

He pulled out clothes, arranged some room for her stuff in the closet, and made plans to keep his very valuable Toy safe. You didn't take risks with possessions like her.

They spent the morning moving her minimal possessions to his apartment. He hadn't known women could exist with so little to their name. Outside of her books, she had two suitcases worth of clothes, three pairs of shoes, and a small box of jewelry. She didn't even own makeup. Shane hadn't been around women in a long while but he remembered their counters of stuff. Toy had none of it. It struck him as odd and it was one more thing to push deep into the well of things to ignore.

Dressed in a sundress, sandals, and with her hair braided back from her face, she came across as fresh and pure. It touched odd parts of him as they walked in the park, looking for the faces and names he'd memorized from various websites - looking for an easy mark.

A large, handsome African-American man sat at a picnic table, a ways away from the mass of people laughing and having fun. He looked bored and almost disdainful.

Bartholomew Boyd, Director of Operations. Perfect. With him, I can maybe figure out exactly what is going on with this little group and maybe get some more insight.

Shane took a deep breath, pulled on the glamour, and dumped persuasion onto the man as he approached.

"Barry, good to see you again."

The man looked at him blankly, then his eyes narrowed. "I'm sorry. I don't believe we've met."

"Sure, we have. I'm Marcus, this is my lovely Toy." He gestured

232

at Toy who smiled sweetly and waved even as he poured on the entrancement, ignoring the oily feeling coating him from the inside of his mind out.

Barry's face went slack, then blank a bit. His eyes glazed over and a half smile appeared on his face.

"Oh, hey Marcus." His voice trailed off after that and Shane backed off the entrancement. If he pushed it too hard the guy would be a drooling idiot for hours.

"Nice day huh? Toy, why don't you go get us some drinks."

Toy smiled at him, with an odd tilt of her head with a strange smile. "Sure." she said and walked over towards where refreshments, including beer on draft, were being served.

"So Barry, I wanted to catch up on Kelvin's plans. Make sure everything is good to go."

"Sure. Magic will be gone shortly; the plan is working well. Eliminate all the Fae, all the mages, and let all the demon hunters get killed. Everyone's on board." He smiled a bright wide smile and chilled Shane in places he didn't think he had anymore. "Hell, he's even working with a demon, playing him, to make sure everything works exactly how it needs to."

Shane swallowed and forced a smile as Toy came back holding two beers, she handed one to both of them. Then she sat down on the table and stared at the trees.

"Bezzid?"

"Yeah, think that's the name, though Kelvin is cagey about stuff like that. Always has all his moves planned out in advance."

"And how is he going to get the demon hunters killed?"

Why the hell do I care? Those people are dead and have always been dead. You don't live that life, get hit with rage, and live long.

Declan's face, the young man he'd known so long ago, flashed in front of him. He pushed it down, away from his memory.

"Mostly incrementally, but some he's converting. Never hurts to have good fighters on your side." Barry frowned, a furrowing of his brows and Shane upped the entrancement, sweating at the power. He could use demon magic so much easier but Fae he

Blood War: Rage

struggled with. It felt different and he didn't have the blood to make it easier to use. Training had taught him how to use it but it would always be difficult. Demon, ah that was like riding a bike.

"Who all is in on the plan?" Shane glanced at the families enjoying a day in the sun. "Them?"

"Not most of them. They think they are fighting the good fight. The ICER agency heads for most countries are on board. We can't afford to allow magic to get any more of a foothold than it already has. That is the reason for the Summit." His voice started to slur a bit and Shane cussed mentally lowering the amount. The man had incredible willpower and fought him.

"We should go now." Toy's voice pulled him out of his reverie.

"What?"

"We should go. They'll notice. You won't learn much more."

"Where can I find Kelvin? I need to talk to him."

"He's already left. But he doesn't have any travel scheduled for a while." Barry struggled even as his eyes clouded.

"What's his address?" That part hadn't been available online and Shane now had a burning need to talk to this guy. Barry said it slowly and Shane sat his beer down, putting it into memory.

Toy rose, taking Shane's arm. "Barry, you should go home. You don't feel good. You drank too much with some friends. Have a good day." She turned Shane and in a causal walk headed away, even as he watched Barry out of the corner of his eye head away from them, stumbling a bit.

Shane shifted his attention to Toy. "Why are you so helpful?"

"Why shouldn't I be? They want to kill all of us."

"We are all already dead. I don't want to save them."

"I know. And it is meant to be. Some things aren't what they are."

He just looked at her and resolved to watch her a bit more closely, maybe get some drugs to keep her asleep when he needed it.

I might have to thrall her. I hate women, they never make sense.

234

Chapter 35 - Doors are made for Busting

Declan waited for the elevator to reach the 7th floor, staring at the glowing numbers slowly rising. Reaching down with both hands in a practiced motion he opened his heavy coat by clipping the sides to the hooks installed for such a purpose. This exposed the combat webbing he wore underneath it for an occasion just like this. He drew the stubby heavy barreled .45 ACP carbine from its sling, and dropped the magazine into his hand, glancing down to look at the round on top.

Armor piercing would be bad here, it'd go right through a wall if I miss. But if I don't use it, and there are more than ring ones I'm not going to penetrate. Damn it, I'm screwed either way.

He chewed on his lip for a minute and sighed, putting it away and grabbing the other magazine, the one with normal rounds that would mushroom on impact. He slapped it back into the weapon and ordered his webbing to make sure he knew where the armor piercing rounds were if he needed them.

The elevator doors slide open with a small ping. He glanced to the left and right and confirmed the hall was clear before he stepped out of the elevator and turned left, inspecting the doors he passed by.

Still not sure about this. I mean, sure you can open portals in buildings but who the hell does it in an apartment building? What sort of moron would want to be trapped with demons in a room? But then again, who the hell is stupid enough to summon demons in the first place.

The door in front of him hummed with the energy of the portal

Blood War: Rage

behind it and he sighed.

I'm never going to quit underestimating the fucking stupidity level of humans.

Raising the carbine in the same motion as he raised his foot, he kicked sharply into the door lock with the carbine nestled into his shoulder.

Ring ones, ring ones, just be ring ones. The familiar thoughts entered his mind as the door flew off the hinges and into the non-warded room.

Damn, she was right. Some idiot was summing demons in his apartment.

Caressing the trigger, two rounds slammed into the first target. A ring one though not a drone, it stood bipedal and hissed at him as he came through. His shots hit dead on and it collapsed to the floor.

Turning, he continued to survey the room. Standing slightly more erect and leaning forward, the butt stock of the carbine stayed nestled tightly into his shoulder, as he took a cautious step into the room moving the weapon to the left and right. *It seems clear.* Moving quietly to his left, keeping the back to his wall, he slid his body around the corner training the weapon forward and reaching around himself in his mind. It was almost as if he could sense behind himself as his eyes searched forward for a target. The hall in front of him led to the small open exposed kitchen. A countertop blocked his view, so he glanced to his right to see an open bedroom door behind the potential hiding position in the kitchen and past the counter in front of him. His gaze locked onto the two demons crouching in the kitchen and babbling to each other.

Fuck. If they are communicating, they are ring two at least. This is not good.

He could see spikes and carapaces over the edge of the counter. Both had the telltale brownish yellow-hued skin of humanoid ring two's, which meant headshots would work.

Perfect, these bastards will go down easy. If this is all I'm facing today, then I'll be done by happy hour.

He moved around the corner, low and quiet, and opened up as soon as he had a shot. They spun but were too slow and the bullets slammed into them, blood spraying everywhere.

Most likely staged here as guard dogs. But guarding what? Where's the portal and the mage?

He moved further into the apartment where the hum of the portal emanated.

A flicker of movement had him ducking and rolling in one motion.

Don't get complacent dumb ass or you'll get your head ripped off.

Declan took his next shot over the first demon's dead body. Another of the dull mushrooming rounds landed dead center into the demon's chest, dropping it to the ground.

Declan shot again at the demon that had moved out of the room to his left and the bullets bounced off the hard carapace. This demon, likely a ring three, was huge and had to bend to make it through the door, which gave him the time he needed.

He popped out the magazine, slapped in the expensive armor piercing rounds, and punched three holes into the head. A spray of blood went out the back side and he just hoped it didn't end up in an innocent bystander.

Yeah but if this guy got out, a lot more people would die.

Crouching even lower with the carbine nestled into his shoulder, he moved the barrel left and right sweeping the room with his eyes, his ears, and his nose. The stench of demons. Left in one place for more than a few minutes they left a telltale scent. It reeked in the confines of this apartment, but he also noted the mingling odors of dried blood, feces and rotting flesh. Somebody, or more than one somebody, had died here already.

Cordy's intel said the demons were here but nobody just summons demons because they are bored. And there was a question of who died.

Suspecting a mage was still cowering nearby, as the portal still

Blood War: Rage

made his teeth vibrate, he reached one hand up. He flipped up the back of his collar and heard it click into place as it attached to the grounding disk at the base of his skull, exposing the silver mesh underlay beneath his leather coat. It was an old habit that provided just a little additional protection against magical spells.

I don't need that type of headache today. No headshots. Nope. I got beer in the fridge but not enough to dull that crap.

Declan could feel the combat mode of his senses kicking in and drawing to him the smells of demon blood and gunpowder - all of it driving forward the urge to kill. Declan stood still for five seconds, letting his senses measure the environment around him for threats before taking another step. Listening for even the slightest out of place sound and breathing slowly in through his nose for the scent of more demons, his eyes searched for the glimmer of active magic. Nothing. Not a sound, not a smell, not a hint of near magic hit his senses.

He had a decision to make. He decided to try one of the oldest tricks in the book. If he was dealing with a human it just might work.

"Alright you stupid motherfucker, come out right now before I just shoot the living shit out of this whole place and leave you to bleed out as a smoking corpse!"

This taunt, to draw out what he suspected was an illegal mage, went unanswered. Still silence. Not even the rustling in the hallways that he suspected would occur, as the neighbors heard gunshots and curiosity got the best of them. They should have been peering into the hallway, opening and closing their doors, or calling the cops. Nothing. No sound at all.

Something is seriously not right about this. Declan tapped his earpiece "Cordelia, ummmm. I think I may have a problem."

Cordelia's voice came in distorted as if the signal was being interfered with. "What's going on Declan?"

"This was too easy and too quiet."

He looked around frowning.

"It was a bust?" Cordelia's warped sounding voice responded.

Doug Burbey & Mel Todd

"No..." Declan looked towards the door as he felt the floor vibrate slightly, as if something very heavy was approaching from the hall. "It's not a bust, it's a trap."

"What? We see no movement on the roof or surrounding building perimeter." Cordelia spoke into his ear.

We? Who the hell is watching me and when was Cordelia going to tell me she has surveillance on me? What the hell...?

Declan's thought was lost as he spun away from the exploding door just in time to be missed by the top half of the heavy wood panel and frame. A hunched over, mud brown creature shoved into the room.

Shit, a Soldier demon.

The calmness in the thought itself was reassuring. Where there should be fear and panic, there was only awareness. The battle sense flooded through his body like a wave of energy, pumping through his heart and into his veins. His mouth filled with the taste of copper. Pupils dilated and took in every detail of color and movement. Muscles twitched under his skin, as if carrying an electrical charge. His mind raced to process his surroundings so quickly, it was if time had slowed. The primordial fight or flight instinct took him in.

Fight. Fight and kill. Pulsed in Declan's brain.

The heavy wooden panel smashed into the wall behind him even as he rolled and oriented himself on the imposing demon. Stroking the trigger of the carbine, he released three rounds into the face of the approaching demon soldier. The first round missed, but the following two rounds penetrated above the creatures armored chest plate and passed through tendrils dangling over its mouth into its softer flesh underneath. A loud screech burst from its mouth. Unfortunately it didn't slow its advance as it plowed through the hall headed directly for Declan.

Subconsciously Declan recognized the screech as a challenge for supremacy or death. Magic and poisoned blood coursed through him, pushing his body to respond to the challenge for supremacy. The battle sense raised his heart rate and surged

Blood War: Rage

adrenaline through his body.

Shit, shit, shit. Need armor piercing.

He quickly hit the magazine release of the carbine with his thumb, dropping the nearly empty magazine of normal rounds onto the floor, while he simultaneously reached his hand upwards for the magazine of armor-piercing rounds in the chest pouch of his combat webbing.

The soldier demon lashed out viciously with its claw-tipped right arm, attempting to eviscerate Declan. He leaned backward and slammed the magazine into the grip stock of the carbine as he felt the demons claw sliding across the side of his coat. He heard it penetrate the outer layer, stopping at the wire mesh beneath.

The demons extended arm attack exposed a vulnerable point in its armor, so Declan leaned slightly to his left and aimed the muzzle of his carbine underneath the demon's extended arm and just above its segmented side torso plates. He pumped four of his armor piercing between the exposed joint and into the chest cavity of this other realm monstrosity. Before his mind could process his next move, the demon's arm flailed backward violently slamming into Declan.

The blow knocked Declan off his feet and onto his back on the floor. Rolling as far away from the demons next attack as possible, he heard the demon stumble as he pushed himself up onto his knees and raised his carbine. The demon swung its body around towards Declan. Lumbering unnaturally, it stumbled on its huge legs as it attempted to maintain its balance as sprays of blood pulsed out of its side.

"All right, drop already you shit!" Declan shouted, more to himself than the threat in front of him. He shot another round into the demon's tendril covered mouth. This time its head snapped backward, with an accompanying audible crack before it collapsed to the floor in a crash of blood and demonic flesh.

Slowly moving forward in a crouch, he kept the muzzle of his weapon pointed at the now still demon's bleeding mouth. Reaching out with the tip of his boot he tapped its leg.

"We done here, asshole?"

The demon did not move. Standing up straight Declan released the magazine catch dropping the mag into his hand quickly, counting his remaining rounds before returning it back into the weapon.

Well shit, this is not good. Now I've got to...

Declan's thought was interrupted by the shouts of a human voice immediately, followed by the rapid hammering of large caliber automatic gunfire. Quickly taking cover behind the kitchen counter rail with his back against the apartment's outer wall, he touched his earpiece as the hammering of sustained automatic gunfire continued out in the hallway.

"Cordy, what the fuck is going on? I just had to take out a damn full on soldier demon that busted ass into the apartment! Now I swear I'm hearing an M240 going off in the hallway!"

"Stand by DK. That's your backup." Cordy's voice now came in clearly but barely audible over the machine gun fire, human shouting, and demonic screeching coming from the hall.

"Backup? I have backup? What the hell!" Declan propped flat on the floor as 7.62 rounds start punching through the hallway walls and into the apartment at chest level. "Cordy, cease-fire, cease-fire damn it! Your backup assholes are about to kill me!"

"Well just hold on for a second, DK. Don't get all pissy on me, I'm a little busy just now."

Oh crap.

Declan kept his carbine pointed in the direction of the large jagged hole that used to be an apartment door as he tried to melt his body lower into the floor when the hallway gunfire abruptly ended. Now at least three separate discernable voices can be heard shouting inside the hall.

"Clear right." Voice number one.

"Clear left." Voice number two.

"Make double fucking sure those targets are down!" Voice number three.

The hammer of a three-second burst of sustained fire rattled the walls of the hallway.

"Confirmed. Clear right." Voice number one yelled.

Choppy three and four-second bursts followed, from where Declan assumed the second voice was located in the hallway.

"Oh yeah, I'm now double fucking sure we're clear on the left again Sir." the second voice calls out.

"OK, let's start processing for cleanup folks." The third voice calmly shouted in what Declan recognized as the 'command voice'. "And, make sure that shithead is zip-tied and gagged tight!"

"Yes, sir." A previously unheard fourth voice responded.

"Mr. Kenner? I'm Mr. Penx. Ms. Bennett asked us to drop by and lend you some assistance." The third voice said from the hallway. "I'd prefer if you did not shoot any of my team, particularly myself. Do you mind if I come in?"

At the mention of Cordy's name, Declan pushed himself up from the ground with a grunt and stood, keeping the counter between himself and the doorway. He quickly exchanged his armor piercing rounds for a full magazine of conventional .45 ammunition.

I think they've already let everyone in the area know something went down here. I don't need to add to the drama, and I sure as hell don't need ballistics tracking back to me.

"Welcome to the neighborhood, Mr. Pink, although from the sounds of it the building manager is not going to be thrilled with your visit. Come on in, but slowly with hands out please."

Mr. Penx rounded the corner of the hall, into what was left of the wall where the doorway stood just a few minutes previously. He kept his hands held out from the side of his body. A M240L short barreled, belt-fed, 7.62mm medium machine gun hung down across the front of his torso body armor. A standard government issue 10mm Glock was on his thigh. His entire uniform was patterned in a relatively old urban camouflage mix of greys and light black. The patch on his sleeve designated him as a member of the International Cooperative Element Responders (ICER) - Tactical. His name tag reads 'PENX'.

Doug Burbey & Mel Todd

Well, if you have to take down a demon with conventional rounds that two-forty Mr. Penx is toting would be a nice bit of kit to have handy. Shit. Now I got gun envy.

"It's Penx, Mr. Kenner, not Pink. Papa, Echo, November, X-Ray."

"Penx huh? Well, that's a bit better I guess. I thought you just drew the really short straw in the government spook name picking contest, ending up with Mr. Pink."

"Don't be an ass, Mr. Kenner. A simple thank you would suffice and Penx is my real name. Ben Penx."

"Sure, it is, Pink. First off, how about you tell me what the racket out there was about and then how you happened to be babysitting me." His voice low and angry as his hands tightened around his carbine. He leaned against the counter trying to look relaxed and nonchalant as rage battled with his control.

The mix of adrenaline and rage bubbling through his system, and the desire to shoot this person who had come into his territory, ate at him. It made him dangerous in a way that he didn't need now.

"Give me a second," he growled out, while raising a hand. Penx fell silent as Declan grabbed a vial of Reset out of his pocket and lifting it, slammed it into his neck. The drug washed through his system, clearing both the exhaustion and the rage that told him to keep killing, to drain the blood and use it.

"Thanks. Now, you were saying?"

Penx nodded at him, his face neutral. "Well, Mr. Kenner, as it looks like we won't get a polite 'thank you' from you, I will just assume you are appreciative of the fact you are not dead right now. While you were taking care of the soldier in here, we were able to take out the additional two ring-one demons and their handler." His voice had a sardonic formal quality that Declan smirked at.

"Handler? Your team managed to grab a ring three demon? Alive? I find that really hard to believe unless you guys have got a lot more firepower out there than I heard. Or, maybe there is some other way to manage higher ring demons."

243

Blood War: Rage

"Come on, let's not be ridiculous. Of course we didn't grab a ring three alive. Although, we did manage to pick up the human weasel that appeared to be watching over this clusterfuck."

"I've got some questions for that son of a bitch," Declan growled and pushed past Mr. Penx and into the hallway. He noted that this entire floor now needed a serious redecorating effort. That is, unless you were into the post urban warfare shoot out look.

I hope nobody sends me this bill. Because I suck at drywall and no way I'm gonna fix this mess.

"Where is he?"

"Mr. Kenner, we secured the prisoner over here." voice number four answered.

Declan moved down the hall passing two extremely bullet-ridden demons and approached the soldier guarding the mage. Declan saw the soldier wore an identical uniform with the same heavy weapons load.

At his feet lay a human in jeans and a hooded sweatshirt, positioned face down with zip ties securing his ankles together and his hands behind his back. There appeared to be a strap across the back of his head securing, of all things, a ball gag in his mouth.

"Really, Sparky? A ball gag?"

"Sir, it's actually really effective. Studies have shown Mages with ball gags in their mouth have extreme difficulties matching orations with the physical motions needed to create magical effects. And it's Sparkazy, Sir. Not Sparky."

"No shit, Sparky. Wait a second, who the hell spends time studying the effects of ball gags on mages? Damn. Never mind. Just roll him over so I can see who the fuck I'm dealing with here."

The soldier reached down and pulled up the head of the quivering, and very young, mage.

"Oh shit, I know this guy."

"Really? You do? That's interesting." Mr. Penx quietly stated from behind Declan.

Strange that I didn't hear him coming up behind me. I must be rustier than I thought.

"Yeah, I know this asshole. I had a run-in with him in my hometown a couple of weeks ago. I thought he was a Fed."

"He's not, Mr. Kenner, although he was reported to have been 'accidentally' killed by one of our agents already. I do believe my boss needs to have a conversation with him."

Blood War: Rage

Chapter 36 - A Fae Walks into a Bar

In the weeks after the MIT incident and running into Declan Kenner at Hunter Gear, Kayter pushed herself harder - push-ups, sit ups, pull ups, going through routines, until by the time she fell into bed each night her body hurt. Nothing she did erased the embarrassment of facing DK at Hunter Gear. Even the memory of him scolding her like a misbehaving child made her want the earth to open up and swallow her.

The worst part? She'd thought she deserved every cutting remark and comment on the sheer stupidity of her actions. It had been almost as bad as having Dad chew her out. Maybe that just made it that much worse. Dad would have stood there and nodded in agreement at everything DK said.

Nights were full of dreams she didn't remember and didn't want. Getting the fading glimpses of blood and demons, she chalked them up to her subconscious also telling her what a moron she'd been.

Maybe I should move on. It's pretty obvious they don't need my help here. So why stay?

The urge to flee her embarrassment fought with the need to prove she really wasn't that big of an idiot. Munching on a power bar and drinking tea she turned on her computer, hoping something would pop up that required her attention, or at least would prove a distraction. The ringing of the phone jolted her from her self-flagellation as she gazed at sensor readings, everything looked normal and boring. Looking at the caller ID she didn't recognize the number but that didn't mean much. A lot of her contacts changed numbers regularly.

"Yes?" She didn't have many friends. Okay no friends, so her greetings were usually rather abrupt.

"Yeah, um, Kayter Reynolds?"

The cold feeling in her stomach cramped at the voice, a man's voice. One she rather hoped she'd never hear again.

"Yeah," her voice resigned as she waited.

Why in the world do I feel like I just got caught putting my sword away without cleaning it?

The man cleared his throat. "It's Declan Kenner. Look, um, you did pretty good the other day, and I might have been a bit out of line at Hunter Gear. So, me and a pickup warrior from the War are meeting at the VFW for drinks. I know you've been there, so if you wanna join us, I'll buy you a drink or two."

Kayter blinked trying to process all the information in those comments. "You don't hate me or think I suck?"

And why the hell did that come out like a request for approval?

She stifled a groan as she let her head thump against the passenger side window.

"Hate you? Hell, no. Why would I hate you? You held up your end of the battle. I think you're reckless and need more team tactical training, but that's cause you're young and haven't worked much with teams. As for suck..." he coughed and laughed. "No. I think you're damned skilled with that blade. Look, we'll be there from about six on tonight. Show up and I'll buy you those drinks." With that, he hung up and she stood there looking at the phone.

All the things he said back at Hunter's Gear came back to her, but this time she inspected them a bit less emotionally.

I did rush in recklessly.

Dad would have beat my butt.

How did he get my phone number anyway? Oh yeah, Miriam.

But never once did he call me stupid or useless. Untrained and a danger to others, yes. But he offered to train me. Maybe?

The thoughts, less emotional and embarrassed, rippled around in her head as she got dressed. Only an idiot refused help. Besides,

Blood War: Rage

riding Midnight usually helped her think better.

Kayter drove Midnight into the VFW parking lot, listening as always to make sure nothing around her implied danger. But all she could hear were the cars in the distance and some machinery running behind the building.

Pulling off her helmet, she locked it onto her bike, set the enchantments and walked in. The deciding factor had been a conversation with her dad a few months before he died. Kayter had asked why he went out drinking with the guys when he hated the bars.

"Kayter, the important thing isn't to have the drinks but to hang out with the people who will die for you. Anything less tells them you don't really value them, or what they do at all."

The words never left her mind, and they drove her to show up here tonight, eat crow, and try to bond with the people she might be fighting alongside. She'd always known to make allies, but anything deeper than an "I'll scratch your back if you scratch mine" sort of interaction seemed beyond her. This, this offer of comradeship terrified her.

The promised warmth and familiar smells helped to relax her. She still didn't know if she made the correct choice by coming here but she'd be damned if she backed down now. When she walked in, she stood up straighter, brushed down her dark jeans, and pulled her jeans jacket out and slipping off her leather one. With a smile on her face that she hoped didn't look too fake, she looked around the VFW.

It had a livelier crowd than last time and she stood a minute, adjusting to the noise, as she scanned the room full of military memorabilia and aging veterans. Her gaze snagged on his bald head and the demon hunter coat draped over the back of the chair. With a stiffening of her spine, she walked towards him.

The man who had held the .38 on the ICER agent last time said something and jerked his head towards her. Declan looked up and quirked a smile at her, waving a hand at an empty chair.

She took the few steps to take in the men at the table. Declan hadn't changed, but he seemed calmer than the barely leashed rage she remembered from the fight at MIT or the odd mood swing at Hunter Gear. There he had come across as a no holds barred fighter, but now? He seemed almost – normal?

No, not normal. He just isn't vibrating with energy anymore. Interesting.

The other man, a good decade younger, with dark hair, a stout frame, and a friendly smile, which he graced her with as she took a chair.

"Nice to see you again, I'm Andrew. We were never properly introduced last time." He held his hand out across the table, winking at her. "Hopefully I won't have an excuse to use my pistol on this sorry excuse for a hunter for getting too fresh with a lady." His teasing remark made her relax even as Declan stiffened. Kayter shook his hand, fighting back a snort of laughter.

"Hey, Kayter here is young enough to be my daughter, if I had kids – which I don't. I'm not trying to get into her pants. You just didn't believe me when I said she kicked demon ass with a sword of all things." Declan leaned back his arms crossed, eyes narrowed.

Kayter shot quick glances at the two of them but shrugged a bit.

"He's right. I did kick demon ass. Though he didn't do too bad. For an old dude." She let the last part slip out and waited to see if she had chosen the right tone. Men were funny creatures at the best of times.

"Oooh, burn. Old dog getting showed up with some new tricks. Maybe she'll get you doing yoga next. The demon fight application of the 'down dog' pose. Naw, you'd definitely sprain something."

"What is this? Pick on Kenner night? Yeesh, invite someone out for a few beers and everyone starts taking potshots. Speaking of which," he raised his hand waving at the bartender. "What would you like to drink? Said I'd buy you one."

"Yeah. Thanks." She settled back, already feeling a bit more at home.

Casey wandered over and placed a steak and fries in front of

Blood War: Rage

Declan and an order of fish and chips down for Andrew. She flashed him a quick smile as he focused on her.

"Hey, good to have you back. I had hoped that jerk didn't chase you away." He said as he grabbed the pitcher off the table.

"That wannabe? Not a chance. I've just been a bit busier than I expected. Declan here is buying me a drink. Lager, dark?"

Casey blinked and then leaned over placing a hand on Declan's forehead. "You got a fever or something? You dying and starting to buy beers for people?"

Declan slapped his hand away growling at him. "I'm not buying beers for people. I'm buying beers for her. She earned them. In more ways than one, " he grouched out. "Now get us another pitcher and her drink, or I swear I'll start singing Casey at Bat."

Casey snorted, obviously unafraid. "I've heard you sing, Kenner. You'd get thrown out of this place by a mob before I could even begin to get upset."

"He's got you there, Declan. You can't keep a tune to save your life." Andrew didn't even bother to hide his smile as he drained his glass.

"Great, everyone's a fucking comedian. I can just leave."

"Hell, no. You're buying me a beer." This Kayter knew how to handle. And she fell into it like slipping on the jean jacket - comfortable, worn, and familiar. "But Casey, can you also put in an order for a burger, fries, and some wings, hot?"

"You got it. Anything else for you two cheapskates?"

Declan and Andrew both shook their heads and Casey moved away, grabbing extra plates and talking to other people as he moved through the tables.

"So, Declan here wasn't blowing smoke up my ass about you taking on a demon with a sword?"

"Taking on? No, I killed three, four?"

"Five actually. Damnest thing I've ever seen. Then there was the one she left in pieces in the courtyard."

"Oh yeah, forgot about that one. What happened to it?" Kayter watched the interaction between the men with sharp eyes.

Doug Burbey & Mel Todd

"Government grabbed it. Ecstatic to have a living demon. How'd you know to do that?" Declan rotated his empty beer glass, a sour look on his face though he perked up as Casey came and sat the pitcher down, with a lager for her.

"Food will be up in a minute," he said before heading on back.

"Do what?" Kayter didn't know what they were talking about. There wasn't much to killing demons.

"To dismember it so the government guys could take it," Declan said even as he poured beers into his and Andrew's glasses.

"Oh, that. I forgot about that one. Didn't do it for that reason." She focused on her beer then shrugged. "It didn't have a head, so I didn't want to take the risk of making what I might assume was a killing blow and leave it behind, only to have it keep its brain somewhere else. And I didn't think I had time to hack it apart, so." She shrugged

Declan grinned at her. "Damn. So, you just removed the ability for it to follow you, maybe hurt you. I'm impressed. Granted, I would have just shot the shit out of it." He grinned at her a bit and Kayter laughed.

Casey dropped off food in front of them and turned then froze.

Kayter hadn't heard the door open, her only chair option had been positioned so the door opened to her side and behind, but with a room full of veterans insisting on the chair against the wall both seemed rude and counterproductive.

Declan looked up and blinked and Andrew froze with the beer halfway to his mouth. A cold feeling creeping down her back she turned following their gaze.

Shock slammed into her and a bit of awe and desire. Sex hadn't been a driving fact in her life, ever. She didn't have time and the imperatives her dad had drilled into her made sex with anyone she didn't trust at her back improbable. All that being said, the man standing in the door made her want to strip off her clothes and do wildly inappropriate things.

No, not a man. A Fae, a fucking full-blooded Fae.

Chapter 37 - Drunk Fae?

"Please tell me I haven't lost my mind and that is an actual Fae standing in the entrance to the VFW," Kayter said. Her voice was oddly loud in the quiet of the bar and Declan winced.

His eyes were locked onto the man and he swore he could hear people's heart beating.

"Not unless I've lost it too and joined you in the insanity," he muttered, pushing his chair back a little.

"I have come to parlay with demon hunters about the most recent incursions. My informants have indicated I can find those odd humans at this location."

"Sorry, none of those here. Wrong bar." Declan said in a loud voice. A wave of chuckles swept through but the Fae male snapped his head towards Declan and smiled.

Ah, crap. Way to go, call attention to yourself by the scary Fae. Moron. Can't keep your mouth closed for anything.

"Hunters. Excellent. I recognize your attire and your bravado. You, I will speak with."

He strode through the tables, the hush making the click of his boots a sharp staccato that echoed off the walls. Declan examined the male as he walked. He really wasn't sure man would begin to encompass what he saw. He was tall, about six foot two, with flowing brown hair that reminded him of good coffee, the type you drank black because diluting the flavor would be a crime. The Fae had vivid blue eyes, tanned skin, and a body that Declan had never had, even in his younger days. Muscled, not slim but not bulky, and he moved like a cat, one that had prey in sight.

I would not want to meet this man in a dark alley without a lot of firepower.

252

The Fae stopped at the table, flashing a smile that looked too perfect to be real. "May I join you to discuss matters of global importance?"

Declan felt the wave of encouragement flow over him and narrowed his eyes.

He has to be using magic but nothing offensive, just persuasion. And global import? What the hell does that mean?

"It's a free country. Sort of." His tone not welcoming, but not quite rude. Kayter scooted a bit closer to Declan, her hands in tight fists on the table.

"Thank you, my good man." The dulcet voice said pulling a chair over as he regally placed himself.

"Oh please, for the love of god, drop the Shakespeare crap."

Something about the Fae toned down, faded. Kayter immediately relaxed, almost sagging in her chair.

Declan bristled.

"Too much? I know humans prefer the drama and elegance, but frankly, it is wearing after a while." He spoke in a much more normal tone, though still oddly formal as he sank down. "This conversation is important. I vow." He glanced up at Casey who still stood there. "Bartender, I would like a drink, well a strong drink. Would you please bring me a bottle of," he bent a bit looking at the wall behind the bar. "Ah, do you really not have anything actually drinkable in here?" His expression made Declan feel like he had just kicked a puppy. Casey didn't seem to fare much better.

"I've got some Laphroaig 18 Year Old under the counter," the words came out as if pulled from him.

"Excellent. Please bring me the bottle and a clean tumbler." He reached into his jeans, which Declan hadn't even realized he wore, and pulled out a wallet, extracting two one hundred dollar bills.

Casey opened his mouth, closed it and shrugged. "Sure." He plucked the two hundred dollar bills from the Fae's fingers and stalked off.

The Fae turned and smiled, something more real but just as potent. Declan stiffened, feeling the magic again.

Blood War: Rage

How much fucking glamor is he using?

The temptation to tell him to drop it tripped across his tongue but he bit it back by focusing on taking a drink.

"Thank you for agreeing to speak with me. The matter is one of great importance." He paused, the slightest flicker of a frown crossing his face. "Well, at least to me." He fell silent as Casey dropped the bottle, still sealed, and a tumbler on the table, a glass with ice cubes in it next to it, then headed back off. Declan noted there was no change included and fought back a smirk.

The Fae unsealed the bottle, poured the tumbler mostly full, and took a large drink, and all of them watched in surprise.

"Not bad, it will at least make this discussion easier." He looked at the three of them, his eyes lingering on Kayter with an odd look.

Bristling for a reason he refused to examine, Declan focused on his steak, cutting it up into bite-sized pieces.

"And what discussion is that?" He didn't look at the Fae.

"About the Fae that are disappearing and the conspiracy between the demons and angels."

Declan jerked and the point of the steak knife slipped into his hand above his thumb. "Fuck," he cussed dropping the knife as he pulled his hand back staring at the blood welling from the shallow cut.

The Fae jerked up straight his eyes riveted on the blood as Declan blotted it with a napkin.

"I didn't realize you had Fae ancestry." There was an odd question in his voice.

Declan looked up, frowning at him. "I don't. Pure human according to the Army DNA tests. Why?"

A frown, that somehow made him look even more regal creased his face. "Odd, I would swear you smell like a relative." He shook his head and waved his hand in the air in an imperious gesture. "I am going about this poorly. I am Duc Artair Niall Donnach. I have resided on Earth for the last two hundred Earth years." He flashed a sudden smile at them and the wave of glamor made it hard to not find it charming. "You may call me Art."

Finishing with his wound Declan put a bite of steak in his mouth looking at the Fae.

How the hell am I am noticing this? I'm still affected, but I know I'm being affected. This is weird.

"So, Art. What the hell are you talking about with a conspiracy between the Angels and Demons? And what about Fae?"

Art finished off his glass and refilled it, a grave look crossing his face. Declan saw Kayter's hand move towards the Fae like she was going to comfort it before she grabbed and stuck it under the table. From the slight shift of her body, he suspected she sat on it. Her other hand wrapped around the hamburger and on the other side of the Fae.

Smart girl.

"That is the problem. We know there are plans going on and that the two sides are communicating, but we don't know what about. But with the sudden influx of portals and demons walking the Earth again, we are worried. Then you weigh the fact that in the last six months over fifty of our citizens, full, half, and quarter blood have vanished, leaving loved ones behind. There must be a connection. Though what they have in common we are unsure."

The words created cold chills running down his back and he shoved a bite of steak in his mouth to give him a minute to think.

"What do you mean half and quarter blood?" Andrew asked and Declan almost jumped. He'd been so focused on the Fae and Kayter he'd forgotten about Andrew.

Art shrugged. "We live a long time and breed, but rarely, but humans are so fertile in comparison, so we have children with humans. Lots by our standards. Given our lives, and that our children rarely live as long as we do, we tend to remain in their lives and in their children's lives." Something real softened his face for a minute. "Our children tend to live well into their second millennia, our grandchildren into their hundreds. We stay in touch and try to help without becoming overly intrusive. Well, some of us do, but a distressingly large number of these relatives have disappeared. If they had died, we assume the bodies would have

255

shown up, but we have not found any."

He polished off the tumbler of Scotch again and Declan noted the level of the alcohol in the bottle rode well below the top of the label.

"So why are you here? There isn't anything we can do."

"Do?" Art rolled the word around as if tasting it. "No, as I do not think you are involved in either the conspiracy or the disappearance of my... our children." He cut off the words and took another gulp of the scotch. "But you fight the corrupted ones and you are aware of the fluctuations in the portals and the currents in your government. Ones such as me can only feel those but faintly. Your government, well most of them, are too suspicious of us to be upfront. Which is funny, considering."

Kayter tilted her head looking at him, licking her lips, but she didn't move towards the Fae at all. "Considering what?"

"Our commonalities. But that doesn't matter anymore, now that we are barely related. But what I am asking, nay imploring - if you see our missing ones, if you hear of their location, let us know. There are families grieving from this loss." He fell silent then took a deep breath. "If you find someone and let us know, we will owe you a boon. A large boon." Darkness flittered across his face, and his voice dropped as his hand tightened on the tumbler. "But know this, those who are behind this, when we find them, will learn that when the Fae turn their abilities to destruction, the Earth itself fears our wrath."

He shook his head, the darkness fleeing from his eyes.

Declan swallowed, that darkness he recognized from the mirror in the wee hours of the morning.

"Here is my card." He pulled three cards out of his wallet and passed them over to each person at the table. "A boon from the Fae is no small thing, and it will be comparable to that which you provide." He finished off the amount of liquid in his glass and pushed back from the table, weaving a little.

As Declan picked up the card he glanced at the bottle. The remains were below the bottom of the label. The card radiated pristine white, and on the front embossed in dark brown and gold lay Art's name, an email address, and a phone number. The card had weight and didn't feel like paper, more like plastic or metal. He wanted to pull it apart and look at it but now wasn't the time.

"I do not see an issue letting you know if we find anything. But I have a request to match what you just asked for."

The Fae paused, swaying just the tiniest bit, which was impressive, If he drank that much he'd be unconscious or dead.

"And that would be?"

"If you hear anything more about the angels and demons and the details, let me know. I don't disagree that something is going on, but I don't know enough to stop it or prevent it from going very wrong."

Art tilted his head to the right then nodded. "That is acceptable. In fact, it would be to our best interest if any collusion ended before they invade Earth. That would give them direct access to our realm and that is not acceptable."

Declan froze, he'd never heard anyone talk about that. The military had talked about it, but publicly no one had really known what the Fae had at risk in this battle. Now he knew. They were protecting their world.

Fuck. Who else knows this?

His mouth was dry, and he fought to swallow. Grabbing a pen from his coat he dug into a pocket and came up with a beer receipt. He scribbled his number on the back and handed it to the Fae who took it from with two fingers, an elegant brow raised.

"That's my number. Call me. I'd like to not die in the next war."

Art inclined his head even as he looked at the scrap of paper dubiously. "I shall see that anything we find is passed on. We would prefer there to not be a next war." He started to go, then stopped turning and looking at Kayter.

"Keep that card handy, mi'lady. You are both rare and deadly, and the turning point for too many things."

He bowed to her then headed out of the bar, weaving a little.

"Should he be driving? And should I get business cards that say something like 'Cold Beer and Dead Demons'?" Declan said turning the Fae card over in his hand.

"He came with a driver," Casey said from behind him and Declan growled.

"Don't do that."

"Sorry." Casey even sounded a bit sorry. "But nah, his driver's been waiting for him. Might as well take the bottle home with you."

"Blech, that is horrid stuff. Swear it tastes like dirt." Declan muttered.

"I'll take it. That flavor is peat by the way." Andrew snaked out his arm and pulled the bottle to himself possessively. "You have no taste, philistine."

"I have taste, and peat must taste like dirt then. Seriously, do I need to get a bunch of cards to hand out to people? Why am I the only one without cards?"

"What did he mean by all that?" Kayter asked, her face pale and brows furrowed.

Too many questions, not enough answers, Declan reached for his beer and focused on the thing that didn't matter.

"Really? Demon Killers Are Us? Or DK Makes Em Dead? How about, We Kill from Hell?"

Andrew ignored him, sealing the bottle of scotch and Kayter chewed on her lip.

Declan focused on his steak and tried to ignore the lump of stress and worry that solidified in his stomach.

"Why do I think Dad didn't tell me something he should have? And I wonder who his father was." Her voice barely audible, but Declan turned to look at her.

"What do you mean?"

"Dad once said he was half angel, half-Fae. He said his mom gave him up for adoption, and his mom was an angel. I thought he was just kidding me."

Her words made him freeze, and he noticed Andrew go stock still also.

"John Reynolds was Fae and angel?"

"Yep. Said he never knew his dad." Her eyes stayed on the door. "Makes me wonder if his dad knew he had a kid. They don't sound like they give them up easily."

Declan just looked at her and wondered when his life had gotten so royally fucked up.

Oh yeah, when the demons invaded and I somehow survived. Really starting to think dying would have been easier.

Blood War: Rage

Chapter 38 - Phonebooth

"Mrs. Lin, please be so kind as to inform our lab manager that I'm heading down for a spot check and will need to make my bi-weekly call while I'm there." Director Ordonio directed his secretary as he walked out his office towards the door to the Pentagon outer A-Ring hallway.

"Absolutely, sir. Please keep it short though, Director. You have a 1430 with that Colonel from the Air Force Air Mobility Command to discuss your requisition of the C-17s for equipment and personnel transport to Fort Irwin California for the ICER exercise next month. The Colonel is questioning the large number of lifts requested for just a single exercise."

"Oh, let's just move that on over to Mr. Boyd's calendar. He loves talking planes and logistics. The Air Force is always questioning things that they don't need to concern themselves with anyway. Barry can handle it."

"Yes, Sir. I'll make sure Mr. Boyd is informed of your schedule change."

"Thank you, Mrs. Lin. Your meticulous attention to detail is the glue that holds all of America's ICERs together. Without you, we'd be no better than the TSA." The flattery made the elderly secretary blush as the Director left the office. He straightened his tie and buttoned the top button of his suit coat, then stepped into structured chaos.

The ring and ramp system of the Pentagon had originally been designed to support not only people traversing floor to floor, but also to allow for vehicles to move VIPs rapidly around the intersecting rings and between floors. Today, even though the vehicles were gone, the halls could barely contain the number of people moving about the daily business of the Department of Defense. Learning the complex numbering sequence of floor/ring/hall/room number that was used on every door, so it could be located in the maze of the Defense Department's nerve center, took new arrivals months to master. Kelvin Ordonio mastered it nearly 30 years ago. He turned and followed the descending hallway ramp away from his fifth-floor outer A-Ring office area. Today he was heading to one of a handful of doors that did not specifically follow the standard numbering system. The Soviet Union had long suspected that the Pentagon contained unmarked, and hidden, sub-basement levels that housed everything from nuclear reactors and weapons to dead alien bodies or brothels for senior government officials.

Silly Commies, you only got part of that right.

The thought amused him as he stopped at a Green Beans coffee cart to grab a quick pick me up before he left the public areas on the way to the laboratory.

"Can I get one of those mochas with the whipped cream and caramel chips please?" The Director ordered his drink from the vendor and felt a light tap on his shoulder, as the vendor nodded his head in confirmation of the order.

"Excuse me, Sir?" A slight young lady in her mid-twenties had moved to his side.

Hmmm... isn't this Barry's latest little tryst? Lisa something... Lisa Redmond... RMD?... No, BMD.

"Why hello, Ms. Redmond. How are things in the Budget Management Division today?'

Lisa blinked at him, apparently surprised that he would know her name, "Umm, oh yes, well Sir. Umm."

Child, do you think I don't know who my directors are fooling around with?

"Now Lisa, it's OK. Remember it is best to formulate your full thought in your mind before speaking." The Director took his coffee from the vendor and thanked him as he paid then turned his attention back to the young lady. "So, what was it you wished to

Blood War: Rage

discuss Ms. Redmond?"

"Um well, sir," Lisa began.

I must really start getting my junior employees into some form of professional speech training. Some of them are more painful to listen to than the damn demons.

"I was just wondering how Mr. Boyd was feeling. He didn't seem to look very well at the picnic yesterday right before he left."

"Oh really?" The Director had been too focused on ensuring he walked around to glad-hand with the hundreds of his employees in the park yesterday than in really keeping track of his senior staff. He knew they would be doing the 'leadership mingle with the masses' act just as he was.

Strange, Barry didn't mention anything to me this morning about feeling ill.

"Yes, sir. He looked rather pale and confused after meeting with an old friend and a little red-headed tramp his friend had hanging off him in the park but he was normal a few minutes earlier."

"An old friend?" The Director's curiosity aroused. Pale and confused are signs of someone who was recently bewitched.

"Well I asked him if he was okay and he said he was fine. That he had a few beers with an old friend and thought he should go home early."

"Oh, yes. Don't worry. Mr. Boyd is back at work today. He just got a little dehydrated is all. Now Lisa, I greatly appreciate your concern and I'll share it with Mr. Boyd. Now I must be heading back to work and I'm sure BMD is eagerly awaiting your return."

"Oh, yes sir! Well, thanks for your time Director, and the picnic was absolutely awesome by the way." The young lady turned and moved into the flow of people walking back upwards to the 5A office areas.

Awesome? No. Barry never drank. Did one of those vile Fae wander into my picnic? My picnic! Did it somehow get its hooks into Barry with that poisonous ungodly suggestiveness? What did it learn? I'll really miss Barry if it did. He was always a loyal employee. Almost a friend in fact.

The Director picked up his phone and hit a speed dial number as he continued his walk down the ramps. "Johnathan, good afternoon... No, I don't need the car today, I'm heading to the Lab... I heard... No, not today. He's covering a meeting for me... Yes, I think Mr. Boyd should accompany you on your next trip to the facility... I suspect you will have a splendid, and uninterrupted, conversation about any new friends he may have in private there... I'm certain... I hope he has the right answers for you and you clear him for a speedy return to work... Yes, severance will be granted if that's the unfortunate necessity." The director hung up the phone and let his smile mask slip and frowned.

Damn, Barry would be hard to replace so close to the exercise. But the ledger must stay balanced and if he's now compromised and likely tainted, he's a liability. There's nothing the Fae can do about the exercise, even if they got everything from Barry. But, the Summit. Ah, that could be a problem. Johnathan will find out what he said soon enough.

The Director entered the control room and waited for the heavy security door to seal behind him. At nearly 18 inches thick, it seemed like it would have been better suited for a battleship than a Pentagon sub-basement room. It was the third one the Director had to pass through to reach this particular cramped control room. The lead engineer glanced over at the Director distractedly as he was feverishly typing commands into his keyboard and barking numbers out to the engineers seated on each side of him. "Good afternoon, Kelvin, capacitors are loaded and we're almost... Fuck, Akber! I said the five channel, not the four! You ignorant ass. Adjust by .097 before you turn us into mush...".

The Director ignored the language and use of his first name in an office environment while his engineer browbeat the other engineer staff into bringing the system into proper alignment. His lead engineer, Doctor John Shotwell, was the only human he had found that could maintain control over the most powerful weapon ever installed underneath the Pentagon. The mechanical and

Blood War: Rage

digital integration to sequence the firing protocols was always a millisecond misalignment away from exploding. A singular weapon with a singular purpose. The Portal Cannon. The massive eight-foot diameter octagonal barrel, eight chambered rail gun spanned a hundred meters in length deep under the office floors. The capacitor bank installation alone had required the repurposing of an entire underground motor pool. Simply to house the energy storage banks required a single, synchronized, eight shot kinetic attack in a ten by ten-meter room. The control room they were standing in was located halfway down the length of the railgun barrels that were obscured behind the wall in front of him.

"Pay attention next time, dickweed." Dr. Shotwell tossed an M&M at the offending engineer then swiveled to face the Director. "All set, Kelvin. Our end is primed for your call. A tad more warning before a visit next time would be swell you know. Akber was rushing his shit and almost turned us into smashed cherry gelatin on accident but we're ready. I can't speak for your freaks down the hall with all their weird voodoo shit, but that's not my business. My business is ensuring I can terminate your call in a few milliseconds if protocols are engaged."

"Thank you, Doctor Shotwell. For obvious reasons I sincerely hope you don't get to see your beautiful creation in use today."

"Ah don't worry, Boss, you'd never know it happened anyway. I'd have to send a crew into the Phone Booth with shop vacs to suck up your misty residue as soon as the Sergeant Major allowed a cleanup crew entry."

"Yes, well, on with it then. Please signal ahead to the "weird voodoo" team that I'm on my way." The Director positioned himself in front of a digital panel adjacent to the massive steel door leading further down the rail guns path. "Lab Engineer, I am ICER Director Kelvin Ordonio requesting access to the Phone Booth by authority of the President of the United States of America." The Director placed his palm on a biometrics panel, feeling a quick prick of a needle that extracted a drop of his blood. His palm and retina were then scanned by the system.

"Lead Lab Engineer, Doctor John Shotwell, confirms, via three-way biometrics, including blood, the identity of ICER Director, Kelvin Ordonio, who has requested access to the phone booth by authority of the President of the United States of America. Access is granted." All three engineers in the control room responded in sequence, "Confirmed." Then typed in independent codes to each of their control terminals.

The Director heard hydraulics hiss as the door braces disengaged and he proceeded through and down the stainless steel tunnel with the door closing swiftly behind him. He moved toward the last door guarded by a single soldier. A series of red LEDs flashed in the hallway as a soft voice stated pleasantly from a recessed speaker, "The range is now hot. All personnel in the phone booth are now considered under the legal jurisdiction of a Final Protocol."

The Director shook his head just slightly. *All this nonsense. So unnecessary. But, this is what happens when you let politicians designate the protocols for government-sanctioned portal openings.*

"Good afternoon, Sergeant Major. How are you today?" The Director addressed the stone-faced senior Army Non-Commissioned Officer standing at the final door to the Phone Booth. The Sergeant Major held a wired analog trigger grip in one hand and had an electrode running out of his uniform sleeve into a wall panel. The electrode was the NCO's second dead man's switch.

"I'm just fine, sir." The soldier turned and looked through a peephole in the last door before moving his free hand to grasp a simple mechanical level in the door. "Seems the mages are ready to open the call now."

"Well then, Sergeant Major, there's no time like the present."

The NCO looked the at Director with cold formality stating "Sir, the Phone Booth is now a live range and you are subject to the legal jurisdiction of a Final Protocol upon entry. I will not be able to hear anything that is said in the Phone Booth. All electronics are

Blood War: Rage

rendered useless when the call is connected. I will only be able to see into the booth though this single armored glass viewport. If at any time I perceive any possibility of a threat attempting to exit the phone booth room, the jurisdiction of a Final Protocol signed by the POTUS, grants me personal subjective authority to release my dead man's switch activating the portal cannon. There will be absolutely no chance of any human, or other, survival within the Phone Booth upon the termination of the call through this process. Do you understand? Please respond yes, or no."

"Yes, Sergeant Major, I do."

The soldier turned and pulled up the door latch then pushed the heavy steel plating inward allowing the director entry into the Phone Booth.

The Phone Booth was a perfect ten by ten by ten clean steel room with only two exceptions. On the wall with the single off-centered door was the eight-foot octagonal barrel grouping of eight independent rail guns, the very end of the Portal Gun barrel. Etched onto the floor were a series of wards to assist the Mages in opening, and controlling, the eight-foot diameter portal to the demon realm that would appear exactly opposite of the Portal Gun's barrels. After he entered the Phone Booth the Director's smile mask fell away, completely exposing a face filled with disdain as he addressed the three mages spaced precisely around the warded circle. It always bothered the Director how many mages it took to hold open a portal of this size but trial and error had confirmed that at least three were always needed. "Open the fucking call right now." The Director growled at the mages.

Soon, soon. After the last call is made I'm going to shove every one of you filthy aberrations into this Phone Booth and let the Sergeant Major send all of your corrupted souls to the true Hell.

The mages did not respond, but the center mage in the portal's key holder position proceeded with a final series of hand motions and completed the waiting link. The wall opposite the mouth of the portal gun became the focal point for a rapidly expanded glowing shimmer. It was as if the very steel wall was now a luminescent liquid plane of rippling energy. The director could feel the jarring screech of the portal's energy in his bones with its incessant hum that seemed to penetrate his skull.

Come on you filthy bastard, I don't have all day.

"Bezzid, don't make me stand here all day. I know you can hear me. You and I have things to discuss." Kelvin shouted at the portal.

The seven-foot bipedal demon, with overlapped armored scales and spikes that looked like a cross between a nightmare insect and giant medieval knight, stepped through the portal into the Phone Booth. The Director had met with Bezzid in the Phone Booth dozens of times now and was no longer shocked at his appearance. He barely moved as the demon emerged from its side of the realm wall.

"What do you want human?" Bezzid's voice rumbled from beneath the tendrils hanging in front of its mouth as the Horde leader glared down at the human ICER Director.

"You know what I want, demon. I want you to meet me on the challenge field of battle like you promised so we can finish this once and for all. You are going to fulfill your end of the bargain. We will put our best against your best and end this. I'm going to destroy you, then fracture the realm wall preventing your filth from ever stepping foot into my realm again."

"You, human, speak like a true Demon. Bezzid has accepted your challenge. Bezzid brings the horde across to destroy you, and your best. Proving to all demons that your realm is now ours and ready for harvesting. Bezzid is pleased that you have taken to the ways of the True Lord. It will not save you, or your kind, but the True Lord may show mercy upon your soul on your harvest day."

"We will see, Bezzid. You are going to fail. Then your overlords will finally understand that nothing waits for your cursed kind here except death and the losses of all your resources."

"Your words speak honor to the True Lord. It shall be a great day when your blood becomes mine. Speak quickly, what is it that you've asked Bezzid here for?" Bezzid began to slowly stroke a single long talon down its arm. The sound of the talon grating

Blood War: Rage

across its armored plates made the director flinch.

Kelvin's face contorted in anger as he pointed at the demonic general and tried to keep his voice calm "I need you to follow the plan. If we are to summon the great battle challenge, then that must be done in accordance with the ledgers. You know this, you agreed to this! Don't mince words with me about your True Lord when you can't even control your minions that violate our agreements. They send dozens of your wretched kind through the portals. I've heard of your attempts to kill the old war veterans. The 'Demon Hunters'. We agreed that it was only a small number of lesser demons that are allowed to cross over. I've taken those resources as my own, destroyed them, and I grow tired of playing games with you. If you wish to waste our time, then you will never be granted the battle that you desire to appease your True Lord. You will never rise above your ranks and will be nothing but an insignificant slave to your Overlord forever."

Bezzid paused for a moment and glanced at the edges of the portal cannon barrel, before answering. "Bezzid understands your words human. Some of Bezzid's sub horde commanders became over-exuberant in their fulfillment of the rage and need of blood vengeance on your warrior clan. Bezzid will ensure they are dealt with. Bezzid expects you to fulfill your end of bargain."

"Have no doubt demon. We will meet you at the challenge field. We will destroy your poisoned blood. It will never be reconstituted to your horde."

Bezzid tilted his head slightly towards the Director, "You are a small and weak human, but Bezzid gives you respect for your understanding of the True Lord. Yes, your death will grant me great power. Your army's blood will fuel my machines. Your words are understood, human. Bezzid agrees the ledgers are to be maintained. Bezzid will fulfill my end of the bargain and keep the numbers of incursions as agreed. In doing so, you must force your overlord to grant you the power to open the great portals, once again allowing for us to meet and decide the final fate of our realms."

Doug Burbey & Mel Todd

"You do that," he nearly spat at the demon, "and I will get the portals open. I will destroy you and your monstrous creations. You will meet your True Lord in whatever hell you believe he resides in. We defeated your blight once and now we will defeat you again."

The plan depended on drawing the demons into the open and into the fight. He needed to prove to all of the world's leaders, that the treaty could never hold and that the demons would never abide by it. Once he, and his like-minded directors, were given unbounded authority they would ensure that the capability of magic was eradicated forever. It was the only way to prevent the demons from ever returning. Even if the ICERS had to kill every single being with the potential to learn magic on Earth. Beezid gave him the perfect opportunity and the perfect justification. When the major demon incursion happened, the ICERS were now prepared to instantly shift all portals to a site of his own choosing. This preplanned exercise will be the ambush in which the demons will be eradicated before they can even comprehend they have fallen into a trap.

"We are agreed, human. Bezzid will maintain my end of the bargain. You will balance your soul with whatever Pagan Lord you grovel to. Soon, this will be done forever."

Kelvin reached up and straightened the knot on his tie slightly then buttoned the top button of his suit coat, "We are done then I believe. Would you be so kind as to get the fuck out of my realm now."?

Chapter 39 - Puzzle Pieces

Toy fit into Shane's life too well, as if she'd always been there. He almost felt bad for still calling her Toy but her name wouldn't stay in his head for anything and Toy did. Either way, he didn't care enough to spend any time worrying about it. Too many other things pulled for his attention.

He had to put together the information Barry had provided and match it up with what that department did. The information made him frown. Worse, he'd finally given in and looked up Declan. Part of him ached to ring up the man who'd been his brother and go get a beer, but that option had turned to ash a long time ago.

Shane sat back, looking at the information on his screen. If you knew where to look, you could find almost anything. Declan Kenner owned a nice piece of property not too far from here.

"Why, DK? What the hell got you back into the demon hunting business? I figured you'd run away to an island somewhere, where no one could ever attack you again."

Most hunters avoided open water; something huge and demonic was still down there, even if no one ever talked about.

It didn't take much more digging. Declan really needed to lock down his information more. He'd created a nice place and the satellite picture hinted that he'd fortified it heavily. The occasional post from the local VFW proved he was there, more often than not. He remained on good terms with at least a few veterans, and maybe a bit more. So he was not a complete hermit. That was good, right?

With a bit more effort, Shane had always enjoyed a bit of hacking, and he found the odd deposits from a government account into his bank.

"Huh. Government is paying you? For what? Who's sending you money old friend?" The words sliced at him as he spoke them, then hung in the air and taunted him.

Was Declan still a friend? Up until the hearings, he'd thought he'd died. Had assumed they had all died. They should have. He almost did.

Shane shook his head avoiding the thought; memories like that were counterproductive. He'd killed their friendship when he'd walked away, so it didn't matter, but, as always, knowledge was power. It took some time, but he finally managed to backtrack it. Everything ended up back at that director and his little agency - International Cooperative Emergency Response.

Declan had somehow gotten mixed up with the guy who was killing or converting hunters. Why? He rubbed his head and shut the browser windows. Declan was the past. All that mattered now was the future.

"Shane?" Toy's voice broke into his thoughts and he blinked, having forgotten she was there. Not good - that was how people got killed. He turned to look at her leaning on the door jamb and looking at him, her green eyes still as guileless as that first day.

I'll never understand women.

"Yes?"

If she wants ice cream or thinks I need to eat healthier, I'll go crazy.

Something in him shied away from the idea of killing her but she was a risk. Risk needed to be removed and dead people weren't dangerous.

"Frax says Bezzid wants to talk to you."

Shane froze looking at her. There was no smirk, no glee, just waiting for him to respond.

"He asked for me by name?" His voice cautious as he scrambled.

"Well, he asked for Marcus Vipsanius. I assumed he meant you." She frowned at him. "Or are you not Marcus Vipsanius anymore? I can tell him no. Frax said Bezzid had questions."

271

Blood War: Rage

"What sort of questions?"

Toy shrugged. "I don't think Frax is told stuff like that. He's kind of like a dog. Bezzid said fetch, he fetched." She blinked at him and he swore for a moment her eyes brightened in color. "Do you want to talk to him?"

Shane rolled it over in his head but in the end no matter the risks, there really wasn't a choice. "Yes."

"Okay, I'll open a portal." She started to wave her hand and he bolted up.

"Not here. Back in the living area."

"Oh, okay." She shrugged and turned back to the living room. "Mind if I make some popcorn?"

Popcorn? Why did she want popcorn?

Shane pushed his mind away from that thought as he tried to focus on how to use this to get the answers he wanted.

"Fine."

"Good, I love popcorn. It never clashes with the blood scent."

Wait! What?

Shane shook his head.

I don't understand women and that one is odder than the rest of them put together.

With quick strokes, he listed out what he knew. Director of a program killing hunters, working with demons, and some sort of Summit where everything would change.

And I still don't know how or why DK seems to be in the middle of this.

He growled at himself and stalked out. Toy sat on the couch with a big bowl of half-popped microwave popcorn in her lap; she stared at the wall.

"Toy?"

"Yes?"

"Why are you staring at the wall?"

"I'm watching."

"Watching what?" He glanced at the wall to make sure it hadn't changed from the beige blandness it had been last time he looked.

Nope, still the same.

"Angels. They are more boring than you think. All that pretty sterility and no joy."

"Uh huh. You can open the portal now." He fought the urge to step back a bit. How crazy was she?

"Sure." She looked away from the wall, at the center of the room, and waved her hand. A small circle appeared and grew to about the size of a large oval mirror like you'd see at a vanity in the old movies. "Hey, Frax?" Her voice was no more excited or worried than it had been when she asked him if he wanted to talk to a demon.

"Yes?" The word had too many consonants, but he could still understand it.

"He's here if you want to get your boss. Or we can watch Stargate."

"Ooh, the swooshy one? Frax would like that, but Horde Lord Bezzid insistent. Bring shortly, swooshy later?"

"Maybe? Depends on our bosses?"

"Understand," the voice replied. Everything went quiet.

Shane stood and waited. This portal was large enough that he would be able to see the demon. Maybe.

"Toy, is this portal like a window?"

She cast him a look. "No, it's like a portal."

He forced himself to take a deep breath and remind himself who he talked to.

"I meant, can we both see each other."

"Sure. You have to stand in front of it there," she pointed at a spot on the floor about five feet from the portal. A bit too close for Shane's comfort; some of those demons had long arms. "Then if Bezzid stands on the other side about the same place you should see each other."

As she talked a figure moved into view on the other side and Shane paled. There had only been a few higher demons seen on the battlefields, and they had killed soldiers by the dozens when they attacked. They ripped open tanks. He rubbed his hands on his pants trying to dry his suddenly sweaty palms.

Maybe this wasn't such a good idea.

The portal pointed at layers of carapace on the demon about where Shane would have expected a belly button on a human. A grunt emerged from the other side and the being lowered until his face peered back at Shane.

"For a deadly race with many formidable weapons, humans are small and soft." His voice was a flat rumble and again Shane felt like he only heard half of what had been communicated.

"Yes, we are. But we know how to use blood and how to kill as well as any demon. So why did you want to speak to Marcus Vipsanius?"

A sharp barking sound emerged from the demon and something that might have been called a smile spread across its face. But with that many teeth and tentacles, humor is not what Shane felt.

"Yes, humans did well. The elemental fire air caused many strange things but what it did to the blood. Ah, if Bezzid had the power to make more of that blood, no boundaries could hold me but that is limited. Bah, not what Bezzid here to ask."

"Really, Francis of the Lighten Up, what did you want to ask?" Shane drawled trying not to show how his mind raced at those strange words.

Fire air, what the hell is fire air?

"Bezzid is still not Francis. Though the concept of lightening up is odd. Do you set the Francis on fire or do you remove layers of carapace to create the lightning?"

Shane blinked thrown off track by the question.

"Neither, it means to not be so serious."

"Ah. Interesting. Bezzid will remember. In the challenge battle for Earth, Kelvin will cheat. That is expected. Hence, Bezzid cheats also. Though it is more of wise planning than cheating. Bezzid asks, how many of these hunters, like the DK, will be facing us?"

Battle for Earth? What fucking battle for Earth? What the hell is going on?

Doug Burbey & Mel Todd

"Why would I tell you? I don't want Earth to be lost to you." Shane countered, trying hard to keep his face neutral though he didn't know if Bezzid could read him. Behind him, Toy crunched on her half-popped popcorn.

"Because Bezzid will make a trade. The Heart of Kali, the demon bible, will be yours for this information."

"Why would you trade that to me, oh great malodorous one?"

All those teeth appeared again. Shane had a flash of what it would feel like to have them sink into his thigh and had to fight back nausea.

"Because you would not have much time, a small span of time or perhaps a medium span, but either way the book would drain you and when Bezzid takes Earth it would be mine again. But you would have your heart's desire, would you not?"

"When would you invade?"

"On the date arranged, of course. This scheduled warfare seems unintelligent, but if humans want to offer themselves to my horde, Bezzid will not refuse. Your human blood is always welcome."

"What would the Heart show me?"

"Everything. It is our creation, our history, our triumphs, our failures, our blood. But over the eons, it has become its own being. When that much blood is used in creation, life can take unusual forms."

The demon lord reached down and picked up an object and held it. Heavy and square, it looked like a book you'd see in a museum. One printed by Gutenberg or some such, and even through the portal, it called to him, the corruptions and power singing a sweet song.

"Stop," Toy's voice said and he blinked, looking at her and realized he'd taken two steps forward which almost put him within reach of a long arm. From the smirk on Bezzid's face, he'd realized that too.

"I'll need to think about it. How can I know if you are telling the truth?"

Blood War: Rage

He smiled with too many teeth and Shane wondered if Bezzid tried to mimic human expressions? If so, it didn't work.

"You cannot. But are you willing to give up the opportunity for this knowledge?" The book appeared again and called to Shane, though he didn't move this time.

"If it just kills me, it doesn't do me much good."

"Maybe you will be smarter than those before you and you will find a way to soothe the heart of Kali." His voice held sweet temptation and Shane narrowed his eyes. The Fae used the same sort of temptation.

"Perhaps. I'll think on it."

The book disappeared and Bezzid shrugged. "Your choice to make for Kali. Don't take much time to decide. The end for you is coming. Soon all your hunters, the ones that try kill my kind, will be gone and Bezzid will have no need to bargain with any."

"Fine, I'll get you the numbers. I'll contact you when I have them. Where is the battle to be?"

Those teeth gleamed in the light from the other side.

"In the white mall, a mighty battle and Bezzid will drink his fill of human blood. But why waste so many hordes if Bezzid can learn ahead of time how many will await our arrival and work on reducing that number? Have your slave contact Bezzid's when you are ready to trade. Maybe you tame the Heart of Kali."

With that, the connection snapped closed leaving Shane standing there staring at the wall.

"Are you going to tell him?" Toy's question, spoken with her mouth half full of popcorn, pulled him out of his reverie.

"Hell no but I want that book."

"It will kill you?"

"Maybe, but it will also tell me how to create my own world, Then I can go there and leave this world behind." He looked at her as he said it, braced for anger, pouting or something.

"Interesting plan," She tilted her head considering him. "A new world. That could be interesting. If the book doesn't kill you, which it will."

276

"Ah, but how fast? Can I learn what I need and destroy it before it kills me?" he asked, even as he started towards his desk.

I have to warn DK. This is all coming to a head and I'm beginning to think I need him and his power to create my world.

"53 hours, 24 minutes, and thirteen seconds of direct interaction. Darn, the portal closed and we were going to watch Stargate. Oh well."

Toy got up and wandered into the kitchen oblivious to the way he stared at her as she left.

Fuck me. What is she?

Blood War: Rage

Chapter 40 – Grilling Up the Past

Declan sat on his back patio, drinking a beer and enjoying the silence. The blessed silence. He stared at the expensive Weber grill wondering if the steak was ready to be turned.

Don't flip it too soon. Don't fiddle. Patience is a virtue. Gordon Ramsey says to only flip twice, and that's just for the perfect grill marks. Oh yeah, gotta make it sexy.

A telltale pop emitted from the rusty old bird feeder hanging from a hook in the yard. Looking over Declan saw a faint blue glow emanating from the metal cage. A simple low magic charm, but unobtrusive and efficient for a warning device. There were several of them spread around his thickly wooded property. Someone had used magic within a half mile of his house. Nestled deep in the woods, with the nearest neighbor 3 miles away, Declan didn't get guests. The charms were proximity alarms. Declan instinctively slid his hand down to his thigh holster just to verify what he already knew, that the Glock was there and flipped open the holster release catch. He slowly withdrew the weapon and sat it on his thigh as he closed his eyes to sense. He took another drink of the beer as he pulled up his external cameras on his phone looking for the intruder then waited.

It only took Declan ten seconds to identify the approaching visitor. The unmistakable musk of a human, dosing demon and Fae blood, with a burnt musk chaser of twisting magic, meant it could only be one type of person. Although confused as to why a mage would be coming to the warded home of a demon hunter.

Knowing that the unwanted guest approached, he stood up walked to his grill with the calm illusion that he was unaware. Sensing the movement coming around the side of his house he

278

made it clear he knew who was there. "What do you want, mage?" Declan said, as he turned to look behind to the approaching man and froze.

The Caucasian man of average height, athletic build, military 'high fade' haircut, a fully non-military 'foo man choo' mustache, wearing jeans and a Guns and Roses concert t-shirt broke into a grin. Above the grin, his eyes glowed a dark unnatural blue.

"Come on DK, who doesn't want a visit from a friend? I came by to say hi. Maybe have a few beers. So, what are you grilling in there?"

The voice slammed into him like a bullet from the past. He closed his eyes as he faced the grill, glad his back was to the traitor.

He's alive. After all these years, he's still alive and walks back into my life now? Why the fuck now?

"Bullshit Shane. One, I don't have any friends."

"Oh, yes you do" Shane interrupted. "You got that hot MILF you work for."

How the hell does he know about Cordy? And she's a mom?

"No, she's an acquaintance and I'm an independent contractor, so I don't work for anybody but myself."

"Whatever she's still hot."

"Two, you never come by just to say "Hi.""

"Three, I told you explicitly that as far as I was concerned you were dead to me and if I ever saw you again I'd kill you." His voice was cold, even as he kept his hand clenched on the gun so Shane couldn't see it shake.

"Why you got to be melodramatic DK? You are so full of shit and full of yourself." Shane spoke as he walked around looking at the place, his body calm and relaxed, but Declan knew damn well he could react with magic in a second.

"That's part of the problem, Shane. I may be full of shit but you're the one who's full of himself." He didn't take his eyes off Shane even as his mind went into overdrive.

"Damn it, Declan." Shane reached into the patio beer cooler

Blood War: Rage

and helped himself to a Yuengling, twisting the top off in a smooth practiced motion pitching the cap in the air. The cap hung in the air slowly tumbling end over end until Shane made a flicking motion with his finger and it continued naturally back to flight in the direction of the bushes. "You can really hold a fucking grudge you know that?"

"It's not a grudge I hold against you, Shane. I'm just done with you. What do you want?" Declan snapped back.

"I've got something that you need."

"I don't need anything that you've got to offer, Shane. I'm not a coward. I didn't abandon my friends and run just because it got real. And I've never needed your magic crap. You know I refused the training, so I've got no use for you or what you're addicted to."

"Too bad. You could have been better than me I think. You were the natural at it. And no one should have walked off Ypsilanti alive. I think the only reason you did it is because of me. You can say thank you now." Shane smirked at him and Declan fought not to deck him. "Now you really need what I have. Information. You may not want it, but I'm going to tell it to you anyway. You may have decided to be a raging asshole about everything, but I still have a heart."

"Me? The raging asshole? Maybe. But I'm not the deserter." Declan laughed sarcastically while slowly moving the Glock back into its holster and snapping the latch closed.

Shane stilled for a second facing away from Declan. He cleared his throat and continued. "You need to know that you've been making some people pretty pissed off."

Laughing, "Well hell Shane, I'm sure that's a long fucking list every day. It was always my best aspect."

"No, when I said, people, I was using that term very loosely." Shane sat down on a wooden slat patio chair taking another long pull off the beer and looking at Declan seriously.

"DK, your name, well the projection of your name at least, is actually passing around some of the inner rings right now. That's not good by the way."

Doug Burbey & Mel Todd

"You mean I've made the Inner Ring Gazette? Or some vibey cross realm communications bullshit that you mages came up with? You guys do blogs with demon land now?"

"Well, you're not far off on that, DK. And no, I don't run a blog on demon information. My website is strictly for porn and you already know that. Man has to have a paying job of course." A sly smile crossed Shane's face and even Declan grinned a bit but he made it go away as he stared at the man he'd once loved as a brother.

"What I'm trying to tell you is things are moving again. I know that even though you act like you're a moron, and pretend not to give a shit, you actually do. The demons are moving around and plotting just like every government in the human realm is. It's a cold war and everyone knows it. You and I both know there's going to be another war eventually, even if everyone else is pretending like there won't be."

"Get to your point, Shane, and that's the only beer you get. I'm serious about that shit. I don't want to make a beer run as I've already had like six already."

Shane took a drag of his beer then sat it down looking at DK straight in the eyes. "The name is Bezzid. It's not well-liked among some of its peers in the realm and it is sure as hell is not going to be liked in the human realm soon."

"Why do I give a shit about whether or not a demon is liked by another damn demon?"

"DK, did you know that demons aren't supposed to like each other by their basic nature? They must compete and maneuver for power against each other if they're not at war with another species. It's like a bloodlust to dominate and control constantly pumping through their veins."

Shane paused, "It's in their nature, above everything else, they must have power and must use that power against someone or thing."

"Why?" Declan asked even as he fought not to deck or hug the man.

Blood War: Rage

Why is Shane really here?

"I don't know. Maybe they get depressed and have to watch reruns of 1970s sitcoms on TV as a punishment. Who gives a shit?! Either way, there's a pretty crafty bastard in the fourth or fifth ring that's planning a play that's going to involve us, one way or the other. But what really worries me is that it's the Director of the ICERs he is colluding with. I'm bringing this to your attention because you've already mucked up a couple of his initial plans. That's put you on his list. There ain't shit I can do about it besides tell you. So, watch your ass. There, I think that's one of the damn favors I owe you cashed in. And I'm not including this beer as I'm taking this one and fuck you, it's gratis."

The ICER's director? Working with a demon? No way Cordy would have anything to do with that. Could he possibly be telling me the truth? Can I possibly trust anything Shane tells me anymore? I thought he was dead, I hoped he was dead.

"Thanks. I appreciate the heads up. I'll watch my back." The words were honest, even as he had no idea what to believe or who to trust.

"I'm not really concerned about that so much, Declan. I just owed you and I don't like to owe anybody anything that can't be paid for in blood. One day you're going to see that I'm right, and I'd love to have you cross over with me. We could do great things together."

"Fuck you, Shane, that's not going to happen. You chose which side you were on and betrayed us. I don't think I'm going to get over that shit anytime soon. But since you brought it up, what is it that Bezzid is planning on doing?"

"He is going to break the Treaty and try to restart the war, and humans are helping."

This got Declan's attention. He stopped and stared at Shane, feeling an involuntary tic developing on his face.

"The treaty can't be broken and you know that, Shane. The Fae enchantment was sealed with blood, then spoken by that ring seven demon committee, and finally blood signed by the ring eight

282

Demon Lord. Only the ring nine demon God can break it itself. And the demons don't know how to talk directly to this "God" even if it really exists. I'm pretty sure that demon buddy of yours doesn't have to juice to pull off some type of bullshit like that."

This can't be right. And after all Shane and I went through together in the war, how can he be nonchalant about wholesale slaughter? How would he know this? Is he that chummy with the demons?

"If he does, rumor has it he has some type of weapon that was derived from the Blood War. He thinks he can use it to launch some sort of blistering attack back into the humans and impress his higher masters after he gets the war started up. Ta Da, instant demon promotion. Were you listening when I said it's in their nature to use power to conquer? I don't know what weapon he's got up his sleeve, but the intel is good. He's definitely got something and don't think for a minute that he won't put it in play."

"Let's say you are right, Shane. Then what do you think we should do about it?"

Shane hesitated for a moment. He finished his beer in a long pull, tossed the can towards the bushes, then with a twist of his hands sent a fluid-like streak of glowing energy forward, melting the can in midair. The bird feeder shrieked and sparked with the pulse of the near-magic release.

"Humanity dies," Shane said softly as he stood looking up directly at Declan. "We won't win a second Blood War, DK. We fought our fight. I'm not going to die here. If you stay, well then you get farmed like the rest of the fucking cattle. You need to seriously rethink your position. I'm almost ready and when the realm veil weakens in the demon assault, you and I need to go. And fucking fast! You have to trust me. It's solid. But if I have just a little more time, I think that together we'll be able to take a few dozen people with us. We will rebuild all of human existence and get it right this time. Without you... well, I'll just start it all over again without bothering with all the baggage."

Blood War: Rage

DK saw the magic-twisted eyes of his best friend glowing sharp and intense. Radiating with restrained power. His combat senses forced themselves forward into his body, tingling and tensing every nerve ending and straining to invoke fight or flight for survival. He tamped it back with deliberate effort and a minor amount of his own inner magically enhanced power reserves.

Shit, I can taste the magic rolling off him. He thinks he can actually do this. Am I more afraid of him? Or a second Demon War?

"Get out Shane. I think we're done here."

Shane smirked at him one last time and turned and walked down his driveway with a saunter in his walk.

His alarm went off and he watched a car pull up, driven by a pale redheaded woman, who waited until Shane climbed in the car. Then she waved at him with a smile and drove back down the driveway. Shane never looked back.

Thoughts roiled in his head and dread tied his stomach into a knot when a whiff of smoke redirected his attention to the steaks.

"Fuck!" He threw open the lid and stared mournfully down at the two hockey pucks laying on the grill. "Dammit, Shane. Those were good steaks." His lost meal was easier to focus on than the words of someone he'd once trusted with his life.

Chapter 41 – Lighten up Georgetown

Declan stood outside the Foggy Bottom Metro Station to get his bearings. According to the mission intelligence summary that Cordy had sent him, this should be a simple cleanup job. Even after the war ended it wasn't unheard of for an occasional stray demon that had survived the battles to have successfully hidden away in the human realm. Some had even been captured and for some ridiculously unfathomable reason been kept in illegal labs to be experimented on or as a perverse sort of pet for a rich idiot.

Always a bad idea, they always get out somehow. Didn't anyone watch those dinosaur island movies?

Declan suspected that the ICER intelligence he received was manipulated. Now he always suspected he was being misled. Cordy briefed him that this was a glorified dog catcher mission. One, or possibly two, ring ones had been making a nuisance of themselves in the Georgetown area. They had been rummaging through trash bins and eating small animals. What brought it to the attention of the ICERs was the upswing, reported by the local police, in finding the bodies of homeless people that had apparently been partially eaten by wild animals. Some rather astute detectives had realized that they might not be dealing with a standard wild-animal-in-the-city attack. They became concerned that this was possibly a case of a stray demon left over from the war. Since that clearly fell in the ICERs jurisdiction, the Washington Police Department decided it was the Feds job to deal with it.

Even with the liberalization of open and concealed carry firearms laws after the war, Washington D.C. was still not

285

Blood War: Rage

considered a very friendly place to go around openly carrying a firearm. To avoid attracting attention Declan conducted this mission with a lighter loadout than normal. He wore his long hunter's coat, as they were still trending in the fashion world, or so he heard. Instead of his heavier load bearing body armor, he wore a more concealable soft Kevlar vest underneath his shirt and jacket. Add that to his jeans and heavy combat boots he did look like a middle-aged man trying to look cool by dressing trendy. This earned him a few smirks from the college set as they walked by but the sultry glance from an attractive brunette coed walking past him did get his attention.

If it wasn't for the fact that I bet you're carrying a lot of baggage, and daddy issues, lady, I might just buy you a drink. Declan thought, as some rather non-parental thoughts crossed his mind while he watched her walk away. He pulled his eyes off the temptation and then took a moment to consider how to proceed with his hunt. With the unfortunate lack of screaming, and panicked, civilians running around shouting "demon!" he was going to have to do this the hard way.

Where would I be hiding out if I was demon lost in the big scary city?

The thought of strolling into one of the numerous Irish pubs in the area, having a few drinks, and just waiting for the lucky break of a screaming and panicked mob running past was appealing. Or, he could try to tap into his reserves and enhance his senses. Maybe then he would catch a break and feel, or smell, his prey. But that would require him to dose on Reset again. Although each time he did, it seemed to take longer to push the rage back.

I definitely do not need to be building up a tolerance. That would be no bueno amigo. Although if I get this shit done quick enough, I might be able to figure out which bar that cute brunette with daddy issues went into. It has been a while.

"Shit. I'm not a monk, though Cordy is probably more in my league." He snorted at that thought. "Please, Cordy is further out of my league than that woman was." Declan looked up and down

286

the crossroads for the metro station. It was a heavy traffic day area with lots of people coming and going, lots of vehicle traffic, and the general chaotic movement of city life.

This was not exactly where I would be hanging out if I was a stray demon from the war that had enough smarts to remain relatively hidden away for the last three years. This little bastard's not going to be making itself a regular around here.

Declan brought up the incident map on his phone and then placed markers on locations that the ICER reports had shown bodies being found. There were six markers in an approximate seven block radius that all took place within the last 60 days, mostly near the Potomac River and canal area.

Well come on, old man, you may as well start with the freshest and work out from there.

After leaving the fourth site, and three hours of walking, Declan began to think he was on a wild goose chase. A conversation with a group of homeless along the Potomac, near the canal bridge, directed him towards something that might pan out. They had confirmed at least some of Cordelia's intelligence. Two of them described a dark reddish porcupine-like creature, around two or three-foot-tall, with six or eight legs, that made a clattering noise when it ran. They claimed it also had a fanged mouth where it's stomach should be. Lately it had been coming out at night and snatching people who were wandering around alone too close to the woods.

Skitter demon. Nasty bastards in a swarm but alone it should be easy enough to take care of.

Declan noted that although they had given the creature's description to the local police, they were apparently discarded as ramblings and not properly recorded. If they had been taken seriously, the police should have dispatched the local Tactical Team, or at least the ICERs should have been called immediately to verify. Even though your average person no longer expected to ever deal with demons again, responsible law enforcement personnel should have taken these reports seriously. Strays still did

Blood War: Rage

pop up every now and then. It was borderline irresponsible that multiple killings, and witness statements of demons in the area, was not responded to sooner.

Why am I the first one to respond here? I really need to ask Cordelia what's wrong with the data intelligence sharing between agencies. This level of incompetent groundwork is bad, even for government bureaucrats. All this damn government propaganda of "There is no more demon threat" that is being pushed nonstop is starting to make people actually believe that bullshit. It makes them stupid. The fools just want to believe it more than accept that the world has changed forever.

Ten minutes later Declan moved slowly through the underbrush of the wooded area along the Potomac canal. Dusk approached and the woods were already starting to darken. He needed to find some trace of where the skitter was hiding so that he could set up an ambush to take care of it when it emerged.

"Now this is what I was looking for." Declan spotted an irregular series of tracks. "Now, unless deer started walking with clawed feet spaced two feet apart from each other. I think I got you, ya little bastard."

He drew his pistol from the holster underneath his coat with one hand and his heavy combat knife with the other. As he began to follow the trail of broken limbs and muddy claw prints in the ground, he let his senses sharpen.

Just a little now, just a little. I don't need much.

The woods began to brighten and amplified sounds began to trickle in as his body responded to its base instinct for survival. He stood for a moment, absorbing his surroundings, when he heard human voices coming from in front of him in the direction the skitter trail was leading him. He began to move as quietly as possible towards the voices.

Crap, that's all I need. Some kind of homeless encampment setting up in a skitter hunting ground.

As he moved deeper into the woods, and the sunlight faded further, he began to see a glow through the trees in front of him.

Then he felt it. The unmistakable pulsing vibration and almost audible humming of the portal.

"Son of a bitch."

Cordy's intelligence is worth a grand total of jack fucking shit. Stray demons can't open portals.

Declan had moved far enough into the woods, closer to the portal, that he could now make out discernible voices.

"But why are there so many?" An agitated human voice was shouting.

"Volget do as need. You keeps open!" The unmistakable growling bark of a demon struggling with a human language responded.

Shit. That's either a ring three or damn smart ring two down there.

Declan dropped to one knee trying to assess the situation and instinctively reached into his coat to grab his rifle.

Dammit, left all my gear in my truck. This was just supposed to be a stray hunt.

A second human voice, barely able to contain his fear, answered the demon "You are just supposed to be bringing one or two skitters. This is way too many!"

" Volget bring, Volget want. You keeps door. Volget go, you keep open. Volget return with more. You keep door for Volget return are raid. Soon back. Skitters guard. Door close, skitters kill all." The demon grumbled back. Declan could hear the clattering of skitters starting to move around the glow in the woods in front of him.

Fuck, there must be at least a dozen, or more, of those things in here now.

Declan backed out of the woods the way he came. He caught glimpses of movement between himself and the glow of the portal between the trees.

I don't have enough firepower with me to take out over dozen skitters and a soldier demon. I should have just followed that brunette to whatever bar she was heading to.

Blood War: Rage

Turning he moved quietly, as fast as he could, to get to the main road by the canal bridge. Declan pulled out his phone and called up a newly added number. "Kayter... Yeah, it's Kenner... Yes, right now... My intel was total crap. I need backup and more damn firepower. Right now... First, stop at the Springfield Metro station where you'll find my truck parked and grab my green bag out of it... Yes, out of my truck. Then bring the bag to me at the canal bridge in Georgetown... With the damn keypad on the door!... I'll text you the code when you get there... Yes, the green bag. Not, the black one... Because I don't want you to blow up is why... Just stay out of it and bring me the green bag... No, I don't need anything from the black bag!... Yeah, I'm staying here to do containment if needed... Yes, fast."

He paced back and forth counting time in his head. How long did he have? How many more would come through? How many people would die because he didn't come loaded to take on a sub-horde element?

The motion of a dark silent bike heading towards him let him blow out a breath in relief and he headed up to where she could park. Declan waited for Kayter to set her motorcycle and remove her helmet before he approached. He noted that in addition to her standard skintight body armor, she also wore a long black trench coat. Apparently, a commercial knockoff of the hunter's coat. He glanced back repeatedly at the edges of the small woods. "Damn, you made good time."

Kayter unstrapped Declan's green duffle bag from the back of her motorcycle and handed it to him with a shrug. "You made it sound urgent and you don't strike me as a nervous nelly."

He glanced at her, then back at the coat. "Okay. I have got ask. What is with the coat?"

"Huh? Oh, just for riding the bike. It distracts people from the silent engine. All they remember is the coat flapping behind me." She stripped it off and put it in one of her saddlebags. "Restricts my movements too much to fight in."

"Thank god. I was worried you were about to try and wear that knock off coat in the fight." Declan stated as he strapped on his own body armor and extracted his Vulture carbine from the bag. Then he pulled all of the remaining magazines from the side pocket, inserted them into his body armor pouches, and set the bag back onto Kayter's motorcycle.

Kayter looked at him, arching a brow. "Do I look like an old man that I need to wear old man clothes in a fight?" She turned and dug in Declan's bag and started to rummage around. "Well, look here. You got some toys!" She turned holding a hand grenade in each hand with a wide grin on her face. "You've been holding out on me."

Declan grimaced, "I don't think we'll need those. But we can't just leave them here in a bag for someone else to steal. Better to have them, just in case we need one anyway. You keep a hold of one and I'll take the other one."

Kayter smiled like she had just been given a pony for Christmas, as she handed the last grenade to Declan who immediately secured it in a grenade pouch on his tactical vest. He then pulled off an empty grenade pouch from his vest and handed it to Kayter. "Okay, make sure this pouch is secured on your harness, snap the clips, make sure they are locked closed. Keep the grenade in there with the flap closed and snapped. Do not, do not..." Declan eyed the now smirking young lady as she rolled her grenade back and forth between her hands. "open that pouch and pull out the grenade unless I specifically tell you to."

"But what if you are dead and you can't tell me?" She said and batted her eyes at him, sarcasm dripping off every word.

"Well at that point I give a rat's ass what you do with it." Declan said as he inserted the ammunition magazine into his carbine and chambered the first round. He paused and looked back at her. "You've used them before, haven't you?" Noting that she had it properly secured it already.

Kayter snorted. "Yes. Squad tactics no. Almost every weapon dad could get his hands on? Hell, yes." She tilted her head a speculative look on her face. "So, what the hell do you have in that

Blood War: Rage

black bag in your truck? A flamethrower?"

Declan attached a flashlight to the front of his weapon's barrel. "No, no flamethrowers. You're never getting a flamethrower."

"What do you mean I never get a flamethrower?" Kayter asked, sounding amused as she withdrew her pistol from its holster chambering the first round. She checked to make sure the safety was set and slipped it back into its holster, then withdrew her *jian* sword. She circled it in front of herself slowly, stretching out her wrists. "If I wanted one, I'm pretty sure I could either buy it or find a vid telling me how to make my own in excruciating detail."

"Because it's bulky, ineffective, hits everything but what you needed hit, and is generally just a stupid idea." Declan responded casually. Taking a cue from Kayter, he started rolling and stretching out his shoulders and arms.

Shit, I hate getting old.

"You suck, Colonel. You're too old school you know. You're completely discounting the aesthetic, and chaos value, of pretty, pretty flamethrowers." The teasing in her voice made him smirk.

Reaching out his hand towards her, "While I'm thinking about it, give me back that grenade too."

"What? No way! You gave it to me all fair and square. I'm keeping. They're too hard to get a hold of for me to give it up. Mine." Her smile made him feel even older. "Just fill me in on what we are doing here."

"Fine, just hold onto it. Inside those woods, along the river, maybe 200 to 250 meters in, there's a mage holding a portal open and we need to shut it down and remove all threats."

"Why the hell didn't you just kill him, closing the portal, before you called me then?"

"Because the mage had a mess of friends in there with him. I suspect there's a high functioning ring two demon with at least a dozen skitters. Last I saw of the demon it had traversed back over to his realm, apparently to bring more back with him, but the skitters are already in the woods. I didn't have enough ammo to

292

Doug Burbey & Mel Todd

take care of all that of my own. So, any questions before we go on there and take care of business?" He had already started heading in, noting she followed him making much less noise than he did.

Damn ninja crap. I'm too old for this shit.

"Yeah, what's a skitter and how do I kill it?" Kayter asked, without any sarcasm.

"Oh, no reason why you should know what those are. Well to put it simply, if you have got arachnophobia you are fucked. It's similar to the demon you chopped up at MIT: Six legs, height is around two feet at the shoulder, prickly spines like a porcupine, can jump about ten feet from a standstill, and will try to land on you stabbing you with its legs because its mouth is underneath its body where a stomach should be. So, consider them highly unpleasant."

Fortunately, Kayter did not seem to be overly concerned with giant demon spiders and immediately got to the point. "Ah, yeah I call them crawlies. So, bullets and sword kill them fine, unless this is a version with armor?"

"No armor. They go down easy enough. You can cut off their legs, stab them through the body, or fill them full of holes with bullets. Usually two or three shots will take one down. It all works. Not the toughest demon to run across but the problem is they tend to have a lot of friends with them and they are damn fast. These little bastards like hiding in the trees so be sure you're looking up, down, all around, all the time. If you see just one, then you probably didn't see the other two."

"Got it, Colonel. Sweep the woods, head towards a portal, kill lots of big crawlies. What about the demon and mage?"

"I'll take care that. You just make sure that once we clear the woods and get to the portal you cover my back while I engage the demon. If I can concentrate on that, knowing you are keeping anything else off me, then I should be able to do it pretty readily."

"Wilco. The mage?"

"I'll make that decision and take care of that when the time comes. There are some things you don't need on you. That'll be on

Blood War: Rage

me."

Kayter looked at Declan's face for a moment then shrugged. "Your call, but, Colonel, I've been doing this a while. I've killed more than one mage. Some people don't realize when they are playing with nuclear weapons, they aren't the only ones that will get killed."

He glanced back at her and gave a short sharp nod, even as he grieved that innocence seemed to be something no one had anymore.

They headed through the woods until he all but tripped over a skitter that darted out of the trees at them.

"Okay go!" No point in subtlety now. Declan raised his rifle and shot two more of the skitters, knocking them back into the trees. Kayter had moved like the star pupil in a classroom full of assassins. Declan had relied on her to clear out the first few skitters they encountered with nothing but her sword as they moved into the woods trying not to draw attention. But after she had taken out the first three individually and they approached closer to the portal, the skitters had located them and were moving forward in a large group towards them now.

"Coming on your left, Colonel!" Kayter shouted as she made quick work of a skitter that jumped at her. She slid her body sideways drawing the blade in front of her cutting off two of its legs before she spun and thrust downwards through the top of its body killing it.

"On it." Declan dropped to one knee and began to his sweep his weapon from the right to the left, carefully aiming his shots putting one or two rounds into each shape as it moved through the trees. Seeing that Kayter had no targets directly in front of her he yelled, "Stay with me, stay directly to my right side." He paused for a minute and looked for new targets. Not finding any, he stood up into a crouch and began to move forward. "Let's go. Head for the glow. I counted five targets down. How many you have Kayter?"

"Six."

294

Doug Burbey & Mel Todd

"Okay, I'm guessing by the portal there should be two or three more. Let's pick up the pace and head straight for it. Remember, you see the demon, you back up. Watch my back and let me take it out. Keep your eyes open as there should be a few more the skitters at least." Declan began to push forward quickly then felt himself getting yanked backward. "Damn it."

"What is it?"

"Nothing, just got my coat hung up in the underbrush. Give me a second." Declan reached down to pull his coat out of the brambles that had grabbed its bottom edge and immediately felt the stabbing pain of a skitter claw, slicing across his hand. "Shit!" Declan pulled his arm back while trying to swing his weapon barrel towards the skitter, he lost his balance and fell onto his back, bringing the skitter with them. He felt its other claws stabbing at his coat trying to puncture through to get a grip on its human prey. Declan shot at its body, grazing it, but that did not slow the skitter. He struggled to get his weapon underneath where he could feel the demon's teeth slashing apart his tactical vest and body armor covering his chest.

I'm going to get killed by a mutant fucking demon spider!

Hot wet blood spilled across his chest and face and he waited for the pain and then death to come.

"You going to take a nap old man? Or are you going to get off your ass and finish the job?" Kayter said as Declan felt the weight of the skitter pulled off his chest. "So, you want to talk about that whole coat thing now? Maybe need a bit more practice moving through the woods in it?"

He felt his face heat as he stood up. "No, I don't think we need to mention this again. Ever. Come on, let's go."

Kayter smiled broadly, "Yes, we shall never again mention my having to kill the big bad spider for you after you tripped on your own coat and fell down."

"I did not... Ugh, never mind. We have killing to do."

Children are going to be the death of me. This is why I never had kids.

Blood War: Rage

They moved towards the glow of the portal now clearly visible through the trees in front of them and they stopped just short of the small clearing. Declan could make out the shape of the human mage, as well as two more of the skitters. The mage was sitting on the ground, chanting softly as the two small demons circled around him slowly. He looked over at Kayter and held up two fingers with one hand while wiggling the fingers of his other hand mimicking a spider. She looked over at his gestures with a shrug of her shoulder and tilted her head at him.

Oh geez, you kidding me?

Declan held out two fingers again. Then pointed at the portal and then used both his hands to make spider gestures. He groaned when he noticed that Kayter was trying to restrain herself from laughing. Just as he was about to conduct a single finger gesture towards her, he noticed her eyes widen and her smile immediately disappear. Declan glanced towards the portal and saw what had caught her attention. Coming through the portal was not just the original ring two demon, but what looked like almost an entire sub horde squad of fifteen to twenty, ring two demon foot soldiers.

Oh hell, we can't wait for them to start to disperse.

Declan quickly snapped his fingers to get Kayter's attention. When she turned her head away from looking at the new arrivals in the portal, Declan noticed for the first time a look of genuine fear in her face. He pointed at the pouch on his now heavily damaged vest, and then unclipped the cover and withdrew a hand grenade, then pointed at her to do the same. The sound of a human scream and a demonic bellow, accompanied by a nearly perceptible wave of empathic energy, jerked his attention back to the portal.

Just a few steps outside of the portal stood a massive, muscled and armored, insect-like demon leader. Declan recognized it as some form of horde lord, a commander by the various splashes of colored paints across the armor-like plates of its body. It was growling and snapping at one of the ring two demons. The ring two demon stooped and tried to back away slowly but appeared to have angered the demon horde commander somehow.

Declan reached down and slid his index finger through the ring of the grenade while gripping the base of it firmly with his other hand, glancing over at Kayter and nodding at her to do the same. He watched as the horde commander screeched and growled towards the other demons while gesturing at the human who appeared to be trying very hard not to run away in terror.

What the fuck is this all about?

Confused, Declan prepared to toss the grenade but did not take his eyes off the portal. He watched as the horde leader grabbed the apparently offending demon by its head, digging its talons into the base of its skull, then it barked some form of command towards the other demons. They responded immediately and re-entered the portal, followed by the remaining skitters.

Declan and Kayter both stood still, just inside the edge of the trees and watched as the horde leader twisted the neck of the lower demon. The snapping of its bones was audible even from their position hidden in the trees. The human mage screamed, causing the portal to flicker, with the momentary loss of its human anchor's attention. The demon leader then easily tossed the dead demon's body back across the threshold of the portal into the demon realm. The mage started sobbing but tried to refocus and hold the portal open while backing away from the demon leader. The demon approached the mage slowly then, to the amazement of Declan, the demon stooped and lowered its face towards the near-panicked human. It held out a talon and lightly tapped the mages cheek, drops of blood appearing with each tap.

Declan then heard clearly spoken English words come out of the tendrils covering the demon's mouth, "Lighten up, Francis," just before it turned around and reentered the portal, leaving the mage and the two hunters alone in the clearing.

The demons uttered phrase kept rolling through Declan's mind.

That's a movie quote that Shane used to use all the time. Why in God's name would I be hearing it right now from a fucking

Blood War: Rage

demon?

"Holy shit! Did you just hear that, Colonel?" Kayter stuttered, her eyes wide. The portal mage turned towards them and drew a small pistol from inside of his cloak and held it in his shaking hands.

"Easy there, buddy." Declan withdrew his finger from the grenade pin and slid it back into his pouch, as he gestured for Kayter to do the same, while never taking his eyes off the mage holding the gun. "I really think we need to talk. No reason for anybody to get hurt here."

"I... Who..." The portal behind the mage collapsed, and disappeared, as the mage's stuttering words betrayed his lack of concentration on holding the realm bridge open.

Declan raised both of his hands in front of him, "Look, no weapons." As he started to take a few steps forward. "Just let me ask you some questions, give us truthful answers, and I see no reason why we can't forget we ever saw you here."

The trembling mage raised the pistol quickly to his own head and screamed "No, I won't be sent to the factory!" then pulled the trigger. The mage's body collapsed onto its knees and then fell forward into the dirt.

Kayter put her hand grenade back in its pouch and drew her sword, "Umm... I'm not sure what just happened. What factory? What we do now? And why did a demon, a high-level demon just do that?"

Pausing a few seconds before he answered, "Well, looks it like our job is done here. Time to go home. Yeah, I'm not sure what just happened here either. My guess is it was nothing good. No, nothing good at all."

Chapter 42 - Playing Batman

Kayter enjoyed running missions with Declan, and the extra money he'd conned out of the ICER agency didn't hurt either. But, it had been quiet for a few days and she needed something to do. Pulling up the computer she started to look and see if any of her contacts had said anything. And she wanted to see if there were any more news stories about missing Fae.

Flipping through programs she pulled up the tracking program that had been running in the background. The tracker program blipped up with multiple weeks' worth of tracking info on it. Kayter frowned as she stared at the computer. What was that from?

Oh yes, that weird government guy. The one that talked about DK.

She reached out about to hit the dismiss but paused.

I already don't trust them. Why not see if they're up to anything?

With nothing else pressing she brought up the map showing his route historically. The VFW she recognized, though part of her smirked at the knowledge his visits were much less frequent. An office building popped up every weekday, while an apartment building showed up every day. Most of the rest of the stops looked like restaurants, stores, boring stuff. She almost hit delete when one weird thing popped up and she zoomed in to look at it more closely.

Every few days, it looked like Monday's and Thursdays he went far away from his normal routes and ended up in an area that looked very industrial. Brow furrowed, she checked the times and saw his car stayed there an hour, then went home.

So, what does a shady government agent do in an industrial

Blood War: Rage

area in the evening? No restaurants, no shops, and he doesn't seem like the type to visit family working the swing shift. What the hell? Though this time Reynolds, use your brain?

The thought was wry and biting, she needed to quit being arrogant or she'd end up dead. With that in mind, she got dressed, planning on nothing but recon. She put on the new body suit Hunter Gear had designed for her. She hadn't had time to play with it, not wanting to risk an untried item on a hunt.

It fit perfectly. Meaning if she gained more than a pound or two it might start to bind.

Note to self, lose a tiny bit of weight, or next time get it made a bit looser.

Her leathers went on over it nicely without binding or catching. It moved well, and Miriam had included some hygiene functions in it if things went really sideways. Underwear and this did not go together.

With weapons and a plan this time, she headed out to the location. Parking in an anonymous parking lot a block away, she slipped off the bike and looked around. It was just getting dark and her night vision rated at the top of the charts. Securing her helmet, setting the magical protection, she slipped into the buildings, blending in with the shadows as she moved towards the buildings.

The address matched up to a squat, two-story building with cars and vans parked out front. Kayter paused, taking out her phone and took snapshots of the license plates, two of which were government.

Inspecting the building, there was nothing about it that said what department or branch it might fall under. In fact she couldn't see a name on it at all, just a door that said restricted. Walking on past, she continued until she ended up a block away, then she circled back. One of the advantages of buildings in America, all of them were required to have multiple exits in case of emergencies. She stood looking at it, reached in and powered her phone off. Breaking and entering weren't her strengths but with her speed and strength, she should be able to pull it off.

It didn't take her long to find the emergency exit, disable the alarms, and jimmy the lock. Learning how to lockpick had been a good choice. The camera angle sucked so she slipped up the stairs, moving slow and checking every corner, ears straining to hear any movement.

At the second floor, she cracked the door a bit after being unable to catch any signs of movements. It opened into an open area that looked like it had been set up for a cubicle farm but they had never gotten that far. Even standing in the door, she heard no one moving around or even the clacking of a keyboard didn't reach her ears. Another glance around showed no cameras, so she moved in, her feet whispers of sound on the floor.

Don't get arrogant. That will get you dead, as you were so eloquently reminded.

Even with the reminder ringing through her mind she relaxed a bit, prowling the open area, but it carried nothing of any activity. To the side were windows and she frowned looking at them. They were too close to be windows to the outside. Reviewing the building in her head, there hadn't been any windows like those looking out.

Dropping to a crouch she moved over to the windows and peered out.

Well, what the hell is this?

Poking her head up she surveyed the area, frown deepening as she looked. People moved around below her, most of them in lab coats, one or two in suits – though those were all back away from anything else, talking with faces that held no emotions.

None of the people talked beside the occasional order to another. Kayter lifted herself up a bit higher to get a better angle into the rest of the room and froze. What had just been out of her sight when she peered over, now resolved itself and her stomach seized.

Strapped to two, no three of the six tables below were people. Their faces slack and IV's attached to each side of their body. They were all pretty, even strapped to a bed and unconscious they

301

Blood War: Rage

possessed a beauty that called to you, and Kayter swallowed hard.

Fae. They have Fae captured. Or at least Faeborn. Oh gods, the missing fae. Oh, fuck me.

Her blood ran cold and she wanted to be sick as she saw the beginning of a war with another realm below her. She kept watching the people below, all men, or at least there weren't any women present right now. The IV coming out on one side was blood pooling into a bag at a very slow rate.

Giving blood equaled a very bad idea for Kayter but she'd seen it often enough to frown at how slow the blood dripped into the bag. The other IV contained a clear fluid that dripped down. The person in the bed had shadows under their eyes so deep she could see them from up here. No way to tell the gender, most Fae tended towards an androgynous facial structure. None of these looked like pure Fae, but they weren't diluted very far either.

Dammit, I should have brought binoculars.

With eyes narrowed she traced up and down each inch of the bodies of the motionless people. Straps secured their arms and feet to the beds, and she saw a bag with yellowish liquid near the end of the bed, barely visible from her vantage point.

Her eyes snagged on what she'd suspected and dreaded seeing. A thick tube ran along the side of the bed and slipped under the blanket about midway down the bed. An opaque white substance moved through it.

Fuck. Feeding tube. This is not good. Means they are keeping them here long term. Which explains why the Fae haven't found the bodies. I wonder if they know these people have been missed?

She kept looking and saw one of the lab coat people swap out a bag and head back to under to where she could not see it.

I've got to get down there, figure out what is going on. I might not be the biggest fan of the Fae, Dad sure wasn't, but this isn't right. And I don't want to have anything to do with starting another war.

Moving quickly but making sure she didn't make any noise, she headed back to the door and the stairs. She needed to get into the

302

other area.

Note – next time see what Miriam charges for invisibility.

The mental laugh helped. Invisibility wasn't possible. Bending light was hard and an enchantment that would do it, well she'd never heard of anyone pulling it off for more than a second or two. Not much use.

The stairwell had almost no signs of use, and with the emptiness of the second floor, she understood why. There might have been more further back on the floor around corners but right now her focus was on what they were doing with the blood. Her bones ached with the knowledge it wouldn't be good.

Getting down to the first floor, she stood by the door concentrating, ears straining, but it all seemed quiet. Taking a deep breath then holding it, she cracked open the door revealing a hallway. She stepped out into it and saw windows and doors a bit further down.

Thinking through the layout in her mind, the person she saw would have entered on the other side of where she stood. With that in mind, she headed to the windows, keeping her back to the wall, then carefully peered around the edge of the window, even as she listened for anyone coming this direction.

Inside was a full lab, scientific equipment, computers, refrigerators and things she had no idea what their purpose might be. The man she had spied stood on the far side of the room. She didn't see the bag of blood but she saw him watching something drip into a vial, a pinkish yellow color. He stood there for another minute, then hit a button, and after a few flashes of light the vial popped out. In an action that looked bored and if he'd done it a hundred times, he grabbed it, moved a few feet over and opened a glass door fridge and put it in a tray. Filling it up. Closing the fridge, he walked back out.

The room looked empty, so she took a chance and slipped inside via the doors near her. The coldness of the room slapped her in the face, but the rest of her body stayed comfortable. With sharp glances, and listening for voices, she headed over to the fridge and blinked at the full trays of the vials.

All were labeled, but the writing was tiny. She pulled open the door and crouched down sliding out one of the trays near the bottom, and grabbed a vial from the back, slipping it into her pocket. She then shut the door and stood, then headed towards the door that went into the room where the prisoners were.

Prisoners seem right, but why? Why risk coming to the notice of the Fae? No one knows for sure what they can do. But if they get pissed it could be very, very bad for us. They know what we can do, but we have no idea what they can do.

Even in her head, she couldn't come up with a convincing argument for them to be here and not in a hospital if something seriously wrong wasn't afoot and they weren't trying to hide it from the Fae.

The set of doors leading out into the open area turned out to be a double set, with a small entryway with bins for lab coats and gloves and booties, not that she'd seen anyone wearing them. The second set of doors were loose and more to separate the area, than to close and secure an area. She could hear the beeps of machines and the murmur of voices in the other area.

Be smart. Not stupid.

Growling under her breath she backed out and headed to leave the building. Going out into that area would have guaranteed someone saw her and even if she'd worn a lab coat, just being female would make her stand out.

Moving quickly, she exited the building and went back around to the parking lot, looking for a place to observe unnoticed. The cars were still there, along with two delivery trucks, and she grinned. One of the trucks, a Freightliner M2, had a flat tire, and from the weeds growing near it, it'd been there for a while. It was well into dark and from the placement of the lights, the top of the truck disappeared into the night sky.

Perfect.

It took less than a minute to jump to the top of the truck and lay down on the filthy surface. Cleaning her leathers as soon as she got back would be mandatory, given the amount of bird shit and other things she refused to think about. Pressing her body flat against the surface, she trained her eyes on the door and settled in to wait.

Every hunter knows how to hold still and wait for prey. Kayter lay there and waited, her awareness soaking in everything. It didn't take long before three men walked out, chatting as they stepped out of the building. Two were in suits, the third had a lab coat draped over his arm. Light reflected off glasses from the lab coat guy and they headed towards the cars parked not far from her.

Kayter quit breathing, worry flashing through her that they might look up and see her, but none of them appeared to have any level of situational awareness at all.

"How much longer do you think our current volunteers will last?" Asked Suit One, he had office boy hair and came across as soft. The way he said volunteers made her skin crawl. Most people used that tone to refer to vomit or feces they'd just stepped in. She'd expected Chad but it wasn't him.

Probably has baby soft hands too.

Labcoat shrugged. "One of them is about done. His blood output is trailing off and I suspect he's about to die. No real reason, but just won't live anymore. We've seen this pretty consistently. Will be a shame though, as his blood is the most potent we have. The other two should be good for another two months before we need to replace them. They're still pretty fresh."

"Hmm, that might work. Rumblings are we might be moving in the next year anyhow, better facility, more volunteers." He paused and she couldn't tell what he did with his hands, but some sort of gesture that seemed more habit than functional. "Either way, we'll need a new shipment of Reset ready to go out relatively soon. The washed-up demon hunters are leaning on it pretty hard and I'd rather they not go off it until we want them to. There are plans to make it very splashy when they lose their crutch."

"Splashy? You do realize that when we flip to providing them with the straight chemical placebo it will work for about a week?

Blood War: Rage

Then the withdrawal will make people on PCP seem calm and logical right?" labcoat asked.

"Exactly. The amount of drama and screaming it will cause should provide the votes we need to shift people to the correct path."

"Huh. If you say so. I don't follow politics. Just make sure to give me a heads up so I'm nowhere near when that goes down. I've got to get going. My wife is holding dinner for me. I'll have a delivery of Reset sent to the office next Monday." Labcoat waved and headed over to his car, a Lexus, and it pulled out.

The other two men stood there for a minute watching the car go.

"Is he that naïve, or does he really think he'll be alive when we close the doors on the project?" Suit Two spoke. He appeared harder, or maybe distant, like he could watch the world burn and it wouldn't occur to him to grab a bucket of water.

"Sure of his own self-importance. Why disabuse of him of that notion? But the more old hunters we get on this stuff, the prettier it will be when we switch it up. We know it will take a week and when the withdrawals hit, it will be fast and very newsworthy, but some lean on it more than others." He paused and Kayter peered harder trying to see the smaller expressions on his face, but the distance and the darkness conspired against her. "Maybe we can get them to lean on it more. Create more situations where they need to fight down the rage. I'll see what we can do. Anything else?"

"No. I have all the detonators set. We can blow the place whenever, a year, six months, tomorrow. They will respond to a code."

"And that would be?"

"Something I'll provide you when we get clearance to blow the place." If Kayter had said that, there might have been humor or teasing? This man, a flat statement.

"I always liked you. You know how to cover your own ass. See you at the office tomorrow. I'll see what I can do to replace the volunteer about to die."

They parted with that.

She lay there for another ten minutes but no one else left the building. She jumped off the top of the truck landing easily and headed for her bike. This vial of Reset, what the fuck was it? And what did it all mean? Kayter had no idea but the sinking feeling in her stomach that it all related to what the Fae had told them. And that whatever the answer was, she wouldn't like it.

Home to clean up, then Declan's. He needs to know about this.

Blood War: Rage

Chapter 43 - Truth May Get You Killed

The alert of his motion sensor pulled Declan's attention away from the football game. More college crap but better than nothing. A flick of his fingers across the remote loaded the camera view on the TV screen. An image of a black bike with a slim figure on it coming slowly down his drive appeared.

Huh, guess she did listen when I told her to come see me if she found anything or needed help. She's got mad skills and in close combat situations she's better than anyone. Well, except Shane but I wouldn't trust him at my back.

He stood, stretching as he headed to the door, almost glad to shut off the painful game.

Really, anyone that names their football team after a turtle deserves to have their asses kicked.

The lame joke made him smirk as he watched the Indian Chief get closer.

Definitely not burning rubber to get here so an unfriendly is unlikely, and probably don't need to start getting loaded for bear. So, beer and try to see if I can try to not make her cry. Granted, didn't do that at the last few times but I think it might have been close at HG. You aren't her dad, Declan. And no child of John Reynolds would be stupid. Act stupid occasionally, but not be stupid. Besides, she's saved my ass once or twice already.

With that in mind, he grabbed two beers out of the fridge and took a minute to strap on his piece. Just because he kinda liked the kid didn't mean he needed to be stupid.

She pulled up to the patio which was just a flat cement pad

Doug Burbey & Mel Todd

with his grill in one corner and a clear view of about 180 degrees of
the possible approaches, especially his driveway.

Declan dropped into one of his chairs, setting the extra beer on
the table even as he admired the bike.

Kayter Reynolds pulled off her helmet, her long multicolored
hair cascading out, looking at him and nodded. "Declan."

"Kayter. Nice bike. Not sure about that enchantment bullshit.
Bit risky, don't cha think?" He took a sip of the beer, never taking
his eyes off her, but he relaxed a bit as she dismounted and walked
over. She picked up the beer and expertly flipped the top off and
took a sip, then sinking down in the other chair and looking at the
view.

"I charge it with my blood, so I don't use much. But the risk is
worth it to not have it noisy as I drive, or risk running out of gas in
a bad situation."

"Point. It still uses gas?"

"Yeah, I keep the tank full, just in case. You know, in case I need
an accelerant, or the magic quits."

"Valid." He fell silent, waiting to see what she would do.
Unfortunately, she seemed willing to sit quietly also. He admired it,
though it might drive him crazy.

"I take it you didn't come out here for the beer?"

"Good beer."

"Hell yes. I'm not spending my money on crap. If I want that, I'll
go down to the VFW and drink that piss water Andrew likes."

Kayter smirked. "Yeah, sounds like something Dad would have
said." She looked around jerking her head back at the blocky
house. "Nice place."

"Should be considering, what I spent on it. You've been holding
your own lately. Don't think otherwise."

Her odd eyes darted over to him, the blue one grabbing his
attention. Then she looked away with a half nod and Declan
relaxed at the acceptance of the apology, one he'd owed her.
Having to spell crap out annoyed him and she had promise.

They sat in silence until she pulled a vial out of her jacket pocket and set it on the table between them. "You see this before?"

"Hey, you got some Reset. High-quality stuff and pure even, if the color is any judge. Mine always seems to be a paler pink. Maybe watered down? Nice." He picked one up looking at it. "Though mine usually come in injection vials."

He glanced over at her and froze, the blood had drained out of her face and her eyes were dilated fully, leaving only mismatched rings around her eyes.

"You know what this is?" Her voice didn't get above a whisper and she never took her eyes away from him.

Cold coiled in the pit of his stomach and he wanted something much stronger than beer. Declan kept his voice even. "Sure. It's a drug to help with the hunters. Helps with stuff. Makes it so I keep my mind, mostly."

Hell, they're even talking about it on TV, likening it to Agent Orange. I've got nothing to be ashamed about unless I snap and kill a bunch of people for no reason.

But he turned his head away and took a long pull on the beer, avoiding the look on her face. It was the clank of her beer bottle that had him look at her. She still looked like she'd seen a ghost.

Her beer had been emptied and he arched a brow. "Want another one?"

"You've used it?"

Declan shrugged. "Not like it's Viagra or something. So yeah. And I have to say it helped. You know what they say, better living through chemicals." He gave her another look. "Are you going to be sick, you're turning green."

Green had crept up the sides of her face but she swallowed hard. "Have anything stronger? I know I need it, you might."

That cold feeling wrapped around his stomach and spine, but he shrugged draining his beer. "Give me a minute." In the kitchen he grabbed a bottle of bourbon, with as green she looked he didn't want to take a chance of his Scotch getting upchucked. Another two beers and two glasses made for full arms as he headed back out, but he'd perfected the skill of juggling multiple drinks a decade ago.

He set the beers down then the bottle, uncorking it, but not pouring anything as he sat back down in his chair, his beer firmly in his hands.

"What's this all about? You didn't strike me as a hardcore booze guzzler. Not that I'm throwing stones or anything. I enthusiastically like my booze."

Kayter didn't answer him but grabbed the bottle splashed two fingers in the tumbler and tossed it back.

Declan snorted as she choked on the bourbon as it burned its way down. "And that is why I didn't bring out the Scotch. I don't abuse the good stuff."

She took a deep breath, set the glass down, and stared out at the trees. "It isn't chemicals."

"What the Bourbon? No, it's decent Kentucky Bourbon. Not super high end or anything, but decent. Picky, picky."

"Reset. It's not made from chemicals."

That icy feeling sank in further but Declan ignored it. "Last time I checked, most drugs are made of chemicals. Cocaine is from leaves, opium is from poppies, chocolate is cacao seeds. Still all drugs." He took a drink of beer, wanting to look away from her, and knowing he had to catch every nuance. "What is it made of, cat piss?"

Kayter turned and looked at him and he wanted to be anywhere but sitting right there. The last time he saw that look it had been on her father's face when he started booby trapping the children and wounded in a last-ditch effort to stop the horde. He'd wanted to die before he ever saw that look again.

"How many have you taken? How many vials of that stuff?"

Declan shrugged. "Ten? Twelve? They seem to last for a while. Not like I look forward to taking them."

Well not too much. It is nice to feel the rage get snuffed out.

She splashed some bourbon in both glasses and pushed one towards him.

Blood War: Rage

"You might need that."

"Really, if it's made of ground-up roaches, I don't want to know." His voice held a note of desperation even to his own ears. He glanced at the bourbon but kept the beer bottle firmly in his hand.

"It's made of Fae blood, well human Fae hybrid's."

Declan felt his mind lock up and the world stopped as he looked at her. "Explain." All humor, everything, drained. At this moment his alarm system had more personality.

"They have people with Fae blood locked up in a factory, kept drugged, and they are draining them dry. When they can't produce any more blood, they dispose of the body and grab someone else. It's made of Fae blood."

Her eyes never wavered even as she drained the second glass of bourbon. DK stood, draining the beer as he did so. With motion full of violence, he chucked the bottle high towards the trees, the second it left his hand he grabbed his .45, raised it and fired. The bottle exploded into a rain of brown shards all over the area.

Slipping the pistol back into the holster, he grabbed the tumbler, and tossed back the contents in one smooth move.

"If she's involved I'll plunge a knife into her ice cold fucking heart. If she knew and gave this to me, I'll feed her to the next demon." DK's voice remained level and quiet. He turned dead eyes on to Kayter and part of him rejoiced as she flinched back. His own human rage pushed back the Rage, swallowing it in cold pure anger.

"Tell me everything. Don't leave out a single detail."

Kayter nodded once, a jerky motion, but she took another mouthful of bourbon and began to talk. Explaining everything. As she talked he sat, the tumbler filled but he didn't touch it as he listened to her talk.

Her color had returned by the time she finished, and she looked at him. "You didn't know."

"You really think any Blood War vet would willingly put the blood of another innocent being in us? I thought drugs, maybe some hard narcotics, but didn't care. Better to get addicted than lose my sanity and take others out with a violent breakdown."

She nodded, the stories were on the news with disturbing regularity.

"It helps?" Her voice low, quiet, but no accusation in the words.

"Knocks it out completely. Almost like it washes it out of my system. It takes time to build back up though I will say each time it comes back a bit faster. But then I've been killing a lot of demons lately and been more exposed to demon blood than I've been in the last few years."

"Who is she?"

"Cordelia Bennett." His voice flat, avoiding any indication about his feelings towards the woman. That power he wouldn't give to anyone.

"The ICER lady? Kinda pretty, about your age? Stacked, smart, and tough?"

"That sounds like her. How do you know her?"

"Don't know her. Just listened in on her at a meeting with that douche bag Chad Morant."

A flicker of humor went through him but it fizzled out quickly. "What did they talk about?"

"You, it turns out. Offering you a way in. Chad didn't want you. She overrode him. I liked her."

"Yeah, I did too. Looks like I need to have a talk with Miss Bennett." His voice warmed a tiny bit, but the grin on his face didn't have anything to do with humor. "If I like her answers, she might still be alive by the time we are done."

"Understood." She sat there for a bit. "Mind if I hang for a bit? This wasn't how I expected this conversation to go."

"We both need food to start. Want some?"

"Sure." Her voice had the same flatness. "How many vets do you think are getting Reset?"

His mind flashed back to the news story and the vet that calmed down as they injected him with something, and the vials that just existed in Cordelia's desk.

Blood War: Rage

"Too many. Most of whoever is left still active with the ICERs or merc outfits, I'd suspect."

"Yeah. That's what I thought. "

He went and grabbed sandwich fixings from the fridge. Then he started planning how he was going to get these Fae victims out, and the pending conversation with one Cordelia Bennet. Sandwiches made, he grabbed his phone and walked back out. He set the plate down but before he could sit back down his phone rang. DK picked up the phone even though the caller said unknown.

"Declan," Cordy's voice rang in his ears. "I have a job for you and need you now. Back up would not be a bad idea."

Chapter 44 – Reset Raid

"Go fuck yourself, Cordelia." Declan said each syllable crisp and sharp and hung up on the shocked silence on the other end. He turned and looked at Kayter, eyes narrowed. "Tell me again everything you remember about the place while we eat. We're going to need our energy. And I need to know the layout, the people, and what to bring."

Taking a deep breath with her eyes a bit wide, the kid began to review all the descriptions, the layout, and the number of people there. As she talked he took notes on his phone and ate mechanically. The floodlights kept his patio well lit but he still paid attention as they ate and planned.

"You thinking 24-hour security?" He glanced at the clock - after 1800. It would be full dark in another hour or two.

"I have no idea. I'd think someone would have to be there for the hostages?" Her voice rose a bit on the end.

"Hostages? No. That would imply they give a shit about them as bargaining chips. These are victims. Period." He knew his voice held darkness and anger, but he'd choose anger over collapsing to his knees and screaming in horror and rage.

Something in her seemed to deflate. "So, no chance there is a good reason they are being held there?"

Declan snorted as he held up the vial. "Not with what Art told us, and the fact they are directing this towards hunters. Then there's the fact that we need it to keep the Rage in check."

Kayter's eyes narrowed but he saw she was paying attention. "Rage? You mentioned it kept hunters stable."

"Yeah, we call it Rage. It's a long-term side effect a bunch of us hunters were left with. We absorbed so much demon blood and residual magic during the war that something in us changed, brought out our darker primal aspects."

Declan swallowed and looked out the window, blood-drenched memories flashing through his mind. "We get pissed and go into almost a berserker mode, except calm, singularly focused, and deadly. It's the dirty little secret among the few veterans left of the Blood War."

Declan broke off, looking at the vial and his gut twisted. He pushed it down and continued. "I assumed it was a drug that helped counteract the effects. If what you found is true, they've been doping me with Fae blood, and that will have other ramifications." The words of the Fae in the bar flashed through his mind again and he swallowed past nausea.

"I see." Kayter stood looking at him. "So, what do you want to do?"

I want to fucking blow up ICER headquarters and kill the people involved in this. But there's always the chance they didn't all know. I really want them to have not known.

A deep breath helped to push it back and he focused on the task at hand.

Fuck it. Do what you can do. Kill who you can kill, figure the rest out later.

"I want to level that factory but we need the information that is there. And need to get those Fae out, alive if possible." Even as he said it, he pulled up the contact list on his phone. "And we're going to need back up."

Kayter arched a brow at him. "I'm not enough? I did well enough with the demons."

"True. But this is us in a confined space full of kill zones, knowing what is coming might be nice. " The number he'd dialed picked up on the other end.

"What up, old man? Ready to move to a retirement home and let me have all your stuff?"

The normalcy of the comment hurt, and he pushed past it, unable to release a drop of control. "I need a spotter. Something bad is about to go down and I'm going to be the one bringing the noise. You in?"

His voice felt flat even to his own ears, but it didn't matter. Keeping the rage, both personal and demon born, controlled took priority.

A pause on the other end, then Andrew replied slowly, "Yes. What do I need to bring?"

"The Bear, something comfortable to go prone on, and patience. Bring your Suburban. We are rescuing people and will need something to put them in."

"I'll be there in thirty." Andrew hung up and DK heard the same lack of emotion that rode him right now.

He shifted his gaze to Kayter. So fucking young but she knew how to fight. Most of the time she had a good head on her shoulders, but he could trust her to kill him if he lost it. And that might be the most important part.

"Come with me. I need to get some supplies before we go do this." He didn't give her time to demure or even speak, turning and striding out of the room. A second later he heard her quick footsteps as she followed him down to his armory.

The biometrics locks into his armory were accessed without conscious thought, as his mind went through what he would need. He'd grab some ammo for Andrew too, just in case, and a pistol.

"Fuuuuck me... You expecting the end of the world?" Kayter blurted as she stopped inside.

"Yup. Every single day." His voice cold and hard as he headed for one of the cabinets. Digging in it he came up with what he'd been pretty sure he had, wireless radio headsets. "Here." DK tossed one to Kayter, who he noted with a bit of annoyance, caught it one handed not even looking at him.

"This place is pretty intense. You could probably withstand a Horde from here."

"Kinda the point. How much ammo you got on you?" He kept pulling out more kit, this would be close in fighting most likely, and he might need to get out in a hurry.

Blood War: Rage

"Not much. The magazine in my .45 and two extra clips."

"Got a speed loader?"

"Not on me." She kept eyeing everything, and DK made sure nothing disappeared off his shelves. Not that he thought she would steal, but he understood the lure of things that caused pain to others.

"Make?"

"Springfield .45 XD MOD," she rattled it off and he frowned. He didn't have one for that specific model.

Heading over to his ammo bench he pulled out something. "Here try this. Universal loader. E-bay crap but it should work."

That pulled her away from her perusal of his stuff as she caught that and flipped a few bullets out, then tested out the universal. "It'll do. Not perfect but faster than by hand."

"Good," he grunted and tossed her two boxes of .45 ammo. "Figure out how to carry that on you."

She glanced down at the hundred rounds then back up at him. "If I have to use this many bullets we are probably dead because they filled the place with reinforcements, instead of just the skeleton crew I saw."

DK shrugged. "Better have it and bitch about it later, than to need it and be without." He didn't look at her but instead he focused on his end game. In a small green engineer bag, he dropped in round balls of C-4, primer cord, and detonators.

"Do I want to know why you are packing explosives?" Her voice sounded behind him, and he flinched.

"To blow up the damn building. Why the fuck do you think?" His voice a bit sharper than it would be normally.

He could feel her standing behind him, looking at him.

I swear, if she is judging me, I will fucking shoot her in the thigh and leave her to deal with the flesh wound.

He stood ready to rip into her, but her face had only a pensive look.

"What if we can't get the prisoners out before we need to blow it."

318

DK's gut twisted. "We will. That is not an option. They are getting out no matter what." He looked at her. "Can you fight in a bulletproof vest?"

"This is. Miriam made it for me. Will protect me from anything we should find there. Anything else, well we will have to hope. The vest makes me too awkward. But you do realize we might not have to kill anyone."

"Do you really think anyone working there doesn't know exactly what they are doing and are fully complicit in it?" His voice harsh, guilt making it even darker.

Kayter closed her eyes. "No. I'm good. Sword is on the bike, so are the extra magazines. I've got some pockets I can get more loose ammo in, but not this much."

"Then here, take this; make sure you can move." He tossed her the smallest tactical vest he had that would give her places to put the ammo, the loader, and the three grenades he handed her.

Her eyes darkened as she took the grenades and her strange eyes grabbed him for a moment. Not sexual, more like knowledge he had no desire to understand threatened to pull him down. He jerked his eyes away and headed for the door even as she pulled the vest on and started adjusting it to fit.

DK made the conscious decision to leave the door to his gun room open. If he got killed while doing this he might as well let Andrew have a way to get in. He wouldn't be needing it anymore. Maybe regardless of how this went down. His life expectancy without Reset could be counted in months if not weeks.

Don't think about it. Not now. Now you have other things to concentrate on.

He heard Kayter coming up the stairs about the time his alerts went off. He pulled up the cameras on his phone and nodded at the sight of a dark Suburban coming up his driveway.

"You riding with us or taking your bike?"

"With all this stuff strapped one me? Riding with you. If one of us gets hurt I don't want to have to worry about leaving Midnight there."

319

Blood War: Rage

DK stopped and turned to look at her. "You named your bike?"

"Yes. You have a problem with that?"

She looked like a kitten as she bristled at him, and a flash of amusement untainted by rage or guilt made him almost smile.

"Nope, just wondering if you were calling yourself Midnight Rider, or something."

Her spluttering, offended noises kept his mood buoyed until he got outside and saw Andrew leaning against his gas guzzler, no smile on his face.

"Grabbed my aid kit too."

"Good. Here's extra ammo." He tossed another two boxes of fifty caliber rounds to Andrew, who caught them much less gracefully than Kayter had.

"Where we headed?" He asked as they piled into the car, after waiting for Kayter to grab stuff out of her saddlebags.

DK opened his mouth and paused looking back at Kayter who was still fussing with organizing and fitting things on the tac vest.

"I don't know. What's the address, Reynolds?"

She pulled out her phone made a few quick swipes and handed it to Andrew. "There."

Andrew looked at it, grunted and put the vehicle in gear. They were silent on the way over. DK wanted to break the tension with jokes or just bullshit, the normal stuff, but all he could focus on were the consequences of life without Reset. A short bloody life.

"I'd park a block or two away," Kayter spoke up. "I'm not positive they don't have cameras. I didn't see any but that doesn't mean anything."

Andrew grunted, and DK glanced at him.

I shouldn't have brought him in. He didn't sign up for this, not like I did. Hell, not like Kayter did. I know he said he'd help, but he already paid his price. Greg knows the score, I should have called him for backup, but he's way too far out to get here in time.

This guilt of getting more friends killed layered on his psyche and he snarled, pushing it back.

I don't have time for this, he's was a fucking pick-up warrior and can make his own damn choices.

"Yeah, take the radio, get your earpiece and find a perch that makes you happy. See if you can see both doors. We won't go in until you let us know you are set.

"Got it." Andrew slowed down and they both slipped out of the vehicle while it was still moving. As they slid the door shut Andrew sped back up, headed down the street. A moment of panic wrapped DK, what if he left and kept driving?

Then I do it myself. But either way, this place will not be standing when done.

He followed Kayter as she slipped through the alley, leading to a door. She stood in the shadows, looking at the door. He took his time to survey the place but she was right there didn't seem to be any cameras.

Crouched in the shadow of a dumpster, he kept his voice down as he asked the questions he needed to.

"Was it unlocked?"

"No, easy jimmy, though. Should have relocked and they'd never know, but the stairs didn't have much traffic from what I could see." Her voice was just as low.

"And nothing on the second floor?"

"No. All on the first and it lets you directly into the labs."

She jerked her head towards a parking lot with one old van, two cars, and he noted she took care not to move her limbs out of the shadows. "That's where they were parking their cars, so I don't think there is much of anyone here."

Is that a good or a bad thing? I want to kill them all but at the same time I just need that place destroyed.

In response, he just nodded and they waited.

Time slipped by and he started to believe Andrew had left them.

"I'm in position." Andrews' voice came over the coms. "Have a clear view of the door to the parking lot, and an angle on the back door. While I can't get a clear shot, I'll let you know if anyone is headed that way. I assume you don't care about people leaving,

Blood War: Rage

only people coming in?"

Do I care about people leaving?

Part of him wanted them all dead. Part of him didn't want any more blood on his soul than what he already had.

"Only if they are coming towards us and armed. Otherwise, just warn us."

"Will do," Andrew replied and DK thought there might be a hint of relief in his voice.

"It's time, Reynolds. Move out." They headed towards the door. He let Kayter take the lead. If she'd already jimmied it once, she could do it again faster than he could.

The door pulled open and let them into a gray stairwell. He waved her to the door after quickly scanning the interior. He signaled her to hold while he placed C-4 at the support point against the far wall.

A quick flick of two of his fingers at her and she pulled open the door. Again, he waved her to a halt and she did as he placed more charges on the support beams. Looking down the hall he moved low, under the window to the far side, anticipating where he would put cameras if he worked here. They moved through the lab and he only paused to place two charges. One he placed under a large compressed gas cylinder with standard flammable label warning and another on a fire suppression main line valve. The lab echoed with emptiness, the only noise the hum of machines, and he sighed with relief.

Kayter waited by the door, her face betraying her thoughts and he ignored what he could see on her face. He rejoined her when the charges were placed, well aware he might be going in for overkill.

Don't care, this place needs to be destroyed. May as well make the boom-boom big and sexy.

He peered out the window into the room Kayter had described and felt his stomach twist in horror. While up this close, he could see the victims. Pale, more than any illness of avoidance of sun could ever explain. They lay on the beds, unmoving and emaciated.

322

Doug Burbey & Mel Todd

Cold clawed at his body and the rage that only Reset could control crept up, and he let it. Everything sharpened and became clear, and he knew the best path. With a quick glance at the girl next to him, he shouldered his way through the first set of doors sweeping the space thoroughly for threats. He waited for Kayter to join him, then he slipped through the second set. The smells of slow death, blood, power, and harsh cleaners assaulted his nose.

He moved through, Vulture upon his shoulder, clearing the room, and ignoring the poor souls in the bed. Movement to his right caught his attention and he turned. A man in a white lab coat was pushing a cart laden with Reset. The vials called to him.

"Hey! What are you doing here?" His voice filled with a mix of anger and worry as he headed towards them.

DK seriously considered just knocking him out, but he reached behind him, under the lab coat, and came back out with a gun. Before the gun even came above his waist DK pulled the Vulture's trigger. The man's head snapped back under the force of the single bullet that shattered his forehead, collapsing it inward in a fragmented mass of blood and bone before he crumpled to the ground.

The carbine's 160-decibel report bounced through the room, and a few of the people on the bed stirred but he kept moving through and clearing the room. No one else seemed to be there.

Too easy. Where are the guards, the alerts? This place can't be that unguarded. This has to be a trap.

"Get them up and moving, there should be wheelchairs around here somewhere. I'm going to finish setting charges." He could feel the mental clock ticking down and it lent speed to his movement, even as he kept looking, waiting for the trap to be sprung.

"I've got them ready to go. But I'll need help getting them out." Kayter's voice rang through the room as he finished setting the last charge. DK turned and headed back to her. He could see her lifting one of the frail bodies into a chair. He paused as he reached the dead body, and the cart standing there. The cart was laden with vials of Reset - vials that would keep him alive.

Blood War: Rage

Thought didn't guide him. He didn't know if he could think but he quickly filled his empty carrier bag with Reset until Andrew's voice in his ear pulled him out of his haze.

"You got incoming and they are fully loaded for an assault."

Chapter 45 – All can die

DK's head jerked up at Andrew's voice on the com. He slung the bag over his shoulder and headed for Kayter and the three victims.

"What door?"

"Five coming in the front, two in the back. Full tac gear, high powered weapons, looks like a full assault team. They're expecting someone a hell of a lot tougher than you." Andrew paused. "Do you want me to take them out?"

Declan grabbed a sheet off one of the bed and picked up the other woman, so frail, so tiny, he knew his touch would leave bruises on her. Placing her gently in the lap of the male Kayter had lifted into the wheelchair, he used the sheet to strap her in. The man put an arm around her, holding her to him.

Grey eyes, cloudy from drugs, looked at him. A slow blink, then he closed his eyes again.

Damn them, no one should have to live like this, for what, to try and control me?

Rage blossomed and this time he let it out, letting the world snap back into the crystal clarity of rage induced combat sensing, and his options unrolled before him.

"Kayter. Take them through the lab to the back door. Andrew, have they breached the door yet?"

He looked around, everything clear as if etched out in high definition. The front door lay in front of them, the rolling garage door locked and still in place. The single door leading to the outside had a frosted window inset in it. He could see the vague image of figures moving in front of it.

"Not yet. Looks like they are getting ready to stack up for a door breach."

Blood War: Rage

"We're headed to the back, as soon as the team actually breaches the front, send the bastards in the back to meet Jesus. The front of the breaching stack won't notice for a few seconds and I'll deal with what is left here in the confusion. Then get your car over here. We have evacuees."

"Roger." Andrew's flat voice pulled back more memories of going through buildings, calling out targets, and a sniper's calm flat voice acknowledging each target he took out. A part of him, a small dark part waited for the guilt, but nothing could get through the rage the drove him.

"Kayter, get clear and push them into the labs. Head for the back door. Kill anyone that survives."

"Kill?" She swallowed hard even as she started to move. "They aren't mages or demons."

"No, but they are here to kill us and that's a good enough reason to waste them. They knew you were here and waited for us. It's an ambush."

"Fuck." He could barely hear her as she went through the double doors, pushing the wheelchair with two victims strapped down on it.

That left him a wheelchair with a male strapped into it, his high cheekbones sharp in his too thin face. DK whirled to give him a good push towards the double doors towards the lab area.

"I'll help," the voice so thin and reedy DK sensed it more than heard it. Either way, he didn't shift his attention as he moved backward, facing the door and braced for the breach.

"Now." Andrews' voice coincided with the door snapping inward. Three men pushed in, moving as a with professional group, guns moving as they scanned. The leader paused for a second as he saw DK.

DK didn't. His Vulture barked out its message and the head of the man exploded. The other two shifted their weapons towards him, but DK had already made it to the doors as he engaged both of them with his carbine.   DK noted the chest of the rearmost soldier essentially exploded as Andrew's fifty caliber Bear started working its ranged death from the rear to the front of their formation.

You're in my world now rookies. Fucked no matter which way you go.

He didn't manage a nice clean headshot like what took out their leader but they went down, one gut shot and the other in the chest just above his ballistic chest plate. Behind him, he heard the distinctive crack of the fifty-caliber sniper rifle and saw another shadowy figure beyond the door collapse and start yelling.

"Clean that up Andrew, nothing gets left behind us."

"Yes, Sir." Came Andrew's robotic reply. Followed by another bark from the Bear.

He pushed open the next set of doors and grabbed the wheelchair, pushing it hard towards the far door where Kayter was pushing hers through.

"Got one of the two. But they have another van pulling up now. Stay or come get you?" Andrew's voice came over his earpiece.

"Come extract us. Kayter, you've got at least one coming for you. You'll need to hold that door until Andrew gets here with the car."

"Got it." Her voice tight but controlled, showing the professionalism he'd seen in demon fights.

DK barely noticed. The need to kill and destroy those that were hunting him egged him on, and he reveled in it.

He glanced at the man trying to roll his chair towards Kayter, but each push of his weak arms barely moved the chair. His mind blared innocent, but the sound of the others coming in through the front door called to him, and he headed that direction. Dropping down to his belly he crawled through the door. The amateur's that they were, they had gathered, glancing around wildly - new people coming in and trying to assess the situation.

Easy. Try to kill me, will you? I don't think so. Not today pogues.

With quick fluid movements, he sighted in, caressed the Vulture's trigger, and moved smoothly the next. The first two shots caused the group to freeze, a sure sign of their lack of actual

Blood War: Rage

combat experience, then they started to move. But by then he'd dropped two more and seriously injured another. He grabbed a grenade, pulled the pin releasing the spoon handle, and started to slow count. When he reached two, he tossed it out and sprinted towards the opposite end of the lab, not bothering to even try to stay low.

He grabbed the guy and shoved the wheelchair through the door as the grenade exploded four seconds later.

Damn, it should have gone off a second earlier. Crappy surplus shit.

But even as he thought that, something in him howled with glee at the screams he could hear behind him.

A man lay dead in the hall, his head all but severed from his body. He stepped over it; that is one he didn't need to worry about coming up behind him.

Kayter stood in the small space where the stairs led up to the next floor. The wheelchair was wedged behind her under the stairs as she faced the door, her sword drawn.

His mouth opened to tell her to get out of the way, but the dead man in the hallway stopped him. Swords didn't create ricochets.

"ETA, Andrew?"

"Five mikes."

DK checked the remote for the C-4. A basic remote and he'd planned to level the building so even if they found a few, they wouldn't find them all. And with as many as he had planted, they'd all die.

The door rattled, and his body reacted, Vulture up and aimed at the door before his mind caught up. Kayter went to the door, her sword ready.

DK fought back a snarl. In this confined space the sword actually worked better, so he waited, regardless of the rage urging him to pull the trigger and spill more blood. He clenched his jaw. He was in control, not the Rage.

A man burst in, gun tracking left to right, which was his

328

mistake. Kayter stood to his right and as he panned towards her, she swung.

Part of DK admired her exquisite control as the sword slashed through the man's neck via the narrow gap between his vest and helmet, ending his life before he even knew what happened. The man collapsed revealing the rest of the squad behind him.

"Down," the word snarled out to Kayter and he fired the second she cleared his field of fire. His nagging had gotten her to respond immediately. His first bullet slammed into the face of the man coming in right behind, shattering his goggles as it shattered the bridge of his nose then penetrated his brain before he had a chance to dive out of the way. The Vulture barked till the bolt locked back to the rear signaling an empty magazine. Declan ejected the empty magazine and quickly replaced it. There were now two dead men lying there but he'd seen at least three more.

"Declan, we have to get them out of here. They're too weak." Her voice seemed to come from a different place and time as he fought to turn his head to look at her.

"Noted. Soon as we kill the last of these fuckers." He stepped out to turn to the right but a man hiding flush against the wall knocked the Vulture aside and slammed at DK's face with the butt of his weapon.

In a move that he knew he'd regret in the morning if he lived till then, DK leaned back, letting his shoulder rest on the wall of the building, the butt of the rifle barely scraping his nose as the attacker became overbalanced.

With a huge shove of his shoulder, he threw himself forward catching the man as he tried to rebalance and they both went down. He heard Kayter attack the ones on the other side, but his vision grayed at the sides and all he could see was the man struggling beneath him. Noise sounded in his ears but he ignored it, needing to destroy this threat, to take his victim's power in blood.

His world coated in red and he slammed the heavy butt stock of the Vulture into the man's face, again and again. He felt the

Blood War: Rage

bones crush between his strikes. The spray of blood urging him to hit harder, even as he licked the sweet salt and copper off his lips.

Damn sad weak human.

The anger of such a waste drove him to hit harder, even after the man beneath him had quit moving.

Now... you...know...who...has...power...me...

A touch on his shoulder had him slashing back with his weapon as he spun, bringing it up to sight on the new threat.

Kayter stood there, well back arms open in a non-threatening gesture. "Declan? Can you hear me?"

Huh, what? Who's talking to me?

DK shook his head and fought to push down the rage, concentrating on a pale Kayter and the idling Suburban next to her.

"Yeah." His voice came out low and thick, almost animalistic and that shocked him more than anything else.

"We need to get the Fae loaded and out of here before more get here. Help me?" Her voice low, cajoling.

DK glanced up to see a white-faced Andrew standing next to the big vehicle looking at him.

"Yes. Hurry up. What the hell are you waiting for? Need me to remind you to breathe too?" He snapped, stalking back to the stairwell and ignoring the blood dripping off him as he walked. The Fae had their eyes closed, which he thought might be a good thing. He pushed the first chair over to the Suburban. Andrew had opened the door and Kayter lifted each of them in with an ease that either meant they weighed even less than he thought, or she was stronger than he realized.

He started to turn to go get the last one when Andrew called back to him. "Jesus, here use this." A blue item flew towards his face and he caught it by reflex. The soft fabric of the towel registered, and he looked at Andrew blankly.

"You're dripping blood. I don't need that in my car." His voice held no humor and DK fought to push the rage down because it wanted to start killing everything.

He stood there swaying for a moment, then snapped open his

eyes that had somehow closed without his knowledge. A few quick wipes got the blood and other substances off his Vulture, and he ran it over his face and chest but suspected he just smeared it around more than anything else.

The remaining male sat slumped in the wheelchair. For a moment Declan worried he'd died but as he moved over, the man's eyes flickered open and latched onto his face.

"That their blood?" His voice a soft whisper.

"Yes." He grabbed the chair and started to push it towards the door.

"Good," the man said a hint of vicious pleasure in his voice. "I hope you hurt them."

"I just might have."

They passed the man he'd beaten to death and Declan felt nothing but numb. They got the man in the car and then climbed in as Andrew started it up and started to drive.

"One second." He fumbled on the outside pouch of the bag that had contained the C-4 and pulled out the remote detonator. When he'd absconded with this years ago, he'd always thought it would be his place he'd blow up, not something from a horror movie.

"Go," he said as he turned to look at the building. More cars were showing up as Andrew pulled away. He watched to time it perfectly and a figure on another rooftop caught his attention. Too far away but the light reflected off glowing blue eyes too bright to be normal and a body he'd recognized at an instinctive level.

Shane? Are you part of this?

He pushed off the thought of watching the men behind them rush into the building and he pressed the button.

"One, two, thr-" The blast wave slammed into their car, rocking it violently. He watched as flames, dust, and debris blew out the sides of the building and it crumpled in on itself.

"What the fuck?" Andrew shouted as he tried to keep control of the car and the entire building started to collapse into itself.

"Holly shiiit! That was way more than what I put in. Those

assholes must have wired the place themselves too. Oops, but damn they are seriously closed for business now." Declan's voice carried and the three Fae, more conscious than he realized, started to laugh. A sharp undulating sound that made the hairs on his neck rise and he turned back to look at them wondering how sane they still were.

The bag of Reset hung at his side, both a life jacket and a weight that could drown him.

He closed his eyes and didn't think as they drove away from the remains of the building, with the Fae still laughing.

They had been driving for about three minutes when Andrew broke the strained silence. The laughing had died down after a minute, and the unspoken words hung in the air like ticking time bombs.

"Where are we going?" Andrew asked not looking away from the road where he drove exactly one mile over the speed limit.

"My place. It's defensible, not that I think they'll attack us there."

"What about these guys? They need medical treatment." Kayter said from the back.

He shot a sharp glance at her. "None of them are hurt, are they?"

"No, not like that. But they are going to require special care to recover."

Declan grunted in acknowledgment, his mind drifting to the Reset and the need for clarity instead of blood. But not here, not in front of these people. He wouldn't take it.

"I'll call that Fae, Art something. He can come get them."

"Grandpa," one of them muttered.

"Then that works even better."

They fell into silence, not speaking until Andrew backed up to his garage. Declan climbed out and opened it up and then the three of them got the pale and shaking people to his couch and recliner. He couldn't even begrudge them for sitting in his recliner when he got a good look at them. Pale, wasted, holes in their arms from the IV's and the location of the feeding tube sluggishly bleeding. He'd seen dead people that looked healthier.

Without a comment, he headed to his vault, tossed the Reset in it, and locked the door behind him. As he came back up the stairs he grabbed his phone and found the card from Art. Dialing the number as he walked back in with all of them looking at him with expressions he ignored, heading for a beer.

As it rang he tossed one to Andrew and Kayter, who caught them but didn't open them. They just watched him.

Get it to-fucking-gether, Declan. You can't dose up before the Fae gets here. That's why he smelled Fae when you cut yourself. Probably not a good idea to let a pissed off Fae think you are a vampire. Get a hold of yourself.

The other end answered as he was about to take a drink and he set it back down, his hand shaking. Reaching down deep he pulled on his own energy and bottled the rage back up. He had to grab onto the counter to stay standing.

"Yes?" The cultured voice on the other end sounded bored and impatient.

"Yeah, I need to speak to Art."

"This is he."

Declan blew out a breath and concentrated on not looking like an idiot in front of the others.

"I found your missing peeps. Well, three of them. One woman, two men. One of them called you Grandpa?"

All the boredom stripped from the man's, well Fae's, voice. "You have them, where are they?"

"My place. They're not healthy. They'll need a hospital or something."

"I have healers. Where. Are. They?" The voice had turned to nitrogen and if Declan hadn't been fighting to stay conscious he might have been impressed.

Declan gave him his address and the line cut off before he could say anything else. He dropped the phone on the counter and drained the beer. It helped. He stood there for a moment then glanced at the two people, friends, staring at him.

"Fae incoming. My guess is they'll be getting here real quick. One of these guys is a relative of Art's I think."

"What was that?" Kayter's voice was quiet. "I've never seen you lose it like that on a demon."

He didn't look at her, just grabbed two extra beers and walked outside to wait.

Chapter 46 – Everyone Lies

He sank down into the chair on the patio, his eyes on the drive to his house. A long pull on the beer in his hand slid down his throat and DK closed his eyes and waited. But the relief didn't come, just the slight numbing of the rage, the pain, and the knowledge he didn't want to face. He set the bottle down on the ground carefully, resisting the urge to chuck it against the wall, to feel it shatter, revel in the destruction.

Picking up glass sucks. Do you really want to be finding glass slivers for the next six months? You already have one bottle out there. Granted I will not live that long, so it might not be an issue.

That almost caused him to chuck it but instead, he grabbed the next beer, twisted the top off, and poured it down his throat. He closed his eyes as he heard the door open and close behind him.

"I'm taking off. Kayter's with the Fae." Andrew's voice still had a flat quality to it and he spoke from a few feet behind DK.

"Kay. Thanks. You did good." DK didn't turn to look at him, instead focusing his attention on the trees and their gently moving leaves and needles.

"Only 'cause we got people out. You need to wash up. You're a fucking mess." His footsteps sounded on the cement, each one sounding like a nail in the coffin that was DK's life. Andrew paused. "Declan?"

"Yeah."

"We're fighting our own people? They did this? They're working with the demons?" His voice didn't shake but DK heard the same emotion that beat at his heart.

"Yeah. I don't know who the bad guys are anymore."

Silence lay between them until Andrew started to move again.

335

Blood War: Rage

"Then I guess I better get a better zero set in on the Bear, it was a few mils off. I'll be over this weekend. We also need more ammo. You need to get the kid onboard full time, get Greg back into the loop pronto and... pull your god damn shit together man."

Something surged in him and he closed his eyes as he heard the door to the Suburban close and then the rumble of the big engine fire up. The vehicle turned and headed down the drive and DK watched him go with eyes that had gotten some dust in them.

Damn wind, always blowing things in your eyes. Need to keep sunglasses out here.

He sat alone, enjoying the false sense of peace that the birds and the music of the trees imparted for a few quiet minutes. Lifting the bottle to his mouth he frowned when he realized it was empty. He set it down and grabbed the next one. He'd need more in a few minutes, but for now the buzz started to kick in and things didn't feel as bad.

Should do it now, while I can still slip in and out without noise.

The beer, the quiet, and feeling the rage trickle away made him almost calm by the time an unfamiliar vehicle came up the drive.

Why the hell didn't I get an – oh. Huh, guess it helps to have your phone with you.

Declan shrugged and took a sip of his beer. Only one left unopened and getting up felt like too much effort at this point.

The big vehicle, a fancy Escalade or something like that with lots of room in back, comfy seats, and cost way more than he'd ever spend on a car, pulled to a stop. The two front doors opened, and Art and another man stepped out. They looked around and headed right towards him.

I really don't have the energy to deal with this shit. Just get your people and go.

Timing it perfectly, he started to talk the minute they were close enough to hear him without needing to shout.

"In through the door into the living room. Your people are in chairs and being taken care of best we can, not being medical people, or having a fucking clue what to actually do. Kayter is in there, she's the one that found them. So, we went and got them. Be nice to her because, besides that, I really don't give two shits anymore." He didn't look at their faces. The trees were much more interesting and less painful than contemplating your own mortality.

The other man grunted and they both headed in the door. Part of him wanted to get up, to follow and make sure they didn't see too much, but it didn't really matter. The bottle was empty again and he frowned. Picking up the last one, he popped it open even as the door opened behind him.

Art sat down in the chair next to him, his face remote and hard.

"They are yours, right?" DK didn't look at Art but he could see him well enough out of the corner of his eye.

"Yes. Is what they said true?"

"I don't know what they said, so I've got no idea." Declan responded, but he knew and he really didn't want to go there.

"That their blood was being used to make a drug called Reset. A drug that pushes down the rage that's a side effect of overexposure to demon blood." His voice held no emotion that Declan could hear.

"Yep." he took a drink of beer to keep any other words locked away.

Art jerked his head in a sharp nod and rose, the door opening again. DK focused on the trees, wondering if the Fae would kill him from behind and if he would actually feel it. Kayter's voice told him the odds of him dying right that second was unlikely. Soft, low voices, reassuring, and odd grunts told him they were carrying out the Fae and putting them in the cars.

Another approaching engine sounded, and he looked up frowning.

When did my place become Grand Central Station? Can't everyone just go away so a man can die in peace? Everyone just get your crap and get out...

He drained the beer even as he rose, trying to focus on the car. A practical two-door sedan in non-descript silver gray pulled up and Cordy climbed out. He went still as her head turned and surveyed the Fae, both wounded and whole.

"Are you guys kidding me with this shit? Blow up one fucking secret government torture cell slash lab, and now they think they can just pop in for a visit without a warrant?"

Rage filled him - watching this woman he'd trusted, he'd liked, and what control he'd found slipped again.

Cordelia stalked over to him, and he tried to enjoy the picture she made, slacks that showed off that nice ass and a blouse made of some soft clingy stuff that draped across her chest. Tried to think about sex, about anything except that she'd probably betrayed him, and he needed to kill her.

Damn, she really is a nice looking woman. Too bad the look on her face implies someone is about to die. Wonder if it's me. And wonder if I'll try to stop her or maybe kill her instead. Or kill her, then just let the Fae kill me. Works...

"So, it's true? Reset is made from Fae blood." Her voice didn't match her face. It threw him off balance.

He glanced over as Kayter and Art helped the last one into the vehicle and felt the rage bubbling back up hard and fast.

"You didn't know?" Accusation laced his words and he faced her head on, his hand tight around the bottle.

"Declan, I swear I didn't know. I thought it was a chemical concoction like Prozac or Valium, or hell, really good weed. I swear I had no idea." Her voice tight and angry as she looked at the emaciated Fae they tenderly wrapped in a blanket.

He focused on her, really focused, and saw the white lines at the corners of her mouth and the circles under her eyes.

Pretty. And sad?

"How did you find out?" He looked at his empty beer bottle mournfully. This would be easier if he didn't have rage eating at him. Maybe then he could not want to hurt her, want to do things that normally would make him sick to think about.

"Grabbed Chad Morant after your little job up at MIT. He implied something before he walked out. It took me this long to validate it. It was buried well. I came here to tell you, but it seems like you already know." She shifted her eyes to him and he flinched away from the warmth in that chocolate brown.

"Thanks for coming out. But nothing you can do. Take care, Cordy. You may be sexy and all, but next time bring a warrant if you're going come by unannounced."

She needs to go. I'm not holding. I'll feel her warm blood on my hands soon.

He turned, intent on his door, more beer lay behind that door.

"Declan Kenner, I must speak to you." Art's voice had gained that surreal quantity again and Declan fought to not turn around and kill him.

All I want to do is drink my damn beer and be left the fuck alone.

He swallowed hand tightening around the bottle until it hurt then slowly turned.

"Yeah?" Anything more was beyond him. Declan looked up and Art's eyes caught him, speared him through his soul and the rage at being vulnerable to this man, to have this being look at him with pity almost broke the control he held himself with. "You should go now." he forced out.

If they don't leave now, they'll just die. I'm done with this all. The Fae blood will make me better.

Something flashed in his vision and he looked to see Kayter tossing Art one of the vials of Reset. It was in a plunger, so not one of the stashed he'd taken from the factory, but from the ones he had in a drawer in the kitchen. Art held it out to him.

"Relieve yourself, Demon Hunter. We must talk."

DK couldn't take his eyes off the vial, the drug that held his salvation and his damnation.

"Take it. We must talk, and you cannot process in his state. What was already put in that vial cannot be undone."

With a hand that shook as if he had the DTs, he reached out and took it. The second his hand wrapped around it, he pulled it towards him, the craving worse than booze ever had been. That terrified him, but not enough to prevent him from plunging it into his neck.

Like an ice cold beer after a day in the blazing sun, the Reset washed through him, cleansing him of the rage and a fair amount of the intoxication. Declan staggered as the pressure he'd been leaning against disappeared.

"There we go..." He blinked and saw Kayter, Cordy, and Art were all looking at him. "Is there an issue?" He snapped as he turned away from all their eyes. "I need another beer."

He stalked into the kitchen, grabbed two more, then stopped and grabbed another two. Feeling more himself now.

No reason to be rude.

The three of them were still standing out there looking at each other with odd looks.

"People... Lighten the fuck up. Here." He handed each of them a beer then went and sat back down in his chair. "Kayter, if you want to, I've got two folding chairs in the closet in the mudroom. You can grab those." He turned his attention to Art, almost resenting the clarity of his thoughts. "Sit. Talk."

Art glanced at the two women who shrugged. Kayter headed into the house, he presumed to get the chairs, and as much as he'd rather look at Cordy and imagine things that would probably get him slapped, he focused on Art.

"You are a strange man, Declan Kenner. But I owe you and my people owe you. I'm well aware of the effects of what you call the Rage. We suffered it too after our war with the demons many millennia ago. We should have offered to help after the armistice was signed. We didn't. I don't know if we forgot or if we never thought you would be afflicted with it also. But either way, I have a solution for you."

Even alcohol lost interest at that and Declan focused on Art. "You can provide a solution for this? For all hunters? Make it so we aren't ready to kill people at the drop of a hat." Hope purged everything and the universe dwindled down to the Fae, the Fae he might be willing to kill for.

Doug Burbey & Mel Todd

Art shook his head. "No. Just for you. I can provide a solution to your issue, but only to you. My family owes you and we will pay the price to ensure you are free of this effect. But we can only give it to you due to the services you have rendered us."

Dashed hopes tasted like burnt ash, dark and bitter on his tongue. He raised the beer swallowing half of it. "Thanks, but no thanks. Too many others deserve to live. I'm the least of them."

"Declan!" Cordy's voice was strident. "Take it. Maybe we can figure out how to pass it on to others."

He glanced at her, wondering how much she heard and then realized it didn't matter.

"Unfortunately, that will not work. It would be a uniquely individualized solution for him alone and it will be very, very painful, much like an addict going through withdrawals. It will merge him with his own magic reservoir and allow him to quench the rage. Humans have been poisoned and the only way to fix it is to balance the magic. Other ways might have been possible once if we had reacted immediately. But now, only those with their own magic and a Fae with the resources to create this balance can achieve it. It may not succeed but you risked your life for my people, with no thought of reward, so I offer it to you."

"Pass," he muttered ignore the sounds of protest from Kayter and Cordy.

Hell if I'll take something that brothers earned also but won't get.

"You have my card. If you change your mind call. The offer is on the table. But know this Mr. Kenner, that if we can't save your body then my honor will require that I save your soul from yourself. You will die as an honorable warrior, not a crazed mindless killer. I will step in and make sure of that personally when your time is nearer." With that Art rose. He glanced at something Declan couldn't see, sighed softly, turned and headed toward the vehicle, leaving his untouched beer sitting there.

Declan sneered and grabbed the beer. "Fae bullshit voodoo and wasting a beer. Not today."

Blood War: Rage

They all fell silent as the big car navigated down his drive and he refused to watch, instead turning back to the trees.

"Declan, you need to take this offer. If only you get saved it is more than nothing." Cory almost pleaded with him.

"Why am I more special than the rest of them? I was no hero, just a dumb grunt caught in the middle who came out the other side alive."

A single male figure approached the group from the side of the house, "Because I need you to live a little while longer, cause a damn horde lord knows your name, and before he eats your heart you're going to help me. Besides, I'm the only one here that's not lying to you and you know it. I've never once lied to you." The voice from his past rolled through all of them. Kayter sprang to her feet drawing the sword in one smooth movement, even as Cordy rolled and came up with her weapons pointed at the man who used to be his best friend.

I really need to learn to not leave my phone in the house.

"Shane...? Oh for fuck's sake already!" Declan exhaustedly lowered his head.

"Well, this kinda sucks. I come all the way out here to talk to you and I find you contemplating death. And not even a cool death with explosions, Filipino hookers, ridiculously expensive scotch, and a monster truck with mounted fifty caliber machine guns. I never thought you were a fucking quitter Declan. Besides, I need your help and not being susceptible to the rage will go a long way to making you more useful to me."

Shane looked around, "I'll be right back." and then turned and walked into Declan's house.

"Ummm, that shifty dude just went into your house. Shouldn't I stop him?" Kayter protested while pointing at Declan's back door.

"Doubt you could," Declan said taking a drink. "He's a no shit battle mage, one of the best, one of the originals. And from how easily he got in here without triggering the magic proximity sensors, he's probably fully juiced up with blood and fully warded. Sit down, not a damn thing we can do about it."

Kayter slowly put her sword away.

The man, Shane, walked back out of the house with four beers. "You're almost out brother. Going to need to restock."

"Got more cases in the garage fridge." Declan said accepting the beer Shane handed him.

Shane dropped casually into the chair the Fae had vacated and set the other beers on the table. He popped off the lid and took a drink. "You always did like the domestic shit."

"Bite me. That is from the oldest brewery in America. It's fucking patriotic is what it is. You can piss off and not drink my patriotic lager then." Declan said but his voice had no heat, nothing but wariness. "Why are you here Shane?" His right hand kept twitching as if he wanted to have a gun in it.

"I need you to help me buy some time. Then you just need to let this world go so we can move on to the next one without all this… ridiculous baggage."

Kayter surged to her feet looking like she might go for her sword again.

Declan raised his hand slowly towards Kayter, "Hold up." then looked over at his oldest friend "I'm listening, Shane. Yeah, I'm ready to listen now."

Epilogue - Demons Have Plans

Bezzid stared at the new list of supplies needed, a sneer lifting hir mouth tendrils.

These damn humans are more difficult now than they were in the past. We should have harvested them earlier in their development but their populations were so spread out there wasn't enough blood to fuel the invasion. Even the simplest computations showed more waste than power gain.

The war machines, and Horde, all consumed power quickly. An invasion's success hinged on a harvest of blood in excess of consumption. A successful invasion meant more power for the sub-hordes and Bezzid needed more power. Bezzid had to break the stalemate to gather enough power and resources ze needed to destroy hirz master's hold over Bezzid's horde and assume hirz position in the greater Horde.

If the cursed Fae had not shuttered their realm from us, we would not need to harvest the humans yet. Both shall fall in time. Then... we shall return our Lord to hirz rightful throne.

Once again, Bezzid glared, frustrated with the computations required to enact his plan.

If only the Overlords hadn't wasted the bulk of the Horde's resources against the humans.

The Overlords refused to authorize enough reconnaissance of the humans. Without that, the Horde didn't understand the development of human civilization and that forced the sub-hordes to cross over unknown battlefields. That cost them dearly, in troops and resources.

Doug Burbey & Mel Todd

Bezzid looked at the computations again then pushed away from the altar. Hirz current form mimicked the bipedal humanoid shape, taller than the tallest human, with hard packed muscles covered in overlapped armored scales. Ze thought it made hir look imposing and the humans seemed to think this form resembled a large insect. Ze still didn't know if that implied respect or not. Pacing the room hirz scales rippled, physically displaying hirz agitation.

Any creature of intelligence would have assumed a gradual technological development progression curve of the human civilization. Of course, we could not have anticipated that humans harnessing of that damned elemental fire weapon and such rapid growth. In less than a hundred cycles they learned to harness the energy of the sun but because they did, we have such devastating losses against the main Horde. Such an irresponsible loss of non-replaceable power. Avoidable if they had not assumed wrongly and had authorized the needed recon.

This wasn't the fault of the dreaded Fae or their interference in the desires of the Horde. This failure lay on the masters who led the Horde. And this was why Bezzid was required by the Lord's teachings to disrupt such inept mastership. The mastership forced upon hir. Ze must consume hirz own master now and assume hirz role to ensure the Lord's return. But to do this ze had to break the chains the Overlords had used to shackle Bezzid.

This ridiculous treaty, signed by the worthless humans and the Overlord Council, brokered by the manipulative and cursed Fae, is a clear affront to all demonkind. Such pathetic weakness must infuriate the Lord. We shall consume their blood and power and then return our kind to its proper place in the realms. We will squeeze every ounce of power from this pathetically weak human race. Bezzid will be with the Horde as we use it against the true enemy, the Fae, consuming every ounce of their magically infused blood to merge with our own. Then, and only, then can we turn the Horde against the next Realm. That of the Angels. Upon consumption of the Angelkind power Bezzid will be at the head of

Blood War: Rage

the Horde that crashes the final barrier, allowing the true Lord to return and grant me my reward. But the numbers are still all wrong and do not assure victory.

The power lost from the last invasion forced Bezzid to contemplate a plan for victory far beyond the mental capacity of hirz useless master. Hirz masters would learn the folly in leaving behind the Lord's teachings and clinging to nothing but the Rage.

Giving all to the Rage, relinquishing all control, made their minds too weak to understand the nuances of the Lord's dictated ways. They have become nothing more than powerful dimwitted juggernauts. But even a dimwitted juggernaut is still a juggernaut needing to be very carefully dealt with. The only way to ensure our Lord's return is to destroy this misconceived treaty with the humans. If only they hadn't forced it on us by signing with blood.

Bezzid grabbed the numbers and looked at them again, frustration battering at him. To make sure hirz throne sat in a place of dominance among the Overlord Council ze needed to find a way to break the humans.

Bezzid is worthy. Bezzid alone has retained the teachings of the true Lord, that we are meant crush all the lesser beings and absorb their power. The way it was always meant to be. If it wasn't for the damn losses of power, weakening the ability to surge the greater Horde. But Bezzid is smarter than hirz master. Yes, Bezzid knows the true way. The Masters have become to heretical and will see the way of the Lord again.

Bezzid noted the changed value of the blood harvested after the humans used the elemental fires, the taint of this unknown magic into the blood enhancing the powers of the Horde had immense value. Again, hirz master's squandered this gift from the Lord in their futile war against the humans. But Bezzid hoarded this tainted power. Let the Master fail, ze would use this power.

Ze had secreted these tainted Harvesters away from the Horde, hiding them in the caverns of his sub-horde. Pulsing with the strange infused elemental power. With this weapon ze would fully consume the humans. With that victory bring power to hirzelf and glory to the Horde. Not only with the use of the humans' clever elemental magic, but with what the Overlords overlooked. A weapon so powerful the council itself thought it would never work and disregarded it as folly.

The greatest weapon to use against the humans was the humans themselves. They were weak and easily manipulated creatures. Willing to betray their own Humanity and be a loyal subject merely for the absurd premise of what the humans would call a 'promise' that Bezzid would grant them power and riches beyond their imagination.

How foolish, and stupid, these humans were to put value in plainly spoken words. No power was carried in these words. The mere fact they perceive such a thing that a "promise" carries weight shows their foolishness. Pathetic little creatures. Summoning me, begging me to take them as my slave, merely in exchange for Bezzid sharing my knowledge of some worthless bits of magics that their pathetic race had never matured enough to learn. Such easily manipulated things they are.

Bezzid barked, something approaching a half laugh.

"Frax, summon the weak realm. Bezzid will contact the human Marcus Vipsanius again. More information is required. Bezzid must see if they have gathered it from their "spies" as they refer to them."

The concept of human spies enthralled hir. Disregarded as a perversion of the logic of power by hir Master, but Bezzid thought creatively, and saw how such lowly humans willingly turned on each other. They would provide what the Horde needed most but lacked in the war. Information.

Ze learned that corruption seeking humans would freely give hir information, again for mere words of promise. Ze began to give them directions. Not only would they tell hir of the workings of the human world, ze could give them guidance on their actions. Like willing slaves, they manipulated their own kind to help hir prepare to push hirz own agenda to gain power. Besides, the lure of Kali's Heart made most of them willing to give anything. Even through

Blood War: Rage

the portal, its siren call could affect them, seduce them.

The treacherous treaty the overlords forced upon demonkind made Bezzid reliant on the humans. Ze had to use the humans to start the portal opening in the human realm and then be secured by his casters from the demon realm side. The treaty had expressly blocked any humankind, or demonkind, from opening a solo realm portal into each other's existence larger than a human sized head. But the exception to the rule was that the willing cooperation of a mage from humankind, and a caster from demonkind, allowed a portal to open within the limits of the power of those summoning it. The human fools thought they may wish to communicate with demonkind for the "common good" in the future. The Overlords thought this may be handy at some point to learn more of the elemental fire they now wanted from the humans to use against the Fae. But Bezzid knew of no better reason to return to the human realm than to harvest their blood and power. Then ze could raise hirz stature and serve hirz true Lord.

A yellow, leathery-skinned demon, with dulled claws standing barely to Bezzid's mid chest, approached and knelt. Frax emitted contentment in his decades of obedience to Bezzid as ze raised hands up.

"Horde Master, portal ready.".

Bezzid pushed aside the simpering caster servant and entered the portal chamber with Frax close behind.

Standing in the middle of the chamber, he let a drop of blood fall on the activation point, feeling the draw from hirz reserves as the portal connected. If hirz personal magic had been greater nothing would have blocked hirz ascension to power.

The small portal glowed stronger and pulsed as magic navigated the distance between the realms, seeking out his intended target on the other side of the veil walls. Bezzid grumbled with impatience for hirz human slave to answer the portal summons.

After a frustrating pause, the reflected face of the human's female mage slave appeared from within the orb. Having to utter a single word to this slave creature was an insult. Such an insult Bezzid only tolerated because it suited his immediate needs. But it would have to be punished eventually. It would be repaid to the Horde when Bezzid ripped the life from this worthless being and consumed hir thereby returning what ze stole.

"Report to me slave." Beezid growled in the best human English ze could manage.

"Oh, you're a biggie. Um… Marcus isn't here. But he did say to be polite and super friendly if you called." The slave's voice echoed through the veil from within the portal.

Bezzid still could not firmly grasp many of the strange words most humans utter. With the ridiculous weakness of the lack of a unified species language, and the human inability to understand empathic thought, he struggled with the nuances in the intent of a human speaker. These annoying traits helped them hide their lies and intent from each other as well as from Bezzid. But even without understanding all the words, Bezzid did understood human speech contained hidden betrayals.

"What is the status of preparations?"

"Grumpy Guss you are. What preparations? "

Bezzid sent forth annoyance, then spiked to anger when ze remembered the human slaves were deaf and blind to the undertones. "Speak clear and true human! Tell me, are we ready?"

"Oh no idea, but Marcus did say that if you got all huffy to tell you that he will get back to you. Where did Frax go? Is he there with you? I like Frax. He's funny."

Bezzid barely restrained hirz rage against the loss of time, a Horde resource that now needed to be replenished after hirz master's latest squandering of blood and power.

"Why?" As Bezzid empathically pushed out his angry disapproval even while though he knew it would not travel across the realms to strike the appropriate fear into his slave, even if ze could sense it. But hirz own body demanded ze project anger and displeasure towards this heretic human female slave regardless.

"All he said was that 'Shit happens.' Do you have pretty flowers

Blood War: Rage

over there on your side? I can't see. Always wondered though. I bet they are neat and pretty."

"Bezzid knows of this 'shit happens' word, you despicable slave. Bezzid understands your words. Shit does not happen to the Horde!"

"Well it appears it happened to the Horde last time you guys crossed over to our realm, from what I could tell."

Every ounce of Bezzid's energy that was focused on repressing his anger so he could tolerate communicating with heretics nearly fractured at those words. Caught off guard, Beezid's body began to shake and without an outlet to unleash on, he would lose control of the portal and his form.

"Frax!" Bezzid bellowed while radiating empathic fury and a demand of obedience.

Frax scurried into hirz master's chamber compelled by the commands radiating from hirz better. Ze immediately prostrated hirzelf submissively in front of Bezzid while radiating the fear and obedience.

Bezzid gestured the portal closed as he roared, then glanced down and thrust both of his clawed hands into the exposed back of his simpering servant. Ze relished the release of pent up emotions and the tactile pleasure of hirz claws penetrating a weaker hordling. Skin, flesh tearing and claws grinding over bone.

How dare this slave insult the Horde? This heresy must be sated.

Bezzid flexed hirz arms and pulled at the back of hir servant tearing it open, breaking hirz spine and spraying hir with blood and gore, as it thrashed under hir in hirz death convulsions. Bezzid felt his fury abate slightly after hirz kill. Hirz thoughts began to clear once again.

More resources wasted. The humankind will pay for these insults. That they are so blind they do not know their betters is not tolerable.

Bezzid closed four wide set eyes as mouth tendrils absorbed the servant's blood from hirz claws. Ze radiated an empathic

350

demand for immediate attendance and centered hirz thoughts as ze waited.

A new servant demon ran quickly into Bezzid's presence. "Yes Lord?" it garbled as it simultaneously radiated willingness to serve and obey. Then the servant started to emanate fear. Bezzid noticed the new arrival glancing at the eviscerated body at the feet of hirz master.

Bezzid pointed a bloody claw at the body beneath him. "That was Frax." Then ze pointed at the newly arrived servant. "Now you are Frax. Have casters start arranging horde portal resources. Soon back to war."

Bezzid turned hirz back on the servant and returned hirz attention to resource computations marking a new pattern on the side margins.

Grast humans! Now Bezzid is one less servant soldier, than a moment ago, for no value in power at all. So wasteful and unthinking these humans are. At least the Fae understand the calculations of balance.

Blood War: Rage

Authors Note:

Doug and I hope you enjoyed this first installment of the Blood War series. The next two novellas will be out soonish.

Blood War: Fight - is the story of the demon's attacking our world from Declan Kenner's point of view.

Blood War: Power – is Shane Gris hunt for the power to make his desires come true, regardless of the cost.

You can keep up with us on Facebook at -
https://www.facebook.com/badashbooks/

Or join out newsletter for hints as to what is coming -

http://badashpublishing.com/?page_id=170

We hope to see you there!

Mel Todd and Doug Burbey

Doug Burbey & Mel Todd

Blood War: Rage

Doug Burbey is constantly preparing to: repel the zombie hordes, defend America from all enemies foreign and domestic (particularly the Hipsters and Fashionistas), brew beer & defeat the Rebel Alliance. Doug grew up in Asia as a military brat, went to college in MI becoming a Detroit Lions fan in the Barry Sanders era, then served in numerous positions and wars around the world with the Army before retiring.

Mel Todd has three cats, none of which can turn into a form with opposable thumbs, which is good. If they could do that they wouldn't need her anymore. While writing and starting her empire, she decided creating her own worlds was less work than ruling this one.